THE PLUTOCRAT

THE PLUTOCRAT

A NOVEL

BY
BOOTH TARKINGTON

GARDEN CITY   NEW YORK
DOUBLEDAY, PAGE & COMPANY
1927

TO

S. K. T.

THE PLUTOCRAT

THE PLUTOCRAT

I

OUT of the north Atlantic a January storm came down in the night, sweeping the American coast with wind and snow and sleet upon a great oblique front from Nova Scotia to the Delaware capes. The land was storm-bound and the sea possessed with such confusion that nothing seemed less plausible than that human beings should be out among the running hill ranges, and not only alive but still voyaging crazily on their way. Tow ropes parted off the Maine and Massachusetts coasts; barges were swamped and bargemen drowned; schooners drove ashore in half-frozen harbours; and all night on the Georgian Banks fishermen fought dark monstrosities of water. But in the whole area of the storm nowhere was the northeaster more outrageous than upon that ocean path where flopped and shuttled the great "Duumvir," five hours outward bound from New York.

Thirty thousand tons the "Duumvir" displaced;
but, as in reprisal, more weight of water than
that every few moments attempted to displace the
"Duumvir." The attempt was for a permanent
displacement, moreover, there appearing to be in the
profundities a conviction that this ship had no rightful
place upon the surface and should be reduced to the
condition of a submarine. The "Duumvir," sometimes seeming to assent, squatted under the immense
smotherings; then, shaped in falling water, rose up
into the likeness of a long white cataract dimly
symmetrical against a chaotic sky. The upheavals
were but momentary and convulsive, however; the
great metal creature shook itself thunderously and
descended again under fantastic clouds of sea; and in
both ascent and descent, sought continually to ease
itself by lying first upon one side and then upon the
other. Under the same circumstances a peanut shell
might have shown a livelier motion; nevertheless,
the "Duumvir" did many things that a peanut shell
would have done, but, being heavier, did them more
impressively.

The impressiveness was greatest in the steamer's
interior where there were vivid correspondences to
what went on outside. For, indoors and off the howl-

ing decks, the "Duumvir" was not so much a ship as an excellent hotel, just now a hotel miraculously intact, though undergoing the extremities of continuous earthquake, and complaining loudly. Great salons and lounging rooms, empty of human life, but still bright with electric light, tilted up cornerwise, staggered and dipped like the halls of a palace in the nightmare of a sleeper attacked by vertigo. Accompanying these fantasies, painted ceilings and panelled walls protested in every voice known to wrenched wood and racked metal; but, for that matter, the whole inner fabric of the ship had become eloquent, squeaking with a high-pitched rancour sharply audible in spite of thunder and roarings without. And within the passengers' cabins, those little hotel apartments that had seemed so pleasant when the ship was at her dock, there were complaints and disturbances not lacking in a painful kind of harmony with the protests of the ship and the contortions of the elements that beset her.

Throughout the long ranges of staterooms there was anguish; but nowhere in the whole vastness of the "Duumvir" did it become more acute than in the prettily decorated double cabin where ceaselessly lurched to and fro upon his active bed that newly prosperous young playwright, Laurence Ogle. His lurching was in spite of him, his passionate desire being for motionlessness; and to secure even a few moments of this he would have given recklessly out of the royalties his play was to send him by post from Forty-second Street. More still he would have given to abandon this first sea voyage of his and to be back upon the unmoving pavement of that street, or to be upon any street or road, or in any alley, or to stand upon a bit of earth anywhere, mountain or plain, or to be in a tree rooted in earth. Nothing had value in his mind now save fixity.

His trunk had been opened and then lashed upright against the wall of his bathroom; but something had gone amiss with the lashings, so that at intervals the trunk presented itself in the intervening doorway, tilted drunkenly to eject sometimes a drawer or a limp garment upon the threshold, and then withdrew into the bathroom, where it produced crashing noises of breakage, to which Ogle was indifferent. Earlier in his retirement he had summoned a steward who proved so unseasoned as to be suffering himself, much too obviously. Ogle wished never to see this man again, and, even if he had cared for his society or assistance, would have had to lift a hand to reach the bell-button. He did not wish to lift his hand; it was already being lifted for him in company with the rest of his person; and the lifting at its climax brought on his worst moments.

He ascended spirally, meanwhile being rocked laterally, and this curving ascent was a long one, both in time and space; then, at the crest of it, there was a moment of poising followed by a descent like a two or three story drop in a swift elevator. The bed sank too rapidly beneath him, going down a little faster than he did, so that until the fall was completed he had no weight; whereas at the bottom he was too heavy, having already begun to be urged upward again. His whole being seemed to consist of nausea and of motion in undesirable directions; and yet, in addition to his poignant sensations, he still had thoughts and emotions.

The emotions were all bitter and the thoughts all upon one subject. He had supposed that when a reputable marine corporation engaged to take him to the Mediterranean it would take him there with some manner of straightforwardness and not upon all these spiral excursions to which his nervous system was by no means adapted. Therefore he hated the ship, not only for what it was doing to him, but for what appeared to be its personal malevolence in deceiving him. This incessant vertical and lateral voyaging, then, was that "luxury of ocean travel" to which the "Duumvir" had invited him in its little pamphlets illustrated by photographs of smiling ladies reading in steamer chairs, placid stewards offering cups of tea or broth, and even of lively couples dancing upon a horizontal ballroom floor—lying photographs which he was now convinced had been taken when the ship lay in harbour.

But even thus betrayed, he was not able to understand how he could have been so gullible as to place himself in his present horrible situation;—"horrible" was his own half-stifled word for it. "Voluntarily!" This was another of his words. "Voluntarily I put myself into this horrible condition—voluntarily!" For he remembered with amazement that he had been not merely willing, he had been eager. He had looked forward not only to other continents, but to the ocean voyage. Chuckling and gloating, how he had bragged of it to unfortunate friends unable to leave their bleak customary work in wintry New York; and only that very afternoon he had taken leave of some of them with what jolly superiority!

That afternoon now seemed to have been an afternoon of the long, long ago; he had undergone so many mortifying experiences and had been through so much trouble since then. His first suspicion that the journey was one of ill omen had come to him when he sat down at his table in the great dining salon; and the suspicion became stronger as his table steward offered him a green turtle soup, for the "Duumvir" was just then riding into tumult and darkness off Sandy Hook. The table was one arranged for four persons, and Ogle had felt some curiosity about the other three, wondering if he would prove fortunate in his table mates; but this interest did not detain him. Indeed, the only mitigation of the ignominy of his flight from the green turtle lay in the fact that the other chairs were not yet occupied. What he needed, he knew instinctively, was neither food nor new acquaintances, but air, fresh air, and a great deal of it. He sought it, and finding it, tried to believe that a few moments on deck would be restorative; but they were not, and neither was the icy spray that drenched him there. He descended apprehensively to his own quarters which were greatly changed since he had taken possession of them in the sweet placidity of the Hudson River. They had become animated, possessed by a demon of animation; and the animation had increased hour by hour, until now, as his blurred eyes half opened from time to time to give him glimpses of whirling walls, ceiling, curtains, and mirrors, the happy pride he had felt upon his first sight of this cell of misery bore the aspect of lunacy.

But his most dreadful thought was that he had committed himself to twelve days of what he now endured. Twelve years would have seemed little longer, for already he was flaccid with the interminable passage of time, and no more than a quarter of the first day of the twelve, each composed of twenty-four unbearable hours, had gone by. Why had nobody warned him not to embark on a twelve-day voyage? Had he no friends possessed of even slight intelligence? He thought of them, driving home in beautiful, peaceful taxicabs from theatres, or lounging in health beside the wood fire in the solid restfulness of the club, and his envy of them was like hatred. "Eleven days!" he gasped, in a wretchedness that foresaw no mitigation forever. "Eleven days and *three quarters !*"

He had always thought himself a resourceful young man; but he understood that under the circumstances resourcefulness was a quality of little practical value. The captain of the "Duumvir" would not be amenable to bribery, nor might all the arts of persuasion induce him to return to New York harbour; and the unhappy passenger had to go wherever this brutal mariner went. It would be useless to offer a resignation; one cannot resign from a boat.

There are people who bear their pains with a better grace when they think of greater sufferings on the part of other people, and so, in a dentist's chair, they keep their minds upon hospitals; but seasickness is a human ill that does not profit by such alleviations. Ogle was aware that other people were as wretched as he; for not far from the head of his bed there was a locked door, which, upon occasion, permitted his room to form part of a suite, and from the other side of this door came vocal sounds of lamentation and rebellion; but whenever he heard them his own misery was automatically increased. Two prostrate ladies occupied the adjoining cabin, he became aware, and although one of them seemed to be helplessly silent, the other was but too frequently audible.

Naturally, he was resentful; and when she moaned aloud, "I *will* die! I *will* die!" as she often did, he felt no anxiety to avert the calamity she predicted.

"Do!" he muttered thickly. "Do die! Do!"

Even if he lived through the next eleven days and three quarters, he would never in his life dislike anybody more than he did that suffering woman, he thought, but presently discovered that he was capable of a deeper antipathy. This was for a visitor who came to cheer the prostrate ladies; a man with a hearty voice of a kind that Ogle detested even when he was well. It was a husky voice, but free, easy, and loud; an untrained voice whose owner had never become conscious of the sound of it in other people's ears. Moreover, it was a voice that burred its r's, shortened its a's, and slurred and buried syllables in the Midland manner. "Middle West people!" Ogle moaned to himself. "Right in the next cabin to me! I've got to listen to them all the way over! That on top of *this* !" Feebly he called upon his Maker.

"Hah, but it's a great night!" the hearty voice exclaimed; and into Ogle's poisoned heart there came a profound animosity; for obviously here was a man undamaged, in perfect health. "Reg'lar January ocean weather, they tell me," this impervious man said cheerily. "Honey, how's Baby?"

The inquiry was bad for Ogle; he was a fastidious young man, sensitive to language, and the words upset him, though he was brave enough to repeat them. "'Honey, how's Baby?'" he whispered loathingly. "'Honey, how's Baby?'" A slight convulsion resulted, and again he called upon a higher power.

"You feelin' any better, Baby?" the terrible Midlander in the next room inquired.

But the voice of the objectionably suffering woman rebuked him faintly. "Let Libby alone. Don't lean over her. You're letting drops of water drip down on her off your overcoat. How'd you get so wet?"

"On deck. I found a door I guess they forgot to lock and went out there. Got tired sittin' around that smokin'-room upstairs; there aren't but two other men up there; all the rest of the passengers seasick, every last one of 'em, the barkeeper says; and those two that weren't didn't show much signs of sociability—Easterners, I expect; scared to talk to anybody. So I hunted around till I found this door that hadn't been locked; and my, *my*, but there's big doin's goin' on outdoors up there! It's a pity you and Baby got to miss it."

Upon this a third voice spoke unexpectedly, a girl's: "Quit calling me 'Baby'!"

It was a sweet and peevish voice; sweet musically,

but peevish in what it expressed; and the bitter young playwright liked it no more than he did the others, especially as it brought a noisy burst of laughter from the visitor. "That's the ticket!" he cried, delighted. "Showin' some spunk to the old man! I guess you aren't so seasick but what you're still able to fight, Baby."

"I told you to quit calling me 'Baby'," the girl's voice said, and there was more than peevishness in it now; it held the resentment that springs from a hatred freshly roused. "I've thought once or twice about jumping off this ship before you get me over there," it continued. "If you don't quit calling me 'Baby,' I will. I mean it. You'll find out!"

"Now, now!" the man said soothingly. "I just came in to see if I couldn't do something or other for you or Mamma; you oughtn't to get so mad, Libby. Don't you want me to go bring you something?"

"No, I don't. If you want to do anything for me, keep out of my sight."

The hearty person seemed to be a little grieved by this, though after a moment or so he was able to produce some sounds of approving laughter. "Well, well! She's got plenty spunk all right, hasn't she, Mamma? Never mind! I'll hop along if you're sure there isn't anything you'll let me do for you. I guess I'll go on back upstairs and sit around awhile some more with those two frozen-faces; I'm not sleepy yet."

"Oh, dear!" the girl moaned. "Can't you stop talking about it and go? Go wherever you want to, so you go! For pity's sake, go and get seasick!"

"*Me?*" He shouted with inconsiderate laughter. "I never felt better in my life. Never even had a good look at the Atlantic Ocean before, let alone takin' a trip on it; never set my foot in anything bigger'n a rowboat, except a lake excursion steamer once or twice, twenty years ago, and yet I'm one o' the only three well passengers out of the whole ship-load! Me seasick? You got to wish worse than that on me before you get *me* down, Baby!"

"I told you if you ever called me that again——"

"There! There!" he said.

But he was interrupted by the querulous voice of the woman who had so frequently threatened to die. "Let the child alone, can't you, Papa? Can't you see you're only getting her more and more upset with you?"

"Oh, now, come!" he said. "Libby isn't goin' to let a little seasickness make her hate her old papa!"

"You know it isn't seasickness that makes me hate

you," the girl said fiercely; and Ogle had an impression that she lifted herself and made an angry gesture toward the door. "Aren't you *ever* going to get out of here?"

"All right! All right! It wasn't *me* that wanted to leave God's country and go scramblin' around over the globe; you got to blame Mamma for that. Never mind; I'm goin'." Then, before the door closed, Ogle heard the husky, hearty voice in a final solicitation. "Honey, you do your best for Baby!"

The miserable young man groaned from the depths. His neighbours were a mother and a daughter, evidently; the daughter engaged in some sort of war with her father, and the three of them outlanders of that particular type to which, of all types in the world, his own fastidiousness found the greatest objection. Before him, if the ship did not sink, he foresaw eleven days and three quarters of physical agony accompanied by the beating upon his ears of family quarrellings in the odious accent to which he was most shudderingly sensitive.

"Rotarians!" he whispered. "'Honey, how's Baby?'" But he was unwise to repeat this paternal inquiry, for immediately he became deathly sick.

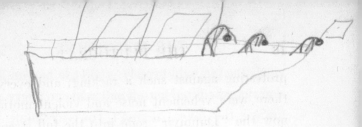

II

IN THE morning a vague and stormy light coming into his cabin from the turbulent day was at intervals almost extinguished by the rushing of gray water over the ponderous glass of the two portholes. He must have slept a little, or at least obtained the relief of stupor, for the daylight surprised him when he saw it; but his surprise, like all else that was his, offered him no pleasure. True, the virulence of his illness had in some measure spent itself; but all his powers were enfeebled; and his interior was like an empty house after a tragedy, threatening to be haunted. Outside his cabin the corridors roared with funnelled wind; bayings and whistlings from obscure sources hunted through the ship like wild hounds and mournful huntsmen; the dark water rushed upon the glass of the portholes ominously, as if determined to get in and finish him; and still he spiralled high, higher than ever, then lurched down and down weightlessly—to rise again. The steamer's fabric screeched rather than squeaked, protesting against such a racking; and everywhere there were vehement noise and violent motion, for now the "Duumvir" rode into the full strength of the storm.

All day wind and ocean struck the ship more and more heavily until late in the afternoon, when a climax seemed to be reached. Ogle clung weakly to the bars at the head of his bed and wondered if even a great liner couldn't be lost at sea. The "Duumvir" was the pride of Italy, he knew;—at least, it was the pride of the Italian mercantile marine, and although he thought of Christopher Columbus he wondered if Italians were still good mariners; for he remembered nervously that Columbus sailed the seas more than four hundred years ago, and a race can lose its cunning. Other people shared his doubts, he discovered, when the rollings and pitchings and howlings were at their worst. All day he had heard nothing from his neighbours, perhaps because other noises prevented; but now, after a protracted out-rageousness of motion and commotion, something of great weight, probably a trunk, crashed sonorously against the separating door, and the voice of the mother of the rebellious girl screamed into the corri-dor.

"Steward!" Ogle heard her wailing. "You man, there! You! Listen! If this ship's going to the bottom oughtn't I to get *dressed ?*"

The steward, an Italian like the rest of the ship's people, spoke no English.

"Madame?"

"Oughtn't I to get *dressed ?*"

The voice of the daughter was heard then, calling angrily: "If he's a respectable man, he'd say you certainly ought! Don't go out there like that. Come back in here and shut that door."

The general uproar, increasing, covered and merged all other sounds, making them indistinguishable; but evidently the mother obeyed, and for the rest of that horrifying day Ogle heard no more of his hated neighbours. The dark came early, and an hour later someone fell against his outer door, opened it, and fumbled along the wall.

"Who's there?" Ogle inquired, though he felt no interest in his own question and cared little what the reply might be.

"Ecco," a mournful voice responded, and the electric light brightened the room intolerably.

"Murder," Ogle said feebly, and, opening pained eyes, beheld his sick steward leaning upon the foot of the bed and looking at him wanly. The man's untidy hair was a lustrous black, and it could be seen that ordinarily he was of a swarthy complexion; but he had no swarthiness now. On the contrary, his pallor was disquieting and so was his expression. "Mangiare?" he said almost in a whisper, and closed his eyes pathetically. "Mangiare?"

Ogle had no wish to comprehend his meaning. "You'd better go away, steward. I don't speak Italian. No Italian. Italian no."

The steward wavered, but tightened his clutch upon the foot of the bed. "Vous voulez manger quelque chose?"

Ogle understood that he was now being addressed in the French language, which he had studied for several years in school and college, but without ever acquiring any great practical facility in its usage. However, he remembered a phrase. "Qu'est-ce que c'est?"

"Voulez manger?"

"Qu'est-ce que c'est?"

The man opened his mouth and with a limp forefinger pointed to the aperture.

"Eat?" Ogle said incredulously. "No!"

"No!" the steward echoed, agreeing; then, balancing, staggering and plunging, made his way out of the room. Ogle wished that he had not come, and that he had not made that gesture of opening his mouth and pointing to it: ocean travel was difficult enough without these pantomimes, the unhappy passenger thought. However, the second night was not so bad as the first, although the storm showed no abatement during the earlier nocturnal hours, and Ogle, himself, did not perceive his condition to be materially improved. His impression was that he lay awake all night, suffering incessantly, everlastingly spiralling, inside and out, and listening to the heavy swish of water upon the glass of the two portholes. Nevertheless, he slept briefly at intervals without knowing it, and toward morning his slumbers grew deeper and longer. When he woke after the longest, two ovals of sunshine were dancing over his floor; the room was bright, the glass of the portholes dry and glittering; and presently, though still a little dizzy, he dared to think that the motion of the ship had grown rhythmic and sweeter.

There was creaking still and some complaint in the vessel's fabric; but the great noises were gone, and in this comparative quiet he heard the opening and closing of the outer door of the next cabin.

"Well, well, folkses!" the loud voice of the hearty Midlander exclaimed. "It's after ten o'clock. Aren't you ever goin' to get up? Upstairs everything's fine—lots o' people out, and it's pretty nearly like springtime on deck. Honey, how's Baby feelin' this morning?"

Ogle sat up in his bed, with his hands over his ears. "'Honey, how's Baby?'" he murmured. "I've got to get out of this!" And with that he felt sufficient life and health returned into him to set foot upon his slowly rising floor.

The hearty voice continued its encouragement in the next room; but Ogle heard it indistinctly, and, as he turned on the salt water in his bathtub, not at all. If he had to listen to any more talk of Honey and Baby he would be prostrated again, he was certain; and to save himself he roused all his powers. So, an hour later, he was enabled to make a somewhat pallid appearance upon deck.

The long promenade, lined with muffled passengers in their chairs, slowly and regularly heaved up forward and sank aft, then heaved up aft and sank by the ship's bows, like a "board walk" at a summer resort made into a gigantic teeter-totter; for the sparkling green sea, laced with white, was still high and lively, showing a horizon like a deep-toothed saw. Many of the shrouded passengers looked preoccupied with introspective doubts; others were serious over troubles too severe and too recent to be so soon forgotten; and, in spite of the sunshine and the inspiriting air, a few lay haggard in their chairs, their anxieties not concealed by closed eyes. Nevertheless, a dozen or more were already briskly promenading; and, as Ogle emerged, a group of chattering young people rushed by him as merrily as if there never had been such a thing as a northeaster off our coast.

He was not yet able to understand their levity; but, having been conducted to his deck chair and neatly enfolded to the waist in a rug, by an attentive steward, he found his cares lighter, and after half an hour or so of what was almost a comfortable relaxation, he accepted a cup of broth from the steward's tray, and drank it with something like pleasure. Life might be worth living after all, he began to perceive, and even the "luxury of ocean travel" not altogether a trap for the gullible. Becoming more and more inclined toward cheerfulness, he first endured, then feebly welcomed, the thought of food, ending by lunching cautiously—yet undeniably taking nourishment—from a tray in his lap. He even went so far as to think of a cigarette, but decided that the time had not yet come for so great a hazard.

Instead of smoking, he found in a pocket of his overcoat a little pamphlet with a printed list of the "Duumvir's" passengers, and entertained himself with it for a time, first looking to see if his own name had been properly spelled. He found it, "Mr. Laurence Ogle," correct, and he repeated it inaudibly several times, wondering how many of his fellow voyagers were interested, or perhaps even a little excited, to find that name upon the list. Probably some of the more intelligent of them were already trying to identify him among the passengers, and although he smiled at his own vanity, the picture pleased him, as well it might. For, although he did not realize it, this thought was a decisive symptom of recovery; he was almost himself again.

What somewhat modified his pleasure was the fact that his name appeared at the bottom of a page. The list was in alphabetical order and he understood that no slight had been intended; but from "Abbott" to "Yountze" he was unable to discover any prestige of celebrity comparable to his own, and although he was sensible enough to understand that of course it was unimportant where a name appeared upon a page, whether at the top, the bottom, or in the middle, still it did seem to him that a little thought might have arranged matters better. Most of the other names were a mere wilderness of the commonplace in which the eye wandered without interest.

There were exceptions, however;—ne .ound one of them not far above "Mr. Laurence Ogle"; and this particular exception arrested his attention as if with a faint strain of music played upon foreign and unfamiliar instruments. "Momoro" was the name; "Mme. Momoro," and, underneath it, "Mr. Hyacinthe Momoro." Ogle murmured "Momoro" over to himself several times, "Momoro—Madame Momoro; Hyacinthe Momoro—Madame Momoro, Hyacinthe Momoro—Momoro." Momoro was the most romantic name he had ever encountered, he thought; a name operatic in flavour and suggestive of high performances in history or even antique legend. Moreover, it might be a name of practical value to him; for if he should ever make use of French "characters" in a play he could call one of them "Momoro." Indeed, Momoro so fascinated him that, letting the list drop in his lap, he began dreamily to

construct some cobwebbings of plot about a charming central figure, "Madame Momoro—Madame la
Marquise de Momoro," he would call her, perhaps.
One of his reasons for being aboard the "Duumvir"
was his belief that he would do well to get away from
plays and the theatre for a while; but the dramatist's
habit of mind prevailed: "Momoro" began to wind
him up as if he had been clockwork. He lay back
in his chair, languidly watching the rhythmic ascent
and descent of the rail against green sea and blue
sky; and before long he was selecting a cast for
"Momoro" which he decided would be an excellent
title. Elsie Grennell, that beautiful brunette, would
play "Madame de Momoro;"—of course a heroine of
that name should be dark.

As the afternoon wore on, the ship's motion became
steadily less emphatic; the January sharpness of the
air grew gentler over the softer sea, yet remained
bracing; more passengers gained confidence enough
to forget their introspections, trusted themselves
upon their feet and set forth upon a brisker and
brisker promenading; the stricken, no longer limp,
began to sit up and look about them; laughter was
heard along the decks. Then, since everywhere this
blither spirit seemed to breathe, Ogle felt it and forgot

his play building. "By George!" he said to himself. "I believe I knew what I was about, after all." And with that he began to feel sorry for his friends in wintry New York, unfortunate people bound down to desks or to nightly work in the theatre, going about through snow in jolting, dirty taxicabs and drinking poisons to alleviate the natural oppression of so dull a life.

He lighted a cigarette, found it fragrant, and, observing with pleasure that of four lively girls passing his chair in a group three were comely and all prettily dressed for sea voyaging, he believed his health almost entirely restored. Earlier in the day these damsels would have had no comeliness in his eyes; he would have looked upon them with distaste; but now, all at once, he thought them charming. He tossed off his rug, and after only a moment of uncertainty as he rose, began to pace the deck like an old hand, experienced in many crossings of the sea.

At least that was his air, convincingly worn; for he had a sometimes burdensome self-consciousness and was anxious to avoid the curious ignominy that attaches to new apprenticeship or to the doing of almost anything for the first time. What he thought of as "gaucheries" were abhorrent to him;

he was determined to exhibit none and to be no parvenu either at sea or in the strange land beyond. Thus, during his protracted promenading, as he encountered and reëncountered the four lively girls, who were going round the deck in the opposite direction, he gave them an opportunity to think a little about the indifferent and easy yet sure-footed stride of an old traveller to whom sea-legs were virtually second nature. Reproductions of his photographs had been printed frequently in periodicals and "rotogravure sections" of late; and he thought it possible that the four damsels had already identified him. If they had, perhaps they had also seen the article about him that called him "the most sophisticated of all our new playwrights"; an article he was glad someone had been discriminating enough to write. Naturally, anybody familiar with it would suppose that a sophisticated playwright like Laurence Ogle had "crossed" three or four times a year during most of his life.

Unmistakably the lively girls took note of him; the elaboration with which they seemed unaware of him and concerned solely with their own private gayeties proved their awareness. Indeed, they could not well lack it; for his good looks were unusual, though he was not impressive in figure, being short and slight. Probably the promenading young women overlooked this defect, if it were one; some quality of knowingness in movement and attire may have successfully atoned in their eyes for a deficiency in height, breadth, and muscular power. Moreover, his symmetrical shapings of feature and pleasant harmonies of dark hair and skin, and his notable, shadowed eyes were all made more significant by those delicate markings that blend into the expression of the attribute young maidenhood most appreciates in the male. One of these maidens mentioned it just after they had come face to face with him for the second time. "He certainly has gobs of distinction," she said. "I adore burning, reserved eyes like that; especially with one of those tiny moustaches. Bet you anything he turns out to be a young Spanish poet in English clothes!"

Other passengers were beginning to notice and estimate their fellow-voyagers, even to venture upon speech with strangers among them; for the "Duumvir" was not a hurried North Atlantic "ferry" merely hustling preoccupied crowds to and fro between commercial and fashion capitals; this was a voyage of pleasure, although its opening pleasantries had been of a humour too rough for its victims to perceive the joke. But with the increasing amenity of the sea and the recovery of something less capricious underfoot and something dependable within themselves, the pleasure-seekers began to catch their first glimpses of what they sought. They dispersed themselves over the ship, taking the air high and low upon all the decks; pulling at weights in the gymnasium; reading or talking in corners of the big salons; contemplating cards or liquor in the smoking-room; or, bending over the little French desks in the writing-room, they began their diaries, and scribbled letters, both diaries and letters opening with accounts of a hurricane at sea, written by the survivors. But at a little after four o'clock most of them were listening to the excellent Italian orchestra in the enormous lounge.

This was the greatest of the great public rooms of the steamer, a tapestried and walnut-panelled room into which a New England village church of fair size might have been squeezed with a little inconvenience to the steeple; and here, as the music began to be heard, the convalesced travellers came to seat themselves in easy chairs grouped about small tables pleasantly accoutred in napery and silver for tea.

Then a prevailing characteristic became apparent in the assembly: the colour of the hair of these adventurers to Africa and Spain and Italy was predominantly gray or white; only here and there did a dark young head or a blonde one enliven the eye of youth looking the place over, hopeful of companions.

In good truth, the pleasure-seekers were elderly, most of them long coupled in marriage; though some were widows, some were spinsters, and a few were worn but hardened bachelors and widowers, travelling in mildly jovial small groups. Their like could have been found in the hotels of California, of Florida, of Georgia and of Virginia and the Carolinas at this season, with youth there as here not much in evidence among them. For youth must be at school or in college, or earning its living, and younger middle age must be providing and storing for the future; but these were people who had provided and stored comfortably enough to grant themselves at least a winter's pleasuring, and now sallied bravely forth to enjoy their own and the earth's fruitions. They were from everywhere in the country, and most of them were wondering a little who the others might be.

From a doorway Ogle looked in upon them thoughtfully. He had a mind to drink a cup of tea and ascertain what music the orchestra might be expected to offer; but they were playing Puccini; nothing intelligently modern was to be hoped of them, he feared; and among the gray heads he saw little to cheer him. These people were well enough dressed and no doubt well enough mannered too, he thought; but their general caste was as discouragingly evident as their age. Successful bourgeoisie, merchants, bankers, brokers, manufacturers, and members of the unsophisticate professions; most of them retired, or else able to leave their businesses or offices to the care of sons and junior partners;—thus the keen young dramatist in the doorway appraised and assorted them, finding them and their wives and the few daughters and young sons who sat among them a dreary spectacle.

Indeed, they oppressed him; he would have none of them, not even though he desired tea; and so, turning away, he walked aft through a corridor and ascended to the smoking-room upon the deck above. He had a friend on board, and there was where he would most probably find him, Ogle was sure; for there was a bar in the smoking-room.

III

WHEN he opened the door his first impression was that someone had been burning incense. It seemed an odd thing to do in a room that had a bar and a barkeeper in it; but these were inconspicuous, the bar being a short one of lustreless dark wood in a corner and the barkeeper a studious young man enclosed, as it might be, in a library alcove, for he was intent upon a serious-looking book. High-backed chairs and deep leather divans permitted the tops of a few heads to þe seen; but there was audible not even a murmur of conversation, and in the centre of the room three ladies and a youth were playing bridge with the noiseless contemplation appropriate to their pastime;—to Ogle's surprise this appeared to be the quietest place on the whole boat. Windows of stained glass sent amber and azure and ruby filtrations of sunshine to swing slowly to and fro upon the walls of dull blackish wood; and the smell of incense seemed not so misplaced after all.

It was traceable, however, not to a censer, but to the bridge table and a cigarette in a remarkable holder of yellow ivory and green jade poised in the interesting long white hand of one of the players. Ogle had never felt anything except pitying amazement for a person who smoked scented cigarettes; but his first glance at this lady destroyed a lifelong prejudice against them; she was instantly of so compelling a presence.

In the dark-walled room with its dark furniture she was as conspicuous as a tall lady in a Sargent portrait. She had a long face, long limbs, a long body; but all with a slender amplitude and no meagreness. Her long aquiline face was not thin, but sleekly contoured, like her vivid hair which seemed to be composed of long, pale bronze threads laid close to one another and polished to a soft brilliancy. And with her length she had grace; her long gestures, as she played, were exquisitely accurate and restrained—Ogle immediately found the word "musical" to describe them—and she sat beautifully poised in her chair, neither resting against its back nor leaning forward to the card table. Moreover, he was as pleased with what she wore as with her grace and lengthiness; a high distinction being marked by that, too, he thought. In a whole ship-load of tailors' woollen "sport clothes," here was a Parisian afternoon gown of bronze green and black and silver, silk and metal and a little lace, worn by one who quietly knew herself to be above both the ordinary conception of maritime utilities and the advice of fashion journals. Her independenc went so far as to treat the smoking-room to a kind of inti-macy; no hat covered the polished pale bronze hair; beyond question this was a woman who would need to know a better reason for doing anything than that other women did it.

Never, Ogle felt, had he known that badgered word "elegance" so vividly expressed to a glance of the eye; though he took more than a glance. She had no definite age; she might have been a marvellous forty or twenty-five; but the latter would have been precocious, the pleased and impressed young drama-tist concluded. For no one under thirty could be so completely what he thought the picture of the perfect woman of the world; and, deciding that she must surely be French, he found it appropriate to describe her to himself in her own tongue. In spite of the difficulty lately attending his steward's attempt to communicate with him in that language, he sometimes used French phrases as the only ones that would fully express his meaning; so now he felt that "woman of the world" was but a pale definition of the Parisian exquisite before him, and in his mind repeated, "Femme du monde"—and added further Gallicism to that: "Femme du monde parfaitement et parfaitement Parisienne!"

She seemed entirely occupied with the cards before her, or else, absently, with the long tube of ivory and jade and the perfumed little cigarette it held; but Ogle nevertheless had the impression that she might be aware of him and of his almost startled interest in her; for although she did not glance at all in his direction she had the cool and competent air of a person whom nothing whatever escapes. So, after standing near the doorway a moment or two longer, pretending to be looking in a general way over the whole room, which was not of the heroic dimensions displayed in the great salons below, he walked on, seeking his friend.

Passing round a high-backed double divan, he came upon two lounging young men deeply sunk in soft leather cushions and languidly preoccupied with amber liquids. Each held a tall glass in his hand, sipping at intervals in a communion probably satisfying, since neither showed any other sign of life; but as Ogle appeared one of them became slightly animated. He was a frail-bodied, fair young man, with a long, pale nose, a faint chin, eye-glasses over greenish twinklings, and, for the semblance of a moustache, a few tiny spikes apparently of fine hay.

"Laurence Ogle!" he said, bestirring himself to extend a hand. "I was wondering when you'd show up. Have something? Anyhow, sit down with us, won't you? This is Mr. Macklyn—George Wilmer Macklyn—you ought to know each other. I was just telling him you were on board."

"He didn't need to tell me," Mr. Macklyn said, as Ogle took a chair facing the divan. "This idiot of an Albert Jones thinks all other people are idiots because he is. I saw that you were to be on the 'Duumvir' in the theatrical notes of a newspaper the morning before we sailed. Naturally I was interested, because I'd seen your new play only the night before. I considered it a very impressive piece of work."

The blond Mr. Jones laughed. "You can believe Macklyn means it, Laurence," he was kind enough to say. "Macklyn is one of those fearful people who are always honest. You know his work, don't you?"

"Ah"— Ogle said, and then after a moment, risked a lie of courtesy. "Oh, yes—yes, indeed."

Mr. Macklyn shook his head, frowning. He was a serious-looking, bushy-browed, swarthy young man; and although for the moment his attitude might be languid his expression was earnest, even severe, seeming to be so habitually. "I fear you say that out of mere kindness, Mr. Ogle. My work is not well known. Necessarily it can be for only the few. I should much prefer to write frankly for the many as you do; but I doubt if I'd know how. It requires another technique, one that I admire none the less. I don't underrate the importance of any man who can reach the mob, Mr. Ogle. The rewards are enormous and the art can be sincere where perhaps it can't always be searching."

"'Searching'?" Ogle said inquiringly; and with no very hearty approval he looked upon this friend of his friend and wondered how Mr. Macklyn happened upon the particular word. "Searching" was precisely what his new play had been called by all of the five most intelligent critics he knew. Not one of them had omitted it, and with so emphatic a corroboration he looked upon searchingness as pretty much his accepted specialty. "You write, yourself, Mr. Macklyn?" he inquired, a little coldly.

"Macklyn's a poet," Mr. Jones informed him. "I thought you wouldn't know his things. Nobody does. He tries to make people notice him by using no punctuation and omitting capital letters; but it hasn't got him very far. I think I'll leave frames off my pictures and see if somebody won't write a few more articles about them."

"You'd do well whether the articles were written or not," the serious Macklyn said. "Does life frame its pictures? Does nature? Albert speaks flippantly of my method, Mr. Ogle; but he knows well enough why I deliberately use it, though it costs me all but a few readers and even some of them read me only to mock. He paints his pictures with the loose stroke of a Gauguin and the colour of a Picasso, knowing that he, too, can reach but one here, another there, and never the mob; and yet he chaffs me for assuming the same privilege. I write poems that have no rhymes, no metre and no punctuation because I am expressing my searchings in that way."

"'Searchings'?" Ogle said. "There might be

several definitions of that word. What kind of searchings do you mean?"

"Within myself. Within life. Within this formlessness we call the universe. Do you find capital letters and metres and semi-colons in passion, in desire, in the disturbing and despairing deep wonder that besets us as we succumb to this shapelessness we call life? Why, even you, Mr. Ogle, popular playwright as you are—you at least broke away from the old, stupid rigidities imposed by the dead art of yesterday when you closed your play without concluding it, so to speak. I thought that was very fine. You not only resisted the temptation for the detestable 'happy ending,' you bravely left your characters just where they were—groping, getting nowhere, caught in the relentlessness of their own blind desires and deafened by the clashings of a remorseless chance from which there was no escape. You showed them struggling, entangled, prompted by only the two primal impulses of sex and greed, as we all are; and you left them to go on helplessly and drearily and wonderingly realizing their own tragic condition, but unable to escape from it. Gorki and Turgeniev and Dostoieffsky would applaud you. It was like some great, gloomy, keyless fugue played upon an organ with no cheap and pretty sounds at the command of the stops. I'm glad of the opportunity to give you my opinion of 'The Pastoral Scene,' Mr. Ogle. I thought it 'popular,' I admit it. 'Popular,' yes; but nevertheless magnificent. It expressed for the many the same ideologism—if I may say so—that I attempt in my own work for the few."

Ogle, at first not too favourably impressed with the bushy-browed young man, began to like him better and to feel willing for him to go on talking. "You're very kind," the playwright said. "As a matter of fact, both the manager and I were nervous about putting on 'The Pastoral Scene' for the very reason that it did not seem possible it would find an audience. Popularity was the one thing we couldn't imagine its possessing, and no one could have been more surprised than I was by its showing that after all there *is* a great sophisticated and intelligent public for an uncompromising realism. I hope you didn't find the play quite without that searchingness you seem to admire in art, Mr. Macklyn."

The serious young man made no response and appeared to be unaware that an inquiry had been addressed to him. Upon concluding his own remarks he had applied himself frowningly to his glass, but without looking either at it or at his companions. Under his bushy brows, in fact, his gaze quickly fixed itself upon the lady whose appearance Ogle had found so interesting.   Her chair was only a few feet from the end of the divan where Macklyn sat and her attention seemed impassively upon the card table; nevertheless, there was something in the sidelong eyes of the poet, as they sought her, that made Ogle suspect this new acquaintance of having talked for her benefit, or at least in the hope that she would hear and be impressed.   Macklyn had neither looked at her as he talked, nor by any emphasis of voice shown himself selfishly unconscious that people were playing bridge close by; but the playwright, accustomed to look for the significant in the small, and marking the sidelong eye, could not resist suspicion. The next moment he found himself suspecting his friend Albert Jones of the same thing.

"No wonder you had doubts of your play's success with the crowd, Laurence," Mr. Jones said; and Ogle, familiar with the speaker's ordinary voice, was momentarily surprised to find it improved to sound a more suave and musical note than it did usually. "It's always surprising to find one's obscure ideologisms appreciated.   Last year I sent a brace of my things to the Salon d'Automne—little pictures analysing a thought of Verlaine's about windows; that was all. When I found the Parisian critics were taking them seriously, I almost fainted away!" And the glance of the painter immediately imitated the glance of the poet, darting sidelong to the lady at the card table.

The appearance of the two adults, Albert Jones and George Wilmer Macklyn, bore no resemblance to that of little children; and yet, somewhat to the irritation of the gentlemen observing them, each of them was so ingenuous as to wear precisely the air of a child who hopes he has said something important and looks quickly to Mamma to see how favourably it has affected her. Unmistakably, they were offering little exhibitions before the unknown lady; and Ogle was annoyed to think that she might perceive that they were doing so and associate him in her mind with blunderers so naïve. She looked clever enough to comprehend performances for her benefit much more subtle than these; and he decided to detach himself in her thoughts from the two performers.

"Oh, I don't know," he said, and, without realizing that he might himself be performing a little, he laughed more musically than was customary with him in moments of amusement. "Ideologism is rather a broad term, after all. We were talking of that the other evening at a country-house dinner. A French officer was staying there—a colonel of engineers on a mission, the Comte du Bourg—and he and I were arguing about the difference between the new ideologism and the old. A member of the Cabinet was up from Washington for the week-end, a very practical man; and he and Du Bourg preferred the old, I the new. As a matter of fact I was rather astonished to find that a member of the American President's Cabinet knew what the word meant. One doesn't look to our native politicians for even the things any fourteen-year-old schoolboy is familiar with nowadays."

With that, wondering if the lady at the bridge table might possibly know the Comte du Bourg, he could not refrain from glancing at her to see if her attention had been at all arrested. Apparently it had not. She sat in profile to him, and a comely long profile her whole person offered to view, ending in a silver-buckled black slipper, tapered from a high instep of silvered silk. But she merely played a card from her hand, and gave no sign that ideologism, old or new, or engineers of France, or statesmen of America, had place in her thoughts.

"Quite a blow we had off the old Hook," Mr. Jones remarked, returning a preoccupied gaze to his glass. "Wonderful how everything's quieted down and keeps on flattening. You could hardly tell now that you aren't on a Fall River boat coming up the Sound. That first night out the only well people on the whole boat seemed to be Macklyn here and me."

"No," Macklyn said, also giving up his scrutiny of the card table. "There was that impossible man who kept blatting at us."

"Oh, I shouldn't count *him*," Mr. Jones returned. "I'd hardly call him 'people'; he's just one of those things our glorious country seems to love to breed. Kept trying to get us to talk to him, Laurence, telling us how he'd never been on a boat before in his life, and how sick his wife and daughter were, but he never touched by a hair; and all about how good business is this year. Pretty awful! By the way, you weren't laid by the heels, were you? Didn't see you about, though."

"No," Ogle said. "I decided to keep below. I'm a little susceptible in a hurricane, and I took that precaution."

"'Hurricane'?" His friend stared at him. "My dear fellow, that wasn't a hurricane. It was only a gale. You've never been in a hurricane at sea."

"Why haven't I?"

"Because, if you had, you wouldn't call a north-east gale one. Why, the fourth time I crossed——" He began a narrative of the sea, including a mathematical description of waves encountered and quotations from the solemn declarations of ships' officers; but the attention he obtained was scant, and presently he discontinued his account and turned, as his companions did, to look at the bridge table.

The lady for whom the three had been all along performing now made her voice audible for the first time in their hearing, a contralto voice of great richness. "Hyacinthe," she said, addressing the youth opposite her with a little sharpness, though nevertheless indulgently;— "c'est à toi, bébé."

"Madame Momoro!" the playwright exclaimed to himself, "Madame Momoro!" This was she whose musical name had sounded a melody to him even from the prosaic passenger list, setting him to build a new play, with her for the heroine. Delighted, he asked for no better. "C'est à toi, bébé," she said. How charming that was, Ogle thought, and how adorable the word! Only a Frenchwoman could have said it.

IV

THE youth to whom this adorable word was spoken, said, "Pardon," absently, and played a card. He was a slender boy of eighteen or twenty, "cameo like" in profile, Ogle thought, finding the young Hyacinthe like Mme. Momoro in that as well as in hair and eyes and gracefulness. The son was the slighter, however, and not so tall; and there was a vertical line between his eyebrows, where a definite groove readily appeared from time to time as he concentrated his thoughts upon his cards. Otherwise his face was of an olive suavity and his reserved expressionlessness complete, though when his long-lashed eyelids were lifted, what seemed to be revealed was not at all the expected innocence of youth, but an intelligence surprisingly seasoned by precocious experience. For if, as Ogle thought, the mother was an ideal portrait of the complete woman of the world, then no less was the son a fine little picture of a man of the world already finished, lacquered and polished at eighteen.

The other two players were thin, elderly ladies in mourning, and gave the impression of being sisters, not only in the grief for which they had dressed themselves in black. Sisters in affluence, too, they appeared to be—not poor even if they owned nothing more than the rings upon their fingers. They were but background dimnesses, however, in the eyes of the three surreptitiously staring young Americans. The beautiful quality of Mme. Momoro's voice when she made it audible had settled any possible doubt about her; for no matter how pleasing the appearance of any person may be, his quality is not to be recognized until his voice is heard; and unexpected voices bring disappointment to many dreamers like poets, painters, and playwrights. But the poet and the painter and the playwright present when Mme. Momoro spoke to her son in the quiet smoking-room of the "Duumvir," heard something even lovelier than what would have sufficed to meet their expectations. Her voice was more than the confirmation of her appearance; and as for Ogle, after she had spoken he felt that to be in the same room with her was like being enclosed with some supreme work of art. He became so acutely conscious of her that it began to seem that he had known her a long time.

Macklyn was the first to turn his head from her. He finished his amber drink, touched his lips delicately with a blue-bordered handkerchief, and said almost in a whisper: "I've written a few things in French. There's nothing else so flexible. Do you speak Arabic, Mr. Ogle?"

"Arabic? No. I've never had occasion to. Why?"

"I thought the item I saw about you mentioned you were going to North Africa. One can't know the Arabs unless he speaks with them. Of course it isn't all Arabic that they speak. By no means! There are some interesting poems in the Kabyle dialects, exquisite, wistful things. I remember one beginning, 'I play my shepherd's pipe on the hillside, and my love hears it among her young goats. How her heart beats as my dulcet sounds reach her ears'— a thing like a Sicilian Pastorale. These things are of the true art; they use no punctuation or capitals, let me tell you. They are not written at all in the original, they are transmitted by word of mouth because they are just cries from the heart. Of course they become conventional when transcribed in French. I suppose you'll go among the Kabyles?"

"Probably," Ogle returned, though he had **never**

before heard of these interesting tribes. He had decided upon his excursion impulsively, only a week before sailing, when the success of "The Pastoral Scene" appeared to be secure; and most of his preparations for the journey had been concerned with a tailor, a haberdasher, and the agent through whom he manœuvred to secure a cabin. "The Kabyles," he said thoughtfully. "I think so. Yes, I should like to learn something of them at first hand."

"You'll find them wonderful," Macklyn assured him. "A noble looking people. If you dressed them properly, for instance—though that would be a pity —they wouldn't look out of place on this boat."

Mr. Jones laughed compassionately. "Queer idea, that, Macklyn. Is it your thought that most of our fellow-countrymen on the 'Duumvir' exhibit a high degree of distinction? From what I've seen of them, they appear a pretty ordinary looking lot of people, I must say."

"Yes," Macklyn admitted, "I spoke hastily. They're on the dead level of the commonplace, with hardly a soul among them one would care ever to see again, judging by appearances and the passenger list. Except Mr. Ogle's and yours, Albert, there wasn't an American name that meant anything whatever or that one had ever heard of before. I'm afraid you're our only celebrity, Mr. Ogle."

Ogle laughed deprecatingly. "That's not always an enviable situation to be in . Conspicuousness isn't invariably pleasant, you know; but I'm afraid you're right about our fellow-passengers I stopped in the lounge for a moment a little while ago; they appeared to be all there and it was rather a well-dressed but unstimulating assemblage—the men drinking tea unwillingly, I thought, but both women and men glad to listen to the obviousness of Puccini. This seems better up here. One isn't deafened, and the room itself is rather well done—for this sort of thing, at least. I mean the panelling and the windows aren't bad."

"No," Mr. Jones agreed. "They're rather good; not bad at all—though of course, as you say, for this sort of thing. And the quiet is really pleasant."

"Quiet?" Macklyn repeated inquiringly, and he set down his glass upon a tabouret before him. "Dear me! I'm afraid it isn't going to be. Listen."

At the lower end of the room an open door offered a view of the after deck and of the vessel's turbulent wake, a white foaming canal dividing the blue ocean almost to the horizon. Macklyn made a gesture in this direction; but nothing upon the sea itself caused him to do so, nor for some moments did anything unusual appear beyond the open doorway. Sounds made a heralding entry there, however; sounds intended to be musical, but unsuccessful in carrying out their intention. Voices rough and loud were approaching, deluded into the belief that harmonies of tenors and bassos were produced. Four men, no longer young but still leather-lunged, were singing— or thought they were:

> "Old Aunt Mariar,
> A-sitting by the fire,
> She wants a drink o' gin
> Though she knows it is a sin,
> Aunt Mariar !
> And for fear she'll make a row
> Let's go take one for her now,
>   Mariar!
>   Mariar!
> Dirty old Auntie Mariar!"

Ogle shuddered, the slight convulsive movement of his shoulders being visible to his two companions who sympathized with his distaste acutely. For the rowdy outburst came with a disagreeable shock upon the quiet room where stained glass swung jewelled lights upon the dark walls, and where Mme. Momoro, taller and more serene than other women, was like some tinted statue of a seated goddess in a still temple. So, at least, she appeared to the three sensitive young artists. If she had not been there, they would have felt the uncouth sounds annoying enough, in all conscience, destroying the feeling they had themselves produced in the place by their low-toned conversation about art; but that these liquorish bellowings of "Aunt Mariar" should intrude upon such a presence as hers was an atrocity in manners but too characteristic, they thought indignantly, of some of their travelling fellow-countrymen.

Meanwhile these outlanders were coming nearer, marching evidently, and shouting their indecorous chorus in imitation of a drum-beat:

> "Mariar!
> Mariar!
> Bay rum in a bottle we'll buy 'er!
> Mariar!
> Mariar!
> Dirty old Auntie Mariar!"

And, with that, chanting vociferously, regardless equally of their own appearances and of other people's prejudices, four red-faced middle-aged men marched in lock-step into the room, and, still uproarious, lined themselves against the little bar.

Their leader, a large man with a broad, smooth-shaven face, the ruddiest of all, outshouted the others. "Forget it! Let your Aunt Mariar alone for long enough to tell George, can't you? What's it goin' to be, gentlemen?"

This voice was familiar to Ogle; he recognized it. "Dear me!" he murmured. "It's 'Honey-how's-Baby' again!"

Albert Jones caught the phrase. "What? What do you mean: 'Honey-how's-Baby'?"

"There's a seasick mother and her daughter in the cabin next to mine," Ogle explained. "A person comes in there to see them, and says, 'Honey, how's Baby?' It's that man there."

"That one?" Macklyn inquired. "That's the same fellow who tried to break in with Jones and me the first night out. He told us he didn't know a soul on the ship except his wife and daughter, but he's evidently picked up some congenial bandarlogs. Look at 'em! It's our most terrible native type, and they all belong to it."

The four noisy men, busy at the bar and uncon-scious of the unfavourable regard bent upon them, abated little of their uproar until filled glasses stood before them. Two, with their heads close together, began to sing, "Yes, Sir, She's My Baby," while the other two, one of whom was the person recognized by the three artists as the most objectionable of all, loudly praised the Freedom of the Seas. He delivered himself of a short oration upon this subject.

"Yes, sir; it's just as you say, the folks at home don't realize that all they got to do, if they don't like Prohibition, is to step on a boat. My case, for instance; why, it's been so long since I had what you might call a regular honest-to-goodness drink I'd about forgot there *was* such a thing! The law is all right on land—I voted for it myself—but it's a grand thing the ocean belongs to everybody. I'd 'a' taken a trip to Europe long ago if I'd 'a' realized how much freedom there was in it. And look how Prohibition habits get into a man, though;—it's wonderful! After I introduced myself to ole Doc Taylor yonder, this afternoon, and met you two other gentlemen, what's the first thing we do? Why, Doc says he's got some stuff in his cabin, and just out o' *habit*, what'd we do? Why, sneaked down there with him just the way we would at home, and sat pourin' it out kind of guilty-like until we happened to remember we weren't doin' anything against the law at all and there was an open bar up here where a man had a right to do as he's a mind to, with nobody on earth to tell him he can't, except his wife; and mine's sick, poor woman, thank heaven!" He stopped the duet, putting a hand upon a shoulder of each of the singers. "Gentlemen, I got a toast to propose. Here's to the Atlantic Ocean, the sweet Land of Liberty!"

"There should be a public executioner on board every liner," Macklyn said in a low voice, but with venom. "It's just such fellows as that who make cultivated foreigners think what they do think of Americans. They think he's typical."

"Well, in a way he is," Ogle returned. "At least he's typical of his own type."

Macklyn agreed, frowning, and the three young men stared sombrely at the typical person. Typical or not, the person's appearance, though more than normally jovial under present influences, was not without some impressiveness. He had been at least mannerly enough to remove his fuzzy green cap as a recognition that ladies were present, and the brow revealed beneath his grayish sandy hair was broad, well-shaped, and even of the kind known as command-ing; the blue eyes were genial but shrewd, and the other features not at all unpleasant;—on the contrary, they were harmonious and what is commonly called agreeable, in spite of the fact that they were so far from producing that impression upon the three pained observers. He was fifty, perhaps, and becoming comfortably convex, though without much risk of being defined merely as a fat man.

His toast to the ocean having been heartily honoured, he instantly commanded a refilling of the glasses. "There's only one thing wrong with this ship," he announced. "It's got oil-burning engines and conservatories and a candy store and hot and cold water and a good steam plant and orchestras and automatic watertight steel bulkheads; but it hasn't got any foot-rail on the bar. If they'd remembered to put one in, ocean life would be just perfect—perfect! But anyway, this is a lot nicer than sittin' in Doc's cabin or listening to high-brow opera music in that lobby downstairs. Let's all take our liquor with us, gentlemen, and go sit down over there on the other side of that sofa and have a nice cosy talk."

The location he proposed for this cosiness was highly unacceptable to the three critics. The divan upon which sat Macklyn and Albert Jones was double, with a high back separating the two long seats; and it was the occupation of the vacant one that the objectionable man suggested to his objectionable party. In fact, he did more than suggest it. Carrying a filled glass in one hand, and with his other propelling before him the gray-haired but obviously elated person to whom he had alluded as "Ole Doc Taylor," he urged his friends to this central position in the room, and, in doing so, passed close by the bridge table With horror, Ogle saw the glass in the outstretched hand wavering over the silken shoulder of Mme. Momoro, and though its bearer avoided catastrophe there, the next moment he bumped heavily into the chair of the young Hyacinthe. "Excuse me, young feller," he said. "I never been to Europe before; I like the ocean fine, but I haven't learned to walk on it properly yet."

Hyacinthe rose, and, accepting this apology with a foreign formality, he bowed slightly and quickly, inclining his body from the waist; then, without any change of countenance or looking at the disturber, sat down again and played a card from his hand.

"You'd think *that* might put the man in his place," Macklyn muttered.

But the man was impervious; his voice filled the room. "Doc, you and Mr. Wackstle and Mr. Brown sit on the sofa. I'm goin' to take this chair where I can get a good look at you, so's I'll know you again and be able to pick you out o' the crowd whenever we all want to go somewhere for a nice song and a little conviviality.   That is, if my wife only stays sick long enough, poor woman!"

Then, seeing his friends disposed as he wished, he seated himself in the deep chair facing them, and, appearing to find life genial and his surroundings benevolent, looked beamingly about the room.   His glance fell upon the chilling faces of Macklyn and Albert Jones, who had turned and were looking at him over the back of the divan; and his recognition of them was cordial.   "Howdy, boys!" he said, with a wave of the hand that included the frigid Ogle.   "I see you never get very far away from the bar." After that, unconscious of any rebuff, as the three heads turned stonily away, his gaze moved on, and, becoming aware of Mme. Momoro, remained arrested there.   "Well, you wouldn't have seen it in the old days," he said, in pointedly approving reference to her; "yet I don't know but what it's right pleasant, after all—ladies sittin' around among us and playin' cards and everything, right in the barroom."

For a moment Ogle held his breath.   It was not a mitigation of the man's offence that he had no offensive intention; lightnings should have destroyed the presumptuous fool. Lightnings failing, something ought to be done about it, the playwright thought; and he had impulses to do something about it himself —and to begin by throwing the fellow out of the room, no matter how difficult that might be. Moreover, his inimical urgings were shared by his two friends; Mr. Jones muttered threateningly, while Macklyn said aloud, "I'll wring the boor's neck, if he makes any more references of that kind."

But the goddess-like lady herself was apparently unaware that she had been blasphemed, and her impassiveness was unmarred by the slightest access of hauteur. Her quiet gaze did not waver from her cards; there was not a flicker of eyelid, nor any deepening in the eye itself; any observer might well have concluded that she had no knowledge of the English language. And thus, the shocked but romancing playwright said to himself, did some ancestress of Mme. Momoro's look in the tumbril on the way to the guillotine, cool, untouched, and untouchable, while the *canaille* surged about the cart, powerless to make her conscious of them.

The *canaille* of the present occasion did not delay upon the subject, but, after a philanthropic smiling upon the admirable lady, went on talking: "No, sir;

the old days were mighty different. Why, you take the people on this ship, for instance. You know it yourself, Mr. Wackstle. You say you been to Europe seven times, and this is the first for me; but I bet there's a mighty big difference between the passengers on this ship and the ones on the first ship you went over on. When'd you say that was?"

"Eighteen-ninety-one, Mr. Tinker."

"Tinker!" Albert Jones said bitterly, on the other side of the divan. "The creature's name is Tinker. It *would* be!"

The creature was continuing his dissertation: "Why, there's more big business represented on this vessel right now than what there was on every ship on all the oceans of the world in eighteen-ninety-one, Mr. Wackstle. You read over the passenger list and look at the names on it that stand for big things and accomplishment all over our country. It took my breath; darned if it didn't! I'll bet it would run into hundreds and hundreds o' millions! I tell you there's some mighty big men on this ship, gentlemen, —men I want to *know* before we land 'way over yonder and get all split up and goin' every *which* direction. For instance, you take yourself, Mr. Wackstle. Soon as I saw your name I told my wife, I told her,

'I certainly got to know that man, Mamma!' Poor woman, she was already about gone even that early, and she couldn't take much notice. But you aren't the only well-known man on this boat."

"No," Mr. Wackstle admitted, laughing modestly. "There's a dozen bigger celebrities aboard than *I* claim to be."

"Well, I won't say bigger," the genial Tinker went on, "but there certainly are others. Take James T. Weatheright, for instance; he's the best-known man in the whole State of New York, I expect. Weatheright's Worsteds are practically household goods all over the world. Then there's T. H. Smith, president of the G. L. and W.; Harold M. Wilson, ex-chairman of the Board of the Western Industrial Corporation; Thomas Swingey, of Swingey Brothers, Incorporated; there's both the Holebrooks of the Northwestern Trust; there's Judge Mastin, ex-general counsel for the Roanoke; J. Q. A. McLean, of the Chicago Milling Company—well, talk about an all-star aggregation, why, when you think of what's represented by a passenger list like that you almost wonder how the United States can go on running with these men out here on the ocean!"

His new friend, Wackstle, chuckled. "Well, I

don't know. You've pretty well covered the list, Mr. Tinker; I don't know of anybody on board you've left out; but when you think it over, most o' the gentlemen you've named are like me, either retired or turned the management of their businesses over to other people, except Smith, of course. He's pretty active in the G. L. and W. still, and it would be a bad thing if this boat went down with him on board. As you say, there's a lot of money represented; but if this steamer did ram into something in a fog and go to the bottom, everything back home would go on just about the same, and I don't believe the public would know much difference—except for T. H. Smith and yourself maybe. He'd be the only headliner in the papers, anyhow."

"What!" Tinker exclaimed. "Why, James T. Weatheright——"

"Yes, I admit there might be front-page stuff about Weatheright; but it wouldn't be heavy. Weatheright turned the worsted business over to his sons more than five years ago."

"Look here! Look here!" Tinker was not satisfied. "I don't want to blow my own horn; but I'd like to say right here and now, *my* town would know the difference if this ship went down. And I don't like to dispute you, Mr. Wackstle, but I guess *your* town and these other gentlemen's towns would, too. Why, you take even ole Doc Taylor here——"

But the person he named was in no mood for so serious a discussion; and he began to sing, "Yes, Sir, She's My Baby" again, Mr. Brown joining him. Mr. Tinker looked upon them disapprovingly for a moment; then his brow cleared, and he sang, too.

On the other side of the divan the music was as little appreciated as the mystifying conversation upon celebrities had been. "Dear me!" Albert Jones complained. "There really ought to be some protection. Somebody ought to speak to the chief steward."

"It wouldn't do any good," Macklyn said gloomily. "They cater to this class of people. All of the liners are full of riffraff nowadays, because a different type of people has begun to travel, made prosperous in these last few years. What did you think of that list of 'well-known' Americans aboard, Mr. Ogle?"

Ogle, who had grown a little red during the enumeration of celebrities, was nevertheless able to laugh in response to the direct question. "Quite a blow to

my vanity, I'm afraid. You said I was for the
many, Mr. Macklyn. This seems to indicate I'm for
the few, after all, like you and Albert Jones."

The sombre Macklyn took him literally. "I
shouldn't mind, if I were you. At least you can say
you never sought the bauble reputation in the Provincial's mouth—or, happily, that you never obtained
it. Naturally, this sort of thing would not be entertained by 'The Pastoral Scene!'"

By an interesting coincidence he learned within a
few moments that he was mistaken. The song behind him drew to a rather hoarse conclusion; a steward brought a tray of copious fresh supplies, prepared
at the bar; then the talkative Tinker began a fresh
discourse, this time inspired by the recent effort to
be musical.

"Yes, sir; that's a mighty good song; I like 'Aunt
Mariar' better, though—more homelike. I heard
some nice music in New York. Got there three days
before we sailed and went to shows every night.
Two nights it was to musical shows; they had a lot
of good music in 'em, cheerful you know, not sad
stuff nobody can understand like that Italian orchestra was playin' down there in the lobby awhile ago
—and more good-lookin' girls than you ever saw in

your life! I don't know where these New York managers find 'em all. Seems like every time I come to New York they've got more of 'em and prettier ones and better dancers. The last night, though, we went to a show without any music, a play—oh, Boy!"

"Was it good?"

"'Good'?" Tinker repeated in a peculiar tone; and he whistled. "I don't know how they get away with it!"

"Raw, you mean?" Dr. Taylor inquired with warm interest.

"Listen!" Tinker said. "My wife wanted to get up and go out right in the middle of the first act; and I pretty near had to hold her down; but after that she was willing to stay to see just how far they *would* go. Besides, nobody there knew us and we didn't have our daughter with us. A friend of mine from my city had been to it, and he told me I oughtn't to miss it. Well, sir, it would pretty near make a horse blush; and *some* of the stuff they pulled—well, the gallery laughed right out! What was funny to me, though, most of 'em downstairs sat as solemn as an egg and never turned a hair. If you'd told me a few years ago I'd ever hear such talk outside of some

old left-over livery-stable in the backwoods I'd 'a'
thought you were crazy! They tell me they're pretty
nearly all like that in New York now; but they'll
have to go some to beat this one! It was certainly
what you might call spicy. Yes, sir, some rancid!"

"Comedy?" Mr. Wackstle asked.

"No, it didn't seem meant to be. They came out
with these things lookin' as serious as a postman in a
blizzard: that's what made the gallery laugh, I guess.
No; you wouldn't call it a comedy, though the hero of
it ran off with his daughter-in-law, a right good-
lookin' actress; but she took an overdose of laudanum
or something and died, so it didn't seem meant for a
comedy."

"What was the name of it?"

"Peculiar name," Tinker replied. "Pasturage—
something like 'The Pasturage Scene.' No; that
wasn't it, not 'Pasturage.' I remember—they called
it 'The Pastoral Scene.' That's it. High-brow *name;*
but when you come to what some of 'em *said* in it—
oh, Boy! not so high-brow!"

The flush upon the outraged playwright's cheek
had deepened. He sat scorching with rage and the
desire to kill. This, then, was what an unspeakable
Tinker saw in a work of art that had cost its creator

so many days and nights of anguished composition! Ogle's staring eye was fixed upon the continuing serenity of Mme. Momoro.   She could not help hearing the loud voice uttering these horrible and unctuous innuendos, and upon such a woman nothing was lost. If she had not herself seen the play, and had nothing to judge it by except this description, and he should be presented to her as the author of "The Pastoral Scene"—— The thought was suffocating, and he was not comforted by the realization that his two colleagues in art were internally raging with him. As it was impossible to walk round a divan and choke a man to death in a steamer's smoking-room, Ogle rose to his feet.

"I think I'll go and dress for dinner," he said huskily.

Jones and Macklyn got up as he did.   "Yes," the latter said.   "This place has become sheerly unbearable."

The three went to the open door, where Ogle half-paused for a cross-shoulder murderous glance at the unconscious Tinker.   The beautiful bridge player sat imperturbable in floating veils of cigar smoke from the divan, which was again turbulent in song. The execrable Tinker, standing, and with a fountain pen for a baton, was apparently conducting a large orchestra. And even outside upon the deck, the fugitive artists were pursued by the hateful chorus:

"Mariar!
Mariar!
Bay rum in a bottle we'll buy 'er!
Mariar!
Mariar!
Dirty old Auntie Mariar!"

V

THE repellent cadence beat upon Ogle's ears, then got inside of them and clung lingeringly there. When Macklyn and Jones, after a few final words about Tinker, had gone below, the heated playwright decided to cool his head with a round or two of the open deck before dressing; and to his disgust he found his step keeping time to the hateful drum-beat chant:

> Mariar!
> Mariar!
> Bay rum in a bottle we'll buy 'er!

The thing was so persistent that when he paused, standing by the rail and looking peevishly out at the flattened sea, the deep pulsation of the ship's propellers throbbed up into his feet:

> Mariar!
> Mariar!
> Dirty old Auntie Mariar!

He went below, keeping time to "Mariar" with every step. It was a curse upon him, worse than

"Punch, Brothers, Punch," he thought; for "Mariar" was odious in its origin; and yet, loathing it, he could not get rid of it, not even in the quiet of his own cabin. Standing before a mirror there, an hour after he had left the smoking-room, he found himself tying a strip of black silk about his collar into a knot the shape of a butterfly, and, as he did so, actually timing the movements of his hands to the beat of "Mariar."   In spite of himself, he brushed his hair with a vocal "Mariar" for every stroke of his brushes;—the wretched chanting had fastened itself not only in his ears but in his throat.   Over and over, he muttered fiercely, unable to stop:

>"Mariar!
>Mariar!
>Bay rum in a bottle we'll buy 'er!"

An interruption broke the spell for him, though not in a manner to please him greatly—the voice of the execrable Tinker, speaking hoarsely with the opening of the outer door of the adjoining cabin.

"Well, well, well, Hon!   How're you and Baby feeling by this time?   Don't you want to get up for dinner?"

His wife's reply was delivered in a thin, high tone

of irritation: "No, we don't! We don't either of us
feel right like ourselves yet, and we're going to stay
here till to-morrow noon and maybe longer. Where
on earth have you been all this time? Never coming
near us since before lunch! We might have been
dead for all you knew or seemed to care. Where've
you been?"

"Why, right on this vessel, dearie. Now,
Honey——"

Evidently he leaned over her with some placative
purpose, for Mrs. Tinker's voice interrupted him,
rising into an outcry:

"Go 'way! I'll be sick again! My goodness!
Why, the whole cabin reeks with it!"

"With what, Mamma?"

"Whiskey!"

"Whiskey?" Tinker's voice sounded incredulous
and plaintive. "Why, no, Mamma! I haven't been
near——"

"What? Don't you stand there and tell me any
such story. Why, the whole place got strong with
it the minute you came in the door. Can't you tell
it, Libby?"

"I certainly can." The girl's petulant voice came
from the other side of the cabin. "It makes me——"

"Now, Baby, now! You don't think your old daddy would——"

"Go 'way from me!" the girl cried. "It's horrible. And didn't I tell you to stop calling me 'Baby'?"

"Now, Ba—I mean Libby—you oughtn't to get to feeling like this toward me. You know I only mean everything for just your own good, and I——"

"Let Libby alone," his wife interrupted him sharply. "You know well enough how she feels toward you; and if you expect her to ever get over it, you'd better not keep trying to talk to her; I've told you often enough! I asked you where've you been all afternoon."

"Why, nowhere except right on this steamer, Mamma. I just been sitting around quietly enjoying myself."

"It smells like it!" she said grimly.

He seemed grieved by her distrust. "Mamma, I've been gettin' acquainted with some pretty big men."

"You have? Where'd you find 'em?"

"Why, Mamma, this vessel is full of 'em! It's chuck full of the biggest and finest men I almost ever saw in one body."

"What on earth do you mean, talking about their being in a 'body'?"

"Me?" His voice grew more plaintive in explanation, and at times he seemed to be distrustful of the pronunciation of a word, pausing and then enunciating with a carefulness that was almost pedantry. "Me? What do I mean by a 'body'? I mean a matter of perfect simplicity. I mean the list of passengers. All you got to do's to read over that passenger list, Mamma, and you'll see."

"I did, and so did Libby. There wasn't a soul on it either of us ever heard of in our lives."

Ogle had recognized her voice for that of a provincial the first time he heard it, and he expected nothing better of her; but her husband was both shocked and reproachful.

"Mamma, I hate to hear you say that; it sounds like you never read a newspaper or took any interest in your own country. You mean to tell me you never heard o' Weatheright's Worsteds?"

"What if I have?"

"Well, it's the very Weatheright that's on this boat. I haven't met him yet; but the gentlemen I've been sittin' with are as fine a small body of men as you'd care to know, and they're waitin' for me now to come back and converse some more with 'em. One of 'em is Charles M. Wacks'le—I mean Wackstle. You've heard of Charles—I mean Charles Wackstle—haven't you, Mamma?"

"No. I have not."

"It's because you don't read the papers, then. Why, Charles M. Wack—Wackstle was general manager west of the Alleghenies for the Mutual Protective for fourteen years. He and the other gentleman I been with are as fine a small body of men as you can find in the whole United States from the Great Lakes to the Gulf, from the pine forests of the great State of Maine to the silver strands——"

"Stop talking like that," his wife commanded sharply. "That's the way you came home talking the last time you disgraced yourself this way, three years ago, on election night."

"'Election night'?" He repeated the words slowly and gently. "'Disgraced myself'?"

"You did! And now you haven't got any more sense than to talk about finding a 'fine small body of men' in the United States, when they're out in the middle of the Atlantic Ocean! It shows pretty well what you've been doing all afternoon, I guess."

"I meant that," he said with grave gentleness. "I meant out here—out here where we are. I said exactly that thing. They're as fine a small body of men as you could find anywhere in the middle of the Atlantic Oshum."

"'Oshum'!" Mrs. Tinker echoed angrily. "You can't even talk! Shame on you!"

"Mamma," he said sadly, "you're not yourself, or you wouldn't speak like that to me, anyway not before Baby. I *said* the Atlantic—the Atlantic Ocean. I don't believe I'm doing any good here."

His daughter agreed with him. "You certainly are not."

Evidently the man became dignified. "The steward will attend to your whishes," Ogle heard him say; and the cabin door closed.

Then the older of the irritated ladies appeared to become uneasy. "If I felt able I expect I ought to dress and go see after him," she said. "You can't tell what kind of people are on this ship. You can't tell who he may fall in with. I'm worried about him."

"I'm worried, too," the querulous voice of the daughter responded. "But not for him."

"Then who——"

"I'm worrying for the people he may fall in with,"

the girl said bitterly. And Ogle, just leaving his cabin to ascend to the dining salon, felt that there might be some points of sympathy between him and this unhappy provincial young lady. A mind so bravely unhampered by the customary filial prejudices seemed to be at least tinged with that modernism of which his own work for the stage strove to be an expression.

He dined alone, the three other seats at his table remaining vacant; and after dinner he found the poet and the painter in the lounge, which was crowded with the same people whom he had seen drinking tea there in the afternoon. A more festal air prevailed, however; there was more movement and friendly chatter; and the evening gowns of the ladies gave the place a gayer colour, though neither Mr. Jones nor Mr. Macklyn appeared to be aware of any improvement. They were in a corner near a passageway entrance, with coffee and cordials between them upon a tabouret, and, leaning back in easy chairs, each displaying a cigarette in a long holder held with somewhat obvious fastidiousness in white fingers, looked coldly upon the neighbouring bourgeoisie. They had saved a chair for Ogle.

"It's the last one in the place," Albert Jones said.

"That orchestra'll be here presently to murder us with some more Puccini and Leoncavallo and Mascagni—even Verdi, if not worse—and of course this type of Americans all adore it. We'd have avoided the place; but we're driven out of the smoking-room for the evening. That gang's still up there and they've got about a dozen more with 'em now, all of the same kind. They didn't go to dinner, and they're singing louder than ever."

"Nowhere in the world nowadays," Macklyn said gloomily, "can one be sheltered from our home-bred boor who carries his native manners with him all over the world. The travellers of every other nation accommodate themselves to the places they're in, and show plasticity—perception of the manners and customs of other people. That fellow this afternoon hadn't the slightest idea how he'd been scorched and put in his place merely by a lady's superb unconsciousness of him. I didn't see her at dinner."

"She has a table on the balcony of the dining salon," Mr. Jones informed him. "It's by the railing; —I caught a glint of that wonderful metallic-looking hair of hers—you couldn't mistake it. She was with the boy she called Hyacinthe; she's his mother and their name's Momoro. I asked the chief steward."

"Momoro," the poet repeated. "Momoro. Yes; it ought to be that. She hasn't come in here. You'd see her instantly, if she were here, crowded as the place is. Over the dead level of these people you'd see her as you see the Nike of Samothrace."

"That's too robust a comparison," his friend objected, "too robust and too active. Madame Momoro suggests power with less amplitude, less motion. She's painted almost as a still-life. Wouldn't you agree there's more of that about her than of the Nike, Laurence?"

"Probably," Ogle answered, a little embarrassed because he knew the statue only through small reproductions in plaster. "Less robustness, as you say, Albert. More reserve and yet a vibration. A vibrating reserve."

Macklyn deepened his habitual frown. "I didn't say she was like the Victory," he explained. "I said you couldn't help seeing her if she were here any more than you could help seeing that figure when you go into the Louvre. She must be a glorious sight in a ball gown. To me she seems carved out of an Hellenic stillness." Here, as he spoke, his frown was relaxed as if by some pleasing discovery, and he repeated the phrase slowly: "An Hellenic stillness.

Carved from a tall, tall block of it." Then, his pleasure increasing, he repeated the words again, letting his voice linger upon them with some fondness. "To me, she seems carved out of an Hellenic stillness."

Laurence Ogle leaned toward him warningly. "*Sh!*" And Macklyn, turning his head, beheld the Hellenic lady and the young Hyacinthe just emerged from the passageway near by. She paused within a few feet of the hushed young men, who, gazing up at her covertly, felt that the poet's phrase for her was justified and Hellenic stillness realized before their eyes. Her lengthiness had no stoop in it at the smoothly carved still shoulders, which were strapped with jet and silver; her head was poised as a tall king's should be, and the long figure of black and silver was a masterpiece of assured motionlessness.

"It's as if some overwhelming great work of art had suddenly been brought into the room," Macklyn said in a low voice to Ogle. "Nothing else seems to have any real existence here, now she's come. I wish I were going to Algeria, as you are. She lives there."

"How do you know?"

Macklyn nodded his head toward a twinkling scarf of mesh and heavy silverwork hanging upon the young Hyacinthe's arm. "Algerian—a very fine one. I've seen one like it at Sidi Okba."

"Sidi Okba?" Ogle murmured, a little irritated by Macklyn's superiority as a traveller. "You have? At Sidi Okba?" Then he divined why Mme. Momoro and her son had come to a halt beside them;—they were looking over the room to discover vacant chairs. He rose impulsively. "Madame,——" he said. "Madame——" He blushed, struggling for French words. "Madame—ah—chaise—chaise ici——"

"Ne vous dérangez pas, messieurs," she said in her rich and thrilling voice; for the two other young men had jumped up, also.

"Mais, madame, nous n'avons pas encore besoin de ces chaises," Macklyn said, bowing. "Nous partons toute de suite. Je vous prie——"

She inclined her head gravely. "You are very kind. Thank you," she said, with a little sibilance, almost as if she said, "Tsank you." Her son murmured the same words, and the little episode in gallantry closed with three solemn bows delivered almost in concert and in the foreign manner felt to be appropriate by the three knightly Americans. When they had departed, as they straightway scrupulously did, to the strains of the Hungarian rhapsody just begun by the orchestra, Mme. Momoro and her son took two of the vacated chairs and turned to watch the musicians. She sat as eloquently impassive as any carven Hellenic stillness indeed; nevertheless, there were slight quiverings and alterations in the contour of her finely outlined lips, and, although almost imperceptible, these delicate shadowings were seen and comprehended by the intelligent young Hyacinthe. He smiled faintly.

"There are some drolleries in the world," he said in French; and Mme. Momoro seemed to acquiesce.

Meanwhile, the three polite young men went for a stroll on the deck, rather elated, though Ogle was disturbed by a detail. "I find I'm a little rusty in my French," he said. "It's quite a time since I've had occasion to use it, and I found myself at a loss, rather, when I began to speak to her. For a moment I actually couldn't remember the word for 'chair'."

Albert Jones laughed. "Don't let that upset you, Laurence. She answered Macklyn in English, you noticed, as soon as he got through speaking French to her."

"Why wouldn't she?" Macklyn retorted, with some warmth. "She knew perfectly well we were either English or Americans.   She'd heard us talking in the smoking-room, hadn't she?"

"Yes; she'd remember that, of course," Mr. Jones said thoughtfully.   "Do you suppose the barbarians would allow us any peace up there by this time? Let's go and see."

Agreeing, his friends ascended with him to the deck above; but long before they reached the smoking-room door they understood that their hopes to find there a quiet nook in which to talk of art—and Mme. Momoro—were not to be fulfilled.   Song still prevailed, and a solo in a too familiar voice, hoarser now, but still from leathern lungs and brazen throat, lamented in ballad form a Kansas tragedy of the long ago.   And then in all that part of the vessel and out upon the salty air through which the vessel sped, and out over the rushing black seas and the shimmering starlit foam that edged them, rolled the chorus of eighteen convivial middle-aged men, far from home and feeling few of their customary responsibilities:

> "Oh, Jesse James,
>   Pore Jesse James!
>   I'll never see my Jesse any more.
>   *Oh*, the awnry little coward
>   That shot Mr. Howard
>   And laid Jesse James in his grave!"

The three young men came to a halt outside the door. "It grows more horrible," Macklyn said. "Let's get out of this."

Then, as they turned away, the too familiar voice was heard again, "Now, gentlemen, le'ss sing something a little sweeter and more homelike.

> "Old Aunt Mariar
> A-sitting by the fire———"

The three returned to the promenade deck below; but it seemed to them that even there some snatches of the detestable song haunted the eddying wind and blew upon their ears. Ogle thought that he could hear "Aunt Mariar" intermittently as he tramped the deck alone, long after his companions had left him and descended to read in bed in the cabin they shared. The curse had come back upon him, and he could not prevent himself from marching in time to it, though what he thought an echo of the orgy going on above may have been not actual sound, but one of those half delusions with which our minds sometimes persecute us when we are in a state of annoyance. This one was persistent enough to follow him, however, even when he left the deserted deck and again entered the lounge on his way to bed.

The concert was over and the great place almost empty; a few people read books or drowsily lounged in easy chairs, and at a card table were seated Mme. Momoro and her three companions of the afternoon, again occupied with bridge. Ogle passed near them on his way across the room, and, as he approached the table, Mme. Momoro, who faced him, looked up from her cards and his eyes met hers directly in a full face-to-face exchange of glances.

For an instant he had the hope that she would nod to him, recognizing him as the person who had addressed her and surrendered his chair to her. If she did thus recognize him and make that acknowledgment, he might dare to bow to her to-morrow, if he should encounter her on deck, and, having got that far, he might hope soon to have speech with her. He had flashlight imaginings of the kind that the dreaming mind of a sleeper groups almost instantaneously into long sequences within the traditioned time needed to open and close a door; and they showed him pictures of himself walking the deck with Mme. Momoro, seated beside her for coffee after dinner, even reading a play to her as she reclined, bright-eyed with sympathetic comprehension, in her steamer chair—and he saw Macklyn and Jones in attitudes of amazed envy in the distance of the long deck.

But his fancies were too fond. Her grave eyes remained grave, and although they may have contained the cognizance that a fellow-being appeared before her, they showed not any light of a personal recognition, but returned unemotionally to the perusal of her cards.

Ogle passed on, apparently cold and no more impelled toward romance upon the sea than was she. Nevertheless, he was strangely disappointed and a little crestfallen. Already, though he was not entirely aware of his own sudden susceptibility, he had begun to have the feeling that the success of his whole adventure to foreign lands depended upon his meeting this remarkable lady. If he failed to know her his great excursion was a disaster at its very beginning.

VI

WHEN he came on deck the next morning at eleven, there ran by the ship a sea of turquoise encrusted with innumerable twinklings of foam opalescent in sunshine. The air, sprung from some aromatic source in the south, was mellow yet invigorating; and Ogle began to regret that already the "Duumvir" was well into the "third day out." But not the weather alone brought about this change in sentiment; indeed, it was not the weather principally; for his thought was less of the increasing balminess than of a fellow-passenger whose acquaintance he had not yet made, though only nine short days were left of their voyaging in company. Macklyn was no longer the only poet on board; the playwright had become his rival, and one reason for Ogle's late appearance on deck lay upon the writing desk in his cabin—an unfinished ode beginning, "O still and stately lady in burnished gold enhelmed." Thus there had been trouble with this poem from the beginning on account of his obstinacy about the word "enhelmed," which was of all words in our language, he felt, the one most expressive of the close shapeliness of Mme. Momoro's coifing, yet has not many twins in sound; and Ogle, as a poet, was not so advanced as Macklyn, but still clung to rhyme. "Whelmed" had been his tentative solution after an hour's fretful experiment, and he still hoped to do better.

No golden helm was visible along the lines of chairs where cheerful voyagers basked and chatted, nor among those who strolled the deck and to-day made bold to show some hint of the climates to which they were escaping; for light fabrics and even white flannels appeared here and there. The four lively damsels brushed by Ogle as he began to pace the immaculate planking; they had found a boy or two and were merry, yet made evident some encouragement to the handsome lone pedestrian; two of them looking him humorously, yet rather pointedly, in the eye, so that he understood he might approach and be forgiven, if he would. These young things, so brisk and boyish, annoyed him; his mind was all upon Hellenic stillness.

Among the strolling or reclining passengers he saw a few whom, he remembered indifferently, he had seen the day before or upon embarking; but Mme. Momoro, her son, her two elderly friends, and Macklyn and Albert Jones were all invisible. Not even the execrable Tinker nor any of his fellow rioters appeared; and the lounge and the other public rooms, when he walked through them, were almost vacant; no one at all was in the smoking-room, not even the studious bartender. The hour for lunch arrived without his having seen a familiar face.

He went into the dining salon a little late, and the tables were well filled, including his own; for as he came near it he perceived that three of the four chairs were now occupied. Two of the people to be his companions there for the rest of the voyage were ladies; and as he approached, with other groups and passing stewards intervening between the table and himself, his first impression was confused and not strongly favourable. The two ladies were obviously Americans, and in dress and looks resembled other American mothers and daughters on board; they were well dressed in the prosperous American fashion of "smartness"; and they were both rather good-looking "in the American way," he thought, discriminating instantly in favour of a French manner of being beautiful. The mother was a dimly pretty exposition of what the dark-eyed, dark-haired twenty-year-old daughter would be at about forty; but his sensitive nostrils at once detected the exhalation of provincialism—and also a pungent discontent. Indeed, as he came nearer, he thought he had never seen two silent ladies more earnestly engaged in expressing peevishness.

A table steward was bending over the occupant of the third chair and trying to explain in imperfect English an item upon the large cardboard menu, behind which this person's face was momentarily concealed from public view. His shoulders were revealed, however, and something in their breadth and thickness disquieted Ogle as he took his seat. Then disquiet became rapidly a sickish apprehension, and apprehension as abruptly exchanged itself for the full shock of dismay.

The person engaged with the steward tossed the menu, which was printed in Italian, upon the table. "Oh, my gosh!" he exclaimed in a voice disreputably hoarse. "Bring us the worst you got, as long as it ain't spaghetti. I been eatin' spaghetti for three days because it's the only thing I know the name of. My gosh!"

It was the execrable Tinker. He and his family

were to be the unfortunate young man's messmates all the way to Africa.

Moreover, he saw no means of escape; every seat in the room and in the balcony above was assigned and occupied, as the Chief Steward had already informed him. His sole recourse would be to effect an exchange with someone; but the only people he knew well enough to approach with such a proposal were Albert Jones and Macklyn, and Ogle was convinced that if he should so approach them, neither of them would respond helpfully or even graciously.

But what dismayed him even more than the prospect of nine long days of enforced intimacy with the Tinker family was what he conceived to be the odium attached to such an association, so sharp were the young man's prejudices. Seeing him in this close association with them at every meal, who could come to any conclusion except that he was a member of the Tinker party, travelling with the Tinkers, at the least a friend of the Tinkers, or, worse, a relative of the Tinkers—or, worst of all, Tinker's son-in-law? Mme. Momoro herself might even now be looking down upon him from her balcony table, wondering if this were true of him; and he cast a pathetic upward glance round the three sides of the balcony visible from his chair; but discerned no glint of burnished gold enhelmed above the scrolled wrought-iron railing.

Tinker addressed him. "Fine morning we've had. Mighty nice bright day!" It was notable how his voice betrayed him with its debauched hoarseness; but what repelled the playwright was the commonplace approach of the provincial, the customary "small-town" manner of opening acquaintance through the weather. However, he said, "Very," and looked up again at the balcony.

Tinker coughed and glanced placatively at his wife; but she offered him no more encouragement to go on talking than Ogle did. She sat with downcast, brooding eyes in the manner of a woman who has lately had much to suffer but more to condemn, and, as for returning her husband's plaintive glance, she made it clear that she had no desire to look at anything so leprous.

The daughter's manner was the mother's emphasized, but with something virulent added. Laurence Ogle had the habit of detaching the observing and note-taking part of himself from his emotions and sensations, a sixth sense that students of their fellowmen acquire; and he was conscious of the emanation of a powerful and unusual hostility from this silent girl. Her hostility seemed directed against everything—against the ship and all the people in it, against every circumstance of life; but most of all, and with the bitterest concentration, against her father. She was sullen and suffering, making both her sullenness and her suffering so evident that a stranger duller than Ogle must have perceived them at a glance; and in spite of himself, his curiosity began to stir. Internal family struggle was his principal dramatic subject, and already he caught a glimpse of such a struggle in progress here—with the girl enraged and worsted. This was his shrewd guess, at least, though he thought she might have a temporary advantage to-day, because of her father's recent misbehaviour.

The father, indeed, seemed to feel himself at a disadvantage; his abased glances at his wife and daughter proved his low estate no less than did his lamentable hoarseness; and there were things about him significant of the struggle an erring man makes to present a fine appearance after sin. A stiff white shirt and collar replaced the softer stuffs he had worn yesterday; his scarf of satin, appropriately black, was pinned with a fine black pearl; he had been to the ship's barbers and smelled too fragrantly of the contact; he was sleeked and powdered and polished; the broad nails upon his slightly tremulous fingers, as he broke a piece of bread, glanced and twinkled like little mirrors.

"Yes, sir," he said. "Couldn't ask for better weather than we're getting now. Seems funny to think of everything back home all covered with ice and snow. You're from somewheres East, I expect."

"Yes," Ogle said.

"Boston, I expect?"

"New York."

"Well, New York's a big place these days," Tinker remarked tolerantly. "My wife and daughter here, though, they like it better than I do. We come from a pretty good-sized town ourselves, and while the population isn't quite as big as New York's yet, it's certainly got every advantage you can find in New York and some ways more. What'd you say your name was?"

"Ogle."

"Glad to meet you; glad to meet you," Tinker said as heartily as his hoarseness permitted. "Mine's Tinker, and this is my wife, Mrs. Tinker, Mr. Ogle. My daughter, Libby, Mr. Ogle."

Ogle made two inclinations of the head and these salutes were acknowledged with a distant formality a little surpassing his own. Indeed, he found in theirs something that appeared to be not so much reserve as a personal reproach, Mrs. Tinker seeming to include every member of her husband's sex in her disapproval, and the daughter perhaps desiring to make it clear that she wished nothing from any person contaminated by her father's introduction. Her dark lashes separated widely for an instant, disclosing beautiful and resentful eyes in which blue fires smouldered; colour came abruptly upon her unrouged cheeks; then she looked down again, and Ogle was surprised by the revelation that this sulky Miss Libby Tinker was one of the prettiest girls he had ever seen.

The discovery failed to please him with her, however, "Middle-West belle" being the depreciative phrase that came instantly into his mind. He had no interest in representatives of that type, although as a playwright he was curious about what he felt certain he had accurately perceived in her—that deep and settled anger with her father. It was, in fact, an enmity, one beyond ordinary family-quarrel animosities, he was sure. It was too fixed and too profound to be the result of any mere mortification caused in her by the man's manners, and, as a spectator of the human comedy, he would have given something to know what inspired it.

"This is our first time over," Tinker said. "I expect you been over often, probably, Mr. Ogle?"

"No," Ogle replied, and was displeased to suspect that his colour heightened as he spoke. "Not often."

"Too busy, I expect. You're in business in New York, aren't you, Mr. Ogle?"

"No."

Tinker nodded. "Professional man. What I thought when I looked at you. I'm a business man, myself. I expect you've probably heard of the Illinois and Union Paper Company."

"No. I haven't."

Tinker looked surprised and a little baffled. "You never did?" he said. "Well, of course New York City's got so many interests of its own, you often do meet people from there that don't get to hear much about what goes on outside their own town. We have representatives right in New York, though: Stone, Tinsdale and Company, thirty-two Broad Street. I expect you've heard of *them*, all right!"

"No, I haven't."

"Is that *so?*" Tinker said. "Well, New York certainly is a big town! Stone, Tinsdale and Company handle a lot of business, and the figures for what the Illinois alone did through them last year would surprise you. I'm president of the Illinois is how I happen to know. I was telling Mr. Weatheright about those figures last night, and he was surprised. You met Mr. Weatheright yet?"

"No. I don't know him."

"I'll be glad to introduce you," said Tinker cordially. "He's a mighty interesting man—plain, too. You'd never know he was a big man from him. No airs or putting on at all; just as simple and ordinary as you or me. There's a number of other well-known men on this boat, too, Mr. Ogle; though I don't s'pose I need to be tellin' *you* that, because of course you know it yourself from the passenger list. What I like about a steamship, it's just the same as a railroad train—you get acquainted with everybody and everybody's friendly and easy-goin'. I've had conversations with as many as a hundred people, I expect, these three days since we came on board. My wife and daughter, though, they've been under the weather. This is the first meal they been able to take in the dining-room." He looked solicitously at his daughter, and there was anxiety in his hoarse voice. "Your digestion feels all right *so* far to-day, don't it, Baby?"

Her response was a momentary glare at him and nothing more. The steward had returned, bringing a large dish of *hors d'œuvres* which he presented first to Tinker. "Are you going to keep the man waiting at your elbow all day?" Mrs. Tinker said sharply. "If you don't want any of what he's got, tell him so and give the rest of us a chance."

Tinker's eyes, genuinely troubled, still rested upon his daughter, and he sighed audibly, then looked at the *hors d'œuvres*. "I'll take a couple o' sardines," he said feebly. "I wouldn't trust any the rest of it."

After that for a time he was pensive and occupied himself with eating. Now and then, as the constrained repast went through its courses, he glanced with a kind of guilty hopefulness at his wife or with a furtive anxiety at his daughter, but received no encouragement from either of them. They murmured together indistinguishably at times, apparently referring to the Italian dishes set before them; but that was their nearest approach to geniality; and as the playwright was trying all the while to show by his manner that his connection with this party was accidental and unwilling, there could not easily have been a more painful little group of people among all the pleasure-seekers on the "Duumvir." Ogle made the meal as short a one as he could with any assurance to himself that he obtained a sustaining quantity of nourishment;—he meant to avoid lingering at the table with the Tinker family, and he was determined not to be seen walking out with them, which would be more conspicuous and therefore worse. He had come late to lunch; nevertheless he was the first person in the room to place his napkin on the table and rise for departure.

Tinker glanced up with more than mere surprise in his expression; there was something suddenly haggard in his look. "My goodness!" he said. "You don't eat much. You through already?"

"Yes," Ogle said, and he added coldly, "I take coffee in the lounge."

It was an unfortunate addition, one he need not have made, since his only purpose was to use the word "lounge" as a chill corrective to the misnomer "lobby," which had irked him yesterday upon the lips of Tinker. Tinker avenged himself at once, although unconsciously; he had been alone with his wife and daughter at the table before Ogle's arrival, and this experience was not one he cared so soon to repeat. He gave the two ladies a hunted look, dropped his napkin upon the floor, and jumped up.

"Wait!" he said desperately. "I'll go with you." And he accompanied the dismayed and red-faced young man in as hurried a departure from the room as could be made without open indecorum. "My soul!" he exclaimed, when they reached the passage-way outside, "I'm glad to get out o' there."

Ogle took his overcoat and cap from a hook on the wall. "I don't care for any coffee," he said. "I'm going out on deck."

Tinker found his own coat and cap. "I'll go with you," he said. "A little fresh air'll do me more good than all the coffee in the world. I sat up kind of late last night, and I ate too many of those hazlenuts and Saratoga chips they keep up there in the smoking-room. It's dangerous for a man to change off from a home diet all at once like that. I'm glad you suggested the open air instead of coffee, Mr. Ogle."

Thus, companionably, he emerged upon the deck beside the annoyed playwright, who saw no immediate means of avoiding his society. "The man seems to believe we belong to the same club," Ogle thought indignantly; and in truth some such conception was not unlike the present viewpoint of his unwelcome companion. For when a man is in flight from his womenkind—and this was Tinker's condition at the moment—he looks upon all other men, even strangers and foreigners, as sympathetic comrades who will instantly comprehend his plight and even dishonour themselves to succour him. The fugitive kept close to Ogle, bumping shoulders with him now and then as they walked down the long deck.

"You may of noticed my wife was a little frosty with me, Mr. Ogle," he said confidentially. "My glory! When she and Baby *want* to do it, they can *do* it, believe me! There was quite a number of gentlemen on this boat sat up pretty late last night; and I haven't seen many of 'em around to-day yet, to tell the truth; but I've seen some of their families, and I guess one or two of those gentlemen got plenty to go through when they do get up. It's a funny thing how some women just naturally can't stand it to let their husbands sit up a little late, even when there's no more object in goin' to bed early than there is on a steamship in the middle of the ocean. That white-moustached ole Doc Taylor's lucky; he's a bachelor and travellin' alone. You aren't married, either, are you, Mr. Ogle?"

"No."

"Well," Tinker said pensively, "of course it's the natural condition, and I've got a mighty splendid wife—I've never been sorry I didn't stop and think twice before we got things settled—but there are a few times in any married man's life when he probably ought to have a little more liberty than he's liable to actually *get*. It don't seem like it's in a woman's disposition to allow it to him." He coughed and seemed to ruminate as they rounded the forward windows of the "Palm Garden" and passed to the starboard promenade deck and the sunshine. "I suppose there's probably some women in the world could understand a man's nature, but likely it's only a few. I expect that one there could, maybe;—anyhow she acts like it to me."

The lady to whom he referred was alone, reclining in a deck chair at a little distance before them; she was wrapped luxuriously in a coat of minks' fur and reading a little book exquisitely bound in green and gold. Ogle had an impulse to turn and run, rather than that she should see him with Tinker, whom the smoking-room episode, if nothing else, must necessarily have rendered offensive to her sight. For the lady was Mme. Momoro.

"She's what *I*'d call a one-hundred percenter for all-round looks," Tinker said warmly. "Let's stop and talk to her."

"What!" the playwright exclaimed. He was horrified, perceiving that she must have heard this genial proposal, since they were within a dozen feet of her and she had looked up to observe them. "No! Don't think of such a thing."

But Tinker had already grasped his arm, turning him toward the recumbent lady's chair, "You're lookin' like the first rose o' summer to-day," he said gallantly and without the slightest hesitation or embarassment. "I feel like the last one myself. I want you to meet a young New York lawyer; his name's Mr. Ogle. Mr. Ogle, this is Mrs. Mummero."

VII

MME. MOMORO was neither surprised nor in any manner resentful of the intrusion. On the contrary, she smiled charmingly up at the dazed playwright and his brazen companion. "Will you sit with me?" she said in her lovely voice and with the hint of mispronunciation that almost yet not quite made "seet" of "sit." She moved her long black-gloved hand toward the vacant chairs beside her. "I am tiring myself to read a stupid little book. When I saw you coming, I hoped you would stop and chat with me." Then with her fine eyes upon the broad surfaces of Tinker's massaged and powdered cheeks, she inquired so gravely that a shrewd compatriot of hers might have suspected a latent drollery, "Your health to-day, it is excellent?"

"Fine!" he said. "Fine!" However, realizing that his extreme hoarseness seemed to contradict him, "All except my throat," he added. "I ate a silver basketful of Saratoga chips last night—awful salty. Affects my larynx."

"Ah, that is bad," she said compassionately. "You will not sit with me?   You both?"

Before replying, Tinker looked thoughtfully up and down the deck, as though his answer might depend upon what he saw.   His purpose had been to refresh himself with a few moments of conversation during which he would remain standing, apparently detained for the casual moment only, and he may have wondered if it were wise—to-day especially—to sit publicly beside a beautiful French lady when two American ladies who did not understand his nature might pass at any moment and draw wilful conclusions.   Nevertheless, he realized that it was impossible to add a great deal to the domestic disfavour in which he already stood; and the French lady's invitation was strangely pleasant to him.   "Well, I don't know," he began.   "I'd certainly *like* to if——"

But the matter was settled for him.   An elderly man with watery eyes and a white moustache came hurrying along the deck, seized his arm, and drew him some steps away for private speech;—this man's voice, too, was hoarse.   "Weatheright's got away from his wife again, and he and Brown and Wackstle and two of the other boys have sneaked up to the smoking-room.   We got to have you."

Tinker returned to Mme. Momoro's chair for a moment, looking serious. "I guess I'll have to leave Mr. Ogle for a substitute, Mrs. Mummero; it seems I got an engagement. It's not goin' to last all afternoon, though!"

With this happy intimation he betook himself hastily and furtively from view, entering the nearest doorway that led from the deck, his questionable medical acquaintance attending him closely.

Mme. Momoro's grave eyes seemed to deepen in gravity during his departure; then she said amiably: "He appoints a substitute without consulting him. I think he must have perceived I am boring myself a great deal to-day."

Ogle, still dazed, murmured, "Ah—I hope not," and could find nothing more intelligent to say. He had begun to understand, however, that his horrified first impression of Tinker's action was mistaken, and that some previous contact had been established between Mme. Momoro and the outlander. Even that big barbarian of a Tinker could not merely walk up to such a woman and begin to talk to her.

"You must not stay because he appoints you," she said. "Perhaps you, too, have friends awaiting

in the smoking-room.   But if you should be so kind
as to wish to remain a little while———"

She looked up at him smilingly, and he found himself in the presence of the opportunity for which he
had longed; but, unfortunately, when he would have
been most debonair he was awkward and self-
conscious.   This was not one of his customary sensations; usually he felt himself to be a person of finer
perceptions, finer manner, finer culture than the
people about him; though his sense of his advantage
over them was a quiet one and wholly self-contained,
he flattered himself.   Standing before the elegant
Parisian, however, the young American was in doubt
of his effect upon her; and uneasily he decided to
adopt the Continental tone of which she and her son
seemed to him so exquisite an expression.

He bowed, therefore, from the waist, quickly and
slightly, as he had seen the young Hyacinthe bow
in the smoking-room; for his association with the
theatre had given him a ready facility in imitation.
"Since Madame permits," he said in a deeper voice
than was natural to him.

Then, as he sank into the long chair beside her, his
complexion, still as pink as when Tinker accompa-

nied him through the dining salon, became pinker. "Since Madame permits" was not in the right key, he feared. It had too much the air of an effort for the eighteenth century, or, what was infinitely worse, it might be a form employed by French chauffeurs and servants. At the best it had an artificial sound even in his own ears as he heard himself saying it, and he wished he had been simpler. "Since Madame permits" might even be as bad, though in the opposite direction, as Tinker's awful "Mrs. Mummero."

But she appeared to find nothing objectionable in either. "You are kind to stay and help me not to bore myself," she said. "My poor little boy, my son, who travels with me, must all day remain in his cabin, writing upon a report for our Department of Education, where he has a little position, poor child; and I have only two other compatriots upon this boat, two ladies with whom we play a little bridge; but one has got an affection of her ear, so her sister stays all day with her. I am interested in your friend, Mr. Tinker, who seems to be such a good friend of everybody. Have you known him long?"

"No, no, no! Not at all," Ogle replied hurriedly.

"Not in the slightest. I haven't any acquaintance with him. I've never even met him. He followed me out of the dining salon."

Mme. Momoro's expression was not always so impassive as when she played bridge, he discovered. She looked at him for a moment with a scrutinizing intensity that made him almost uncomfortable; then her gaze relaxed and she smiled faintly. "He is very amusing," she said. "He is a type I did not see in New York or Philadelphia or Boston, which were the three cities I have visited in your country. I did not go to Washington; but I have been told I might find your typical American there—somesing like Mr. Tinker perhaps. You agree?"

"Believe me," Ogle entreated her earnestly, "he isn't typical."

"No, I suppose not. You have so many, many people; but there could not be a great number of this kind. I should speak of him as typical only of your ruling class, perhaps."

"Our 'ruling class'?"

"I get my ideas from my son," she confessed. "He is a student of peoples. But I agree with him that all nations are governed now by the gentlemen of commerce. I am afraid you must submit to being ruled by your Mr. Tinkers even in your land of liberty, because all the world must submit to the same thing. Hyacinthe instructs me that owning riches means the control of wealth, and so it is power. Mr. Tinker gives me that impression. He is a man with power, and all that he really respects is the other men with power who rule your country with him."

To the incredulous playwright it seemed that she spoke with a kind of admiration. "Frankly, Madame Momoro, he conveys a very different impression to me. In fact, I'm afraid that what I see in him is not so much power as noisiness."

"Yes?" she said; and she laughed. "He is much, much less noisy to-day than he was last night! Oh, *very* much!"

"Did you hear him?" Ogle asked, a little surprised. "When I went down to my cabin rather late, you were playing cards in the lounge with your friends, and I wonder——"

"Yes?" she said, as he paused. "You came through the lounge rather late? You noticed that I was there?"

He looked briefly into her eyes, which were somewhat metallic and inscrutable for the moment.

"Yes," he said slowly, "I 'noticed' that you were there, Madame Momoro."

She gave him a grave little nod of acknowledgment. "That is flattering. What do you wonder?"

"Nothing—except that it was quiet in the lounge and I wonder how you heard the noisiness of the smoking-room."

"I think," she returned, gazing before her out to sea, "you are really wondering how I met Mr. Tinker."

This was so shrewdly the truth that Ogle blushed again and became a little confused. "I didn't mean to ask such a thing," he said. "I didn't intend——"

But her quiet laughter interrupted him. "It was droll!" she said. "When we had played our last rubber, Hyacinthe asked me to go to the smoking-room to have a liqueur and a cigarette. *Never* did you hear so much noise as there was in that place when we sat down—never! Some thought themselves to be singing; you could not understand how they could have such a belief. Then all at once Mr. Tinker shouted louder than all of them together: 'There is a lady present,' he told them, and, 'Maybe she don't care so much about music as we do.' And he came over to where I sat and asked me if I wish to make them 'shut up,' because if I do, he will, whether they wish it or not. So I said no, they must sing all they like; and he said—he said——" Here Mme. Momoro was suddenly overcome with mirth. She pressed her two long hands upon her cheeks, laughing between them. "He said he had already perceived I was 'a girl like that'! He pronounce' me a 'regular' somesing—I cannot say what. So he told us his name and the Ill—Illi—Illinois Company; he is the president. And he seized upon my hand to shake it up and down in your American way, and he shook Hyacinthe's hand; and then he asked our name and brought the gentlemen—most of them— to where we sat. 'This is the Mr. Somesing of Booffalo who makes all the worsted,' he told us; and this is Mr. Somesing from Tchicago who is president of some letters in the alphabet; and this is Mr. Somesing from somewhere else who has such a big, big Trust Company——'" Laughter threatened her composure again; but she was able to continue: "Even though he was a little—well, we must say he was a little exhilarated, if that is a proper word— you could see he admires those gentlemen because they have power, like himself. It was very interesting."

"'Interesting'?" Ogle echoed. "I must say I think you take a gracious view of his impudence, Madame Momoro."

"Impudence? No, no!" She became serious again. "It was like a passage in Homer, or in some Gothic poem perhaps, where the great chieftains are introduced, one after the other, and the poet tells how mighty each one is and where his home-land is and how many followers he has. You don't see how precisely like that it is?"

He shook his head. "I fear you have learned to love satirizing Americans."

"But no! I am not satirizing. I truly think what I say."

He laughed, incredulous. "You won't judge the rest of us by such people, I hope; though foreigners are apt to get the impression we are all like that. One trouble with our country is that each generation produces a new brand of parvenu for the rest of us to live down. The foreigner sometimes mistakes the latest type of parvenu for our 'best people' and for typical; and so he draws the conclusion that we have no culture, no art, no literature. I admit that so far, in the European sense, we have nothing that may be called literature or architecture or music or painting or sculpture; but we are working toward them, and in one or two branches of art I think we may be thought pretty completely arisen."

"Indeed, yes," she responded generously. "In New York there is some interesting architecture quite native and not borrowed from us, and I saw some fine collections of paintings. I am sure you will have an American art some day."

"I think we already have," he said. "That is, I think we have in one or two branches. Ah—the stage——"

"Yes. Yes, truly!" she agreed with a gracious show of enthusiasm. "I saw some of your actors, some of the best, I was told, though I do not remember their names. They were excellent. Some of them might be thought of highly if they would come to France and act there, I am sure. It was a pleasure."

He frowned, seeming to concentrate upon the expression of his thought. "I meant not only the acting, but the whole art of the theatre. I really think we have arrived in that. Just in these last few years we seem to have made a really tremendous advance. Until even that recently our American theatre was frankly—well, lamentable."

"You are fond of the theatre?"

His frown deepened. "Fond? I don't know. There are times when I think I hate it—because I tire of it, I suppose."

For a moment neither of them spoke; and during the silence she cast a thoughtful sidelong glance or two at him as he sat frowning at the horizon of blue water. Then she said: "Mr. Tinker spoke of you as a lawyer."

"I am not. Of course the man knows nothing about me whatever."

"May I be so intrusive as to guess your profession? You are a dramatist?"

"Yes," he said. "Probably you didn't understand my name when he mentioned it—and perhaps it may not mean anything to you, unless you saw most of the New York plays. I am Laurence Ogle."

She repeated the name slowly. "Mr. Laurence Ogle. No. I am sorry."

So was he, for he had hoped that she might have been taken to see "The Pastoral Scene." As she had not, and might possibly remember Tinker's horrible smoking-room interpretation of this masterpiece in the new manner, the author decided not to mention the title. Instead, he offered a generalization.

"Outside of New York there is no feeling for art in America at all. Our plays find almost no audience beyond that centre. You can judge for yourself what such people as those you saw last night would make of anything with any depth or of anything really poignant or searching. I have just said that such people are not typical; but I admit that they are fairly characteristic of the newly prosperous vulgar so numerous among us. Suppose you put a play before them in which you expressed a sense of the tragedy and mystery of life; of the chaotic war always just beneath the surface of life; of the monstrous formlessness beneath the struggle that goes on near the surface—you may imagine what they would make of it! To please them you must offer a pretty little romance about money and marriage. If you write of humanity they think you are either prurient or insane. Fortunately, in the last four or five years we have either discovered or educated—I do not know which—an audience in New York that cares for an art somewhat more sophisticated than would delight these morons."

"Morons?" She repeated the word thoughtfully. "Morons. I do not know it. It means?"

"Defectives," he explained. "People whose

mental development has been arrested since child-hood."

"Ah, yes." She was silent for a moment or two, appearing to be occupied in adding "moron" to her vocabulary. Then she asked: "You are going to Italy, perhaps?"

"Later, I may," he said. "I came away for a winter's rest. I'd been working pretty hard, and I don't care for Florida or California. I may go over into Italy before I sail for home; but I thought I'd just run over to Algiers for a month or so."

"You have been there, Mr. Ogle?"

"Algiers?" he said unwillingly. "No. That's one reason I wanted to go there, because I hadn't been;—it's pleasant to go to a place where one hasn't been; and Algiers seems a little off the beaten track for tourists. Of course I hope to avoid tourists as much as possible."

"So?" she said, and seemed faintly surprised. "That is difficult nowadays, I am afraid, no matter where you go. Why do you object to them?"

"Why? Dear lady! Do you need more than the sample of their manners on this boat to answer that?"

"But on this boat we are *all* tourists," she said. "I am one myself."

"That is rather different," he returned. "I do not mean people of the world who happen to be travelling."

"Then what do you mean?"

"Well—to put it briefly, such people as the Tinker family. But to save our nerves, don't let us talk of them; it is enough that we have to see them and hear them. Do you know Algiers, Madame Momoro?"

"Oh, yes; it is where I am going now."

"It is?" he said, delighted.

"Yes. I am going there with the two French ladies who are here upon the boat; they have a winter villa in Algiers. But Algiers is not Algeria, Mr. Ogle. You will see somesing of our great province there, I hope."

"I don't know. I haven't made any definite plans. What is it like?"

She smiled; then with a slow gesture of her slender, long hand she waved his glance toward the length of the horizon line from east to west and back again. "Ask me what this ocean is like and I could answer you because I could say, 'Well, it is all like that, except for changing weathers, from New York until we come to Gibraltar.' But if you ask me what Algeria is like I can't tell you so easily and perhaps I can't tell you at all, because, for one thing, it is Africa. I think you can't tell much about Africa, no matter how much you talk of it or how many pictures of it you show, except to someone who has been there—and him you do not need to tell because he knows. But I can tell you one thing about it, Mr. Ogle."

She turned from the sea to look at him, and, returning her grave regard with some intensity, he asked: "What is the one thing?"

"I think," she said slowly, "you will be glad afterwards that you went there. I think you may find somesing in Algeria, Mr. Ogle."

"You mean local colour, types, landscape?"

She still continued to look at him, and he thought that into this fixed gaze of hers, very pleasant to him, there came a mysteriousness, something impenetrable from the depths. "Well, I mean—somesing!" Then she laughed. "Do you know if Mr. Tinker goes there, too?"

"Heaven forbid!" he said.

VIII

THE fervour of his exclamation made her thoughtful again, and for a time neither of them spoke. They looked out to sea, but not into infinitudes of space, for the sea was visibly finite, and the immense globe of water, curving its long horizontal arc against the encircling sky, was like a great round crystal within a luminous blue shell. Stillness seemed to abide there at the crystal's edge in a frozen serenity; but that this far edge must be in movement, too, was proved by the motion near the travellers' eyes;—the rim of the deck, slowly dipping and rising, alternately disclosed and concealed the westward-running little sparkling seas as they were swept into foam and green whirlpool by the majestic passage of the "Duumvir." This activity in the foreground of what they saw and the delusion of fixity in the distance brought to the mind of Mme. Momoro a comparison that pleased her companion doubly; once for itself and again because it seemed to show that Tinker, as an episode of their conversation, was definitely disposed of and forgotten.

"How still the ocean seems to be, far, far away out there," she said. "Stiller than glass, stiller than ice— oh, still as death! Less alive than death, because it looks as if never, never at all, had any life been there and never, never could be any. One must think that only where our ship is can there be any life, or anything have power to stir. So always when I am on a ship that is solitary on the ocean, I think it is very much like our planet. The world is a great busy thing whirling and rushing on through emptiness; but so lonely because it seem to be the only thing alive in a space of death that has got no end. From the earth at night you look out on the sky and the stars, as we look out now from this ship. The sky and the stars are so quiet, so still—oh, so very still!—so you say, 'The earth is all alone on its journey through all this stillness, this terrible stillness of the sky!' But I think that must be wrong: I think it must be like what we see now. The waves near the ship are all dancing; so they must be dancing yonder where they look so still. There are great fish in the water over there and millions and millions of little water animals you would need the microscope to see. So it must be in the stars and sky when we think our world-ship is the only thing with life and everything else is death. We are wrong, I think. Everything is life and nothing at all is death." She turned to him suddenly. "Do you think so?"

"I do," he answered earnestly, leaning toward her a little. "I do—since you show me how to think so."

She smiled, but glanced away from him. "I am afraid you may mean you think the sea is making me sentimental, Mr. Ogle. Our little world of the ship is coming very much to life since all the people have had their lunch." She added this commonplace to her reverie; but her gaze went back to the sea.

Passengers had come out from the dining salon and the lounge in increasing numbers; and many of them now read in their chairs or wrote letters upon books and magazines supported by their knees. Some of them leaned upon the rail, chatting or scanning the sea in hope of whales or porpoises; others covered themselves with rugs in the long chairs and lapsed into drowsy apathy; but most of them became cheerful itinerants, making the everlasting round of the deck and seeming to take a lively pride in their pedestrianism.

Among these, though they were not equipped with

such a pride or any of the common cheerfulness, Ogle
took note of two ladies whom he recognized painfully,
in his own mind, as Honey and Baby, his table companions.   They passed recurrently, making the round
again and again, arm-in-arm, with no visible pleasure
in their performance.   Mrs. Tinker's expression remained no less aggrieved and disapproving than it
had been at the lunch table; and the profile of her
daughter, as it moved across the playwright's range of
vision, between him and the sunny azure of the afternoon sky, showed even an increase of resentfulness,
he thought, though the silhouette was undeniably a
lovely one, and, except for its sullenness, might have
been a very model of piquancy.

But this pretty Miss Libby Tinker was more than
sullen; she was highly irritable, as she made evident
in passing Ogle and Mme. Momoro for the fourth or
fifth time.   She switched away to a little distance
from her mother, though without interrupting their
forward progress—the movement was to rid herself
of the fond maternal arm.   "For heaven's sake,
don't hang onto me!"

Mme. Momoro detached her thoughtful gaze from
the sea to look after them.   "Your American young

ladies are the most independent in the world," she said. "They are always showing us that."

"Some of them," he returned quickly. "But please don't take an ill-mannered provincial for a sample of our American ladies."

"No? It is very puzzling."

"What is?"

"What you have just told me. Because wherever I have gone in America I have been told I must not take any of the people I have noticed as samples. It is very hard to discover America." Then she smiled. "If Mr. Tinker should be going to Africa I do not know what *he* would get from it, but I would like to see him there."

"You would?" Ogle had thought they were rid of the unpleasant subject, and he was a little nettled by her tendency to revert to it and even dwell upon it. "Why on earth should you?"

"But why should I not?"

He frowned. "Well, frankly, it seems a little grotesque."

"Grotesque?" she said inquiringly; but the word seemed to please her, even to amuse her pleasantly, and she repeated it. "Grotesque. Yes, I think it might be. One might think of him in that way—upon a camel at Touggourt or out in the Desert, for instance. I am sure he would ride upon one and perhaps have his portrait painted as he sat upon one."

"He would!" Ogle said grimly. "That is, he would if he thought he could use it for an advertisement."

"All the same it would be interesting," said Mme. Momoro. "I have a little weakness for the grotesque."

"Have you?" He turned to her earnestly, and found her eyes benevolent. "I didn't mean the man would be anything so distinguished as grotesque. It seems to me he would be only annoying. I meant that something else struck me as grotesque."

"Somesing else besides Mr. Tinker in Africa? What?"

"Well—well, frankly——"He hesitated, a little embarrassed, and then decided to be bold enough to go on with his thought. "Frankly, it is rather curious to me that a lady of your type—though I don't mean you belong to a type, Madame Momoro—it is a little strange to find you apparently without the—the prejudices, perhaps I should say, that an American of your class would feel. I hope you'll forgive me for seeming personal; it is only in appearance that I do seem so. I'm not really personal in my meaning. I——"

"I understand," she said gravely. "Say what you are thinking."

"Then since you do permit me—well, frankly, I'm puzzled that you're so charitable as to be amused by such people. They belong to an objectionable bourgeoisie with which we ourselves avoid contact. We are never conscious of them unless we travel and then we are but too unhappily made aware of their existence. They swarm in politics and in business; they thrive upon a horrible ceremonial known as the Great American Banquet; they read mystery stories, buy maroon velours furniture, call their advertisements 'literature,' and speak of a tragic drama as a 'show.' They are blissful when a brass band plays 'In The Gloaming.' If it plays 'Suwanee River' they cry. Their religion is to pay for their wives' pews in expensive stone churches full of 'art glass,' and their patriotism is to bellow at a cultivated Chinaman that they are one-hundred-per-cent. Americans. We think they're rather terrible, Madame Momoro."

"You say—'we'?" she said inquiringly.

"I mean simply, Americans of good breeding and

some experience of the world," he explained. "What distresses us is to see foreigners getting their idea of America from the Tinkers; and what I meant by 'grotesque'—well, frankly, since you do permit me to say so, it seemed grotesque that you could be so gracious as to find the man amusing instead of awful."

"Why?"

"Why?" he repeated. "Why, because anyone can see at the first glance that you are at the most extreme opposite pole from such a creature. Because you are so preëminently everything that he is not, and he is so vulgarly everything that you are not."

"Ah, but he did not seem to me vulgar," she said. "I cannot understand. Why should you think I am so different?"

"What! Why, I've never seen anyone like you before in my life," he informed her earnestly. "When I came into that room yesterday afternoon and saw you sitting there——"

He paused, and she looked at him inquiringly. "Yes? I was sitting—where? You mean when I played bridge in the afternoon perhaps? I think you came in a doorway facing me."

"You remember that I did?" he asked, his earnestness so increasing that his voice became a little husky. "I thought then that you were a woman who saw everything while looking as though you saw nothing."

But she did not take this as a tribute. Her eyes opened wide; and her lips parted, too, in sudden laughter. "I seem so vacant?" she cried. "*That* is how I look?"

"You look——" he began ardently, and then checked himself. "Ah, Madame Momoro, you might not let me tell you how I think you look! You might say I do not know you well enough."

"So soon I should be saying that to you?" she asked gaily; and to his thrilled delight she added, with a quick flash of her eye to his, "Well, there are nine days left!" Then, as she unfolded the rug that had been about her and rose easily to her fine height, she said: "Do you care enough to know me better to walk with me a little while on this eternity of cycles we call a deck?"

"Do I!" the happy young man exclaimed, though it is possible that he would have preferred to go on knowing her better, seated. She was taller than he and he had to look up to her as they walked.

He had also to lengthen his stride and make it a

rapid one to keep pace with her, he discovered; for although she appeared to be moving not even briskly, she swept onward with a graceful and tranquil speed that inspired poetic improvisation in one of two astonished young men who emerged from coffee in the lounge, half an hour later.

> "The unhurried golden huntress
>   Great Diana gliding swift—
>   Oh, swift as light!
>   Between two close-set clouds———"

This was the black-browed Macklyn's spoken thought of her as he and Albert Jones, deciding instantly upon a promenade for themselves, more moderately followed the fast-moving pair. Then the poet became prosaic. "How in the name of a name d'you suppose he's ever managed to meet her?"

"I'd like to know that myself," said the envious Jones. "He's always lucky, that fellow. His new play is running like wildfire and people make a great fuss over him;—everybody tells him seriously he's a 'great artist'; and he's even lucky enough to believe it. Now he's had the prodigious luck to meet this one wonderful-looking woman on board, and he'll probably also be lucky enough to interest her and monopolize her. Anyhow, he'll try to; you'll see.

She's got him on the hop to keep up with her, though, and for his sake I hope he's lucky enough not to know he looks rather like her poodle trotting beside her."

Macklyn was fairer. "Oh, no, He's a distinguished looking person, that Ogle; handsome, too; and you can tell he's 'somebody.' Even if he is a bit shorter and nearly trots as you say, he can afford it, because he's too significant looking to be even a Diana's poodle. Where do you suppose they're heading for now?"

The question was drawn from him by a change of movement on the part of Mme. Momoro and the playwright, who were leaving the promenade deck and ascending an open companionway to regions above. Albert Jones proved himself equal to a shrewd guess.

"They're going up to the smoking-room," he said. "Women smoke anywhere nowadays, of course; but for some inexplicable reason you'd find that many of these elderly American ladies on board object to the sight of one of their sex doing it in the open air. Mme. Momoro wants a cigarette; but she's been in America and she's so completely a woman of the world that she understands this curious prejudice. Shall we go up there, too?"

"We might as well," Macklyn assented. "He'll probably treat us like a couple of outcasts; but we may as well try it out.   Anyhow, he can't stop us from looking at her.   I think you're an adroit person, by the way, Jones."

"Why?"

"To reason it out why such a woman wouldn't smoke on deck if she cared to.   Ogle prides himself on being an analyst—you can tell he does from his play—but I doubt very much if he'd have been able to fathom a delicate bit like that from merely seeing Mme. Momoro bound for the upper deck.   I'm sure he'd never have guessed it."

By coincidence, Ogle was just then guessing in a directly opposite direction, and not at all to his own pleasure, though he followed Mme. Momoro with alacrity.   As a matter of fact, she had offered him precisely the explanation diagnosed by the astute Mr. Jones—she wished a cigarette, and perhaps some of the American ladies would not be pleased to see a woman smoke on the open deck, though she had herself observed young American and English girls thus freely disporting themselves.   But Ogle, in spite of himself, could not avoid an uneasy suspicion that she had become curious to know what the man Tinker was doing. The execrable one seemed to have indeed a grotesque fascination for her; she had mentioned him again, several times, during their flying promenade; and the young playwright was distressed to discover this singular and almost unworthy predilection in a lady who had for him so compelling a charm.

Something more than charm she had for him, in fact; though he did not yet realize the condition into which he was lapsing. He hurried after her swift Diana gliding and his eyes were fixed upon that inscrutable head enhelmed in burnished gold;—thus, already glamoured, he followed her, if not like the leashed poodle fancied by his jealous friend, at least like an ardent servitor of the hunting goddess. And this was only "the third day out"; while nine were left, as she had reminded him.

IX

IN THE smoking-room, Macklyn's prophecy that he and Albert Jones would be treated as outcasts seemed in a fair way to fulfilment, and as a measure of self-respect they seated themselves at some distance from the chairs occupied by their fortunate friend and the glamorous French lady. Ogle had not been aware of their entrance, so deeply was he engaged with her; but after a time his glance wandered to them as he talked, and he gave them a preoccupied nod; then immediately returned his gaze to what was undeniably better worth its while. He was speaking earnestly, but in a low tone inaudible to them, for to-day it was possible to converse quietly in that room, although eight middle-aged men (all of them hoarse) were present, including the vociferous Tinker.

This afternoon the pastime of the barbarians was neither musical nor bibulous. The eight sat about a green-covered round table within a leathern seclusion of chair-backs; they concentrated their minds in successive deliberations upon compacted hands of cards, held close to their fronts; they pondered, they considered, they breathed solemnly, they smoked cigars as with a grave unconsciousness that they did so. Then, from time to time, looking up, they regarded one another with a peculiar scrutiny, profoundly insincere; but when they spoke it was only to murmur technicalities. Before the strangely quiet and thoughtful Tinker there glistened upon the green cloth a toy castle made of celluloid disks built into many little towers brilliant in clean colours; moreover, he was the only warden of such a keep. No other of the eight thoughtful men had similar defences before him. And ever and again, through the slowly dispersing layers of cigar smoke, there were cast upon Tinker's bright towers reflective glances in which there was a hint of acidity.

"I suppose it's a relief that they sang themselves voiceless yesterday," Albert Jones said to his friend. "But as a spectacle I can't say I find them much more stimulating to-day. Poker is our national card game because it suits the temperament of our sterling business men precisely; their form of relaxation, it seems, is to prove to one another that what they essentially are is wolfish.   To me it's rather a painful sight."

"You aren't compelled to look at it," Macklyn suggested.   "There's something else in the place."

"Thank you," Mr. Jones said gratefully.   "I'm trying my best not to let her know how much too well aware I am of that fact.   How old do you suppose she really is?"

"I don't suppose.   A few women in every century forbid such suppositions: the Empress Elizabeth, Ninon, Diane de Poictiers——"

"Eve, herself, no doubt," the painter added, "to say nothing of the wife of Menelaus.   Madame Momoro looks twenty-six or a glorious thirty, as you choose, but can't easily be under thirty-eight if she's the mother of the full-grown youth travelling with her; and I should say there's no question but that he's her son—he looks it perfectly, and she called him 'Bébé.'   Probably she's forty; she might be more. Without any doubt at all, she's years and years older than Ogle—as much as ten or twelve probably."

"So?   Well, he doesn't know that," Macklyn observed.   "He doesn't know anything except that she's listening to him.   She's a woman who casts a spell, and he's spellbound; no question.   I'm not an expert reader of lip movements, but I have an impression that he's quoting rhymed and metrical verses to her."

"He is," the painter whispered. "Listen."

The poker table had become deathly silent in some crisis of suspense; the noises of air and sea through which the "Duumvir" rushed were closed out by the panelled walls; and though the throbbing of the vessel's heart was always beating up from fathoms underfoot and faintly vibrant even here, the stillness of the room permitted some phrases spoken in a lowered voice to be heard by the two intent listeners. They caught but a little; for the card players completed their crisis with an outburst of exclamations all bitter except one, which was uttered in the hoarsest voice at the table: "Push, losers, push!"

"Yes; he's reached that stage already," the painter said, alluding not to the triumphant Tinker, but to Ogle. "It's verse. Something of his own, do you suppose?"

"I do indeed suppose so," Macklyn returned, thus supposing accurately out of his own experience. "And addressed to her or descriptive of her, I haven't a doubt in the world. By George, but she's giving a wonderful performance!"

"Why 'performance'?"

"Because she's had so many such things written to her—of course she has; just look at her!—she wouldn't care a rap for a million of 'em. Yet she's letting him think she does, in her impassive way, which isn't impassive, after all, you begin to observe, as you study her more closely.   She has that cool surface—a statue with an almost glossy patina; but as you get used to her, you begin to feel that she's a woman almost on fire, not with her emotions, but with the incessant vibration of her thoughts. She's thinking about everything all the time; but what she's really interested in just now, over that beautiful long cigarette holder of hers, is the poker game."

"I believe you're right at that," his friend agreed, concentrating his greenish eyes behind the thick eyeglasses he wore.   "She's really paying Laurence precious little attention and probably doesn't know what he's saying."

But here the envious young man was mistaken. Mme. Momoro's glance undoubtedly passed over the playwright's shoulder to the green table as he talked; but she was a woman capable of doing two things excellently at the same time.   "That is delightful of you," she said, as he concluded his quotation.   "I am sorry you did not write more. You see what a thirsty vanity I have; I am insatiable of any flattery, no matter how unfounded it is, so I am like a poor soul in the Desert far away from any oasis and trying to drink the water of a mirage. Besides, one knows that writers must be always writing—even if they can find no more to write about than a stranger on a big ship full of people. But when you see the Desert you will not write of ladies, Mr. Ogle; you will write only of that."

"What did you mean," he asked. "when you said some people change in Africa?"

"Well, don't some people change all the time, even though a very little, everywhere? So, if you are always changing a little, then finally after many years of changing little by little, that makes an immense change, you see. There are some who change nowhere, it is very true; but that is the people who become fixed and rigid as soon as they have passed the changes of youth; they are made of plaster of Paris. But people like you, who follow one of the arts, they remain always young because they are always plastic; so they must have to change a great deal very often, because the impressions made upon them by different things are always changing. You cannot constantly make impressions upon a piece of wax without altering the essential shape of that piece of wax. Such people are very, very susceptible to their surrounding, and they are different in different places. Well, there are some places that have unearthly beauty, places of so strange an enchantment that plastic people, when they go to one of those enchanted places, they become different from themselves very quickly and they will see everything as they have not seen it before. They will believe that what they always thought black is now white. Someone you thought he was a giant he will seem a little pygmy; and perhaps some pygmy look a giant. Such places where there is a spell that will change a plastic person like you in this way, there are not many of them; but one that I know is Capri and one is Taormina and one is Constantinople, and one is almost wherever you wish to go in Africa. You see they will put a spell upon people who can be bewitched, and the others will not be touched."

"You think I am one who can be bewitched then?" he asked, and he added, a little dramatically: "You have already discovered it?"

She laughed, declining to take this as seriously as he seemed to hope she would. "You wish again to be kind to my vanity, since I have described it to you as insatiable," she said lightly. "But what you really think is that I am fantastic when I speak of the witchery of those beautiful queer places. I am earnest, though. I have known a man to come down from a high mountain altogether a different person from what he was when he climbed up. And yet, after all, such an enchantment only accomplish' what happens to us in time without it. If we live a little while in this world we find that what we once thought black is truly white—we do not need to go to Constantinople for that! We find that someone we thought always a great, kind soul is sometimes a little spider. Toward people we cannot help but change, because we all have so many faces and everybody is like a manufacturer of masks; he has a thousand, but will show only one at a time, hoping you will like it, and so how can you ever know him? Yet each mask is a real thing, and so nobody can ever know one another, don't you see? And sometimes the mask a person show', it is a mask just to make you angry, and in a little while there is another to please you, like that young girl who was rude to her mother and would not allow her to touch her arm. She showed a mask of anger—she can afford to show so ugly a mask, because she is so pretty that even her rage is pretty, too; but the next time we see her she may be wearing the mask of a gentle angel. Which one is she, herself? If you meet her at El Kantara you may think her the angel."

For a moment Ogle was puzzled. "The young girl who was rude to her mother," he repeated; then he remembered. "Oh, you mean 'Baby,' this fellow Tinker's daughter."

Mme. Momoro laughed and her glance, passing over his shoulder, became more luminous. "Is she his daughter? Poor man, does he call her 'Bébé'? How pretty! What is her real name?"

"I'm sure I haven't the slightest idea," Ogle said coldly. "I fear that it would take more than an unearthly landscape to give that young lady the appearance of an angel in my eyes," he added, "or, for that matter, to make me care to notice what appearance she bears at all."

"Take care!" Mme. Momoro warned him gaily. "You cannot tell what you may become when you get away from this ship, Mr. Ogle, for the ship is still America. You have really not left home yet, all of you Americans."

He leaned a little nearer her. "Would you care to prophesy? What do you think I will become?"

He asked this in a low and impressive tone; but her glance still crossed his shoulder, and she spoke a little absently. "What you will become? You are charming, so you must take care to change only to become more so. You must take care——" Then, as she watched the card table where another crisis impended, she paused. Suddenly she clapped her hands triumphantly. "Oh, see! See!" she cried. "What a magician! He win' everything!"

The eight middle-aged men broke out in commotion. "Push, losers!" the victor croaked loudly; and there were things said that should not have been. The players began to rise from their chairs, fumbling in their pockets, tossing bank notes and gold and silver upon the table and accompanying this outpouring of cash with loud abuse. At the same time Tinker, flushed and openly hilarious, gathered the money together in handfuls which he stuffed loosely into his pockets, and in reply to all insults he maintained a continuous husky shouting: "Hair o' the dog! Hair o' the dog! Wait for the hair o' the dog!"

But the others were noisily preparing to go on deck or return to their families. "You're nothing but a murderer," Mr. Wackstle informed him harshly. "'Hair o' the dog'? No, thanks! We'll get even with you after lunch to-morrow, and I've had enough hair o' the dog already."

Tinker did not stop shouting, and two stewards were already on their way bearing trays of wide-topped glasses brimmed with amber sparklings. "Everybody!" the uproarious victor commanded. He waved a steward toward the repellently staring Macklyn and Jones. "Those boys, too. Everybody, now! Just one hair o' the dog that bit you."

Mme. Momoro was mystified. "One hair of the dog," she repeated, turning wide-eyed to the playwright. "What can that mean—one hair of the dog that bits you?"

"This," he explained as one of the stewards presented a tray before them. "No! Certainly not!" he said to the man indignantly. "Take it away."

"No, no!" she cried quickly. "It would hurt his feelings, and he is so kind." She took one of the glasses from the tray, lifted it near her lips, and bowed smilingly to Tinker. "To the magician!"

He immediately left his companions who were departing after a brief and discourteous acceptance of his hospitality. "Magician?" he said loudly for their benefit as he came over to her. "Who? Me? No! I was just showin' those poor childish old men a few o' the rudiments; but naturally I had to charge 'em a little something for the lesson. They're all mad anyhow because their wives won't speak to 'em to-day; but glory! they haven't got anything on me in that line: the big trouble with *me* is, mine *does!*" Then his glance, roving jovially about the room, fell upon the poet and the painter, sitting coldly aloof. "Here, waiter!" he called to one of the stewards. "Didn't you hear me tell you to fix those two boys up like the rest of us?" With that he pushed a chair innocently between Mme. Momoro's and Ogle's, seated himself in it, and addressed Macklyn and Jones directly: "There's only the five of us left, it seems like. Whyn't you boys come over and join us? Five people's just enough for a nice cosy little party."

The two friends looked at each other hastily, then at Mme. Momoro, and came to a quick decision. Simultaneously they accepted filled glasses from the steward and the invitation from the barbarian, who received them with cordiality. "Sit down, boys, sit down," he said, and as they bowed in a manner a little suggesting that of the young Hyacinthe, he presented them informally. "Mrs. Mummero, it's a couple of Eastern gentlemen I been talkin' to a little, off and on. Easterners are likely to be kind of frozen-face until you get to know 'em, Mrs. Mummero; their climate makes 'em suspicious; but after they find out you aren't goin' to steal their shirts off of 'em they're just the same kind of human beings as anybody else. You been over in God's country quite some little time, Mrs. Mummero?"

"You mean——" she began, somewhat blankly; then she understood, and laughed. "Oh, in America? Only three months."

"Just for pleasure, I expect," he remarked, nodding. "Well, I wish I could speak French as well as you do English; I don't hardly speak it at all—just 'polly voo frossy' and 'nix ferstay'; that's about all *I* know. How 'n the world you ever pick up so much of the language in that little time?"

"Oh, no," she protested. "I have been often in England to stay a long while there, and when I was a little girl I had an English governess. Yet even still I make mistakes in my English sometimes, I am sure."

"At that," Tinker returned affably, "I bet you wouldn't make as many as I would in French, if I ever tried to talk it much. I expect if I'd had to wait to learn French I'd never 'a' started for Europe at all, and I expect it was about the same with these boys here, too." Thus he generously shared his linguistic defects with the three young men, who were sitting somewhat rigidly in their chairs and showed no enthusiasm for his reference to them—though one of them was relieved to hear Europe and not Africa mentioned as the Midlander's destination. Ogle had feared that the Tinkers might intend to land at Algiers instead of continuing with the ship to the Italian ports whither most of the passengers were bound; and, although he understood that the French possessions in North Africa were extensive, his prejudice had now become such that he began to feel the need of a spaciousness more than Continental to contain him and the Tinker family at the same time, with any pleasure to himself.

Now that a prospect of eventual relief was before him, however, he relaxed enough to say: "I should hesitate, myself, to speak French in Madame Momoro's presence—and even English!"

She gave him a little bow, and explained to Tinker:

"I have told Mr. Ogle that I am very susceptible to flattery. I provide myself with it wherever I can, and I am so childlike I relish it—even from the untruthful."

"I bet you hear a plenty!" Tinker exclaimed. Then, over his amber glass, he looked at her with a beaming admiration and said in a tone of amiable inquiry: "Widow, I expect?"

To the three sensitive young men the very air seemed shocked by the impact of so grossly naïve a personality; but the response of the desecrated lady left them nothing to wish for, though it was as personal indeed as what elicited it. "But you, Mr. Tinker, if one is to judge by some remarks you have made, you are not in the least a widower."

"*Me!*" he shouted, without the remotest consciousness of having received a reproof. "A widower? I guess you wouldn't think so, if you'd heard a few things I heard this morning after I came on deck! The trouble with steamships is, no matter how big they make 'em they'll never be able to make 'em big enough for a man to get down town before his wife wakes up the morning after he's been out a little late with a few congenial friends. Widower!" He laughed in rueful jocularity, and passed to another aspect of this suggestion. "I expect you wouldn't think I'm a widower if you knew what'd happen to me if it got out that I was sittin' up here right now talkin' to as good-lookin' a woman as *you* are, Mrs. Mummero!"

At this she surprised and a little grieved the majority of the impromptu party by a laugh of frankest pleasure. "You are an extraordinary man, I see. When a woman says she exist' only to hear pleasant things, no matter how far from the fact, you are shrewd enough to believe she has told the simple, shameful truth. Yes, you are very extraordinary, Mr. Tinker."

"Think so?" he said, and he was modest enough to utter a deprecatory laugh. "I guess nobody'd have to be very extraordinary to say a good many of that kind of things to *you !*" Suddenly he sighed, but as with some physical reminiscence not to his taste; he passed a handkerchief over his forehead and set his untouched glass upon a tabouret. "Oh, dear me!" he murmured. "It don't look so good to-day. What I really need is a little fresh air."

"Why do you not go to take it? ' Mme. Momoro asked him with a kindly solicitude.

He brightened, looking at her appreciatively. "I believe I would," he said, "if I could get anybody to

go with me to keep me from jumping overboard;—
I feel kind of despondent.   I expect you and I could
find a place out here on the top deck among all these
boats where my family wouldn't be liable to come,
and we could sit down and get a whole lot of ozone."
He rose, looking at her in genial confidence.   "How
about it?"

Again it was time for the lightnings to destroy this
man.   Playwright and painter and poet, already uneasily aware that the outlander had been monopoliz-
ing the attention of the tolerant lady, now were sure
that his hour was come.   He had gone too far; and
for the incredible audacity of his proposal, as well as
for the offensive artlessness with which it had been
made, he would now be beautifully and permanently
annihilated.   But as the three sat hopefully ex-
pectant, Mme. Momoro smiled amiably and rose.

"If you think it will be of benefit," she said.   "I
am always a philanthropist."   And with a charming
nod of farewell over her shoulder, she moved at once
toward the open door.

"My glory!" Tinker said, as they stepped out
upon the small after-deck beyond.   "I feel any
amount better already."

He was tall enough to look down upon her, and he

did so gratefully. She took his arm, and they disappeared from the sight of those within the room.

Unquestionably some sense of bafflement remained behind. "Now, why on earth," Albert Jones inquired, "would such a woman do a thing like that?"

"It's simple enough to me," Macklyn said. "You wonder how she can let the creature address a syllable to her, and not freeze him so solid he'd never be able even to look at her again. I suppose that's what you're wondering, both of you, isn't it?"

"I do," Ogle admitted. "I do indeed. I thought —— I thought——"

"Yes; one knows what you thought," Macklyn interrupted a little crisply. "But I'm afraid Madame Momoro has seen quite a number of men like you, Mr. Ogle, and like Albert and me quite as well. But this Iroquois from the prairies is a new type to her, and she's interested in specimens. We're of her own class; she intuitively knows us too well to be interested in us when there's an unknown specimen at hand. I don't think we need to feel mortified because she prefers half an hour or so of microscopic work, tête-à-tête, to a general conversation—especially as Albert and I didn't even offer her a sample of our own and never opened our heads. She had no reason to suppose we were prepared to offer her any more entertainment than that, even if she sat here all afternoon."

For himself and his friend Albert there appeared to be more consolation in this viewpoint than for Ogle, who had been two hours engaged in offering her entertainment; nevertheless, he accepted the theory of her interest in specimens and found a slight solace in it. But another thought of Macklyn's did not add to the clarity of the playwright's mind, already somewhat painfully mystified.

"There was one inconsistency I don't understand," said Macklyn. "When he delicately asked her if she was a widow, she scolded him with that retort to the effect that he had been complaining publicly, as it were, of his wife. Of course the creature himself hadn't any idea he'd been scolded; but that's beside the point. Why should she resent his asking her if she was a widow and then not be offended, even be pleased apparently, by his much grosser references to her personal appearance and his charming implications of his wife's jealousy? That's what I don't see."

Neither did the playwright nor Albert Jones; there appeared to be no solution.

X

AT DINNER that evening, though Miss Olivia Tinker's manner had not altered, the rigour of her mother's was observed to be greatly relaxed. Tinker, still smelling faintly of perfumed hair tonic, wore the air of a quietly righteous man who has proved himself sterling in the teeth of misjudgment, and that this was a hypocritical exhibition for his wife's benefit Ogle well believed; but at least it seemed effective. She rallied her husband upon his fine appearance, accusing him of wishing to appear young enough to dance with girls of eighteen or nineteen in the "Palm Garden" after dinner; and the playwright perceived that although between the husband and wife there rankled some obscure difference concerned with the sullen daughter, normally Mrs. Tinker was fond of the man, perhaps sometimes even proud of him.

Ogle was not so narrow-minded as to find it impossible to understand how a provincial wife could entertain such sentiments; her consort was no doubt

eminently presentable among their own kind. He
was robust, but by no means shapeless; his broad face
retained enough comeliness for a middle-aged woman
still to think of him without much self-deception as
"handsome"; his hair was yet darker than it was
gray; and there emanated from him, all in all, an
expression of power and energy, of which even his
severe young critic could not be wholly insensible.

Moreover, the critic could find no fault with the
creature's excellently made evening clothes;—so far
as mere appearances went, there was little reason for
the most fastidious person to dread being thought a
member of the Tinker party: Mrs. Tinker and her
daughter were as knowingly dressed and coifed as
any of the modish ladies on board, if one did not include the supremities of Mme. Momoro. Indeed,
Miss Olivia Tinker, revealed by a cloth of gold evening gown, was so lovely in spite of her ever smouldering sullenness that any young man facing her across
the small table might have been thought fortunate.
This one was far from thinking himself so, however;
for no matter how well they appeared to the eye,
these people annoyed him even when they were silent,
and when they opened their lips except to eat he felt
himself perishing of their Midland way of speech.

Mrs. Tinker, having already unbent to her husband, was able to include others of his sex in her forgiveness. "It's been a lovely day," she said to Ogle. "I suppose you've been enjoying it on deck, prob'ly?"

"A part of it, yes."

"I guess you behaved better than my husband, then," she continued. "I expect about everybody on board knows what a bad man he is by this time. I never did feel so disgraced in my life, and there've been plenty times at home when I've felt disgraced, too."

"You don't mean by *me*, Hon, do you?" Tinker inquired reproachfully.

"Don't I though!" she exclaimed; and she turned to Ogle, a mild waggishness in her eye. "You couldn't guess how that man's been behaving all afternoon! He's nothing but a robber, and I expect a good many gentlemen on this boat think so, too. He's a wicked man, and if I were you I wouldn't have anything to do with him."

"Look here!" her husband protested. "I don't see what cause you got to complain."

"He means he's got a bad conscience," she explained to Ogle. "The gentlemen in our town say he has a contract with Satan whenever he plays cards; and he gets so scared it might turn out to be true he always comes and gives Libby and me his winnings, and we put 'em in a box for our Community Chest fund. What he brought us just before dinner this evening would almost pay our whole subscription for a year. Yes, sir, this bad man's been sitting up in that stuffy smoking-room every minute of this whole afternoon from lunch till dinner-time, playing poker. I wonder they don't put him off the ship!"

"Now, Honey, Honey!" Tinker objected plaintively; and then, catching Ogle's cold sidelong glance, he favoured him with a slight but detestable wink. Being fellow-men, they were comrades in the deception of women, it implied; and Ogle was implicitly trusted on that account never to reveal the goings-on with a superb French lady that had taken place during an afternoon supposedly devoted altogether to cards. Thus the creature exhibited himself as more and more abhorrent.

The young man looked away without making any response to the wink except a slight hardening of his expression; and as he withdrew his glance he was surprised to encounter the full gaze of the girl across the table. It was the first time during the meal that she had looked up from the plate before her; and she immediately looked down again, leaving him a little disturbed, for there had been something brightly scornful in her eyes. Astonished, he was almost sure she had expressed herself injuriously;—it was as if she let him know she understood perfectly his opinion of Tinker, and added that although she herself hated her father, she despised Ogle for thinking what he did of him.

The playwright could not at once rid himself of the feeling that in the straight encounter of their eyes, his mind had met that of this silent girl and had been held in contempt. It piqued him, and he mentally asked her a question: "Since you feel so bitterly toward him yourself, what are you reproaching *me* for?" He would have put that into his glance if he could when she looked up again; but she did not do so, not even when he rose to leave the table and bowed to her and her mother.

This time, Tinker remained fearlessly with his womenkind;—most wives pardon victorious husbands, and his winnings for charity to-day had obviously atoned not only for the means by which he got them, but for his last night's meandering from the path of virtue as well. "See you later," he said cordially,

unaware that the two slight bows of departure had
definitely not included him.

The spacious lounge filled rapidly after dinner;
but Mme. Momoro was not to be seen there; nor in
the "Palm Garden," where there was dancing later;
nor in the smoking-room, which was almost vacant
all evening, though three young men haunted it
hopefully from time to time.   The youthful Hyacinthe appeared on the promenade deck alone, wrapped like an American collegian in a coat of coonskin
and pacing composedly;—he was unaware of being
an object of interest, or that he was kept in sight dis-
creetly but without intermission until he retired to
his cabin.   Not until late in the evening did Ogle
despond, and then an uncomfortable suspicion came
into his mind.   Still roving bleakly on deck, he
glanced for the fiftieth time through a window of the
lounge and came to a halt.   There were only two
people in the place: Mrs. Tinker busy at a writing-
desk, and her daughter seated near her and looking
with an air of permanent stubbornness at nothing.

In his wanderings about the ship the playwright
had not seen Tinker.   Could that imply a possible
coincidence?   With a most distasteful impression
that it could, he decided impulsively to show the

lonely and unhappy girl before him a slight conventional attention: music from the "Palm Garden" was still audible. He went into the lounge at once, presented himself before her and asked her to dance.

She gave him another queer look, as brief as the one he had caught from her at dinner and as eloquent, but not less hostile. "What do you mean by *this?*" it seemed to say, and to add: "Intruder!" Then, with instantly downcast eyes, she seemed to consider his invitation unfavourably, for she frowned; but abruptly she rose and without any other sign of consent and without speaking at all, went with him, and they began to dance.

Nothing could be asked of this provincial Olivia's dancing, her partner was forced to admit to himself: she gave him no more trouble than if she had been a floating roseleaf in flight on the air, here or there or wherever he would, at his wish. But she did not look up again, and he had a fine view of dark eyelashes against new ivory; she did not look up even when he spoke to her. "I haven't happened to see your father anywhere about the boat since dinner," he said, as with a casual commonplace of humour. "I don't suppose he got off at a way-station, do you?"

"He said he was going to bed," she replied, and added nothing whatever to the information.

Then, as the information itself was all her partner really wished of her, and as she seemed to wish nothing at all of him, neither of them thought it necessary to say anything more until the dance ended. When it did, she turned at once to the door and without seeming to notice that he was accompanying her, went straight back to the chair in the lounge near her mother.

"Thank you," she said, when she reached it. "Good-night."

Her brusque abruptness, something to which young ladies had never sought to accustom him, he found a little startling. However, it gave him his release, and he accepted it with a bow as cavalier as seemed appropriate, and went away to see if by any last chance Mme. Momoro had made her appearance in the smoking-room during his absence. But again he was disappointed; Macklyn and Jones had gone to bed and the place was now wholly deserted except for the watery-eyed, ancient man Taylor in apathetic conversation with the barkeeper. Ogle retired quickly, disheartened by the sight. It was not until late the next afternoon that he saw her again.

He had passed her empty deck chair many times; but at last it was occupied, and his heart quickened at sight of her as he came nearer. He had other symptoms, also, of what had begun to be the matter with him: his self-consciousness increased uncomfortably and he was disturbed by the mortifying alacrity with which his colour heightened, as he was himself too well aware. For with all his sophistication, he had never overcome a girlish misfortune of blushing whenever he was most anxious to appear austerely self-contained.

That was how he wished to appear now, especially as the chair upon Mme. Momoro's right was occupied by Albert Jones, and that upon her left by Macklyn. In his thought he reproached her for this; it seemed to him that she must have connived; and since he had not seen her for more than twenty-four hours she might well have provided a kinder opportunity. So, as he came near, he merely lifted his cap from his pink brow, and to emphasize his reproach, would have walked coldly by; but they hailed him.

He joined them; accepted the foot-rest section of Albert's chair, and was gently reproached for having so long made himself invisible. Mme. Momoro accused him of evading her; but in this he feared to trust her sincerity; and then, in view of what she lightly made known a few minutes later, he began to suspect that her accusation had contained an element of humour.

"Tell me," she said: "Is it true that everywhere in the United States the ladies are the tyrants and the husbands like slaves of the harem who are allowed to go out to work, but only under supervision? Is it true that those poor husbands must always say to the wives, 'At such and such a time I was at such and such a place for such and such a purpose'? That extraordinary man told me this, last evening, up yonder in the corner of the boat-deck where he says he is 'safe.' He insists to me that those are the conditions of marriage for all American husbands: they must account to the wives for every moment, and if a husband speaks at all to any woman not in his family, he must tell every word the woman has said to him and every word he has said to her. I could not believe it, and I asked him some questions about it again to-day. He said it was true, and that no husband could go alone to call upon a woman unless his wife first instructed him to do it. Otherwise the wife would murder the husband; and when I said I think he does not speak the truth—for I am a feminist, you see—he said it was better for the husband to be murdered than to have the wife say the things she would say in such a case, because to listen would take all the rest of the husband's life."

She leaned back in her chair, laughing. "What a man! He is so amusing in what seems to be such a strange frankness, and because you cannot tell whether it is frankness or not, or if he is joking, or what it is at all. Never have I seen such a man in my life! Can it be true what he tells me?"

She addressed the question to Ogle; but he did not seem to hear it, for he was too greatly preoccupied with the revelation of her recent whereabouts:—the theory of Mme. Momoro's interest in specimens was plausible, yet hardly seemed to account for the number of hours she had too evidently spent in studying this single abominable one. Then, as the playwright sat staring plaintively at the smiling lady instead of replying, it was Macklyn who explained that the views of Tinker were not to be thought representative except of the Tinker walk in life. What the man said was true enough of countless Tinkerish couples; but these formed an inferior populace with which members of the caste of her present auditors had little to do. So the poet informed her, with some emphasis.

She was only the more amused, and expressed a doubt of his authority. "I think you are a bachelor," she laughed. "He told me he knows almost everybody in great sections of North America, and he declared that upon the whole of that continent there are absolutely no exception to what he says of husbands and wives, unless there are a few in Mexico and one or two among the frozen Esquimaux." Then, observing that the three young men were unable to laugh with her, but remained serious and almost disapproving, she must have resolved tactfully to make them forget a subject plainly unsympathetic to their natures. She began to speak of other things, and spoke so well that she succeeded with two of them.

Something in the aspect of the water, as the running little seas tipped themselves with bright rose-colour from the western sun, reminded her of a voyage she had made in the Indian Ocean; and she began to tell them of it in her thrilling voice: cholera had come on board her ship in this Oriental seafaring; but it was not discovered until it had made headway among a crowded steerage of Far Eastern Mohammedans returning from Mecca. Then the ship's engines had broken down and could not be repaired for days— days of torrid heat, with molten gold from the sun, she said, poured upon their fevered heads. Two of the passengers had become insane; one, a girl whom she knew, had flung herself into the sea in the unbearable heat of noon, drowning before she could be reached; and the sea-burials over the vessel's side were hourly, day and night. But all the while, and through all the terror, she told them, the sea was incomparably beautiful and the nights were an enchantment of big stars close overhead with such meteors flaming and hissing from among them as she had never seen before or since. It was like a strange, strange conception of Gustave Doré's, she said; and except for the anguish about her she might have enjoyed it, because she had not been frightened, and it resembled, she thought, a great artist's dream of hell.

Her audience sat motionless, held as much by her voice itself, perhaps, as by what she said; for it was a voice with mellow hints of music in its every tone. They hung upon her narrative as if Paganini played it to them upon his violin; and when she concluded— with a little trill of her rich laughter and a final gesture of her shapely long hands—only the young playwright still retained a troubled thought of Tinker. She left them then, and as she went swiftly down the bright deck toward the sunset she did not seem to go to dress for the evening, though that was how she had explained her departure. She seemed to be flying home appropriately to the great, round blaze of the sun into which her tall figure appeared to vanish, as the three, with blurring eyes, stared after her.

This was Macklyn's expression of her manner of leaving them; and Albert Jones agreed. "Yes," he murmured, wiping his glasses. "A woman with wings! A woman with wings!" Ogle said nothing; for the voices of the sea and the pulsation of the ship's vitals were mocking him, and through and through his head, from ear to ear, they seemed to beat a hoarse, intolerable chanting:

> Mariar!
> Mariar!
> Bay rum in a bottle we'll buy 'er!
> Mariar!
> Mariar——

He turned from his enthusiastic friends and walked away without any of the usual explanatory mutterings.

XI

"GROTESQUE" had been his word for the puzzle of her behaviour, and with "Mariar" persistent in his head he feared it was now the right word for his own condition. Never in the young playwright's life had he been so fascinated by a woman, or so piqued and mystified by one. He had no interest in the sea, or in the unknown land upon the other side of it whither he was bound, or in the ship, or in the ship's passengers, save only one. Day and night she was the provoking apple of his mind's eye; he could get no rest from his thought of her, nor any satisfaction in the thought; and when he was with her he felt himself to be clumsy and brooding.

What irked him, too, he could never be alone with her—only the accursed Tinker seemed able to accomplish that. From the moment the execrable one had introduced Albert Jones and Macklyn to her they were barnacles. If she sat in her deck chair, Jones was fast to a chair upon her right, Macklyn clung upon her left. When she went upon her sweeping promenades they kept themselves undetachable alongside. In the lounge for music or coffee, or in the smoking-room or wherever she appeared, they appeared also. In the evenings, if she watched the dancing in the "Palm Garden"—she declined to dance, herself—they watched with her. Only once again before land was sighted did Ogle contrive to be alone with her, and then not for long. It was the day before they reached Gibraltar.

"Thank heaven this part of the journey's almost over," he said gloomily.

She looked a little hurt, though perhaps more humorously so than really. "You find us very tedious?"

"You know what I mean, I think, Madame Momoro."

"No. I cannot imagine at all."

"I think you can." He was so serious that she laughed compassionately, whereupon he made bold to touch her arm. "Please don't laugh," he said. "I'm glad we're near Gibraltar because two of my friends are landing there; and I'll be glad when we reach Algiers because after that you won't sit in a corner of the boat-deck with Yahoos any more."

She frowned as if puzzled. "Yahoos? I do not know the word. What is that?" Then comprehending, she laughed. "Oh, I see. You mean yesterday afternoon when I was talking there again with Mr. Tinker, and you passed us and looked so cross you wouldn't speak. Why didn't you join us?"

"For one reason, I couldn't quite believe I was wanted."

"Oh, but I should have been charmed," she protested. "That man, he is so amusing one would love to have a companion to enjoy him with."

"I find I have quite enough of him at the table," Ogle said coldly. "That is about as much as a civilized being could be asked to stand of him, I think."

"I am not civilized?" she inquired; but she was not offended, for she laughed, and little lights danced in her clear eyes. "You do not see the real man at your lunch table or at dinner," she added, not waiting for his reply. "I have been able to catch a glimpse of your table sometimes, looking down over the balcony railing. I can see he does not talk so much when he is with his family; you all four look very solemn. But when he is not under the eye of his tyrant women—oh, then he is entertaining to me; he is extraordinary!" And she concluded with a question in a tone of childlike naïveté: "You don't like him?"

Ogle stared at her. "Pardon me," he said. "I'm not precisely in the habit of being laughed at, Madame Momoro."

Then she thrilled him, although she laughed; for she touched his hand lightly with the tips of her fingers, and said: "You are a dear!"

That was all;—the indefatigable pair, Macklyn and Jones, came up just then and ruined a beautiful moment for him. And to increase the coldness of his sentiments toward them, this was all they accomplished; because she departed at once to visit her friends, the elderly French ladies, in their cabin, where one of the sisters was still afflicted by an abscess of the ear. After that, as she explained, she must prove her devotion to Hyacinthe and allow him to read to her his report upon public education in America, which he was preparing for the French government.

This report of the young Hyacinthe may have been a compact one, or perhaps he had only written a little of it; for certainly the reading occupied no great length of time. Prowling uneasily about the boat-deck, not quite an hour later, the playwright heard a rich, low laughter unmistakable anywhere in the world, and, following the sound, came upon a nook between two lifeboats where sat the elusive lady with Tinker.

She was anything but embarrassed. "I told you it needs two persons to enjoy this extraordinary man," she said gayly. "To believe what he tells me would need perhaps a thousand; but one more might be at least a little help. I insist that you join us."

"Sit down, sit down, young fellow," Tinker said cordially, and he waved his hand toward a folded camp-stool leaning against the white wall of the wireless operator's room near by. "I just been tellin' Mrs. Mummero some simple God's facts about a few things in my part o' the country, and she thinks I'm makin' 'em up. She don't know a thing about the United States; all she saw was just New York and Boston and Philadelphia and hardly anything to speak of, of *them*, nothing but a few hotel clerks and some pink teas. Well, she began to talk about how much of a place Paris is—she seems to think a good deal of Paris and some the other towns they got over in Europe;—but I told her she never in her life saw a real town yet, and she never *will* see one unless she comes back and gets to the other side the Allegheny Mountains. I told her to come out my way and *I'd* show her one!" Then in his enthusiasm he leaned toward her, beaming broad admiration upon her. "I'd certainly like to take you around *my* city!" he said.

"Such a proposal!" she cried. "Mr. Ogle, you must stay to save me. I might accept!"

But Ogle was already moving away, and did not look back. He made up his mind to stop thinking of her, to banish her entirely from his mind, and, feeling restored to freedom by this resolution, sat down comfortably upon a coiled hawser and wondered why he had not sooner set himself at liberty by so simple an act of will. The sun was bright and under it the whole circle of the sea lay sparkling; balmy airs encompassed him; he was once more his own man. Congratulating himself upon the ease with which he had dispersed the fascination, he began to realize that he had been almost in love with Mme. Momoro. Then his chin sank, his hands clenched, and he groaned half-aloud.

"How can she?" he whispered bitterly. "How can she treat me so!"

At dinner that evening Mrs. Tinker was in great

spirits. She nodded at the placid hypocrite across from her and said to Ogle: "Do you know what this wicked man has been up to? Robbing those poor gentlemen in the smoking-room again the whole live-long afternoon. Well, Libby and I'll just have to stand it, I expect, because he stole more from 'em to-day than any time yet, and I'm going to endow a new ward in a hospital when we get back home. What's more, the first place I'm going to look for when we land from this boat, it's a jewellery store!"

There had been no card game at all in the smoking-room that afternoon, as Ogle knew; and he found a momentary satisfaction in the thought that Tinker's hypocrisy was at least expensive.

But this pleasure was fleeting; the man was probably "made of money." One day the playwright had heard the manufacturer of worsteds and the Wackstle person talking of Tinker in the lounge. The two men evidently had known something about him before they encountered him on this voyage, and it was clear that they thought well of him. In fact, the worsted magnate had spoken of his "respect": "I have a great respect for any man that can build up a really big business out of nothing the way Mr. Tinker's done these last fifteen years with that paper com-

pany. It was just about up the spout when he got
hold of it, and I understand he never borrowed a
penny for it but backed it with his own capital entirely. It must be a great satisfaction to a man to
feel he's made such a position for himself in the world
of business."

Ogle thought wonderingly of this phrase, "the
world of business." He had always been aware that
there was such a world and always felt about it what
his father felt about it before him. His father had
been a rather embittered and radical assistant professor of English; and Laurence had gone from the life
of the university into what he felt was the forefront
of the theatre and studio life of New York. So when
he thought wonderingly of that phrase used by the
worsted man, "the world of business," his wonder
was that of the mountaineer who sees pedlars
greedily bargaining over their packs far below him in
the haze of the plain. The world of these business
men, the Tinkers and Wackstles, and worsted men,
was a strange gloom, as he thought of it—a smoky
twilight wherein they groped ignobly for money and
incessantly babbled in their own dialects about their
grubbing. To them it was a real world evidently;
they passed the word from one to another when one

of them got money in quantity, and they had their own murky little trading celebrities, dismal bragging beings wholly unknown on the heights above, And it was with one of these that Mme. Momoro preferred to spend hours alone!

"Preferred" was the galling word in Ogle's mind. For it had become clear to him that although she was "nice" to him and to Macklyn and Albert Jones, and, when she had nothing more to her taste to do, gladly made herself their gay and sympathetic companion, what she preferred was Tinker.

All in all, the young man felt that he was getting a rather severe lesson in both the variety and the singularity of human tastes and viewpoints. Upon the matter of their singularity, moreover, he received further enlightenment as he was preparing to retire, this last evening before the "Duumvi " left the Atlantic for the Mediterranean. For days he had heard nothing through the closed door between the adjoining cabin and his own, except commonplace fragments from Mrs. Tinker concerning dress, to which Olivia responded in monosyllables; but to-night the elder lady was more discursive.

"One thing I've been sort of disappointed about, so far," she said. "I always heard you were likely to meet so many interesting people on these big liners, especially going to the Mediterranean. Of course most of these on board are well dressed, and they're all well off, no question, or else how could they be here? But I certainly don't agree with your father: he says they're the finest lot of people he ever saw—he always says that, anyhow, wherever we go, because he always likes everybody—but I never did feel that just succeeding in business and showing it in their clothes makes people interesting. What I mean is, you can look over this whole boat and you'll scarcely see a single intellectual face."

The daughter's response was characteristic of her mood. "I wouldn't want to see it, if there were."

"Well, I would," Mrs. Tinker returned. "At first, from his looks, I thought that little fellow might be going to turn out right cultivated; but he hasn't made one interesting remark the whole way over. He don't seem to know anything about anything at all."

There came a sharpness into the daughter's voice. "Oh, yes, he does. He knows he's wonderful."

"It doesn't look like it," her mother returned;— "the way he and his two funny-looking friends keep

hanging around that adventuress!   I do wish I knew
who she is: I'll bet she's got a history behind *her !*"

"Perhaps in front of her," Olivia suggested, and
could be heard to yawn.   "She's beautiful."

"She may be," Mrs. Tinker admitted cautiously;
"but she looks like a woman to me that'd always be
up to *something* or other, you couldn't tell what.
Anyway, the thing that's sort of disappointed me so
far is, I thought there'd be so many cultivated-looking
people on board, and except that second head-waiter
in the dining-room with the eyeglasses, I haven't seen
a one."

The light clicked out upon that, and the incensed
young man heard no more.   Inevitably and by every
possible means, it seemed, these Tinkers, middle-
class Middle Westerners, of whom he had never heard
two weeks ago, were ruining his voyage and his temper, and actually interfering with his life;—at least,
thinking of Mme. Momoro, he went so far as to put
the matter in that extreme way.   He could only
pray for haste to Algiers and his departure from the
boat and all contact with such people.

But in the morning for a time the engrossing lady
made him forget his ill-humour.   He stood with her

upon the forward gallery of the promenade deck, and, although Macklyn and Albert Jones and other passengers stood with them and even pressed upon them, he stood nearest her, and his shoulder touched her arm.   Before them the bow of the "Duumvir" flung aside a bluer sparkle of water than they had yet known, and there opened a majestic avenue between the giant headlands of two continents.   Upon the left, flat-roofed Spanish villages rose from the sea and massive square white towers stood beyond upon hills of unfamiliar shapes and colours.   On the right a long parapet of ominous mountains, gray and mysterious within a veil of blue haze, ranged down the Straits as far as the eye could reach.   It was to this long and somehow disturbing highland barrier that Mme. Momoro directed Ogle's attention.

"Africa!" she said, in a low voice.   "That is Africa!   Anything could happen behind those mountains, one feels.   The stranger it could be, the more one would expect it.   These are the Pillars of Hercules; and just here, on this side, is Spain.   It is barren, perhaps; yet it is beautiful and smiling, too. But there, that huge sculptured shadow in the high air—that is Africa!"

She said the word "Africa" in a way, as he

thought, he had heard no word spoken before in all his life. She little more than breathed it; but it was as if she breathed the whole stories of Cleopatra and Carthage in the one lingering low sound.

"It is magnificent," he said, deeply moved; and added in a husky voice for her ear alone: "Your thought of it, I mean. I feel your thought of it in your voice, and I understand. And you—you are more than Africa!"

Onward sparkled the flying bow of the "Duumvir," opening headland upon headland on the leftward shore until almost abruptly, there, gigantic before them, they beheld old Britain's Rock climbing the brilliant sky of Spain.

"My golly! *that's* familiar," a hearty voice said from the clump of passengers behind Mme. Momoro and Ogle. "What an ad! What an ad!"

Tinker's enthusiasm was for the genius of a commercial organization in his native country; and a moment later he was heard again jovially extolling it, in reply to a remark from Mr. Wackstle.

"Yes, sir; certainly it's impressive; but if it hadn't been for that ad how many people do you expect would ever 'a' heard of it? The only thing that disappoints *me*, I always thought they had their sign painted right on the Rock like it is in the pictures. I'm goin' to sue 'em, when I get back, for false pretences.   It ain't there!"

"Pop-*puh!*" Mrs. Tinker, excited by these first moments in the Old World, so new to her, scolded him amiably but with a loud shrillness. "If you don't look out, Mr. Wackstle will think you really don't know any more than you sound like you do."

"Well, I don't—not much.   Was this where Napoleon landed from St. Helena or something?   What ever *did* happen around here, anyhow?"

XII

OUR human nature has many humorous ways to betray us, loving to cajole our eyes from knowing what they see, and leading us (especially when we travel) to mistake what is within us for a quality of our surroundings. So it was with Mr. Laurence Ogle's disappointment in the picturesque town of Gibraltar: he believed that he saw the place; but what he saw was a discoloration of it worked by his own mood. Macklyn and Albert Jones were to depart at once for Seville; Tinker certainly would be unable to escape from his family duties; and the playwright had hoped for a beautiful day ashore with Mme. Momoro alone, or, at the worst, with the quiet and discreet young Hyacinthe as a chaperon. Moreover, she had encouraged him in this hope, giving him a deep quick look to go with the rest of the encouragement, a look of some gravity. "We could drive to Algeciras," she suggested, and asked gently: "You would be willing to take me into Spain?"

"Willing!" he said. "Ah, very, very far into Spain!" He told her he had always owned many bright castles there; that since he had met her he was engaged upon a new one much brighter than the old; and he was fortunate enough not to suspect that something of the kind might have been said to her before. She had been several times to Gibraltar.

This was the most of his good fortune, however, for while he waited with her, as the passengers were descending to the tender to be taken ashore, an elderly lady appeared upon deck, with her bandaged ear concealed by a mourning veil. Accompanying her were her sister and the young Hyacinthe in solicitous attendance; and at once, upon sight of this group, Mme. Momoro informed the crestfallen playwright that her plans to visit his Spanish castle were cancelled.

"But if those ladies intend to go ashore and look about, surely your son——"

"No, no, no!" she said quickly;—she seemed to be a little shocked by the suggestion. "Mademoiselle Daurel and her sister, Mademoiselle Lucie, are our dearest friends; they are my hostesses in Algiers. We are travelling with them; we went to America with them. They are very nervous and not strong;

they depend greatly upon me. I am sorry, but I must go." He had not seen her so serious, and as she hurried away from him she gave the impression of a person who has been urged to do a frivolous thing at the sacrifice of an important one. So his new castle came down about his ears, and he went ashore carrying the ruins with him.

He said a gloomy good-bye to the painter and the poet among a mildly clamorous crowd of guides, passengers, pedlars, and drivers on the pier. Albert Jones was going to Seville "for a bit of painting perhaps," he said; Macklyn would accompany him there and later across to Florence, where they would take an apartment or possibly a villa together. Ogle promised to find them if he came to Italy after his African adventure, and also to send them news of himself and of Mme. Momoro when he reached Algiers.

Then, unexpectedly rather regretful, he watched them as they drove away, rattling and rocking in an absurd little surrey with a gayly shabby fringed top, a gayer and shabbier driver, fringed himself at the elbows, and a feather-plumed, aged little horse spasmodically brisk in a gesture of departure. When they were out of sight Ogle bethought him of an omission—his friends had forgotten to leave an address where they might be reached by letter. However, he was not inconsolable; he hoped Algiers would offer him things more interesting to do than writing letters.

Alone after that, he strolled up into the town to make a dull day for himself. Everywhere and delighted with everything were the "Duumvir's" passengers; and he could go nowhere but to be annoyed by their exclamations of discovery. They discovered the shops, the tea-rooms, the strange, pleasant colours of buildings and shutters, the incomparable sleekness of the horses held in waiting for British officers outside a club, the robed Moors from Tangiers across the way, fine old sherry, lovely gardens, and the eloquent drowsy little graveyard in the sunshine below the old town gates. Here, among the epitaphs, Ogle would have lingered, for he thought the inscriptions touching, and saw that something of England's history was written there; but he fled from an invasion by the families of Mr. Wackstle and the worsted magnate.

Most of his fellow-travellers, he observed, were now upon a footing of cheerful acquaintance with one another; in fact, he was the only person of the whole ship's company who went about Gibraltar alone, hailing none of his fellows and being hailed by none. This was his own choice; yet he could almost have wished that nature had made him a little less exclusive. He had always been exclusive; he had been so in college and in the career he was making for himself now in New York; but his exclusiveness, absorbed in boyhood from his lonely and satirical father, had no ordinary snobbishness in it. The assistant professor had despised "good family" almost as much as he had despised riches; and he had taught his son that the only aristocracy was one of culture—and there were only a few members, anywhere, apparently.

Laurence had never been able to look upon people generally as his fellow-men. On the contrary, he saw almost all of them as caricatures of what he felt they should have been; and since he by no means looked upon himself as a caricature, he naturally could not meet many of them upon a congenial basis of equality. Sensitive and lacking a strong consciousness of mortal fellowship, he found contact with the great majority disagreeable; almost invariably they offended some delicate prejudice of his; and, as he thought of them, they had only a surface existence, never going "deeply into life," as he did. There was a somewhat fashionable phrase he used both in speaking of people and in thinking of them, a complete definition forbidding all further research; and he thought nothing of applying it to a whole shipload of human beings, or, for that matter, to all the inhabitants of broad areas in his own country. Indeed it is probable that he had called more people "quite impossible" than had all of his most fastidious and talented contemporaries put together.

He belonged to a few clubs; but was exclusive within them; he went to dinners where he was a lion among ladies, as he was, too, at tea in the afternoon sometimes; and his acquaintance was principally with people who held exclusive views of literature and the arts—the only subjects upon which views were of real importance, they felt—but even among these exclusives he was exclusive. In his work in the theatre he had made not a single warm friend among the managers and actors, and only a few among the actresses. These people were his instruments and necessarily he must work with them; but he seldom became at all intimate with them. As a matter of fact, Albert Jones was the most intimate friend he had and the two were not very closely intimate, at that. Moreover, since his father's death his nearest relatives were some cousins in Rhode Island whom he had never seen; and after he had been nearly run down by an automobile in Gibraltar, he became a little more gloomy when he thought that if he had been killed, those unknown cousins would have inherited the royalties from "The Pastoral Scene." Probably the Rhode Island cousins and the manager of his play would have been the only people much interested; though no doubt the manager would get all the "publicity" he possibly could out of wide-spread obituaries.

Thus this lonely young man had all day grown more and more disgruntled with Gibraltar, with life, and almost with himself; and he was not the less so because the automobile that spared him by a hand's breadth contained the Tinker family returning from an excursion into Spain as far as Algeciras. Tinker shouted jovially, waving in greeting a spiked stick decorated with gay ribbons and designed for the bedevilment of bulls. Also, he wore a bull-fighter's hat, purchased simultaneously at the bull-ring and so strikingly incongruous upon his Midland head, that Ogle spitefully hoped Mme. Momoro would see him in it. She did, as it happened, only a moment later and under the playwright's eye; for she came by, just then, in one of the gay, shabby little surreys, with Mlle. Daurel beside her and her son and Mlle. Lucie Daurel in another surrey behind them.

Mme. Momoro gravely and slightly inclined her head to the Tinker automobile, not as if in a personal greeting, but in the manner of a lady whose courtesy extends itself to acknowledge the presence of people recognizable as fellow-travellers. Then, to Ogle's chilled surprise, this same distant formality was visible the next moment in her return of his own salutation. Usually she greeted him with a brightening vivid recognition that seemed to say, "You, at last! How charming!" Mlle. Daurel, sitting beside her, austere, dryly pallid, and infinitely remote, had such a frigidity of look as he had never seen upon the frostiest of American women; she suggested the snow on a faraway mountain peak, never thawed and very old. And Mme. Momoro seemed to have caught from her a little of this icy remoteness and to have become again the wholly impassive statue she was upon his first sight of her in the smoking-room.

He went to brood upon this in a tea-room; then returned in a launch to the "Duumvir," where he found a sprightly show of embroidered Spanish shawls en-

livening one side of the promenade deck and many
passengers chaffering with the swarthy merchants in
the sunset. Other swarthy merchants, rocking up
and down in rowboats on the gilded sea far below,
offered baskets of fruit and branches of oranges; and
the small globes, brilliant among green leaves, constantly ascended from sea to deck, for they were
pulled up on long strings by the purchasers. Both
sets of merchants should have appreciated the mag-
nificence of Tinker, who was still wearing his enormous Spanish hat and bought shawls and oranges,
the one as readily as the other. Of the shawls he
bought the four with the longest fringe, this appearing to be his standard, though they were also the
most splendid in colour—"gaudiest" was Ogle's word,
as he stood by, morbidly observing. Mrs. Tinker
selected one of the four for herself, and the other
three were for the daughter, as Tinker made known;
he could be heard loudly instructing a steward to
convey them to her in her cabin.

"Tell her they're from her old man," he called
after him; and then, going to the rail, he began to
shout, "Polly voo frossy" and "Nix ferstay" at the
fruit sellers, and to shower down coins among them,
laughing uproariously as they scrambled to catch

the money. And as the baskets soared upward to
the steerage passengers for whom he bought the fruit,
he directed the distribution, not moving from where
he stood and bellowing over all the clamour of the
recipients and of the boat pedlars. "Hay, there!
That feller in the velveteen pants didn't get any!
Hay! You! Don Gonzabo! You with the whiskers! Send up that basket to the feller in the velveteen pants! You sabby? *Hay*, there! You no
speakee? Oh, you do! Three cheers for Christopher
Columbus!"

Everybody was laughing at him; and Ogle turned
away, ashamed that an American should be making
a spectacle of himself before these foreigners.   Mme.
Momoro was one of them, though she did not appear
to be observing the spectacle, nor indeed to be conscious of either Tinker or himself.   She stood beside
Mlle. Lucie Daurel, who had not the frosty remoteness of her older sister, but showed an almost
child-like eagerness in testing the effect of a darkly
gorgeous green and black shawl upon her friend.   The
effect was dashing, unquestionably;—wrapped in this
shawl the long and graceful Frenchwoman became
at once a Spanish portrait, superb in colour and contour against the blue mountains that loomed beyond

the vessel's rail. Ogle wished to tell her so; but the distance she had put between them when she bowed to him so coldly was now emphasized by her apparently complete unconsciousness that he stood near her. He had the painful impression that she did not wish him to speak to her.

Mlle. Daurel bought the shawl, and that evening in the lounge it was draped upon the back of Mme. Momoro's chair as she sat at bridge with her son and the two sisters. But by this time the "Duumvir" was again at sea, steaming deeper into the Mediterranean under warm stars, with the lights of Spain behind her; and Ogle was becoming unhappily confirmed in his impression that the amazing lady's attitude toward him was not what it had been no longer ago than this same day's morning.

He sat near her, with coffee upon a little table before him; and as he almost faced her his eyes were upon her over his cup whenever he brought it to his lips—and at many other times, too—but never to meet her own; for she gave him not a glance, nor seemed to know that he was in the world. Her whole consciousness appeared to be engrossed with the cards and with a constant solicitude for the sisters Daurel. The elder still wore her costume of the afternoon with the mourning veil pushed back, and once, when she put her hand to her ear under the veil as if in momentary uneasiness, Mme. Momoro quickly took her other hand in both of her own and looked at her with the glowing intensity of one who takes upon herself the pain of a friend and so banishes it. At another time, when Mlle. Lucie shivered after the opening of a door to the deck, Mme. Momoro wrapped her instantly in the new shawl; and, again, when the older sister found something amiss with the score, which was painstakingly kept by Hyacinthe in all their games, his mother spoke to him in French with a severity of tone that made him blush. But never once did she glance toward the lonely young man, who all the while watched her covertly and with an ever-deepening pessimism.

His fortune was no better the next day;—when she walked the deck it was at a slow pace, suiting her fine stride to the deliberate movements of one of the sisters Daurel; if she sat in her chair it was with one of them, or both, at her side; and in the evening the four played their eternal game until midnight; then she accompanied them on their way below and did not return. The day after that, the last day of his voyage, she was no kinder: he was as effectively separated from her as if she had been upon another boat with all the depth of the Mediterranean between them; and his consequent suffering surprised him, it was so sharp.   Two weeks earlier he could not have thought it possible that he would this soon be going about with something like an actual aching in his chest because a Frenchwoman, heretofore unknown in his life, preferred the society of her son and two elderly compatriots to his own.

Then when "the last night out" had come—that night so unbelievable during his early physical sufferings—and when she was again inaccessible at the bridge table, he began to feel desperate.   He wrote a note consisting of the fevered inquiry, "What have I *done?*" and directed a steward to place it under her cabin door.   After that he went out on deck and walked violently.

His pace and the vigour of it were such, indeed, that when he rounded the after corner of the ship's house and collided with a lady who was coming almost as rapidly from the opposite direction, he struck her so shrewdly that she staggered backward, and was in the act of falling when he sprang forward and caught her in his arms as the only means of keeping her upon her feet.   It was Olivia Tinker.

"Let me go!" she cried instantly, even before she regained her balance.

"Certainly!" he said indignantly. "I beg your pardon." And he stood away from her. "I was only trying to keep you from falling."

"Good heavens, you don't need to explain *that!*" she exclaimed. "I didn't suppose you——" She stopped, apparently because of embarrassment.

He was embarrassed, too, and not pleased that he should be so on account of little Miss Tinker. She was of his own height; but he thought of her as "little Miss Tinker" and thus she had sometimes been mentioned in his talks with Albert Jones and Macklyn. It angered him with himself that his *savoir faire* could be impaired by little Miss Tinker's first implying that he had caught her in his arms because he wished to, and then reproaching him for explaining that his motive was utilitarian.

"Good-night," he said stiffly; then lifted his cap and went on; but he had not gone far when he began to fear he had been rude to her; and the thought of her lovely, unhappy young face touched him. He knew her opinion of him, for he had heard her express it to her mother; but to-night, in his own unhappiness, he discovered that he forgave her for it.

Something in this unhappiness of his—for he perceived that his feeling now amounted to unhappiness—made him think that another unhappy person would be congenial to him; and, as he came round the forward promenade deck and met her again, he stopped her.

"Miss Tinker, would you care to go in and dance?"

She looked at him for a moment, and then brusquely asked him a strange question: "What for?"

"I beg your pardon," he said, bowed, and would have gone on; but she detained him.

"I meant I didn't care for anybody to be polite to me," she explained, her voice still ungracious. "If you'd like me to dance with you because you want to dance and don't know anybody else to ask, I will."

"I think I could know other people to ask, if I wished to," he said. "I asked you because I——"

She interrupted him. "All right; it doesn't matter. Why should anybody ever bother to explain anything? Besides, I like your dancing." They were just outside the Palm Garden door, and she dropped her wrap on a deck chair as she spoke; he opened the door for her; she went in quickly and turned with her hands outstretched to him.

They danced through four intervals of music; and
though neither of them had more to say to the other
than when he had danced with her before, her eyes
were not so continuously downcast as they had been
on that previous occasion; she looked at him several
times with a clear, deliberate gaze in which her sullenness always smouldered; and although he knew this
smouldering had nothing to do with him, her eyes
disturbed him, as they always had disturbed him
when he encountered their full revelation. She had
no right, he felt, to look as though she understood him
—and understood him contemptuously at that—when
manifestly she could not, and knew nothing whatever
about him. She did not even know that he was a
playwright and in his own way—so far from her
little way—a celebrity. Nevertheless, he would have
gone on dancing much longer with her when she
stopped; for he had never danced with anyone who
made him feel so much inclined to dance forever.

"No," she said, when he asked her to wait for the
music to begin again. "That's all."

Then, not looking to see if he followed, she went
out to where she had left her wrap. He reached it
first; put it about her shoulders; she said "Thank
you," and without turning her head walked a few

steps away from him as if to leave him definitely. But she stopped suddenly, and came back to him.

"I think I'll say something to you," she said. "I'll never see you again, because this is the last night; and I'd like to have it off my mind. It's about my manners on this trip. You know what I mean because you've had a sample of them at the table twice a day, and what I want you to understand is that they're my own responsibility and not my mother's and father's. They brought me up to be decent to everybody, and it's been the fault of nothing but my own beastly state of mind that I've behaved as I have on this voyage. It's my fault, not theirs; I want you to understand. I'm telling you this because I'll be able to feel afterwards that at least I made some explanation of my own rotten table manners and have that advantage over you, because though yours have been as bad as mine, you haven't dreamed of making any such explanation and never would. And I oughtn't to go without telling you that it's only I who've realized that your manners are as bad as mine. My mother and father haven't understood; they just thought you didn't know anything."

With that, she looked him full in the eyes once

more. "Good-bye," she said, not ungently; and left him.

Angry and a little dazed, he stared after her, regretting that his sympathetic quest for solace in another unhappy person's society had been so ill-advised. Yet there was something curiously piquant in the most insulting thing she had said: "They just thought you didn't know anything." The girl herself, then, thought he did know something; but she evidently believed that it was better to know nothing than to have manners as bad as her own. "Silly!" he said; but was not quite sure that this settled anything.

He descended frowning to his cabin, there to discover something that immediately banished both his irritation and the erratic Miss Olivia Tinker from his mind. Upon his desk there lay a thin blue envelope addressed to him, and on the single sheet of paper inside it he found written in a delicate hand:

You will understand? Ah, you will be kind! Write to me at Villa Colline des Roses, Algiers.
AURÉLIE DE ST. D. M.

He understood nothing except that an enchantment seemed to be just before him; and his lightened heart would not let him sleep until near dawn.

XIII

HE SLEPT late into the morning, undisturbed by a great to-do and the moving of heavy trunks in the corridor near his cabin; and he finally awoke into a curious, unfamiliar stillness. There was no throbbing from the ship's vitals, and for a few moments the silence was like the noon pause in a village. Drowsily he became conscious of a far-away tooting of little horns; and then, close by, he heard a creaking of wheels and voices shouting vehemently in French just below the open portholes of his cabin. These sounds must be illusion, he thought, for they came from where he had grown used to the liquid rushing and flinging of the sea; it was difficult to understand what Frenchmen and creaking wheels were doing in the water. Suddenly and startlingly there came the loud sonorous braying of a donkey; and at that he sat up, wide awake, in his bed and looked out through the portholes.

What he saw was a white-and-gray town rising upon a crescent of hills in terrace on terrace of thick walls and flat roofs, strangely massive and venerable

to an American eye.   Old-looking domes bulged up
from the flat roofs here and there; the general white
and gray was spotted with hazy blues and pinks; and
he had distant glimpses of the great leaves of palm
trees fluttering in the breeze.   Everywhere shapes
and colours were strange to him; the "Duumvir" was
at a dock in Algiers.

When he came forth into the brilliant Mediterranean sunshine, and had been waved onward by a
man in a French uniform at the head of the pier, he
realized that this was the last of the "Duumvir" for
him.   He was not yet free of some physical reminis-
cences of the sea, however; his eyes retained the ship's
habit of motion, and the solid way before him seemed
slowly to rise and fall in the rhythm of the rising and
falling deck; the ground felt strange to walk upon.
This sensation was much more acute than it had been
at Gibraltar, where it resembled a slight occasional
vertigo;—here he was like a skater, walking with
strangely weightless feet difficult to direct after a
long day on the ice.   They seemed unable to carry
him forward with any proper speed, baffling him as if
he were trying to hurry in a dream, and what he saw
was dreamlike, too.

Before him, beyond the dock, there was an open

space of ground thick with dust, and there came from it to whine at him, and to pluck at him with old apes' hands, five or six figures almost indistinguishable from dust.   They wore ragged headgear of cloth, and about their bodies were torn swathings the colour of a coffee sack, not the colour of a new coffee sack, but of one that has lain years upon a trash heap, a colour soon to become familiar to him.   Other figures like these stood to stare at him in an inhuman, strange-dog manner of staring; and they and the beggars were brown people, so strickenly old, so strickenly nondescript, that, except for a gray beard or two among them, he could not tell which was man and which was woman.

Close by him a shabby gypsy played a guitar, and, in dusty velvet and flying ribbons, there danced a fandango in the dust to this tinkling a fantastic yellow midget woman two feet high, jerkily galvanized like a mechanical doll upon a music-box.   The gypsy confidently offered his hat to Ogle for a contribution; the beggars whined importunately at his elbow and plucked at his coat; an unpleasantly dapper guide with a waxed moustache and a breath all garlic joined him officiously;—everybody seemed to feel rightfully entitled to a little of his money.

He gave coins to the gypsy and to the Arab beggars, repulsed the guide, and discovered among some waiting automobiles the omnibus and porter of the hotel in which he had engaged rooms by cable. The porter, a handsome person with brass buttons upon his bright blue coat and gilt braid round his cap, made everything simple for the traveller, relieved him of all care for his bags and trunk, put him into the best of the automobiles, and bowed profoundly as it moved away.

It moved rapidly—Ogle at once perceived that he would have no complaint to make of slow driving in Algiers—and he was borne flying up and up hill through the newer French part of the town. The streets that he saw, though foreign enough to him, might have been streets in almost any city in France, except for the palm trees here and there and the veiled women and Arabs among the French pedestrians on the pavements and in the trolley-cars. The playwright's most exotic journey until now had been to Montreal, and all he saw upon this swift drive wore for him the air of exciting novelty; he took delight in the apéritif drinkers upon the pavements before the cafés; in the strolling French cavalry officers, brilliant shapings of colour, though not so brilliant as the Spahi beneath whose scarlet cloak light flickered from spurs on boots of red Morocco leather; but, above all, Ogle was fascinated by the robed and turbaned Arabs, the robed Jews and the hurrying veiled women. He had never been among robed people before, and he decided at once that trousers, except upon ladies, had ruined the beauty of occidental life.

The car swept him through a gateway, then through a mysterious and bosky garden beyond, and in the midst of the garden came upon the hotel. The walls were half covered with scarlet and purple blossoms of climbing vines, and before it there was a balustraded white terrace whereon a majestic black-bearded merchant, in a turban and white robes just immaculately out of the Arabian Nights, displayed embroideries for the benefit of a dozen or so English ladies and gentlemen. These were seated about painted little iron tables and enjoying coffee upon the terrace after lunch, though not making their enjoyment at all obvious.

When Ogle, having himself lunched excellently, joined them there a little later, he had already made up his mind that his coming to Algiers for a rest had been an "inspiration." Algiers was French—he pleased himself by thinking that he had seen a dozen

Madame Bovarys in his drive from the pier—but it was also the Orient. He seemed to feel a breath of the East upon his cheek, to smell incense through grilled windows, and to hear the plashing of fountains in hidden moonlit gardens where sang amorous nightingales among the heavy fragrances of strange flowers. So he said to himself that he stood at the scented gateway to Araby. No doubt this same scented gateway to Araby had been discovered by other young travellers in the same spot; but Ogle's Araby had a special perfume for him—Mme. Momoro was there and the terrible Tinkers were not.

At five o'clock that afternoon, having wandered dreamily through the higher streets of the town, wondering where he should find a villa garden gateway inscribed "Colline des Roses," he stood leaning upon a stone wall and looking far, far down upon the sea. From this height the great "Duumvir" looked like a small model of herself, appropriate for a steamer agent's office, and the deep blast of her signals came but faintly to his ear. Then, as she stood out to the open sea, the flat blue of the Mediterranean wrinkled obliquely back from her bow and a narrow white lane was left behind her, so that as she drew farther and farther away the ship appeared to be only the pointed head of a white arrow so long that it was feathered at the shore. "Good-bye!" Ogle said, and for a moment he thought of a pretty and sullen girl who might be on her deck—and perhaps looking back. Probably she would never understand that she had reached the climax of her bad manners last night when she "explained" them and added her queer insult to what she seemed to believe was an explanation. But he did not think long of Olivia Tinker. "Now for to-morrow!" he said exultantly.

He meant Mme. Momoro; and in the morning he wrote to her as he breakfasted on a little balcony overlooking the hotel gardens. He merely asked if he might not see her that day, and thought the request eloquence enough; but the address "Villa Colline des Roses" appeared inadequate to him. His balcony, where he sat in the comfortable sunshine, was by the open window of his bedchamber, and a French *femme de chambre*, who had just said to him "Good-morning, gentleman," was busy within the room. He called to her and showed her the envelope. "Will that do?" he asked. "Could a messenger find this place without having to know the street and number?"

"Monsieur?" She looked seriously at the address, appeared doubtful; then brightened, "Ah!" she exclaimed, making an important discovery in spite of his handwriting. "Colline des *Roses!* Ah, Colline des *Roses!* Oh, *Colline* des Roses!"

"Do you know where it is?"

"Where is Colline des Roses? Everybody can tell you, gentleman. It is where live Mademoiselle Daurel and her sister."

"Do you know them?"

"I?" she said. "No, no! I know some pipple that work for them. They have two chauffeur'; one is marry with my cousin. Their cook I know, too. You are going there, gentleman?"

"I want to send this note there."

"The concierge at the bureau, he do it for you, gentleman." She looked again at the envelope. "Oh, it is for Madame Momoro! Ah, Madame Momoro!"

"You know her?"

She laughed. "No, gentleman. I have seens her. Very—very *gentil*. You know what *gentil* is? Beautiful lady! She is here with them last winter and in the spring. You see Mademoiselle Daurel and her sister, they are very rich pipple. Always they were rich; but now they have a brother has die in

America where he was so, *so* rich! And they went there when he has die, and they get everything belong to him. So now they come back to here, maybe they are going to make Monsieur Hyacinthe Momoro to be their son."

"What?" Ogle was astonished. "You mean they want to adopt him?"

"I don' know what that is to say," she returned apologetically. "How you say? 'Adupp'?"

"Adopt," he said. "It means to make someone who really isn't your own child be the same as your own child, by law."

"Yes, law," the woman nodded eagerly. "Yes, that is it. That is what they think to do. Everybody in Algiers know' all about it, gentleman; but I know more than other pipple because it is my cousin who marry with the chauffeur. My cousin tell me Madame Momoro want that very, very much. She love him a great, great deal, Monsieur Hyacinthe Momoro, and she think he is not so strong. If Mademoiselle Daurel make him her son, then perhaps he don' have to work. Mademoiselle Lucie Daurel wish very much to make him the son; but she must always do what her sister is telling her. Mademoiselle Daurel, she always take' a long time

to make up her mind; but my cousin a week ago she
is telling me that now they will be at Colline des
Roses again, and her husban' think they will ad-
adupp—is that the word?—he think now they make
Monsieur Hyacinthe Momoro their son. Who can
tell?''

Then she returned to her work, and Ogle sat a
moment longer, looking thoughtfully at the envelope
before taking it to the concierge.   He had heard that
French servants were great gossips and far from accurate; but this one seemed to have a reliable avenue of communication open to the villa "Colline des
Roses"; and he wondered if the frost-bitten Mlle.
Daurel had a prejudice against Americans. She
oughtn't to have, he thought, in view of the fortune
that had come to her from the country of the Americans; but it might be possible.   In fact, it might be
what that note so beautifully signed "Aurélie de
St. D. M.'' had entreated him to understand.   And
as he thought of it, this explanation seemed more and
more plausible; Mme. Momoro was so anxious for
the adoption that she had feared to lose influence
with Mlle. Daurel by letting the icy old woman see
she had made friends with any of the hated race.

If this was true, he hadn't much chance of seeing Aurélie de St. D. Momoro at "Colline des Roses," he feared; and ruefully he began to wonder if she would dare to let him see her anywhere.

Another thought troubled him a little. On the "Duumvir" she had no air of indolent luxury; she suggested great energy under easy self-command; yet undeniably she suggested luxury without the indolence; everything she wore had been as rich as it was exquisitely made; and he had seen beautiful furs upon her, and once or twice, in the evening, some fine jewels. Moreover, Hyacinthe Momoro, in a quiet way, was a finished portrait of the youthful exquisite; Ogle had noticed his flat watch of platinum, his white gold cigarette case with a coat of arms in enamel; everything belonging to either mother or son was of the elegance that is most inordinately expensive; and yet they could not be rich. If they were, why should Mme. Momoro be so anxious for her son's adoption? Ogle remembered the fond compassion with which she spoke of the boy's small position in a bureau of the government and of the hard work he did upon the report he had been writing in his cabin. Thinking of that, the playwright felt that he had begun to understand her better; he became sympathetic and ardently wished to tell her of his sympathy.

Unfortunately, the opportunity to do so began to appear remote; no reply to his note arrived that day or the following morning. Then, after haunting the desk of the concierge until noon, he sent her a second missive inquiring with some insistence why he was treated so enigmatically. "You said I should learn much in Africa," he wrote. "Are you assisting the continent to teach me that I am so insignificant I no longer exist at all? You asked me to understand. I can understand that since I belong to the Western Hemisphere I am unfortunate enough to incur the prejudices of your friends; but I do fail to understand that a place so well equipped as I have every reason to think 'Colline des Roses' should not contain an ink-stand. You ask me to be kind. Good heavens! How is one to be kind to the Sphinx? That great figure is another ornament of this continent, I learned in my childhood; but as it is still something like two thousand miles from me I fear the difficulty in showing it any very striking benevolence may be too much for me. Yet it seems no farther away, nor no more stonily perplexing, than you are. Why?"

An hour after he had sent her this appeal, a card was brought to him as he sat at his table-d'hôte lunch in the hotel dining-room. "Hyacinthe de St. D. Momoro" was the name engraved, and it brought the ever-ready colour into the young American's cheeks. He immediately left the table and went out to find his caller; but Hyacinthe was not to be seen in any of the Moorish public apartments, nor upon the terrace. Ogle went to the concierge, as he had already learned to do in all emergencies.

"Monsieur Hyacinthe Momoro is gone away directly," he was informed. "I think he don't call to see you; he just call. Leave card for politeness."

"But didn't he say he wanted to see me? Didn't he leave any message?"

"No; he don't say anything at all; jus' say his card is for Misterr Uggle," the concierge replied; and he added, with what appeared to be a rather cynical amusement: "He look very bad."

"Ill, you mean?"

"No; he's not seek." The concierge laughed. "He has a glooms. Might be, he's getting a nerves attack."

"What about?"

"I don' know," the man said; and, losing interest

in the subject abruptly, he turned to serve an English guest who was querulous about a noise made by the steam pipes in the billiard room.

"How can you expect a man to make a decent shawt in such a din?" this sufferer inquired and added bitterly: "I *ask* you!"

Ogle lingered a moment, but decided to return to his unfinished lunch. Evidently the *femme de chambre* had not greatly exaggerated the fact when she said that "everybody in Algiers" was familiar with the affairs of the sisters Daurel and their visitors.

On his way back to the dining-room he passed the entrance to the hotel restaurant, a smaller room; and although the painted glass doors were closed, sounds from within reached the corridor distinctly enough to let him know that compatriot tourists were lunching there. "Alley vooze on!" he heard a male voice exclaiming in pain. "Don't pass that cheese anywhere near me again; it's worse'n a dead snake. My Gosh!"

Ogle quickened his steps; the voice was "Middle Western" and reminded him of Tinker's—a jarring note in Algiers. He did not wish to be reminded of Tinker, who was by this time a jarring note in Naples, no doubt; but happily Naples was a city upon another continent; and so far, in his rambles down into the town, Ogle had encountered no more than four or five of his recent fellow-passengers. The "Duumvir" had left only a few of them in Algiers, and those he had recognized were of the quietest and grayest. Of course other ships arrived, he knew, and would inevitably deposit Tinkers and Wackstles and worsted men; but they could be avoided. Africa was larger than the "Duumvir."

After lunch he went down the long hill to wander about the lower town, where he had found himself most fascinated, for there the oriental life thickened and the occidental thinned out to almost nothing. But to-day he walked absently, preoccupied with his broodings. It was evident that Mme. Momoro had sent Hyacinthe to leave a card at the hotel: Was that her way of signalling that the reproachful note had been received and had gone to the mark? The gloom of Hyacinthe could not have been caused by his polite errand certainly; and it must have been extreme since the concierge had noticed it and had laughed about it. Was it a French habit to be cynically amused by other people's depression? For the concierge's amusement had indeed appeared to be cynical when he suggested that his youthful fellow-

countryman's low spirits might be due to an attack
of nerves.

Thus puzzling, the absent-minded pedestrian wandered on among strange, narrow streets, and presently found them so queer that they offered him a
new puzzle to solve. The people about him were
swarthy, but not brown; they wore gaudy stripes
upon their robes; the men were hawk-nosed and
black-bearded, and the women he saw were not
veiled. What puzzled him was the fact that the
faces seemed familiar to him, and so did the garments; he had that disturbing sense, like an elusive
half-recollection, of having been in this place and
among these people long, long before, in his childhood
or in a previous incarnation. For a time the solution
evaded him; then all at once he understood, and
laughed to himself. This was the Jewish quarter;
these Jews of North Africa were just what they had
been two thousand years ago; they wore the same
dress and lived as they had immemorially lived.
Time had no meaning here; and he had casually
stepped back into the Bible. The scenes about him
were from the Old Testament; and that was why he
felt he had been among them before: they were like
the coloured illustrations in an elaborate "Children's

Bible" he had been given when he was a little
boy.

Pleased, he went on, climbing up and down stone
steps, penetrating dark thoroughfares so narrow that
they were but passageways, and presently found
that he was away from the Jews and among a different people.   Most of these were as squalid and soiled
as the mere deep holes they seemed to live in among
the thick-walled buildings.   And here the streets
appeared to be brown tunnels, with intervals of
meagre light where the vault was broken; and upon
each side of him were mysterious and ponderous
old green doors, or open low black archways where
foul-robed brown men sat in the dirt with massed
dates, or a few dusty vegetables, or perhaps a
dozen copper or brass pans for sale beside them.
Some of these streets were silent and almost empty
and some were swarming and clamorous.   Piteous
tiny donkeys and lean goats were everywhere; and
once Ogle was pressed to the wall by the passing of
an enormously fat gray-bearded Arab almost wider
himself than the street he rode in.   For he was
mounted, so to speak;—a donkey, almost hidden under the man's burnous and not larger than a collie, incredibly bore him over the uneven stones that were

slippery with a dreadful filth. The huge rider gave Ogle a hard look as he squeezed by him, and spat noisily, seeming to express an unfavourable opinion in that manner.

This hard look remained in Ogle's mind as he went on. The eyes of the beggars at the dock the morning he landed had something of the same hardness, even while they entreated him; and he saw it now in the glance of every man who looked at him in these streets. It was an expression that excluded him from all fellowship, and it was worn by the raggedest and most debased of the people who took note of him. Here, as he went farther, nearly all were debased as well as ragged, clad in unbelievable patchings and fragments of every hue, but mostly of that repellent tint of ancient coffee sacking he had seen upon the beggars near the pier. Obviously, there was not a soul he met who did not a little more than despise him; for there was something beyond mere hating and contempt in the look—and it was always the same look that he got from all of them. It did not alarm him, although he realized that he had wandered into what must be the worst part of the Arab quarter, and the concierge had advised him rather emphatically not to go into the Arab quarter at all without a guide.

He was not timid; and the ugly look interested him. It seemed to him a little like the look he would himself turn upon a large rat, a rat large enough perhaps to do some effective biting, if attacked.

The analogy was perfect, he thought; they looked upon him precisely as men look upon a rat. It was a curious sensation to be alone among people who looked at him like that, to be among these degenerate brown rags of human beings who were not so debased in their own eyes but that they utterly excluded him from the right to claim to be a part of humanity. To their way of thinking he was evidently not a human being at all; he was an intruder with money in his pockets for which they would gladly have cut his throat; but nevertheless and always a rat, worthy of nothing better than annihilation even if he were naked among them. He remembered what Mme. Momoro had told him one day: that Africa might make a change in him, and that he might discover something there; and he wondered fantastically if she had meant that he would discover himself to be what the mongrel eyes of these slum Arabs so clearly informed him they thought him. Certainly she herself was not treating him as if he were wholly human, he thought with no little soreness.

Meanwhile, the way before him grew fouler. Unpleasant smells had beset him from his entrance into this quarter; they had grown more and more powerfully unpleasant as he progressed; and now, quite suddenly, as he turned a narrow and crowded corner, a scent of Araby struck him that was like an explosion in his nostrils. It was the great chief ancestor and Beelzebub of all demon smells, he thought, a Goliath among smells; and he turned back from it as from flood or fire; for it was not to be borne except by people inured and hardened by bitter experience. But when he turned he found that he had been followed; he had a train of unscavenged riffraff the most leprous he had seen, and they filled the narrow passageway behind him.

They had been whining and chattering at him; but as they had kept behind him, he had not been aware of them, for there was other chattering everywhere in this dark byway. Now, when he sought to pass through them they kept close, so that he could not; and pressing near him they set up a loud clamour half-imploring, half-sinister. Therefore he turned again, and with his handkerchief to his nose, faced the mighty smell and went into it. He walked as rapidly as he could; but his followers were nimble and more than kept pace with him. They clamoured in his ear, breathed upon his neck, plucked constantly at his light overcoat, from the pockets of which they pilfered a pair of gloves, matches, and some copper coins; they pressed upon him hungrily and caught at his sleeves with sore hands that made him shiver. Other creatures of their kind joined them, all chattering, whining, and plucking at him; and some squeezed by him from behind and got before him, walking backward so that he had ado to get ahead, for he had become the centre of a rabble.

The way was now up hill through a street vaulted overhead and not distinguishable from a noisome tunnel; but at a hundred yards or so before him it seemed to emerge to a brighter open space, or hilltop, and he thought if he could arrive there he might possibly find a French policeman, or get some help to shake off these leach-like tormentors; but they on their part seemed bent upon preventing him from reaching the open space. More of them crowded from behind him, and, coming in front, set their hands as if persuasively upon his chest; they ceased to walk backward before him and but slightly gave way as he pushed them, until finally they had him at a standstill.

"What the devil do you *want?*" he shouted angrily. "Get out of my way!"

They clamoured the louder, pressed him the closer, and, as he put his hand in a pocket of his trousers for coins, another hand accompanied his and clawed the coins from his fingers before either hand emerged. He felt contaminated; he was furious and now began to be a little frightened, too. The face nearest his— and it was near indeed—was not all of a face; but the bloodshot eyes of it were passionately alive and held that excluding look in which he had been interested a little while before. So had all the other bloodshot eyes close to his own that look; and it was the look that frightened him.

"Get out!" he shouted, though their chattering, close to his ears, made it difficult for him to hear his own voice. "Get out of my way! Get *out*, you dirty brutes!" And helplessly he began to swear.

Then suddenly the pressure of unclean bodies against him was withdrawn; the plucking hands ceased to touch him; the voices were gone from his ears. Brown feet fled noiselessly down the way they had come; rags flitted into holes, and, like shredding mist, the rabble vanished.

From the brighter open space above, there came

marching down the tunnelled street a queer procession. At the head of it an aged and blue-black negro, his broken lips frothy with unholy excitements, beat upon a tom-tom hanging by an old scarlet rope from his shoulders. He wore a tall headdress made of the crackling skins of cats, glittering with broken bits of mirrors; about his waist there swung some dozens of jackals' skins; his warped legs and great flat feet were bare. He pranced as he marched, beat pompously his tom-tom and shouted over and over, in a profoundly dissipated old voice, as a herald clearing the way imperiously for those behind: "Bo' jour, Messieurs et Dames! Tout le monde a droit! Bo' jour, Messieurs et Dames! Tout le monde a droit!"

At a little distance behind him Ogle discerned the figures of two women in European dress, walking with a tall young man who carried a heavy stick; but marching before these, almost abreast of the barbaric negro, prancing in step with him and evidently delighting in him, there came a stalwart man, middle-aged but visibly active and audibly deep-lunged. "Bum joor, Mushyoor a Dam!" he shouted as he came. "Toolamond a drot, whatever that means! You said it, grandpa! I'm gettin' to speak so much

French I can hardly understand myself! Keep your
old drum a-goin', Uncle Remus!"

He stopped short at sight of the lone American.
"Well, where in the name o' conscience did *you*
come from?" Then he turned to call to those behind
him: "Honey! Baby! Look who's here!"

The elder of the two ladies greeted Ogle as if he
had been a cherished friend whom she had long
warmly hoped to meet again some day. "Well, if
it isn't just too wonderful to see a familiar face in a
place like this!" she cried. "We thought you went
on with the 'Duumvir.' We didn't *dream* we'd
ever see you again!"

Olivia confirmed this. She had begun to blush
brilliantly as soon as she saw him. "Indeed, we
didn't!" she said hurriedly. "If we had, I would-
n't——"

She stopped there, leaving him to comprehend that
she wouldn't have insulted him if she had known his
foreign destination to be the same as her own. She
wasted her pains, however, for Ogle was not listening
to her. He was looking at Tinker and fearing that
this was going to be worse than the beggars.

XIV

THE English player of billiards who had complained so earnestly of the noise in the steam
pipes was querulous about many things; daily
in the table-d'hôte dining-room he could be heard
fretfully instructing the maître d'hôtel upon the
correct temperature for wines, upon the natural laws
governing the density of soups and gruels, and upon
other matters vital to happiness. No one in the large
room could fail to be as well instructed as the person
to whom he spoke; and his penetrating voice, high-
pitched and bird-like, ran continuously in a repeated
little tune always ending with a lifting note as of
inquiry, though his purpose was far from being either
musical or interrogative. Fair, thin, high-nosed, he
suggested a fine old Colonel by Du Maurier; and
Ogle, after solving a little problem concerning his
name, was impressed by his distinction.

Three middle-aged ladies and a long-nosed girl,
all of pleasant outdoor complexions and strong tastes
for old and unshapely clothes, revolved in close orbits

about the querulous gentleman, whom one of the older ladies called "my dear." The other two and the girl, however, always addressed him as "Swilliam," which was what puzzled the young American, especially as their table was near his, and he heard "Swilliam" constantly. Finally he sought enlightenment from the concierge, and was pleased to learn that his neighbour was General Sir William Broadfeather, a personage of even more important achievements than Ogle had supposed.

Sir William, with his small flock about him, was waiting for tea in one of the heavily draped Moorish public rooms of the hotel; and the playwright, returning from a drive he had taken to air himself after his encounter with the beggars, dropped into a chair across the room from the English party and tapped upon a table for a waiter.

A white-jacketed youth approached inquisitively. "Yes, gentleman?"

"Du thé," Ogle said. "Avec du toast et des petites gateaux." He had been studying a French and English "Conversation Book" in the mornings.

"Yes, gentleman," the youth returned politely "Tea and toast and some small cakes for one. Immediately!"

He went away, leaving Ogle a little discomfited, though what had just happened was a set-back by no means uncommon among linguists. But the American, blushing, hoped that Sir William and Lady Broadfeather had not overheard the injurious dialogue. He was strongly conscious of them and conscious of himself as well, wondering if they approved of him. He hoped they did.

Tea for either himself or the English party was slow in appearing; and presently Sir William beat startlingly with a walking-stick upon a large brass tray that had been placed before him on a Moorish table of ebony and mother-of-pearl. The brass was highly resonant;—people sunning themselves on the terrace looked in through the open door, seriously concerned to discover what might be the matter; and the concierge and a porter hurried apprehensively from the office.

Sir William rose and began to pace the floor. "My dear man!" he said, addressing the concierge in a falsetto wail. "Is one to have never the slightest attention in this hotel? A most dreadful liar dressed as a waiter promised us our tea half an hour ago, and we've not got it. We've not *got* it!"

The concierge spoke soothingly; but Sir William

would not be soothed. He repeated, "But we've not *got* it!" over and over again as argument in rebuttal to everything the concierge said, and when two waiters appeared with trays he still insisted in a voice that could be heard over half the hotel: "My dear man, it's all very well for you to tell us we *shall* get it; but I tell you we've *not* got it!"

He subsided then into his chair; but was insufficiently appeased, for he said, "Perfectly monstrous!" in the act of sitting; and said it again as the tea was being poured for him. "Perfectly monstrous!" One of the ladies said, "S'William," placidly, either as agreeing with him or to placate him; and at intervals, as he drank from his cup, he said, "Perfectly monstrous!" and the lady said, "S'William," in the same placid manner.

There was something fine about all this, Ogle thought; these English had no craven self-consciousness such as he found in himself. They were so secure of themselves that they were never worried by the possible opinions of spectators;—in fact, they were unconscious of spectators; they knew what they wanted and thought only of that. They had a poise founded on the centuries; a poise unattainable by his own fellow-countrymen. And while he was engaged

with this thought, the fellow-countryman with whom
last of all he would have had General Sir William
Broadfeather and his ladies behold him conversing
came breezily into the room on his way to the elevator. Ogle looked at the wall, hoping not to be
recognized by the back of his head.

  He looked at the wall in vain. "Well, I declare!"
Tinker exclaimed. "Do you drink *tea?*   My soul!"
And he sat down cordially in a wicker chair near the
playwright, who began to feel that Fate had become
too ironical to be borne. This Old Man of the Sea
was now fast to his shoulders upon the land; and
there seemed to be no way to escape him. What
Ogle wished to say was, "Let me alone! I have no
desire for your society or even for your acquaintance!"   But he was weakly incapable of so honest a
course; he could only fall back on a feeble coldness,
wholly ineffective, as he had been but too reliably
informed, because Tinker blandly mistook it for
mere stupidity. To one so sensitive as Ogle this was
not a pleasing mistake; he would strongly have preferred to be thought brutal; but as he had no talent
for open rudeness, he could only sit and suffer.

  "Tea!" Tinker repeated with loud incredulity.
"I thought hardly anybody except women and Eng-

lish people did that. There's some English people
got rooms near us on our floor, and they were havin'
tea on their porch up there yesterday afternoon when
I was tryin' to take a nap;—I didn't see 'em, but
something must 'a' gone wrong, or it didn't come in
time maybe. My glory! You'd 'a' thought they
were being murdered. There was one tin-voiced old
fellow—my soul! You could 'a' heard him cackling
a half-a-mile!" He threw back his head and laughed
noisily; then became somewhat more serious, as if
doubtfully seeking information that must prove
whimsical if true. "Tea! You *like* it, do you?"

"Certainly."

"Well, that's funny," Tinker said reflectively, and
his seriousness increased. "Listen!" he said. "Ain't
this the doggonedest place you ever did see? Look
at that sewer where we met you this afternoon, for
instance. Why, the United States army ought to
come over here and clean it up! If we had a sink of
iniquity and disease and dirt and crime like that right
in the middle of *my* town, it'd last just about fifteen
minutes! We went all through part of it after we
left you, and our courier told us it was the best part.
My soul and whiskers! He's a mighty nice man,
though—for a foreigner. He's a full-blooded French-

man; name's John Edwards. That old darkey we had cake-walkin' around with us stuck to us all over the show: he was the nearest to a human being I saw in the whole place. I liked him; he was the only soul we met that had a laugh in him; the rest of 'em looked as if they'd cut your throat for a plugged nickel. Full-blooded nigger he is: not an Arab at all; this John Edwards says he belongs to some nigger tribe of sorcerers or something; but all the sorcering he did for us was to beat his drum and yell 'Toulamond' and pass the hat—he did *that* often enough! Funny about you being in our hotel all this time and us not knowin' it. I expect it must be because we been eatin' in the restaurant and you in the tabble dutt. John Edwards says that's the way to pronounce it, 'tabble dutt.' That's right, isn't it, 'tabble dutt'?"

"I believe nearly so."

"In *our* country," Tinker went on, "of course we most always call it 'table doat'; but this John Edwards says it's 'dutt'—or pretty *near* like that any way; and he ought to know, because he's a full-blooded Frenchman. He speaks English pretty well, too; but I been talkin' to him for about three days now, and listen! that isn't like talkin' to somebody that knows what the Pirates did to the Senators last season! No, sir! My! but it's a relief to get with somebody from God's country again! How're you standin' it: all this bottled water and buyin' your own soap and everybody jabbering around in foreign languages with all this 'We, we,' and 'Mon doo' and 'Mercy, mercy!' and everything? You gettin' along all right?"

This he asked in the sympathetic tone of a hospital patient who puts such an inquiry to a fellow-sufferer from the same disease; and he seemed to take Ogle's brief "Quite well" as sufficient reply; for he went on: "Well, I haven't got any fleas yet, myself; but my wife, she says *she's* found one or two on her. She likes it over here, though. She kept goin' on this afternoon about how 'picturesque and foreign' it all was and everything; and the only time she got dampened at all was just a little while after we left you this afternoon. We ran right spang into a smell —well, I've smelled smells; but *this* one—oh, Boy! I turned around to this John Edwards. 'Listen!' I told him. 'Get us out o' here! I don't care about how picturesque and historical everything is and all, get us out o' here.' You talk about smells, why, as long as I've lived, never in my life did I——!"

He paused, leaned over and put his hand solemnly upon Ogle's knee. "Son, when I get home if anybody ever tries to tell me anything about smells, I'm goin' to say: 'Listen! Don't try to talk to me on *that* topic, because *I've* met the *King !*'"

When Tinker called him "Son," Ogle glanced wretchedly across the room at the English party to whom the hearty Midland voice could not fail to be audible; but they were preoccupied with their own affairs. General Broadfeather had discovered that some marmalade he had ordered was not quite to his taste. "A bit tweaky," he pronounced it; and one of the ladies disagreed with him. "Tweaky? You're too funny, S'William!"

Tinker, too, had paused to listen to this simple little dialogue, and his untrained Midland ear failed to identify it as being of his own language. The pronunciations were unfamiliar to him, the cadenced inflections confusing. "A bit tweaky" he heard as "beet tweekeh" and "you're too funny" as "yaw tewfenneh." The strange sounds and the people, as strange to him as what they uttered, interested him a little.

"French family, I expect," he said, his glance resting upon them speculatively, and, while Ogle's flesh

crept in horror, he added in his big voice casually:
"Funny names they got for each other. Seems she
called that old bird 'Swillum.' What you suppose
it means in our language, 'Swillum'? I never——"

But Ogle clutched his arm. "Hush!" he whispered. "They're English. My heavens! Haven't
you got any eyes and ears? English!"

"Think so?" Tinker responded, mildly surprised;
and he added, "We got a Jew in my town was born
and grew up in England; *he* talks kind of funny, too,
even yet. Mighty smart man though. Insurance."
He took a cigar from his pocket and lighted it, apparently as a sort of punctuation marking the change
of subject. "Well, sir, this John Edwards tells me
there's been a lot of history happened around this
neighbourhood. He says there's been ancient Romans and Spaniards and Turks and Mohammedans
and pretty much everybody all over this part of
Europe."

"This isn't Europe." Ogle corrected him with
some sharpness. "This is Africa."

"Sure it is!" Tinker laughed and rubbed the back
of his head. "My wife tells me that about a dozen
times a day. I haven't forgot my geography, I
guess; but you always hear people talk about goin' to

Europe, and you're always expectin' to go there yourself some day, so I can't seem to get it out o' my head this *is* Europe. Well, I expect it's a good deal the same thing in the long run—both of 'em just dirt and old ruins and backward kind of people mainly, I guess. I leave it to my wife and Babe to know all about the history and picturesqueness of it. She and Babe certainly have read up on it, too, though Babe won't *say* much. She——" he checked himself, chuckling a little painfully. "I expect I got to quit calling her 'Babe.' She certainly gave it to me red hot for calling her that in front of you this afternoon!"

He chuckled again, but without much mirth, and for a moment or two his cheerfulness of expression was gone; he looked troubled. "I'm afraid she isn't havin' as good a time as I kind of hoped she would," he said, almost as if to himself; then with renewed briskness he asked, to the young man's surprise: "You seen anything o' Mrs. Mummero since you been here?"

"No," Ogle replied shortly; and prompted by a sudden queer suspicion, he said: "Have you?"

Then, with a pained alarm that became all too quickly an unhappy conviction, he saw the broad and comely face before him heighten in colour and become illuminated by a surreptitious amusement. "I'll tell you," Tinker said unctuously;—"but don't you ever breathe it to a soul: my wife would just fairly scalp me alive. Mrs. Mummero certainly knows her way around! She took me a drive day before yesterday to see some monkeys, about fifty or sixty miles, I guess; and yesterday she got me to come and eat lunch with her at a hotel up over the hill here."

"What?" Ogle gasped. "You say she——"

"She's a wonder!" Tinker said earnestly. "You talk about brains; why, that woman's got more brains in her little finger than a whole Bankers' Convention in their heads. She's——"

He was interrupted. His daughter, coming from behind him, touched his shoulder. "Mother wants you to come and dress."

"Murder!" he exclaimed, jumping up guiltily. "How long you been standin' there? Did you hear what I——"

"I did not," she said brusquely. "I'm not interested in what you say."

"Well, that's lucky—sometimes," he returned; and

favouring the playwright with a companionable wink, he said affably, "See you later," and went away.

Olivia turned to go with him; but, as if it were distasteful to her to walk with him even so far as the elevator, she swung about toward the opposite door, hesitated, and after a moment, came back to Ogle. He had risen upon her advent and was still standing, staring pallidly after Tinker.

"I don't think you understood what I said to you this afternoon, Mr. Ogle."

"What?" he said blankly; then amended his manners. "I beg your pardon. Will you have some tea?"

"No, thank you. I tried to tell you something when we met you in the Arab quarter this afternoon, but I don't think you understood. You were looking at my father. I don't think you paid any attention to what I was trying to say, you were so busy despising him."

"I beg your pardon!" he said again. "I think you are mistaken."

"Do you?" She uttered a short and rueful laugh. "We won't argue it; I understand perfectly. I'm not very decent to him myself, and of course you know it—you'd be blind if you didn't;—but I don't despise him, though perhaps I hate him. That's my own affair. What I wanted to tell you was that I shouldn't have said what I did, the last night on the 'Duumvir,' if I'd thought I'd ever see you again."

"I know that," he said. "You told me so then."

At this she drew an audible quick breath and her eyes opened wide. "I suppose you think I'm merely making it an excuse to speak to you again!"

"Not at all. I meant I understood that you wouldn't have expressed your opinion of me except as a valedictory. You didn't need to explain it again."

"I did need to!" she said in a low voice, fiercely. "You might have thought I knew you were leaving the ship here, and so *might* see me again. You might have thought I said it only to make you think about me. Girls do that sort of thing sometimes; you *might* have thought that."

He was nervous; what he had learned from Tinker had dazed him, and now Tinker's daughter irritated him. "Believe me," he said; "I haven't been thinking of it at all, and it's not very probable that I ever shall."

Her cheeks as well as her eyes showed her resentment then, and some violets at her breast moved to her quickened breathing. She gave a half-smothered little outcry. "Oh! How much you're like them! We're going away to-morrow, and this time I *know* I'll never see you again, so I can add a little to what I told you on the boat. How *much* you're like those people we saw to-day "

"Am I? What people?"

"Those horrible creatures in that Arab slum," she said. "I thought of it when we got among them to-day and they were all staring at us. You have just their look in your eyes when you look at my father or my mother—or at me!"

Then, with her own eyes not smouldering now, but seeming fairly to blaze blue flame into his, in her hot scorn of him, she turned on her heel and left him.

He abandoned his tea as it was, half consumed, and went out, furious, to the terrace. She had succeeded in making him so angry that for a few moments he almost forgot the shock her father had given him; but as he paced up and down in the falling dusk, his temper cooled in one direction and began to grow warm in another. The insults of the bad-mannered American girl were easier to bear than the unfathomable double-dealing of the exquisite French lady.

Thus, this shift of temper having rapidly taken place, the heat within him grew fiercer and fiercer until, an hour later, he was angrier with Mme. Momoro than he had ever been with anyone in all his life before.   At least, that was his own unhappy impression of his state of mind.

XV

IN THE morning, having slept little, he beheld
from his balcony the magnificent departure of the
Tinkers. A quarter of an hour earlier a deferential formality attended the setting forth of the Hereditary Prince Orthe XVIII of Fühlderstein and his
bride, who had been spending part of their honeymoon in Algiers. The manager of the hotel and
the concierge, with the two chief porters, the *maître
d'hôtel*, two *valets de chambre* and an agent of police,
all bowed respectfully as the amiable-looking young
couple were driven away in an Italian touring car;
but this, as the melancholy playwright observed, was
only a one-act curtain-raiser, as it were, preceding
the full-sized drama of the American family's departure. Looking down from his stone-railed box,
he saw the brisk yet imposing arrival of two long and
powerful French automobiles, new and glistening;
one a landaulet, the other a limousine. The chauffeurs, trim young men of capable appearance, jumped

down, and, with them, the good-looking courier Ogle
had seen in charge of the Tinkers the day before.
More 'impressively, there descended from the landaulet a stout and smiling man who wore a white
camellia upon the lapel of his frock coat and a broad
black watch guard across his white waistcoat. The
playwright recognized him as M. Cayzac, the chief
personage of the tourist-agency and branch banking-
house to which his letters were consigned.

M. Cayzac was apparently in high spirits, yet solicitous that all might go well with so important an
undertaking as he had on hand this morning;—the
manager of the hotel came forth to salute him, attended by the concierge; and the three conferred
seriously, the gestures of M. Cayzac meanwhile
becoming fluent, vigorous, and almost operatic.
Then porters appeared, laden with small trunks,
large black leather bags, rugs, fur coats, hat boxes,
vacuum bottles and lunch baskets, for this was a
motoring expedition of wide scope and no small moment; that was to be seen with half an eye. The
trunks were strapped to the back of the limousine
and upon its roof; the bags, boxes, bottles, furs, and
baskets were stowed away inside; and while this was
being done more employés of the hotel began to ap-

pear and collect themselves gravely in small groups
between the landaulet and the principal entrance.

There was a pause; then a bowing began near the
doorway, and Mrs. Tinker came forth, whereupon
M. Cayzac rushed to her and gracefully kissed her
hand—an act of courtesy visibly embarrassing to
her; indeed she seemed doubtful of its propriety.
He also kissed the hand of Olivia, who followed her
mother, looking prettier than ever and not quite so
resentful as usual, Ogle thought.

Now a mild commotion was perceptible, and
Tinker appeared, wearing a gray ulster over his
travelling clothes, for the morning was brisk; his
hands were full of paper money, and his great anxiety, obviously, was to get rid of it. Since it was
pink in colour and flimsy in texture, possibly he did
not regard it as money at all, but merely as an en-
cumbrance. However that may have been, every
polite assistance was rendered him in his determina-
tion to depart without it; and when he had finished
by pressing the last of it upon the manager, he seemed
to feel, and was, relieved. Moreover, in this imperso-
nation of a Christmas Tree moving between the door
of the hotel and the landaulet, he inspired, for himself and for the golden land whence he came, a pas-

sionate enthusiasm combined with a beautifully concealed amazement.

The manager presented bouquets of violets and roses to the two ladies; a gardener presented them with two bouquets of greater variety; the *maître d'hôtel* presented Mrs. Tinker with a dozen jonquils; another gardener presented Tinker with three camellias, which a *valet de chambre* reverently pinned upon a lapel of the gray ulster. Then, when Tinker and Mrs. Tinker and Olivia were seated within the landaulet, and the courier had taken his place beside the chauffeur, the manager, the concierge, the *maître d'hôtel*, the three clerks from the bureau, two chief porters, two waiters, four *valets de chambre*, and two gardeners stood bowing their adieus; but those of M. Cayzac were vocal as well as gesticulative. With amiable fervour, he made what had the air of being an oration of tribute, as the two cars began slowly to move through the garden; and a clapping of hands and something like a slight cheering from the waiters and porters and gardeners encouraged his effort. Guests of the hotel, American, English, French, Italian, Greek, and Turkish, leaned from their balconies and came out upon the terrace, wondering what potentates incognito could thus be honoured.

M. Cayzac waved his arms ardently. "Bon voyage, Madame, Mademoiselle et Monsieur, et merci mille fois, Monsieur Tankaire!" he cried in conclusion. "Au plaisir, Monsieur Tankaire!"

And Tinker, leaning from the window of the landaulet, and waving his soft hat, shouted cordially in return, "Alley vooze on! We, we! Mon Doo! Mellican man say velly much oblige'! Goo'by!"

The expedition passed out of sight round a turn in the garden driveway, tooted its small brass horns at the gates, then was forth upon the adventure; and the hotel employés returned gayly to work, affluent even beyond expectation. Ten minutes later, General Sir William Broadfeather, with one of the middle-aged ladies and the long-nosed girl, got into a small touring car; a porter and the concierge seeing them off; and to each of these Sir William gave a silver coin, but not until the engine was in full agitation.

Ogle, returning into his room pained by the contrast—for again it was the Americans who had made spectacles of themselves—found the gossiping *femme de chambre* engaged in making his bed. "Good-morning, gentleman," she said; and, with a bright glance at him she added: "Las' night I have seen

my cousin that is marry with the chauffeur at 'Colline des Roses.' You know what happen, I think?"

"No. I don't know."

"Well, my cousin she don' know herself," the
femme de chambre admitted. "Her husban', 'e don'
know too; but is somesing."

"Something happened at the Daurels' villa, you
mean?"

"Yes, surely," she said, and nodded three times for
emphasis. "Surely is somesing happen. It has
been going to happen all the time since they were in
North America, my cousin she think; but now it
happen the most of all. It is yesterday and the day
before. Mademoiselle Lucie Daurel, she cry very
much and Mademoiselle Daurel is angry—*oh*, she is
angry! They hear her say that Monsieur Hyacinthe
Momoro is a bad, bad boy! Bad!"

"What!" Ogle exclaimed. "How on earth is he
'bad'? What's he been doing?"

She shook her head. "Nobody can tell. The
servants in the 'ouse, that is all they know, but they
say Mademoiselle Lucie cry so much because she
think 'e is bad, too. Mademoiselle Daurel tell her
so before they arrive; but she won' believe. Now she

cry because she mus' got to believe it. You see Madame Momoro?"

"No."

"Well, maybe she is going to tell you what happen. Maybe she will tell you when you see her; I think not."

Ogle thought not too; but his greater doubt was that he should see her; and after Tinker's naïve disclosure he was no longer sure that he indeed wished to see her. He was morose that morning and inclined to be a woman-hater, as he walked down the long hill to M. Cayzac's office. M. Cayzac was there, somewhat pompously affable behind his desk; but the letters Ogle expected had not arrived, which made him anxious; for they should have reached Algiers by this time, if sent by way of Havre and Marseilles, as he had directed. He took a taxicab back to the hotel and found the terrace occupied by only two people:—one was the Arab merchant, asleep in the sunshine against the wall, and the other was M. Hyacinthe Momoro.

Tilted forward in a painted iron chair, the youth sat with his elbows upon the white stone railing of the terrace balustrade and stared vacantly into the garden. His attitude was one of blank dejection; and, on the part of this quiet and rather lonely boy, it was not without pathos. Moreover, when he turned his head at Ogle's impulsive "Hello there," violet tintings under his eyes suggested to the playwright a suspicion that Mlle. Lucie Daurel might not have been the only one to weep, of late, at the villa "Colline des Roses."

Hyacinthe rose, bowed in his formal way, and stood silent, as if respectfully waiting for the older man to say something more.

"You didn't happen to be calling on me again?" the American inquired. "I'm sure I hope so."

"You are very kind," Hyacinthe returned. "No. We have come to stay in the hotel a few days. Then we mus' go to Marseilles."

"'We'? You mean your mother is here with you?"

"In the hotel. Yes, she is here."

Then it appeared that Ogle's doubts about wishing to see Mme. Momoro again had not been well founded. "I wonder if there is an hour when I might call on her," he said. "I wonder if I might——"

"I will ask her," Hyacinthe said quietly, and went

straightway upon this errand. He returned within three minutes and reported a favourable response. "She will be very glad."

"She will? When?"

"At any time to-day. Now, if you wish."

"Thank you. Then now, if you think——"

"I will show you," Hyacinthe said.

He led the way into the hotel and to the second floor, where he knocked upon a door and then, without waiting for a response, opened it, and stood aside while Ogle entered.

Hyacinthe did not follow him. "My mother will come very soon, I am sure," he said, and, having closed the door, went away.

The room was a small salon furnished in the Moorish manner of the public apartments downstairs—that is to say, it was Moorish after a Gallic interpretation, and reminded Ogle of "oriental rooms" he remembered seeing in a few American houses in his childhood. Here, however, where veritable Moors walked the streets, it seemed less out of place; though after what he had seen of the Arab quarter it did not have the air of being truly Moorish; for it was clean and comfortable and odourless.

Before him, as he stood, there was a doorway with

a portière made of painted bits of hollow reed and green and rose glass beads strung upon long cords; he was conscious of movements behind this gay curtain, and presently a faint spiciness seemed to drift out from it upon the air as if released from an opened vial of scent in the room beyond. Someone spoke softly in French; it was a woman's voice, perhaps that of a maid or a *femme de chambre* of the hotel; and Mme. Momoro's deeper tone replied to it quickly, her words indistinguishable—but when the rich sound of that low and hurried music came to his ears, the young man waiting felt the warm colour rush upon his cheeks and temples.

She had treated him abominably; he was sure of that; and yet now, when he heard her speak again and knew that in a moment he should see her, he could not for his life keep himself from blushing. Then an exquisite, long white hand, smooth and without a ring upon any of the shapely fingers, grasped some strands of the beaded curtain as if to open a passage through it; but Mme. Momoro paused invisible, speaking again to the woman beyond;—and Ogle, looking at that beautiful hand, began to tremble.

The next moment the portière rushed aside with a

clattering of beads; she swept in, long, graceful, swift, enhelmed in her pale gold and dramatically intimate in glimpsed lace and a silken robe that swathed her in a fantasia of sombre colours. With the beautiful hand outstretched to him, she crossed the room; and then, tragic and sweet, stood looking down into his eyes.

"My poor friend!" she said. "You must forgive me. I have not been very happy."

There was a lingering skepticism within him, even though he blushed and even though he trembled; but he could not doubt that she told the truth when she said that she had not been happy. Her face was almost haggard with the traces and shapings of emotion, and yet these traces and shapings were indefinite; they gave her no lines, and marvellously no age; it was as if she had been misted over with sorrow, not marked.

She retained his hand and led him to a chair close beside another. "Will you sit and listen to me?" she asked; and as he obediently did as she wished, she released his fingers from the gentle pressure with which she had enclosed them, turned away, walked to the window, and there turned again to face him. She lifted her arms high in a gesture eloquent of her inability to express what she felt, and, as her hands descended, clasped them behind her head. "Oh!" she cried. "I think it would be very difficult to believe. No one could believe that such a woman as she exists!"

"Do you mean Mademoiselle Daurel?" he asked.

"Who else? You do not have such people in America! No, nor in England. Nowhere else but in a Latin country could you find natures so extraordinary."

"What has she done?"

"It is incredible," Mme. Momoro said, seeming not to hear him. She came back to the chair beside him, sank down in it, and then, not looking at him but before her, said again: "It is incredible."

"I'd like to ask you something," he began huskily. "On the 'Duumvir,' was it on her account——"

"Everything was on her account," Mme. Momoro said bitterly. "Everything! How long I have devoted myself to her! Always I have proved it; and I don't say that always she has been unkind to me, because often she has been very kind—except for her jealousy. That has grown insufferable. You see, she is old; she has been very spoiled all her life— so many, many years in everything she has had her way. Even in the War she lost nothing. So everybody must do each little thing exactly as she wishes. My friend, you saw how it was upon the steamer: after she came out of her cabin again, I did not dare to speak to you. It was for fear of displeasing her; for fear she would make a terrible scene with me. I was afraid even to look at you!"

Ogle was still capable of doubting her. "But you weren't afraid of looking at—at that Tinker!" he said. "You certainly——"

"No, no!" She turned to him, surprised. "Not after she was well again. Until then, yes; but not after."

"What!" Ogle cried indignantly. "Why, he told me himself you've been going about with him here in Algiers. He said you——"

"Oh, in Algiers; yes," she returned frankly; and in spite of her tragic overcasting, there was a twinkling in her eyes. "I could not resist that! Algiers is larger than a steamer. I told dreadful lies at 'Colline des Roses' and ran away to be with him because I thought if I could be amused I could endure a little longer what that terrible old woman was making me suffer. It was because with him I could laugh a little bit and forget Mademoiselle Daurel."

"I see!" Ogle said grimly. "With me you couldn't hope to be amused. So you didn't even answer my note."

She put her hand lightly upon his. "I knew he was going away in such a few days, and you were going to stay in Algiers." Then she smiled faintly and said in a wistful voice: "Sometimes, can't you understand, a woman like me *must* find something to laugh at to keep from crying?"

"But why couldn't you have written me at least a word of explanation, when you had all that time for him?"

She laughed ruefully, shook her head, and removed her hand from his. "You don't understand; perhaps you couldn't. I was in that house: I didn't dare to write a note. I didn't write to Mr. Tinker; I had promised on the boat to meet him at M. Cayzac's office. But what you must think of, please, it is that I knew you would stay in Algiers a long time; I knew I would see you. But I wish to be frank with you: he interests me, that man. I like him very, very much."

"Yes," Ogle said coldly. "I think you've made it apparent."

She gave him a long look then, and smiled sorrowfully. "I am afraid you resemble other men in one thing: you would not allow a woman to be your friend and still be herself, with her own mind and her own likings. No; those things, they must all be *yours!*"

"Not at all. Only——"

"Only it is true," she said. "Very well. There is a simple solution; we need not be friends." And she rose, offering him her hand.

He stood up, to face her. "Your solution mightn't be so simple as you think—for me. Unfortunately, no matter how you treat me, I haven't been able to get you out of my head since the first moment I saw you, not for an instant. Yet I don't understand you. I don't know you. You mystify me in everything. You write me asking me to 'be kind,' begging me to 'understand'—and then you freeze me because an old woman is 'jealous' of you, you say; and after that you 'don't dare' even write a word to me; and you drive all afternoon with another man. It doesn't seem to me you've given me much chance to be your friend."

She looked at him thoughtfully. "Then I will now," she said; and they sat down again. "I will try to make you understand. Mademoiselle Daurel has been much more than jealous of me. The proprieties of an old Frenchwoman of her type who has never married are beyond anything you could ever have known in your own country. She is fanatically religious, and a great part of her jealousy of me is for my soul."

"For your soul?" he echoed; and he frowned in more puzzlement. Yet, remembering the withering frostiness of Mlle. Daurel—that look of a very old Puritan, dead—he had a gleam of light, and he consented to smile. "She is afraid you may not go to heaven?"

Mme. Momoro laughed painfully. "She knows that I am damned. But she wished that I do not lose my soul altogether, so that I may at least reach purgatory after an eternity of hell."

"What in the world do you mean?" he cried; for she was serious.

"It is very simple. I am divorced. Colonel Momoro was not Catholic, and there was a person he should be free to marry. So it was done. Well, you see, the Church will not recognize such a divorce, and because I permitted it, Mademoiselle Daurel believes that I was placed in defiance of the Church, and damned—but because I haven't married again I still have a soul. I may reach purgatory, if I am always careful—careful beyond anything you could guess of carefulness! She has long wished for me to become a nun."

"What!" he exclaimed. "You aren't in earnest?"

But he saw that she was, and he knew too that what she was telling him must be true; her eyes were wholly truthful and so was her voice. "Mademoiselle Daurel believes that only as a nun could I make my soul safe for purgatory," she said. "You see it has been unfortunate that gentlemen sometimes think me worth speaking to. And whenever she discovered that they did and that I answered them— well, she would pray for me all night! That, I could endure; but unfortunately she would make me pray with her. What horrible nights!"

"Make you?" he said. "How could she make you?"

At this she coloured a little and looked down. "I hoped—well, I must be frank. In part it was inertia and the habit of friendship; people you are with a long time can make you do a great deal; you bear many things rather than quarrel. But in part I own to you that it was—well, it wasn't noble. Both of them adored Hyacinthe, and they have no nephews or nieces. You see, I hoped they might think of him when they made their wills. I would undergo great sacrifices for that." She looked at him, and suddenly her eyes and lashes were brilliant with tears. "Do you think it is very brutal of me—to have been so great a hypocrite for my son's sake?"

When she looked at him as she did look then, through that quivering diamond brightness, he had no more doubt of her at all; he was overwhelmed by the thought that the superb creature, always until then so bravely and surely poised, now wept before him, trusted him with her tears.

He caught both her hands in his. "Aurélie!" he said. "I think only—only that you're divine."

She drew her hands away, laughing ruefully. "No. You think I suffered all that because I am mercenary. That is what you think."

"Never, never!" he protested. "I do understand. Give me the chance to be kind, as you asked me."

"Do you truly wish to be?"

"You know that I do."

"Then don't distrust me any more," she said; and her wan smile ineffably touched him.

"You'll have no more distrust from me," he said. "Was that the last thing you had to bear from Mademoiselle Daurel—distrust?"

She shook her head, and her lips set angrily. "No! She wished to take my life from me. They would do everything for Hyacinthe—only I must give him up! Well, I have borne ten thousand things; but that is what nobody must ask a mother to do. I will do anything—anything in this world; but I will not do that."

"I don't understand," he said, puzzled again. "I thought——"

"She wished to take him away from me; that is all. The first day we were again in Algiers both those women came to me and they propose' to me that they will adopt Hyacinthe. I am to be no longer his mother."

"What? Why, I thought——"

She sprang up, not noticing that he had spoken. "They have taken everything from me—my friends and all this time that I have given them—and now they want to take all that I live for! They will give him everything except his mother and me everything except my son. No, no! That was the end of those people for me!" And again she strode across the room, lifting up her arms on high. "No!" she cried loudly. "Nobody can be my child's mother except me. There are other things beside money that he could starve for." And once more she turned to the young man. "Do you think that is selfish? Do you think Hyacinthe himself would consent if I did? Never! Ask him!" She strode back to her chair, sank into it, closed her wet eyes, and touched them with a handkerchief. "You will think I give you a scene from some drama of the emotions, I believe," she murmured. "The Aurélie Momoro you knew on the ocean didn't seem to be so excitable a lady, I am sure." Then she opened her eyes, laughed ruefully, and said: "Well, the scene is over. I am rational. What shall we talk about?"

One thing he might have liked to talk about, incidentally, was the gossiping of French servants. The cousin of the *femme de chambre* had been sufficiently far from the truth in her account of poor Hyacinthe's "badness," he perceived; and he wondered if this lower-world rumour could do the boy any harm. Probably not, he decided; especially since Hyacinthe and his mother were so soon returning to France;— then the thought of their departure gave him the subject she asked for.

"Why are you going to Marseilles?"

"It is only *en route*. We go at once from there to Paris."

"Well, why are you going to Paris?"

She made the effect of shrugging her shoulders, but without actually moving them; her hands were lifted a little distance from her lap, then dropped. "Why go anywhere? In six weeks Hyacinthe should be in Paris to make his report; it is as well to go now."

"But it's winter in Paris, isn't it?" he urged. "And here it is so beautiful! You have six weeks. Why not spend them here?"

"Algiers?" she said, and shook her head slowly. "Algiers is nothing. You should not stay here long, yourself: there is so much for you to see."

"I shouldn't care to stay long," he told her gloomily, "if you aren't going to be here. Shall I come to Paris?"

"No, no! Nothing is there now but rain and snow, and it is dark by four in the afternoon. It would be wicked for you not to see Algeria. You should go to Bougie and to Biskra and the Desert and to Constantine and across into Tunisia and——"

He interrupted her. "No, I don't care about it. If you're to be in Paris I shouldn't be interested in those places."

"You shouldn't?" She laughed, and with the tips of her fingers touched his shoulder indulgently, as if she patted a petulant child. "You must not be ridiculous, my friend. I think sometimes you don't know quite how young you are. You are what ladies love to call 'a nice boy'; but perhaps you have still a little to learn and a little to see. You are in a country that is the Arabian Nights, and you aren't 'interested'! My dear, go and get an automobile and leave Algiers behind you. Go up into the Djurdjurra Mountains among the Kabyles and down to the Desert. After that, write to me and tell me, if you can, that you were not interested!"

She was herself again, cool, faintly amused, kindly impersonal; and he was piqued by the change. "I'm not what 'ladies love to call a nice boy'," he said, with a little indignation. "I'm a rather tired, rather lonely man of the world. I'm tired because I've worked too hard, and I'm lonely because I'm not able to like many people, which I realize is a fault——"

He was going on; but she interrupted him. "*Do* you realize that? Aren't you a little proud of it, my dear?"

"That's the second time you've called me 'my dear'," he said sharply. "I wish you wouldn't. It sounds as if you were my aunt. Well, you're not."

"No," she said gently. "I hope I am your friend.

I shall—I shall regret to be so far away from you day after to-morrow. Day after to-morrow is not long; it always comes so quickly."

"If you will regret it, why do you go?"

"Because I can't stay here. It is not pleasant to be where I might see people who——" Threatened by a sudden tendency to sob, she stopped speaking and covered her face with her hands. "I can't—I can't stay here," she murmured brokenly.

Upon that he was at last dazzled by an idea. "Then why won't you go with me?"

"What?" she murmured. "Go with you? Where?"

"Wherever you want to. To those places you said I ought to see. We could take a motor——"

"No, no! I couldn't." She dropped her hands from her face, and turned to him, smiling sadly. "I am not very conventional; but neither am I eccentric, and I fear such an expedition might have an air of some eccentricity."

"Aurélie!" he cried. "You're merely mocking me. What would be either eccentric or unconventional about a motor trip with your son and me? Be serious."

She frowned, smiled vaguely at him, then rose and

walked about the room; paused by a table and let her fingers drum upon it an accompaniment to her perplexity.

Meantime he urged her. "We'll go anywhere you wish to go—anywhere. *I* don't care where we go. It won't matter." He came to her where she stood. "It won't matter to me where I am, if I can see you, if I can listen to you, if I can be with——"

But at that she laughed outright; and when he seemed astonished that she did, and a little offended, she put her hand upon his shoulder with a charming complete friendliness. "My dear," she said, "you must not be cross with me if I call you that—like your aunt—and even if I laugh. You see——" She broke off, and then, with a coquetry that enchanted him, she said: "Well, you don't want us *both* to be ridiculous, do you—not upon an expedition among the Berbers? Go and find Hyacinthe!"

XVI

AGAINST the white dust outside the garden of the inn at Tizi-Ouzou, six brown camels ambulating through the noon sunshine offered a prehistoric silhouette to the eye of the traveller. Immense burdens, covered with old sacking, rose bulbously from their backs and weighted their lean sides; dusty brown men in brown burnouses walked beside them carrying long staves; and on high the philosophical heads of the camels drifted slowly forward, thoughtful above earthly drudgeries and lost in curious revery.

Soundless as a caravan in a dream, this silhouette would have floated on unseen by the party of three motorists lunching in the garden of the inn, if the youngest of them had not happened to turn his head. The other two, a lady of arresting comeliness and a pleasingly dandified dark young man, were deeply engaged in talk over their luncheon of omelette, roast thrush, salad, and champagne. The lady sat with her back to the road; the camels were therefore not visible to her; and although the young man must have seen them if he had looked beyond her, looking beyond her was something he had no desire to do. Food, moreover, appeared to be something else for which he had no desire; and while his charming friend, unembarrassed, ate with an appetite almost robust, she proved herself at the same time unfailingly capable of returning his devotional gaze with a grave sweetness.

Hyacinthe called their attention to the silhouette in the noonday sun beyond. "Some camels for Mr. Uggle," the youth said; and he added mildly, "If he wish to look."

"Camels—for me?" Ogle inquired, a little startled. "How could that be?"

"I mean they are the first we have met," Hyacinthe explained. "You will see them all the time by-and-by and get used to them; but when people come to Algeria they always get excited the first time they see a camel."

"Oh, yes," Ogle returned. "I understand what you mean." And he looked absently out at the grotesque figures slowly passing. "Very interesting."

Mme. Momoro turned to look, and she sighed with

pleasure. "For me, I never get used to them. Probably these do not go to the Desert, but only to some agricultural work not far away; yet the sight of those animals is always romance to me, more than romance. When they keep their strange voices quiet like that, they are something moving without any reality, just things swimming by you in a dream. They make no more sound than the clouds over our heads up there in that still sky. In the Desert at night a thousand of them could pass close by your tent, and you would never know anything had been near you. They are just queer shadows left over out of some earlier age of the world; and now we have begun to travel into that earlier age of the world where they belong. You will see; but not to-day."

"Not to-day?" he repeated. "Aren't we to travel into an earlier age to-day?"

"Indeed we are," she said; "but not into the age of the camel." She laughed. "What you shall see to-day is the age of the goat. Look yonder in the air." She pointed to where a pale blue profile of mountains rose out of the haze of the plain and were almost merged into the sky. "Before dark you shall see the Kabyle people at home and look far, far down on mountain tops where they have their cities."

"Look down on mountain tops?" he said. "Is it aviation?"

"Almost," she laughed, and warned him gayly: "You must not be nervous."

He laughed too, and still thought the warning merely banter after lunch when they resumed their journey. He sat with her in the small enclosure of the landaulet M. Cayzac had sent to the hotel for him the day before; Hyacinthe had taken his own place in front, outside the glass, with Etienne, the driver; and behind these two the little interior was like a tiny bright house on wings. At least to the mind of one of its occupants it was such a house, a flying glass cottage where he was to live a glorious month with Mme. Momoro, proprietor of her time, calling her Aurélie, and lost with her out of the world.

He wondered what Albert Jones and Macklyn would think of this fortune of his, if they could hear of it; and he was pleased to imagine their incredulity. In fact, he felt a little incredulous himself, and, remembering his first sight of her, that impassive statue set where the stained lights swung slowly up and down upon the dark panellings of the "Duumvir's" smoking-room, he could easily have believed that he had indeed left the plausible actual world behind him and but played a part in a fantasy made of his own fond imaginings.

Nothing outside the open windows of his flying cottage seemed to belong to the plausible world that he had known until now. The shapes and colours of everything, the trees, the wayside shrubs, the infrequent stone houses and stone sheds, the very texture and contour of the ground, all were unfamiliar. Robed men in turbans and swathed men in ragged headdresses worked in the fields, tended sheep or goats on the hillsides, or trudged along the road, laden themselves or driving laden asses; and a troop of cavalry, brilliantly blue and red, trotted down a crossroad. Then a Spahi on a white Arabian horse came galloping out of the distance far ahead, a mere flicker of colour at first, but growing brighter and more definite and enlarging swiftly until, with the wind making white flames of the horse's mane and sculpturing the Spahi's cloak into a great scarlet wing, he flashed gloriously by.

"Broadway was never like this!" the playwright murmured, congratulating himself upon his present whereabouts and his remoteness from that dreary field of his labour.

Except for a single anxiety connected with this

selfsame bleak Broadway, he believed that for the first time in his life he was finding an unflawed happiness with nothing whatever to ask from the whimsical gods. The single drawback was no doubt an insignificant one at that, he told himself; the letters he expected had not arrived in Algiers; but although their importance to him was financial, and not to be disregarded, he had left careful directions for their forwarding, and M. Cayzac's clerk, a responsible young man, had assured him there would be no error. Ogle did not greatly disturb himself; to let a futile anxiety intrude upon fairyland would be ridiculous, he thought.

From time to time they would see, far ahead of them, Arabs driving flocks of sheep, cumbering the road; and when the automobile howled the long warning of its coming, the shepherds, peacefully trudging until then, would instantly leap into frantic action;—they did not look back, but went at the sheep as if Satan were behind them; and Ogle loved to see the flying draperies of these figures, small in the distance, like Tanagra statuettes come to life. But when the car overtook Arabs on donkeys, as it did almost continually, the picture was different. Bitterness visibly appeared upon the peaceful scene:

arguments began; flails rose in the air and descended; then the long ears inevitably had their way and the riders sat morosely until the machine had shot glittering by, trailing its whirling cloud of dust.

Mme. Momoro was delighted with these triumphs of intelligence over men. "Always, always, always you will see them do that," she told Ogle. "You are going to pass thousands of these little donkeys and every one of them will do the same thing. You shall not see one of them all who will be different. As soon as he hears an automobile coming, every donkey in Africa will make ready to defend himself like a good fencer on guard. Nobody can stop him, and his master can sit on him and beat him and tell him all the bad things Allah will do to him; but the donkey believes in a right higher than his master's words or his master's club, and he will never yield his faith in that right of his to a moral independence. He is brave, too, you see, and he will not put himself to the trouble to run away from just a terrifying sound like our siren; he will stay and see if the bugbear means to attack him. So he whirls halfway, with his head and the front of him off the road, but with his behind legs facing us, ready to fight if we swoop at him as we pass. You will see them do that from here to Timbuctoo and from Timbuctoo to Bagdad, every one, always with the fighting legs to the road. He is ready to fight if he must, you see, or to depart at a right angle if that appears the only wise thing to do. It is the most admirable trait, and we all should learn it of them."

"I learn of you, Aurélie," Ogle said. "I think I'd much rather learn of you, my dear."

"I must always think you a flatterer," she returned amiably. "Your opinion of my superiority is a little overwhelming. Also, I understood our journey was to be neither eccentric nor unconventional; I fear it might seem both if you call me your dear."

At that he felt a little rebuffed. "You mind it?"

"Well——" She gave him an indulgent smile, in which there was something a little too maternal to be quite to his liking. "You told me I must not be your aunt; but if you call me your dear when anybody is listening, I think you must put that word with it."

"What word?"

"'Aunt,'" she said. "You will much better call me 'dear Aunt.'"

"You love to mock me!"

Then, seeing that he frowned, she laughed, and touched his arm. "Look," she said. "There is

where we are going. Do you see?" She pointed
before them to where the landscape of another planet
seemed to make its appearance in the distant sky
of this one. High over the haze of the plain and
poised upon blue ether, there hung a fixed apparition
of shining white precipices and snow and ragged
colossi of gray rock.

"Yonder is where we shall sleep to-night," she said.
"That is the Djurdjurra, and now you are going to
see how an automobile turns itself into a chamois."

As a matter of fact, they had already begun the
long and steep ascent of the foothills. Etienne was
busy shifting his gears; and within twenty minutes,
as Ogle looked down from the window beside him, the
plain seemed to be a long, long distance below. On
the road and upon the hillsides, they began now to see
people whom he perceived to be more and more unlike those of the plain, for these were of a white-
skinned race; there were reddish glints in the hair of
some of them, and the faces of the women were tat-
tooed upon brow and chin, but unveiled. Moreover,
except for the tattooing, a few of the women were
comely in the shabby, gypsy brilliance of their wind-
blown draperies; and the shifting groups of them,
moving at ease along the skyward edge of the precipi-

tous road, reminded the playwright of exotic ballets with clamorous scarlets and yellows and sea-greens tossing against a back-drop of luminous blue.

He spoke to Mme. Momoro of this resemblance, and added: "The way they look at us isn't very like the smile of the ballet, however. It seems to me I've never had so many hard looks in my life as I have since I came among these Mohammedan peoples."

"Yes," she said. "They mistake us for Christians, you see."

"Certainly you're one," he retorted with some sharpness, "since you refuse to marry again."

She laughed. "I have not boasted to you of any invitations, have I?" Then, rather hurriedly, she returned to the less personal topic he had introduced. "For myself, I like their hard glances. It gives me a sense of freedom to be among people who absolve one of all responsibility to be polite to them; they so openly look upon us as strange, bad animals. Yet of course it must be a little surprising to you to have women staring at you with the expression of these Kabyle ladies, as if you were not a charming young man but a wild rabbit they might devour but would never pet."

"No, it's more as if one were a rat, I think," he said. "It does make me a little uncomfortable, though not because my vanity is upset by the ladies thinking so ill of me."

"What then?"

"Well—" he pondered a moment—"there's a provincialism about them that seems abysmal— belonging to an age more primeval than those ages of goats and camels you mentioned. I suppose the inhibitions I dislike most are those of provincialism; and here are actually white and rather fine-looking people so stonily, so anciently provincial that they don't even recognize us as belonging to their own species." He told her to look at a tall man observing them from the hillside they were just then rounding. "See that fellow. He's actually fair; his eyes are blue and his hair is almost a light brown under that wisp of gray rag about his head, and his moustache is reddish. You could take that chap to a tailor's and a haberdasher's and a barber's and have him done for the perfect picture of a New York or London club window—all except his eyes. They're too primitive, too abysmally provincial. His eyes would keep him out of any club, because it's the very essence of provincialism that the provincial soul, in excluding the rest of the world from its own province, excludes itself from the rest of the world."

Mme. Momoro clapped her hands. "Bravo! You say it as if at some time you must have written it and committed it to memory." And when he blushed in some confusion, "Never mind," she said consolingly, "it is quite true that the provincial excludes himself. You worship cosmopolitanism then?"

"Not worship," he rejoined, "and not exactly cosmopolitanism. But I do like a little sophistication in the people I associate with."

"But sophistication is always provincial."

"What!" he cried. "It's always the reverse."

"No; because nobody can know intimately a great deal about the whole world. The greatest cosmopolitan knows a little about a great many parts of it and can adapt himself to many kinds of people; but in his one lifetime he can't become a sophisticate among these Kabyles and among the Esquimaux and the Patagonians and Samoans and Javanese and Japanese and Russians and Portuguese and Chinese and Sicilians and Spanish and the French and Germans and Italians and English and Americans. A lifetime isn't long enough, my friend. You have told me of the great difference between your New York and Boston—things so very confusing to a Frenchwoman that I could never become sophisticated in them. Cosmopolitanism is a little knowledge about many places and kinds of people; sophistication is a great deal of knowledge about a very few places and a very few people, usually about one place and one kind of people. It is exactly what is possessed by that tall Kabyle we just have passed. He is splendidly sophisticated about his own place and his own people; and if you tried to make friends with him he would despise you not only for your religion, but because he would see that you are unsophisticated; he would wish to laugh at you for not understanding a single Kabyle dialect, or knowing any of the important people, or how to eat, or what one says to a stranger. And if you tried to walk where he walks when he goes to his house he would be disgusted with you for being so provincial that you couldn't follow him except on your hands and knees."

Ogle frowned, not greatly enjoying her definitions; and she was so kind as to pat his hand, which pleased him not much better, since he felt sure she would have done as much for Hyacinthe, and in the same manner. "Confess that you couldn't," she said.

"Look down out of your window and see if you could go to his village without crawling to it."

Ogle did as she wished, and he shivered. While they talked the automobile had climbed rapidly and was now high upon the mountainside, flying along a narrow road with no parapet—an ascending highway bordered by illimitable air. Looking down from his window, which almost overhung the alarming edge of the road, the young American glanced into a blue void with depths of dark twilight. Out of this gulf there rose, though with its rounded crest far below him, a steep mountain; and upon the summit there was a cluster of stone houses, all of one story and showing never a window or a doorway.

"You see you are looking down upon mountain tops," Mme. Momoro said. "That is probably our friend's village, and to reach it he will need to do some going down and going up that the best Alpinist would not despise. His mountain is like a great cup upside down in an enormous basin, and his village is on top of it, to be safely provincial. You will see many of these villages, all on mountain tops for the same reason. It is a glorious view for us superficial cosmopolitans. You think so?"

"Ah—well, yes," he said, but with no very firm conviction.

In truth, this drive was beginning to seem almost a little too adventurous. He was no mountaineer; he had never liked to look from the upper windows of a skyscraper; and the height and depth of the gigantic, ragged world about him now offered him a new experience, of which he was far from sure that he wished to take advantage. He had no desire to look down again over the unprotected, sheer edge of the road, and began to understand that his companion's warning at Tizi-Ouzou might have been not wholly a bantering one.

He was not timid; but he was a townsman; worse than that, a literary and theatrical townsman, spending most of his life writing in a secluded room, or, when his work was in the theatre, advising actual people how to speak and move like the fancied people he imagined principally out of his reading. Of course he thought he imagined them out of "life"; and, with the aid of what he read, he did study the people about him; but nearly all of these had been bookish or theatrical, or both—not perceptibly resembling the undomesticated-looking Kabyle tribesmen now rather numerous upon this unreassuring road in the sky. Ogle was a realist: he had been almost hotly praised for the unmitigated realism of his "Pastoral Scene"; and there was a pastoral scene about him now—at least there were goatherds upon the vertical mountainside pasturages; but this was a pastoral scene of unmitigated romance, and romance was not his specialty. He did not even believe in its existence; therefore its intrusion upon him naturally began to affect his nerves; and what also disturbed him was his conviction that if accident befell the automobile here, leaving its occupants stranded, the neighbouring Kabyles would prove to be people of few inhibitions and little capacity to remain mere unselfish spectators of the disaster.

But for that matter, although it was only too easy to imagine an accident to the automobile, it did not seem probable that much would be left to worry about afterwards. If the wheels should leave the road, there was nowhere for them to go except down, with nothing substantial to interfere for the first half mile or so. He bitterly inquired of himself how intelligent beings could have wished to build such a thoroughfare and why anybody cared to travel upon it, especially with the rapidity this accursed Etienne seemed to think appropriate for motor mountaineering. The car swung upon hairpin turns at crazy speed; it charged toward right-angled shifts of course with the gulf straight before it, and Etienne, one hand off the wheel and his head turned, gesturing earnestly as he discussed with Hyacinthe something far, far away upon another mountain. When Etienne did this Ogle thought it best to close his eyes; but at other times he preferred looking at Mme. Momoro to looking at the scenery.

"It is a wonderful road," she informed him. "Of course in mere altitude it is not so prodigious as some of the Alpine drives; not nearly equal to the Stelvio, for instance. Yet I think it is more thrilling than the Stelvio or the St. Gotthard or either of the St. Bernard passes, for here you are always able to see the great contrasts of height and depth and you have more extraordinary vistas, because in the Alps so many of them are shut off by the closing in of the mountains about you. Then in Switzerland the roads are too civilized; nearly all have walled parapets, or stone posts at the edge, which will help to keep you from going over the precipice if you swerve, while here there is nothing at all, and that makes it more exciting. I have always thought this the most glorious of all mountain drives—especially when we go fast, as Etienne knows I like to. Yonder is one of the finest vistas. At one time you can see a whole long valley with mountain after mountain rising up from it, each of them with its Kabyle town upon the top and most of the summits lower than we are. You are wasting your time looking at me, my friend; you must not miss this valley below us."

He was obedient and glanced down briefly. "Yes; it's extraordinary," he said, and, finding himself a little dizzy, looked forward to steady his eyes.

Before him the road still zigzagged up and up, until, high above it, perched on unending perpendicular pinnacles of rock, he seemed incredibly to see regular walls and shapes like houses. "My heavens!" he exclaimed. "These Kabyles haven't got a town up *there*, have they? *People* don't live up on the end of a lead pencil a mile high like *that*, do they?"

She laughed happily. "Not Kabyles; no. Those are French up there. It is where we are going."

"What!"

"But only to pass through," she assured him. "We go on a great deal farther. Michelet is much higher. That is only Fort National."

"Oh, it is?" he said feebly.

Michelet was their destination for the night; and he began to wish that Mme. Momoro had not felt he should see it. In a continent so extensive as Africa were there not plenty of interesting places upon pleasant normal ground, down near the likable level of the sea? And he began to wonder if he had been wise to put the planning of the expedition so completely in her hands, without knowing a little more about it himself.

At a sharp spiral of the road, where the grade was unusually steep, he was relieved for a moment to find their pace slackening down to a full stop; then Etienne backed the car to gain clearance for the turn; and Ogle, horrified again, could not to save his life refrain from looking out of the little rear window. He looked into a dismal abyss; and became decisively unsettled in his mind: it began to seem to him, as it had seemed on the dreadful first night of the "Duumvir's" passage, that his whole journey was a mistake, and that he should never have left Broadway. His unflawed happiness of an hour ago, already a little marred by his companion's remarks upon sophistication, was all gone. So readily do we become again the children of environment, so quickly may mountain or sea or plain alter what is deepest and sweetest within us; he sat beside the lady whose image had been thus lately the one star flaming in his soul and wished that he were four or five thousand miles from her, having his hair cut in a basement barbershop he knew on Fifty-ninth Street;—love can be that peculiar.

When the grisly backing was over and the car sped on again, up slope, over slope, he looked steadily through the glass at the backs of Etienne and Hyacinthe, and hated them both for their insane unconcern—and for talking. Here was a chauffeur, it appeared, who could not answer the simplest question without removing at least one hand from the wheel, and, at the most hideously inappropriate moments, both of them! Hyacinthe, moreover, habitually so silent, must choose this particular time and no other to become morbidly interrogative concerning a landscape that should never have existed at all, even in an abnormal imagination, and much less should be made a subject of gesticulative discussion during the harebrained process of scaling it.

Mme. Momoro adored every inch of the drive. "You are missing the most superb view by not looking out of your window," she said to Ogle, and she leaned partly across him to look out of that window herself. Two hours earlier this exquisite nearness, this touch of her shoulder would have enthralled him; the delicate spice of the scent she used would have been a moonlight serenade translated into odour and enchanting him; but his imagination had become so enlarged upon the only subject concerning him now that he squeezed himself against the back of the seat and leaned the other way behind her, lest her added weight should induce the lurching machine's centre of gravity to shift dangerously to his side of the road.

When she contented herself again with her own window, he was somewhat relieved, but not durably. Even with his eyes closed he could make himself a little dizzy by merely imagining that he had them open, and since he could not keep himself from such imaginings, a slight vertigo was almost continuous. Presently Etienne had to turn out to pass another automobile, and, at the worst possible moment, Ogle looked out of his window and down—because he could not help it. Thence onward he lived through a nightmare.

Higher and higher this impossible road went climbing; and ever higher the car ascended it. Snow-covered peaks rose beyond a monstrous gray hole in the world, and being upon the very rim of this

Titan's excavation, Ogle had just closed his eyes after one unavoidable and stricken glance into it, when Mme. Momoro gave him an affectionate and enthusiastic pat upon the shoulder.

"It will be glorious to-morrow morning," she said. "Glorious!"

"What will?" He spoke gruffly; for he was thinking again that he had never heard of this revolting Michelet until she told him he must go there. Now she was taking him there, and he was shivering inside his ulster, bitterly chilled by the cold air of the high altitudes. More, he was dizzy, and his loathing for mountains had become so great as to make him a little sick. Ever since she had so oddly spoken of sophistication he had been disturbed by the thought that after all there might be a lack of sympathy between their two natures; and now, when every moment proved to him by his own sufferings what a profound disparity existed in their tastes, the lack of sympathy began to appear vital. So strange in effect upon the sensitive young man was this ride to Michelet. "What will?" he repeated. "What's going to be so glorious to-morrow morning?"

"Why, when we come down the mountains again."

"What!" He opened his eyes and stared at her. "Have we got to come *back* by this same road?"

She laughed in gay surprise. "Why, what other way could there be, my dear?"

It was of no use for her to call him "my dear," even though her inflection just then was by no means that of an aunt. At this moment he almost hated her.

XVII

IN A corner of the public room of the inn at Michelet there was a small fireplace, and here, after dinner, Laurence Ogle sat alone, huddling within the limited area of heat given forth by two chunks of root hissing mildly among ashes. He was still chilled, and had declined to accompany Mme. Momoro and Hyacinthe upon a walk outdoors to obtain a moonlight view of snowy peaks, although she assured him that it would be magnificent and that the Jungfrau itself could do no better for him. He was cold, morose, and surprised at the strange fluctuation in his feeling for her;—the thought of the morrow's descent filled him with horror. By moonlight, or by any other light, he wished to see no more of mountains than was involved in getting down from these he was now unluckily upon through no fault of his own. He preferred to stay as close as possible to the fire, where he had what there was of it to himself; and, shivering upon the tepid hearth, he satirically addressed to the universe the remark that this was Africa, the land of torrid heat.

At a little after nine o'clock he heard Mme. Momoro return, her rich voice sounding cheerfully from the hallway in conversation with several unmistakably English voices. Evidently, other tourists had been forth for the moonlit view, and she had made acquaintances. One of the English voices, a man's, he had somewhere heard before, he thought, though for the moment he could not identify it. It was a tenor voice of a tinny quality, and easily ran into falsetto. "Most remarkable!" it exclaimed. "Most indeed! Quite an experience for my wife and my secret'ry, Miss Crewe, as well as myself. Quite indeed—Teen-Kah."

At least that was what Ogle understood the English voice to say; and he supposed "Teen-Kah" to be the name of one of the moonlit Djurdjurra snow-peaks the party had just been observing. "Teen-Kah" was probably what the Kabyles called the highest and most outrageous of their mountains. "Teen-Kah sounds like what such people *would* call a mountain!" he thought sourly; and toward them and all their mountains and Teen-Kah in particular—since it was probably for the view of Teen-

Kah that he had been dragged here—he felt the most virulent antipathy. Kabyles! He remembered Macklyn's telling him on the steamer that he ought to see something of the Kabyles; and he wished that he had the poet's address in order to telegraph him that he had indeed seen something of the Kabyles—and enough, too, in one afternoon, thank you!

"Quite, indeed—Teen-Kah," Sir William Broadfeather repeated, as he opened the door for Mme. Momoro to enter the room.

Lovely in dark furs, her cheeks glowing, she came in laughing; but when she saw Ogle's attitude of depressed intimacy with the slowly charring roots, she uttered a little cry of commiseration and crossed the room to him so swiftly that she was beside him before he could rise. She put her hand affectionately upon his shoulder. "My poor dear child!" she exclaimed. "Don't move; you are still frozen. I shall have the porter make a better fire for you." Then, as she went back to the door, she said to Sir William: "One moment, and my son and I will be delightedly at your service."

Sir William, removing a long tweed cape of elderly appearance and disclosing himself in a fuzzy short coat and knickerbockers, stared after her appreciatively. "A charming woman!" he said with warmth. "She tells me you had a bright day of it all the way up. We had a bit of a brush of snow, ourselves, the day we came up. Still, it's quite a jolly little motor climb. Pretty hills."

"Hills?" Ogle said. "Hills?"

"Yes," Sir William returned. "Pretty ones." Then he seemed to feel that decorum permitted him to revert to the more important subject. "A charming woman!" he said again. "A delightful woman, your mother!"

"What!" The playwright gazed at him, openmouthed. "I beg your pardon. What did you say?"

Sir William smiled upon him almost fondly. "Charming. A most charming woman, your mother."

"Dear *me!*" Ogle said. "Madame Momoro isn't my mother."

"No? Ah—I understood——"

"No, no!" the young man insisted. "Not at all, not at all!"

"No?" Sir William was surprised; but seemed to feel that he must yield to an indubitable authority.

"Then I suppose not," he said rather reluctantly. "You see my wife and Miss Crewe and I had gone out for the view, if you understand; and we saw this lady and a young gentleman with her looking at the same view that we were, you see; so we fell into talk quite naturally; but almost directly the young man returned to the inn. The lady spoke of him as her son and as I hadn't got at all a good look at him, when we came back and the lady spoke to you so solicitously, and what with the difference in your ages—though I must say she could be thought as young as yourself; a most remarkable and charming woman, too, I must indeed say!—naturally I assumed you were the youth who had been with her and were consequently her son. I see my mistake: you are of course a young friend of her son's."

"I'm travelling with them," Ogle returned; and he felt that upon his cursory view of General Broad-feather in Algiers he had thought too highly of him. "We are upon a motor journey together."

"Quite so," Sir William said benevolently. "After we had talked for a time with Madame Momoro we made bold to introduce ourselves to her, and she was so good as to mention her name and tell us something of the route she is following. We have been here four days, if you understand, and four days is something a little more than sufficient, you see; but happily for ourselves we are leaving to-morrow for Bougie, as she is. I ventured to express the hope that we might lunch together to-morrow at Yakouren, you see, and share the same table in the evening at Bougie, and indeed, in a general way, rather maintain a liaison between the two automobiles, as it were, from time to time, during the remainder of our expedition to Biskra. Ah—Madame Momoro was so charming as to appear agreeable to the project. In the meantime, as I proposed a few rubbers of bridge for this evening, she was generous enough to say that she and her son would be delighted to encounter my wife and me in that pastime."

Ogle's impression had always been that the English were a conservative people, slow to make friends, and with strangers reserved even to the point of discourtesy. Now he perceived that either this was a great mistake or that General Broadfeather was a supreme exception. Seldom in his life, the American thought, had he met a man who proposed so much intimacy upon so slight an acquaintance.

"You play?" Sir William inquired.

"Bridge? No."

"Ah! One sees that Madame Momoro must play an excellent game, though perhaps her son's youthfulness may not make him so formidable an antagonist. One sees instantly that Madame Momoro would do anything well—anything! In half an hour, if you understand, she told one more of the curious history of these extraordinary Stone Age mountaineers, the Kabyles, than one has been able to learn from all the guide-books. You have found the Kabyles doubly interesting in her company; one would know that without the asking."

Ogle was tempted to give him an honest opinion of the Kabyles, and so strong was his inclination that he might have yielded to it, at least in part, but he had no opportunity. A porter came in just then with better supplies of wood for the fire and behind him appeared Lady Broadfeather, who had replaced her outdoor wraps with a Cashmere shawl. Sir William graciously took it upon himself to present Ogle to her as "Mr. Uh, a young friend of Madame Momoro's son"; then Hyacinthe came in with his mother, bringing cards and counters.

The fire, more generously served under Mme. Momoro's direction, presently became rosy; and after a time Ogle felt warm enough to withdraw to a

table against the wall and write a long and urgent
letter to the manager of "The Pastoral Scene." He
had finished it and was looking absently and somewhat discontentedly at the bridge players, when General Broadfeather, gazing at the cards in his hand and
apparently having no thought for anything else in
the world, unexpectedly said, "Ah, yes—Teen-Kah!"
He seemed unaware that his remark had been per-
tinent an hour earlier, but not since then; for he
repeated it: "Ah, yes—Teen-Kah!"   Then he added:
"One imagines America must be more and more extraordinary.   The evening he was here Teen-Kah
talked to me at least two hours about the enormous
city he lives in, and the Illinois and Union Paper
Company.   One felt desperately ignorant never to
have heard of either.   Most extraordinary person—
Teen-Kah!"

Ogle caught the briefest flicker in the world of
Mme. Momoro's glance toward himself; and then, as
first suspicions faintly sickened him, he understood
that "Teen-Kah" was no Kabyle mountain, nor
even a Kabyle chieftain, but only General Sir William
Broadfeather's pronunciation of the name of a person
more objectionable than the worst of the mountains
or the wildest of the chieftains.   Tinker had just

been to Michelet.   And after brooding upon this intelligence for only a few moments, Ogle came to the
pleasant conclusion that the expedition to which he
stood in the somewhat lavish relation of host was
virtually a searching-party on the Djurdjurra mountain trail of the president of the Illinois and Union
Paper Company.

This was a conclusion involving no little mortification of spirit for the young man who sat so quietly
at the writing-table against the wall.   Mme. Momoro looked at him several times as he continued
to sit there; but he seemed to be engaged in examin-
ing the address he had written upon the envelope of
his letter.   However, after half an hour of this rather
meaningless scrutiny, he got up and with a murmured good-night, left the room and went to bed.

In the morning he did not speak to her of what lay
so heavily upon his mind; he suffered from it and
from his horror of mountains, as they rode down
slopes that stupefied him, but he suffered in silence.
He had a premonition that she would herself open the
subject, though he hoped she wouldn't until they had
passed the grisliest part of the descent; and she fulfilled both his hope and his premonition.   It was not
until they had turned aside, below Fort National,

from their road of yesterday, and were upon a saner highway among more amiable hills that she asked him why he was so quiet.

"If you do not talk to me I must think one of two things."

"What two things?"

"Either that you are not well or that you are angry with me."

"Not at all. I am perfectly well."

"Ah, so?" she said. "Why are you angry with me?"

"I'm not angry."

"What then?"

"Nothing!"

She looked at him, considering him thoughtfully; but he did not meet her eyes;—instead, he sat staring moodily before him. "My dear," she said, "you remember something I once told you of the great effect places may have upon people? I told you that Africa might make a change in you—and already it has."

"Not at all."

She laughed sadly. "Yes, you would say not. But you are like the man I told you of. Do you remember? He went upon a high mountain, and when he came down he was not at all the same person he had been before then. It has happened exactly to you. You are not the same person you were yesterday before we came up into the mountains. I feel the difference like a blow in the face, and I know that I am riding beside a stranger. What has happened?"

"Nothing at all. It happens I've never been among mountains before, except on a train, and I find they get on my nerves a little; that's all."

"I am so sorry," she said gently. "Indeed I am sorry. You were cold, too—shivering by that poor little fire last night. I know. I understand. You hate the mountains, you hate the Kabyles—and you hate me!"

"What nonsense!" he said impatiently. "There's nothing whatever the matter."

"My dear! Do you think I can't feel it?" She was silent for a moment, seeming to ponder upon some perplexity; then she laughed as if at an absurd idea intruding upon her. "It could not be——No, you would never be so foolish as that!"

"As what?"

"You could not be cross because these English are to lunch with us at Yakouren?" She looked out through the small window behind her. "Yes; they are following.   You could not be so absurd as to object to my consenting to that, could you?"

"Not at all," he returned gloomily.   "I don't care who lunches with us at Yakouren—or any other place!"   Then he was a little ashamed of himself; for even in his own ears what he had just said had the ring of sulking eighteen.   "I mean it isn't your fault that you overwhelmingly fascinated that pompous old General at first sight.   Whatever our ages, we succumb to you immediately: we can't help it and *you* can't help it!   So far as I can make out, he intends to attach himself—from now on."

She laughed.   "You are a funny young man, and he is a funny old one.   I was polite to him.   How can one be otherwise?   But I shouldn't have given up my evening to play bridge with them, since you don't play.   I thought it would amuse Hyacinthe; he had gone to his room to work again upon that tedious report, and so I——"

Ogle interrupted her petulantly.   "I wish you'd understand that I haven't the slightest objection——"

But she, in turn, interrupted him.   "What is it that you do object to?   I came with you to be really your friend, and friends should make us happier."   Then she spoke as if to herself.   "What is it—what *can* it be that I have done?" And when he would have said "Nothing!" again, she checked him, lifting her hand. "Wait! Let me think." She put the tips of her fingers to her forehead, and pressed them there, remaining silent for a moment or two. Then she made a sound of wonder and discovery. "Ah! It *could* be that!"

"It could be what?"

"Look at me," she said; and when he obeyed he saw little shadowy compressions as of a repressed amusement at the corners of her mouth, and her beautiful clear eyes were brilliant with laughter unsuccessfully hidden. "I know now," she said. "It is because Mr. Tinker and his family have been at Michelet. You are absurd enough to think I wished to go there because of that. You think I hoped they would be there. Confess it."

"Does it need to be called a confession?" Ogle asked, keeping his gloomy eyes steadily upon her. "I think you missed him by about a day. I think he told you he was going there."

At this she laughed aloud, and her laughter was genuine. "How could he tell me where he was going?"

"How could he tell you!" Ogle exclaimed indignantly. "Presumably with his voice."

"He couldn't," she cried, "because he didn't know himself!"

"Do you mean to tell me he didn't know where he was going?"

"Not the least in the world!"

"You expect me to believe it?"

"He didn't," she insisted, still almost overcome by her pleasure in Tinker's unspotted ignorance. "He only knew he'd never heard the names of the places and couldn't pronounce them if he had. His wife had been to Cayzac, and Cayzac had given her a courier who would take them to see what Mr. Tinker calls 'the sights'; but what these sights were, or where, he had no more idea than a stone! So how could he tell *me* what he didn't know himself? You Americans are the most wonderful people!"

Ogle believed her. "Tinker *wouldn't* know!" he thought. But her added exclamation nettled him.

"I wish you wouldn't so often call me 'you Americans,'" he said. "There are about one hundred and twenty millions of us, I believe; and really we aren't all exactly alike. I don't think of you and the *valet de chambre* who brought my hot water this morning as 'you French.' It might rather be more agreeable of you not to say 'you Americans' in a classification of myself with that Tinker."

He spoke the unpleasant name with vehemence, and as he did so, Mme. Momoro, still laughing, called his attention to the roadside. "Look!" she bade him. "Look at those people there upon that rock. Quickly!"

He turned to the window and beheld a dozen Kabyles, men and boys, emerged from a cluster of stone huts and grouped upon a shouldering rock, close by, to observe the passing of the automobile. Frowning, they stared unwinkingly at it and its occupants; and the eyes of all of them had that hard exclusion Ogle was beginning to know so well. Then, as the car came opposite the rock, almost all of them lifted their right hands, palms outward, in a gesture that might have been thought one of greeting, except for the fierce stare that forbade such an interpretation. Ogle already knew the gesture; it was a forefending against the evil fortune that might be an emanation from the Christian outlanders in the automobile.

"These Kabyles are like the rest," he said. "Why did you wish me to look at them?"

"It was to remind you of their eyes," she said gravely. "Your own had the same look a moment ago when you asked me not to speak of you in the same breath with that poor Mr. Tinker."

"Indeed? That's rather odd," Ogle returned; and he smiled faintly. "Another lady told me exactly the same thing in Algiers."

"Another lady?"

"Someone I think you don't know," he said; and did not further satisfy her slight curiosity upon this point.

But, although at the moment he took the coincidence lightly, it annoyed him by remaining in his mind and recurring to him at intervals throughout the morning, so that by the time they stopped for lunch at the Arab village of Yakouren, he had begun to think of it rather poignantly. The provincial American girl and the experienced French woman-of-the-world had both made the same unpleasant personal comment upon his eyes, and while he liked it from neither of them, he bore it better from the "little American."

Then, wondering why the slurring comparison seemed less offensive coming from Olivia Tinker than from Aurélie Momoro, he did Olivia the justice to remember that she had some warrant to resent any-body's instinctively looking like an Arab whenever she herself or her mother or father was in sight. For upon this double testimony he realized that he must indeed admit having worn an Arabian expression at such times, and he found himself thinking a little more tolerantly—almost with favour—of Olivia. She was ill-tempered, rather evidently because of some grief or rebellion within herself; but she had made no pretense of liking him, and at least had not told him he looked like a Kabyle or dragged any senile British generals around after her while she was his guest upon a motor trip. "Besides," he added to himself, as a final explanation of his more severe present hurt, "I never *did* care for *her!*"

In this there appeared to be an implication that at some time in the past he had cared for Mme. Momoro.

XVIII

THEY came to Bougie at sunset, and in that warm but fragile light the town seemed not so much built as made merely of colour and painted, a plaid of old rose and faint green and gray, upon its Mediterranean hillside. Here the senile British General proved too violent a pedestrian for the sedentary young American during a stroll—or what Sir William remarkably called a stroll—up and down the steeply slanting streets in the twilight. Mme. Momoro swept ahead with the tall Englishman; Lady Broadfeather and Miss Crewe, chirruping to the polite Hyacinthe, kept nearly up with them; but Ogle fell behind, and, when the dark came on, found his way back alone to the hotel, out of breath, tired, and more disgruntled than ever.

At dinner, however, he found that it was possible for him to become even more so. Upon the wine list the General discovered a red Beaune, a dear lost love of his, he said—and not only said, but copiously proved by wearing his lost love's colours, ere long, as

his own complexion.   Meanwhile, he became so
gallant in his praise of the French lady that Miss
Crewe looked faintly surprised, though Lady Broadfeather did not.   Time after time, he proposed Mme.
Momoro's health in the brave eighteenth-century
manner, always brightly ignoring the fact that the
ceremony had already been performed.   "To Artemis!" he said, and visibly was pleased to think this
an original inspiration.   "To Artemis, light-footed
on the hills, if you understand.   When goddesses
come to life let it be our mortal privilege to offer li-
bations and quaff nectar to them!"   He also drank to
Hyacinthe, who rose and bowed, but seemed slightly
embarrassed by the compliment.   "To your good
health, young gentleman!   You are the Mozart of
bridge.   We must recognize precocious genius as well
as goddesses."   And a little later, he called Mme.
Momoro's attention to an amiable-looking young
couple dining at a table across the room.   "Other
potentates are dining in Bougie this evening besides
yourself, august Artemis.   Those two young people
are the hereditary rulers of the old and independent
principality of Fühlderstein, Prince Orthe the Eighteenth and his bride.   They were staying at our hotel
in Algiers last week.   Curious how one encounters

people again and again in this part of North Africa—
or, rather, it's less curious than it is inevitable, since
everybody follows the same path and makes the same
stops. That reminds me, if you understand; I have
a little plan for lunching by the wayside to-morrow
on the road to Setif. We could have the hotel put
up lunch for us and we might make a little picnic of it
in the Gorge du Chabat el Ahkra, you see. If you
and your son and Mr. Uh think well of it, I'll instruct
the *maître d'hôtel* about the hampers. What do you
say? Shall we make a sylvan festival—Artemis and
fauns and wood-nymphs banqueting in Islam?"

Mme. Momoro, nodding and smiling, told him that
nothing could be more delightful; then she gave Ogle
a quick little look of appeal, as if to ask him how she
could have extricated herself with any courtesy. A
little later she gave him another such look when Sir
William, having finished his coffee, set his cup down
decisively, rubbed his hands, and exclaimed, "Madame Artemis! Master Mozart! Now to the
bridge!"

Ogle made no response to either of the plaintive
glances. He looked over her head, said nothing, and,
as soon as the party left the table, went up to his
room.

There, without turning on the light, he sat for a
little while on the edge of his bed; then he got up and
stood looking down upon a dim little square before
the hotel, where two or three ragged Arabs and a
few cats seemed to be holding inexplicable converse
together. The young American at the window did
not puzzle himself over the argument apparently
taking place between men and animals below him;
he had just solved a puzzle of his own and was not
attracted to another. The significance of the presence in Bougie of the Fühlderstein bridal couple had
not been wasted upon him, and neither had Sir
William Broadfeather's comment upon it. "One
encounters people again and again in this part of
North Africa. . . . Everybody follows the same
path and makes the same stops." Tinker himself
didn't know where he was going—that was probably
quite true; but Mme. Momoro knew. Everybody
followed the same path; and of course she knew that
was the path upon which Cayzac would set the
Tinkers.

The young playwright began to be borne down
under the conviction that his fate as a traveller, and
perhaps as a human being, was inextricably bound
up with that of the Tinker family. The gods of

spiteful comedy, at play in the African sky, had looked down upon him and with malevolent laughter had seen to it that there should be no escape from his aversion; it was a question of a few days, perhaps of a few hours, when the Old Man of the Sea would be upon him again. There was no longer a possible doubt of Mme. Momoro's diplomacy; and Ogle underwent the experience of knowing that he was being used—not a comfortable experience for a young man by no means selfless or lacking a fair opinion of his own significance.

In the morning, if he chose, he could assert himself; he could say, "No; we aren't going to lunch with Sir William Broadfeather in the Chabat. We're not going on to Setif and Biskra and Batna and Constantine and the rest of it, looking for a person named Tinker—who has his family with him, by the way, and is therefore in no pressing need of our society. We're going back to Algiers." For a little while he thought he had determined upon this virile course and took a grim pleasure in thinking of it—until he realized that he wasn't capable of saying such a thing to Mme. Momoro. Here he fell short as an analyst: he didn't know why he wasn't capable of it; he knew only that he wasn't. But there were other reasons

why he must go on as she had too adroitly planned:
the concierge of the hotel had handed him a telegram
from Cayzac's offices and it informed him that his
rather anxiously expected letters had been received
in Algiers and forwarded to Biskra. It might take
them some time to be returned to Algiers; he was
now within two days' easy motoring of Biskra; and
the letters were growing daily more important to him.

Humiliating as it was to be used—and used by a
woman to whom he had shown only the tenderest
chivalry—he must continue to be used. Then, having reached this enfeebling conclusion, he thought
of the Arab donkeys and their unfailing behaviour,
which was what Mme. Momoro had prophesied of
them. What a reproach to him! For they were
ridden, yes; but at least they showed a fighting heel
to the road, rider or no rider. He had none to show;
and with a sickish laugh, he found himself facing a
deduction that in spirit he was not their equal.

From a little distance there came on the night air a
sonorous palpitation: the rolling of drums and a chal-
lenging music from the bugles of a detachment of
French cavalry on the march. The sounds, so mar-
tial and stirring, roused him from his distressful reverie; and as he stepped out upon the small balcony

beyond his window, bugles and drums grew louder, and men and horses began to pass a corner beyond the open square. They were but vaguely illuminated by a single street lamp, and he could see little except soldierly outlines, twinklings of metal and moving sleeknesses of light upon the horses; nothing was definite in the darkness except the clean rattle of the drums and the brazen clarity of the bugles. Then abruptly these fell silent and another music set the pace—the African oboes and tom-toms of an Arab cavalry troop following the French to barracks. The tom-toms, beating with their ominous monotony, were like a pulsation in this Arab earth, Ogle thought —a barbaric heartbeat he might have heard in that earth every moment since he had set foot in Algeria, if he had listened; and over the tom-toms the oboe pipings rose and drooped in strange quarter-tones, singing uncivilized messages in the united voices of new-born babies and old cats wailing out of Egypt.

Morose as he was, the young American on the dark balcony found himself fascinated by that wail and by the throbbing of the tom-toms. He could bear a little more of this Africa, he thought, even though he must see it in the society of a lady who was betraying him.

XIX

IN THE morning when he asked for his bill, he was surprised to find as an item upon it, "Speciale Diner for six persons," at a price equally special; and, beneath it, another even more striking, for this one referred to a number of bottles of "Beaune Rouge 1907." That vintage, moreover, was evidently all that Sir William had said of it; the hotel authorities, who should have known, heartily agreed with him upon its worth.

"This is a mistake," Ogle informed the landlord, in the "Bureau." "General Broadfeather would be annoyed, I think, if I paid more than half upon these items. It was his proposal that our two parties dine together, and I think you'd better transfer half the amount to his account."

The landlord looked blank. "How can I? He is gone two hours."

"That's singular," the American said. "Did he look over his own bill before he left?"

"Eh? Did he? I escape with my life!"

"Then he must have misunderstood. It's rather

odd he———" Ogle was puzzled. "Singular!" he
said. "Did he have lunch put up to be taken in his
car?"

"No, gentleman. He did nothing."

"Singular," Ogle repeated thoughtfully; and he
paid the bill.

Outdoors, in the morning sunshine, the automobile
was waiting for him. The chauffeur and a porter
were strapping bags upon the roof; Hyacinthe stood
pensively regarding an unlighted cigarette; and Mme.
Momoro, already in her accustomed place in the car,
gaily waved her long black-gloved hand and smiled
a greeting to her preoccupied squire as he appeared.

"Broadfeather didn't do anything about lunch,"
he informed her. "He has two hours' start of us,
and if you expect to carry out his idea of hard-boiled
eggs and sandwiches and wood-nymphs and fauns
and so forth in the Gorge du Chabat———"

"No, no; I don't," she laughed. "Those English
will not be there, thank heaven! We will lunch at
any place where there is food. Get in and let us forget the English."

He obeyed half of this request; but, when they were
again forth upon the road, reverted to "the English."

"Then you knew the Broadfeathers had started a long time ahead of us, I take it," he said.

"At least I was certain they knew I hoped they would! Last night I think he drank too much. After we had played bridge for a time he was so confused he didn't know how to count. One moment he would be almost quarrelsome with poor little Hyacinthe and the next he would be—with me—too pleasant! He became—well, I must call it odious; and we had to stop playing. I am afraid his poor, round, little, old wife must have been very mortified; and I hope she is giving him such a day of it now as he deserves. We'll not see them again. Do you object if we don't talk of him? It was a little painful."

Ogle had his own reasons for regarding the subject of General Sir William Broadfeather as a little painful; but he acquiesced without mentioning them. "Very well," he said, and, as he added nothing to that, she looked at him inquiringly.

"You are hating me again? Have I done something more?"

"Not at all."

She shook her head and sighed. "I shouldn't have come with you. You are not happy."

"I'm quite all right."

"No," she said. "I don't know what has happened; but somesing has changed very much." She spoke with a sorrowful conviction that proved itself well-founded in the utterance of a single word. Upon the "Duumvir" and in Algiers, and, indeed, until the ascent of the Djurdjurra, he had thought her most irresistible of all whenever she said "somesing"; and once he had spoken of this to her, telling her he found the word, on her lips, "adorable." But when she said it now, his emotional experience took the form of a wish that she might be content to say nothing at all.

"I should never have come with you. I should ——" Her voice trembled, and then suddenly she sank back against the cushions, her hand pressed upon her forehead in an impulsive gesture of pain. "Ah! I should have known it!"

"You should have known what?"

"That you might come to look upon me and poor Hyacinthe as an imposition upon you." She drew in her breath sharply, then straightened herself to her usual erectness. "It *is* one, too."

"An imposition? No, indeed!" he protested with some apparent warmth. "You mustn't say such things."

"Not if they were true?" And when he would have protested again, she checked him. "No. You see you offered me an escape, and I was weak enough to take advantage of it."

"You mean an escape from Paris in winter-time?"

She shook her head. "I must make a confession to you. The escape was from much worse: it was from the long tyranny of Mademoiselle Daurel. You write comedies—or tragedies, it may be;—but you don't understand women's quarrels, because even the most adroit man can't understand them. When men really quarrel it is over; they have done with each other; but it isn't so with women. When I said we would go to Paris I knew that before we should *quite* leave, Mademoiselle Daurel would make overtures, and I was afraid I would be weak enough to listen. My feeling for Hyacinthe might conquer; so we should have gone back to that old life of petty persecution. It has happened before, you see."

"You've broken away and gone back before this, you mean?"

"More than once. The last time it was because— ah, a man could never understand how a woman's hopes can chain her to a persecution! I had this hope for Hyacinthe: Hyacinthe's work is drudgery; he is unhappy in it, and since our friend who gave him that appointment is dead, he has no political influence to go higher. He is very quiet, but he is clever; he knows music; and a Parisian impresario wishes him to buy an interest in his office for one hundred thousand francs. It would be heaven for Hyacinthe, and one hundred thousand francs is nothing to Mademoiselle Daurel. I was so absurd as to say to her that she might be happier to do a little for him in her lifetime. She was infuriated!"

"Why?"

"Because she thought it might allow us to escape from her. That terrible old woman——" Mme. Momoro again caught in her breath audibly, and for a moment could not speak. "It is incredible, but there are some old women like that. They are unable to exist unless they have somebody beside them whom they are keeping in torment. I think she can't live without me. So I felt that just to step into an automobile with you—well, it was simple enough to seem an escape. It was to go out upon the road like a gypsy. Gypsies are hard to find, and they are free. You can't understand what it means to be free from such a pressure, or how happy I've been these quick little days away from it. But—well, I thought it was what you wanted. I thought I could be——" Her voice trembled again; but she laughed bravely and went on, "I thought I could be—well, entertaining to you. You see, I didn't know you hated—mountains!"

"I don't in the least know what you mean," he said valiantly. "I'm stupid and silent sometimes without reason. You mustn't think——"

But she interrupted him. "You mustn't struggle so hard to be kind; we can't be impositions upon you any longer."

"What a horrible light that puts me in!" he protested. "Merely because I'm a little quiet——"

"No!" she said with sudden sharpness. "I shall sail from Tunis for Marseilles as soon as there is a steamer; but to get to Tunis I am afraid I must go as far as Biskra with you; that is only one more day. I leave you as soon as I can, you see, which should be some consolation to you."

"Then you say good-bye to me at Biskra?"

"Because it isn't possible sooner!"

The sharpness of her tone, unfortunately, roused a sharpness in him; and his sense of being used rose suddenly above the treacherous sympathy he had begun to feel for her. He spoke with bitterness.

"I see! You feel pretty sure he'll be in Biskra."

She stared at him. "I think you may mean Mr. Tinker."

"Yes."

She said nothing; but, after looking at him expressionlessly for a moment or two longer, made an odd movement as if she had forgotten that she was in a moving vehicle and meant to rise from her seat and leave him. Then she leaned forward, her hand uplifted to tap on the glass before her and her lips parted in the impulse to speak to the chauffeur.

Ogle caught the uplifted hand and held it.

"Aurélie!" he said. "You can't get out here on the road."

"Why not?" she asked fiercely. "There are some things one prefers to others." Then she released her hand from his, put it over her eyes, and again sank back upon the cushions. "Just a second," she murmured. "Sometimes one must think a little."

"I hope so. Certainly before one does anything absurd." He went on talking, as men do when they begin to feel remorseful. "I don't see why you resent my inference; surely it wasn't an unfair one. However, since you do resent it, I'll gladly apologize and withdraw what I said. I didn't mean to——"

"Thank you," she said; and she laughed helplessly, as if in apology for the tears that now trembled upon her eyelids and the emotion that kept her from speaking. She sought her handkerchief vainly for a moment, a search always disastrous to the strength of a gentleman witnessing it; and, when she had found it and used it, gave him her hand without looking at him.

"Please forgive me," he said huskily; for the pathetic trustfulness of this final gesture necessarily completed the unmanning of him. "Could you? And forget it?"

"Of course," she murmured; and she pressed his hand fondly before gently withdrawing her own. "We must both forget a little, my dear!" And with that, she brightened, once more bravely smiling upon him. "We are spoiling a beautiful day with our nonsense. You are going to see the Gorge du Chabat el Ahkra—hillsides covered with apes, but no English—and then a great desolate plateau coloured in pastel. We are on our way to the Desert! Could we be happy again—for a little while?"

He assured her that they could and he almost believed it. Late in the day, by the time they reached Setif, that bleak little city of the Atlas plateau, he believed it with a better conviction; Mme. Momoro showed herself never more charming. She was even the more so because, during this day and the next, she seemed to lay aside every vestige of the delicate coquetry that until then had been the elusive spicing of all her manner with him; she became wholly the gentle gay companion, anxious that he should miss nothing, living in the humble hope that he would be pleased, frankly tender with him—or merry with him, if that was his mood.

When he was cold upon the plateau beyond Setif, in the morning, she put about his shoulders a fur coat of her own that she insisted she was too warm to wear; and she did it almost by force. She sang Arab songs to him in a thrilling low voice he could just hear; she made word pictures for him of the Phœnician merchants who had once travelled this way, and of the coming of the Romans, and then of the overrunning Eastern hordes under Sidi Okba devouring the very fertility of the earth and leaving only the tumbled rocky débris through which the long road wound its way down to El Kantara and the gates of the Desert.

Something of the spell that had been upon him returned; and he wished again, as he had wished at Tizi-Ouzou on the first stage of their journey, that this dreamlike wandering with her might be for ever. But by the time he realized that this was his true desire, and spoke of it to her, the second afternoon of their two days of mild motoring from Bougie was on the wane; Biskra was not many kilometres ahead of them, and, although the car had run smoothly, Mme. Momoro had begun to look a little fatigued.

"I do wish that," he said. "I wish we could go straight on down into the Desert and never turn back."

"It is difficult motoring," she returned. "And what of the dramas you write? Won't you be expected to come back to New York some day to write new ones?"

"I suppose so. It seems pretty far away and unreal—all that—and insignificant. If I should go back——"

"Yes?"

"I suppose since your conscience won't let you marry again——"

"No. Not even if I were honoured by an invitation!"

"Then I wish"—he paused and laughed musingly —"I wish you weren't a woman, but a boy, so that you could go with me."

At this her look of fatigue deepened a little. "It is curious," she said. "When a man becomes interested in these platonic excursions, he always wishes that the lady were a boy; he never wishes to be a girl. I fear I should be a 'boy' a little mature for you, my dear."

"I believe you often deliberately try to make me feel idiotically young," he returned with some annoyance. "Why do you——"

"But you see our journey would be very improper if you weren't. It is one thing for me to travel with my son and his young friend; but quite another thing for me to travel with a gentleman and use my son only as a chaperon. I am much more conventional than you suspect. You see, you *must* be young—or I shall have to stop the car and get out, as I threatened to yesterday."

"You're mocking me again. Sometimes I have a feeling that from the very beginning you've done nothing else. Is it true?"

"No," she said, and without complicating her reply by any explanation, she changed the subject. "Look before you. I promise that you will like it better than the mountains."

Her promise was already fulfilled. They had come through many miles of dismaying mountainous desert and were in a gorge of tumbled, bright-coloured rocks. Now they passed a charming French inn, and just beyond it the barren gorge culminated in one of those dramatic climaxes that Nature, laughing rather mockingly, sometimes throws into the faces of human contrivers of climax and motoring playwrights. The automobile ran out through an appalling gateway of savage, gigantically ragged stone, and suddenly was in the green oasis of El Kantara. Hundreds of palm trees tossed their great feathered leaves above flat-roofed mud houses and long mud walls; there were glimpses of white-robed figures, mottled with orange sunshine and violet shadow, as they moved in the cool green avenues; somewhere a tom-tom throbbed, and there was the tinkling sound of running waters.

Mme. Momoro turned smilingly to her startled companion. "Your first oasis!"

"It's worth it!" he exclaimed impulsively, not realizing that his meaning might be construed as not impeccably gallant. She gave him a quick side glance, which he did not notice; but although her fine

eyebrows showed the slightest elevation she said
nothing.

Beyond the Arab town they passed the long, white-
washed wall of a fort; and near the gateway a Nubian
sentry stood blacker than black lacquer against the
intolerable whiteness of the white wall under the
African sun. Ogle was enraptured with him. "Look
at that!" he cried. "It's a blot of printer's ink on
white chalk. Or it's as if you saw the glaring white
wall through the hollow eye-holes in a mask of blue-
black enamel. This is getting to be a show!"

"Wait," she said, and a little later, as they came
down a gentle and curving slope, she tapped upon
the glass before them. The chauffeur stopped the
car. "Now," she said.

But she had no need to tell Ogle to look: he was
leaning forward, staring with all his eyes at the unending level of the pale blue horizon—for, except that
there were no tossing waters near him, he might have
been again, with this same companion beside him,
upon the deck of the "Duumvir," looking out to sea.

"It's true then," he said. "I've always heard that
the Desert looked exactly like the ocean; but most
things like that turn out to be untrue when you come
to them yourself. I suppose that blue ocean yon-

der——" He hesitated, doubting; the illusion was so strong. "I suppose that ocean yonder really *is* the Desert?"

"Yes," she answered, and she sighed as if relieved to have come to it. "It is the Sahara."

XX

A T BISKRA, Mme. Momoro went at once to her room to rest; and for the first time since Ogle had known her she looked as if that was what she needed. She had always seemed not only inexhaustible, but unimpairable, and her vitality like a strong metal so brilliantly polished that its surface could not be flecked; he was astonished and distressed to see her drooping. "I hope she's not overtaxed her strength," he said, expressing his concern to Hyacinthe, his guide to the branch-office bank where his letters from America awaited him. "I'm afraid she——"

"My mother?" Hyacinthe said inquiringly. "You think she has travel' too much for her strength?" He smiled faintly and shook his head. "She is twice as strong as you or me. She would walk from here to Hammam Meskoutine in five days, go into the hot baths, lie down ten minutes and come outdoors looking like a new gold coin just from the mint. After dinner she will be ready for bridge all night, if there is anyone to play with."

The banking office was closed when they reached it. "We arrive too late," Hyacinthe said; and he read a note upon the door. "You cannot have your letters to-morrow either. It is a holiday. I am sorry."

They walked back to the hotel through a street of bazaars, where they were invited by brilliantly gowned merchants to drink coffee; and Hyacinthe declined these invitations with a politeness somewhat indifferent; but he showed more animation in dealing with street pedlars and beggars. Wicked-eyed brown youths in dirty white burnouses kept at Ogle's elbows offering him daggers ground from old files and sheathed in red leather;—"Fi' franc! S'ree franc! Aw franc!" they insisted, holding the barbaric little weapons almost upon his face. "You *buy*, gentiman! Aw franc!" Two stalwart Arabs, dragging a piteous blind man between them, walked backward before him, whining ardently for alms, making it difficult for him to move without stepping upon their bare feet; and child beggars, in rags constructed apparently of matted dust, clung to his coat, wailing loudly, "Good morny, Mister Lady! Good morny, Mister Lady! Panny! Panny! Geev panny!" Other beggars and pedlars, with draperies flapping on the wind out of the Desert, came hurrying from the distance like hungry birds.

Hyacinthe dispersed them. He flourished his light walking-stick threateningly and astonished his companion by the savage harshness of his voice, though Ogle could make nothing of the words he used. "It was just some vile expressions in bad Arabic," the youth explained. "You must learn them, if you are to have any peace in these places where the tourists come. I will teach you at dinner." They had reached the arcades beneath the long veranda of their hotel; and he paused, sighing. "Now I will go to my room and get out the manuscript of my terrible report and play with it some more."

"Play with it?"

"Why not? None of my superiors will pay any attention to it; nobody will ever read it; but one might as well do it properly. It takes the place of solitaire for me, I suppose—like my important governmental position itself."

"You hate it, I'm afraid," Ogle said.

"Hate it?" Hyacinthe shrugged his shoulders, smiling faintly. "It is so nearly nothing. How can one hate nothing?"

In spite of his experienced manner and the veiled

cool precocity of his eyes, there was sometimes a plaintive wistfulness about the boy that made Ogle pity him and wish to be of use to him. "Of course that means you do hate it, Hyacinthe," he said. "Why did you get into it?"

"A friend of my mother's was so kind as to appoint me; but it was only two months until he drove his automobile into another one at one hundred fifty kilometres an hour. After that he was not in a position to do anything except for the director of a— how do you say it?—a place where they burn dead people. He had expressed that wish. So I am still doing the nothing to which he appoint' me."

"But your mother told me there was a chance you might go into something with an impresario in Paris."

"Did she?" For an instant Hyacinthe looked at him with a bright, interrogative sharpness; then he cast down his eyes. "Well, I might believe in such a chance—if it happen'!" he said pessimistically. "Good-bye until dinner." But after he had turned away, he turned again. "The sunset will come before long, and you know it is famous here. You couldn't do anything better with your time than to spend the next hour on the roof of the hotel."

His light sketch of his patron, Mme. Momoro's

friend whose political influence appeared to have been important, preoccupied the mind of the young American as he ascended the broad stairway. The meagre outline of this influential person did not seem to hint the portrait of an elderly philanthropist; and Ogle's imagination flashed out one of those inexplicable pictures, sometimes the result of only a barren word or two: he seemed to see a thin blond man of forty with a pale high forehead, a handsome comic-tragedian who drove a racing car insanely through the French sunlight and had reasons for trying to forget himself and for hoping to be forgotten. There was something interesting about a man who bestowed government offices, went into an automobile collision at ninety miles an hour, wished to be cremated, and was devoted to Mme. Aurélie Momoro. But she evidently had not cared to define him except as a friend who was dead; Hyacinthe, moreover, was a master of reticence; and Ogle comprehended that a piqued curiosity to know more of the cremated gentleman would probably never be gratified—which was indeed a well-founded bit of comprehending.

The roof of the hotel, an ample flat expanse, was unoccupied when he arrived upon it, though chairs and benches were hospitably placed for observation of

the celebrated sunsets. This evening's had just begun to be foreshadowed in elusive changes of colour
upon the Desert, the distant mountains and the deep
green oasis; but it did not promise well, Ogle thought;
for the foreground, near the hotel, was as damaging
to beauty as were the commercial exhibitions murdering the landscapes of his native country. Covering the walls of garages and the sides and fronts of
buildings, enormous painted signs advertised the
merit of French aids to the tourist upon his travels,
and suggested to the mind of the playwright the
"show business"—with the Sahara Desert as an
adjunct of the show. "Saharan sunsets turned on
promptly at five forty-five," he said sourly to himself. "It's too bad; one would never have thought
it of the French. I don't believe Tinker himself
could have done worse!"

A structure like a minaret rose from the roof; he
climbed the winding interior stairway, and came out
of a small door upon a narrow gallery built about the
four sides of the slender tower. Then, moving to the
southern side, he looked out upon the great show to
the east and south; for although the too-enterprising
advertisements in the foreground prevented his
escape from the idea that it was a show, he admitted

that it was a great one. The mud-walled town of Old Biskra, just glimpsed among green-feathered groves of palm trees and shot with silver glints of water, lay far below upon the south; but it was not in the south, nor in the west toward the sun itself, that the dramatic beauty of the Biskra sunset came to its climax. Standing upon the southern side of the gallery, he turned his eyes to the east and realized that there was what he had come to see. For there, like a high coast line beyond a wide bay, a long spur of the distant barren mountains ran down into the flat Desert; and this whole great range of rock had just become magnificent. In its incredible opalescence, he recognized that topmost ecstasy of colour, the Pink Cheek in which the Arab glories.

Even the ugly wall of an ugly room grows beautiful when the diffused late rays of a setting sun gild it and overlay the gilt with subtle tints of rose and with star dust; but the long, long rays that reach the Pink Cheek vibrate through the infinity of the Sahara before they glow at last upon the great rocky spur. Ogle had seen trees in the sunrise after a New England ice storm, and had thought their fairyland glories of iridescence the most startlingly beautiful sight of his life; but now, as he recalled the picture, their crystalline brilliancy seemed of too hard a glitter. Massed forests of such trees, all ineffably veiled in gauzes of faint gold and lilac, and running down from the sky into a flat amethyst sea, might look like the Arabs' Pink Cheek, he thought; and he admitted to himself that his gaze was spellbound. He wished never to stop looking.

Then, in his mind, addressing an invisible person, he said gratefully, "Thank you!" It was Mme. Momoro he thanked, for having brought him here.

Someone else was spellbound not far from him, for he heard faintly upon the air a little "*Ah !*" not vocal but just breathed, a sigh of wistfulest delight. He could not see who uttered this slight sound; she was upon the northern side of the gallery, he upon the southern, and the walls of the minaret rose between them to support a small dome overhead; but he knew that this intruder upon the spell that bound him was a girl; and for no intelligible reason in the world, he had the curious impression that she was Olivia Tinker. Nothing could have been stranger; he was not so familiar with Olivia's sighs that he could identify her by the sound of one, especially when it was a sigh of pleasure.

Other sounds, footsteps upon the stairway and

lightly murmured exclamations, indicated that the
person who had said "*Ah!*" was joined by friends—
two of them, Ogle thought—on her side of the gallery.
There were some moments of silence, and then a
woman's voice, softened by emotion, and at the same
time a little elocutionary, repeated not quite accurately a quotation with which Ogle at one time in his
life had been familiar:

> "The day is done, and the darkness
> Falls from the wings of night
> Like a feather is wafted downward
> By an eagle in its flight."

The person who had said "*Ah !*" was not pleased.
"Oh, *dear !*" she said. "Mother, that's perfectly
terrible! It isn't getting dark in the first place; and
in the second it isn't 'like' a feather; and in the third
it isn't 'by' an eagle. How on earth could an eagle
waft a feather?"

Mrs. Tinker laughed. "You needn't be so particular, Libby." Then evidently she turned to a third
person. "You'll have to get used to my daughter's
agonies over her poor father and mother, Mrs. Shuler.
She's doing her best to educate us; but she's a great
deal more patient with us lately, since we've been

down in the Desert to Touggourt. This trip's doing her a lot of good."

"It is not!" Olivia returned instantly; but she moderated her denial, accompanying it with a friendly murmur of laughter that seemed to contradict her own contradiction and support her mother's statement. "Anyhow," she added, "this sunset doesn't need any poetry to help it out. I'll let it alone, if you will, Mother."

Ogle's first feeling was one of keen sympathy with her point of view; his next was a brief wonder that his destiny had again meaninglessly posted him as an eavesdropper upon the petty dialogues of this mother and daughter; and this was succeeded by a slightly deeper perplexity that he should have recognized the girl's presence through so slight a sound. Then he solved this riddle—not happily. That Olivia and her mother stood within a few feet of him upon the gallery of the tower failed to surprise him, and so he realized that he had expected to find the Tinker family in Biskra.

He had pretended to himself during the latter part of the journey that Mme. Momoro was not coming here on that account; he had done what he could to aid her in her deception of himself; but he knew now that he hadn't thoroughly fooled himself, nor had all her beautifully acted diplomacies really cajoled him. This was where she had planned to meet Tinker and the meeting was at hand, though Tinker himself might not know it. Ogle thought it somewhat probable that he didn't; and, within the sound of Mrs. Tinker's voice—a voice precisely appropriate for the reading of the Secretary's Report to the Ladies' Entertainment Committee of a Church Fund Drive in the Midlands—the young man was bitter yet hopeful enough to think that her husband's immediate future might be a little complicated and uncertain.

She was speaking of him to her friend. "I do wish he could ever learn to follow the example of a gentleman like *your* husband, Mrs. Shuler. Only last night I said to him, 'For goodness' sake, Earl,' I said, '*why* can't you behave a little like Mr. Shuler?' I thought that might have a little weight with him on account of his having met Mr. Shuler at that convention in Minneapolis and his admiring him so much, besides the coincidence of happening to meet him again in a queer place like this, way off from everywhere and all; so I just said, 'Since you admire him so much, why can't you *behave* a little like he does?'"

"Mr. Shuler admires Mr. Tinker, too," Mrs. Shuler

returned warmly. "He told me he considered Mr. Tinker one of the ablest and most important men in our whole part of the country. He told me Mr. Tinker isn't only head of the paper company, but that he owns the gas plant in your city and's built up I don't know how many industries all around the state. He says Mr. Tinker is just a marvellous man, and that he's had so much success almost anybody's head would be turned by it. My husband says that's one reason he admires him so much, because his head *isn't* turned. He's just as simple and affable as if he wasn't anybody much at all, and Mr. Shuler says that's perfectly wonderful in a man that has five or six thousand people working for him in his different plants. And he says he never in his life saw a man with so much energy and——"

"Energy!" Mrs. Tinker exclaimed, interrupting. "That's the very trouble, Mrs. Shuler. What I said to him yesterday, I said, 'Why can't you do the way Mr. Shuler does and go and take a nap after lunch? Why can't you show a little common sense?' Not he! Every place we've been, the first thing he'd find out would be whether they had a water-works and an electric-light plant and a sewage system; and if they had, he'd drag our poor courier to look at them with him. 'Look here, John,' he'll say—he calls him 'John Edwards' because his real name is Jean Edouard Le Seyeux and Mr. Tinker said the only thing to do with his last name's to forget it—'Look here, John,' he'll say, 'I don't care where the Romans or the Carthaginians or the Mohammedans or anybody else left some old foundation stones lying around, there's a water-works in this town and we're going to get up and go look at it at seven o'clock tomorrow morning, before we leave here.' And then when they'd get through, heaven only knows what *pourboires* he'd give all the workmen, Arabs and everybody! Even Le Seyeux shakes his head over it."

Mrs. Shuler laughed. "I guess you needn't worry about *that*, Mrs. Tinker," she said admiringly. "My husband told me that Mr. Tinker built and practically supports a big hospital and two trade-schools for workmen's children in your city."

"That's very different," Mrs. Tinker returned primly. "When it's for good causes like that, I never make any objection; but I think it's perfectly criminal of him to spoil all the French hotel servants the way he does—and these Arabs. What he's done since we've been in this place alone makes my hair curl to think of it! Besides what he just *throws* around, he's sent bournouses and red Morocco boots and tunics and brass belts and boxes and boxes of dates to every one of his department heads and foremen and——"

Olivia interrupted plaintively: "*Couldn't* you stop talking about Papa—for just a *little* while, Mamma?"

"Yes, dear," her mother said soothingly. "It's a lovely sunset, and we ought to just watch it in silence. I never saw such colours in my life,—so many different shades and all! It's so interesting, I think, after reading 'The Garden of Allah', though I don't like that place much; it seems so creepy." She lowered her voice a little. "As I was saying, you can't do anything with him, Mrs. Shuler. I wanted him to take a little rest to-day—not he! He got to talking to a young couple in the garden here yesterday afternoon—Austrians or Polish or something, but they speak English, he said, as well as he does himself—and he took a fancy to them and sat with them after dinner in the coffee-room and told them all about what Africa really needs in the way of American machinery and so on;—you know his way. So to-day he got 'em to go off on a long camel ride with him. He had lunch taken along on some other camels to eat somewhere in the Desert—you never saw anything more like a circus parade in your life, except it was so kind of wild looking it almost scared me. Heaven knows where they were going or when they'll be back! He——"

Olivia interrupted again. "I give up!" she said, and she laughed. "Mrs. Shuler, if you expect to see what's left of a Desert sunset, you'd better come down to the roof with me and leave Mother up here. Papa bought her an absolutely impossible girdle of enormous clumps of carved amber and ebony in Touggourt, and she likes it. Sometimes she won't speak to him or of him at all; but just after he's got her something she likes you can't possibly stop her! You'd better come with me."

A moment later the door opening upon the gallery clanked and she could be heard descending the spiral stairway. At the same time, Ogle became aware of a vague commotion of sounds from the direction of a dried river bed on the edge of the oasis, and, looking that way, he beheld a cloud of dust, in the midst of which were glints of barbaric colour, gleamings of brass, and the tall shapes of camels.

Mrs. Tinker's voice sounded eagerly. "Look, Mrs. Shuler! There he is now! He's just getting back from the Desert."

XXI

THE distant cloud of dust containing Tinker's caravan, Tinker himself, his Austrian or Polish friends, Jean Edouard Le Seyeux, and others, crossed the dry bed of the Desert river, where stands the white-domed tomb of the marabout, and, making its way into Biskra, disappeared among the mud walls and palm trees of an Arab outskirt. But although temporarily invisible from the tower, its progress could still be followed by the increasing uproar travelling with it. A confusion of shrill voices, cat-like oboe pipings and the thumping of tom-toms were commingled upon the air; and down the street before the hotel ran the wicked-eyed sellers of knives, the trinket vendors, beggars, pedlars, and flying groups of brown children in tatters, hurrying passionately toward the commotion; blind men were dragged by at a run.

Then, at a corner below the hotel, the caravan turned into view, and, with little half-naked brown boys and black boys turning somersaults in the dust before it, swung barbarically up the broad white road. In nucleus it consisted of four camels of majestic breed, loftier than other camels and imperially conscious that they were. They were attended by smaller camels, upon which sat white-robed servants, and by brown men on Arabian coursers, by hairy old men on hairier donkeys, by musicians, clamorous pedlars and beggars, by goats, dogs, poultry, and the general vociferous rabble.

Capering fantastically before the procession and beating a tom-tom, a magnificently robust gray-bearded negro conjuror roared lunatic jocosities and caught tossed coins between his teeth;—he wore a headdress three feet high of yellow skin flashing with little mirrors; his skirt of jackals' skins leaped to his dancing, and, as he danced, he continually made convulsive obeisance to the potentate from afar, whom his prancing heralded and hoped to placate. This was Tinker, bareheaded, with a scarlet burnous over his shoulders and his trousers rucked up to his knees, riding at the head of his caravan high upon a gigantic white camel. He had been to Sidi Okba, where he had apparently bought everything that was for sale; silver-spangled shawls and scarves hung from the camels; great brass platters were borne upon them like shields; attendants carried bundles of red leather, laces, and outrageous weapons.

Up and down the street groups of tourists were standing to stare; British, wearing pith helmets, monocles, and puttees; French in white flannels and straw hats; open-mouthed Americans; mounted French officers in scarlet and blue drew rein; and from the doorway of the hotel came the landlord, the concierge, porters, waiters, immaculate Arab guides in white and brown, all deferential and hoping to be useful.

"Isn't it perfectly *awful!*" Mrs. Tinker said to her friend—and yet, though she meant what she said, there was somewhere at the bottom of her voice an elusive and just detectable little note of humorous pride. "I'll certainly let him know what I think of him for making such a spectacle of himself! The idea of his wearing one of those red things like that! He just can't help buying 'em wherever he sees 'em; and the trouble is, he hasn't any self-consciousness, Mrs. Shuler. If he felt chilly he'd put it on; he hasn't the slightest regard for appearances, because he honestly never thinks about 'em. Probably he's lost his hat, and I do wish he'd pull his trousers down! He hasn't the slightest idea how ridiculous he looks—and he wouldn't care if he had."

Ridiculous was how he looked to the burning eyes of the young man on the opposite side of the tower gallery. That is, at first Ogle thought him ridiculous; and injured vanity was not assuaged by the thought. It was to lay siege, then, to this buffoon, that Mme. Aurélie Momoro had travelled the long way from Algiers, dragging with her a spiritless serf whose hand or shoulder she patted now and then as a reward for paying the tavern bills! From her window somewhere below she was probably looking out now, and not one whit turned aside from her purpose to captivate that absurdity upon a white camel; she would care no more how ridiculous he was than she had cared how chivalrous and delicate the gulled serf had been with her!

But, continuing to look down upon the caravan, as it slowly swung up the street, drawing nearer, something about it daunted the sore spirit of the watcher on the tower. Against his will, he perceived a kind of barbaric stateliness, and lost his conviction that either the procession or its master was ridiculous. Moreover, he recognized the young

"Austrian or Polish" couple Mrs. Tinker had mentioned as members of this expedition. In the thin and rosy light of late sunset, riding well, no more incommoded by the swaying of his huge beast than he had been by that of the "Duumvir," Tinker came up the street at Biskra with the Princess of Fühlderstein upon his right hand, Orthe the Eighteenth upon his left, and the mob rioting hopefully about him as he laughed and scattered down silver coins among them.

There was something, then, not so ridiculous as formidable about the big, broad-faced Midlander; and the playwright felt the hovering of a Punic resemblance. For thus, with boys and black conjurors tumbling before him, with the rulers of States riding beside him, with tom-toms beating, and the rabble clamouring, some great scarlet-robed Carthaginian, master of six thousand slaves at home, might have ridden in from the Desert two thousand years ago. In fact, the disgruntled observer was able to perceive a further Punic resemblance, more painful: a great Carthaginian Barca—Hamilcar or his gorgeous son Hannibal—thus riding in from the Desert so long ago, might very well have encountered here a tall Beauty of the Gauls, who had travelled down from the Mediterranean seeking him everywhere and at last waiting at this oasis, sure of charming and enslaving him. Biskra might have strange surprises for industrial princes, whether of seagirt Carthage or a boosters' town on the Midland prairie.

"I'd just like to know what he's got to say for himself!" Mrs. Tinker exclaimed, as the caravan stopped before the hotel and her husband and his guests were assisted to descend. "Let's go down and see, Mrs. Shuler. I only hope he's tired enough to lie down awhile for a nap before dinner."

Her hope was a vain one; for they were met at the base of the tower by Tinker, divested of his burnous, supplied with a hat and in lively spirits. He came briskly out upon the roof arm-in-arm with a middle-aged companion of his own sex and similar nativity. "Look here, Mamma!" he shouted. "Mr. Shuler saw what I've got for you downstairs, and he says his wife's goin' to be mighty jealous. I had 'em carried to your room for you; and you and Baby'll find 'em laid out on your bed, I expect. You might pick out a shawl for Mrs. Shuler while you're at it. Anyhow, you better go look at 'em."

"There'll be time enough for that by-and-by," his wife returned severely. "We came up here to see the sunset and I certainly don't want any more shawls and neither does Libby; maybe we can coax Mrs. Shuler to accept 'em *all !* What have you got to say for yourself—behaving like a circus clown before the whole place like that! And, by the *way*"—here her tone became more emphatic—"I thought you told me that young lady with the light hair was a bride."

"She is. They're a bride and groom on their wedding trip; they told me so."

"Then why didn't you let 'em ride next to each other, the way honeymoon couples like to? Why'd you have to go and push your old camel in between 'em? So you could talk to the bride better? What are their names?"

"I don't know," Tinker answered, and he rubbed his head. "That's been botherin' me all day. I asked him about fifteen times; but it was so foreign sounding, and he'd always sort of smother it when he said it, at last I gave up tryin' to get it. Mighty nice young couple, though."

"Yes," Mrs. Tinker said with some tartness, "I noticed you seemed to think so—especially the bride."

Mr. Shuler laughed waggishly. "That's right, Mrs. Tinker, give it to him! You'll have to keep your eye on him. I met Charlie Wackstle in Naples as my wife and I were coming down here, and he told me quite a good deal about Mr. Tinker's capers on the steamer. You'll have to look out for him!"

Tinker protested with an affectation of jocosity, under which a keener ear than Mr. Shuler's might have detected a little genuine alarm: "Now, that'll be enough, Mr. Shuler. Our friend Wackstle's a splendid man—just splendid in every way—except he's never spoken a word of truth since he was born. Listen! When that Wackstle came into the smoking-room and said it was a nice bright day outside, everybody there would send for their rain-coats. Listen! I've always believed George Washington was dead, but if Charlie Wackstle *said* he was, I'd telegraph to Mount Vernon and tell George I was comin' to visit him! Listen! If Charlie Wackstle ever told the truth in his life——" He paused. An Arab servant stood before him, offering him a small white envelope. "What's that? For me? I don't know anybody here." However, he accepted the missive and opened it.

Mr. Shuler cackled gayly. "Billy-dues already! It's certainly a little suspicious how heavy he puts it on about Wackstle being such a prevaricator. You'll have to keep your eye on him, Mrs. Tinker!"

"Indeed I know that," she said. "Who on earth would be writing to you in a place like this, Earl?"

He put the note in his pocket, laughing evasively. "Oh, it's what Mr. Shuler said," he returned. "It's a billy-doo. I can't keep 'em away from me!"

She frowned. "I asked you who's it from."

"Now, Honey!" Then he laughed louder. "I believe you think it's from that little, light-haired bride. Well, on my word, it's not;—as a matter of fact, it's about something entirely different."

"Well, what?"

"Maybe I'll tell you some day, maybe not, Mamma." He became fondly taunting, as if humouring Mr. Shuler's joke. "Anyhow I got to go 'tend to something."

With that he moved toward the stairway to descend; but she detained him. "What do you have to——"

"Oh, it's nothing, only I got to look after it myself. See you downstairs pretty soon."

"But I want to know——" She checked herself and stood looking after him as he disappeared. Then she turned to her companions. "I *know* it's that note," she said.

"You'll have to keep your eye on him," Mr.

Shuler repeated, unable to part with this humorous device. "Somebody's probably trying to get him away from you, Mrs. Tinker."

"Somebody's probably trying to get him away from some money. Somebody's always after him for *that !*"

"Well, he's still a pretty good-looking man, Mrs. Tinker. You'll have to keep your eyes open."

"Indeed, I'll do that!" she said; and this, for a time, was the last heard from her by the young man upon the gallery overhead. She moved away with her friends to occupy some chairs at a distance from the tower, and only the indistinguishable murmur of their talk was audible.

XXII

THE rosy incandescence of the Pink Cheek had grown fainter and duller, until now, with sun and short afterglow both gone, the great spur was no more than a cloud of gray ashes lying upon the darkened plain. In the Desert, nearer, were the low brown tents of some Nomads whose supper fires glowed in garnet points against the dun-coloured sand. So were there hot little points burning in the gloomy soul of the lonely young man upon the tower. His dream was "all over," he said to himself—for it is the habit of young gentlemen of his age to speak to themselves of their dreams—but even as he came to this dream's end he was not quite sure what it was that he had dreamed.

What had he asked of her? This he asked of himself, and elicited no immediate reply. He had spoken to her of marriage, regretting that her convictions did not permit her to entertain the idea; but when she had twice answered—apparently with mere gayety, to be sure—that she did not boast of her invitations, he had not increased the number of them. Asking her to marry him had been no serious part of his plans; but he sadly suspected that if she had wished him to ask her she could have made him. His feeling for her, until it began to alter, had been a delighted kind of reverence; she fascinated him and allured him; but what he had liked best was looking up to her, seeing her as a beautiful, wise-spoken, oracular statue, gracefully empedestalled above him. And as he thought of her thus—as he had first thought of her on the "Duumvir"—he found the answer to his question. What had he wanted of her? He had wanted her to let him worship her. And so this playwright, who in his trade practised "unmitigated realism," confronted his romantic idealism at last upon a minaret rising over a Saharan oasis. He found life impossible because a woman indefinitely older, but indeed definitely more experienced than himself, had been too practical to allow him to continue his worship of her. He tried to be fair to her; she had given him glimpses of agony when she spoke of her life with Mlle. Daurel; and he understood that to escape from some of the hardships of life many people will strive more wildly than to escape death; but such salvation as she played for in this flight to

Biskra was grotesque. And so was his adoration grotesque; for he had asked to worship a woman whose one desperate desire was money. Then, too impulsively, his eyes were brimmed against the young twilight stars, and he would have shed actual tears of self-pity; but he saved himself from this climax of imbecility by paying himself, in a whisper of extortionate painfulness, what was really a great compliment, though he did not mean it so.

"Jackass!"

With that word still in his mind as his best definition of himself, he came down from the tower, but did not descend into the hotel. If he went to his room, he knew that he would throw himself face downward upon his bed; and he felt that already too many attitudes of his had been abject, and that he might profitably omit this final prostration. He walked to the northern parapet of the roof and looked down into the Arab town.

Just beneath him was a lane separating the hotel from some native courtyards, and, within these courtyards, in the dusky twilight, women were crouched formlessly over braziers of reddening charcoal; camels were ruminating; and an evening peace seemed to have descended as part of the routine of the hour. It was not allowed to be broken by a tall negro whose dress consisted of a torn red jersey, a circular apron of jackals' skins, and a few necklaces of teeth;—he rapped upon the closed green door that gave entrance to one of the courtyards, then, in a subdued voice, uttered a monotonous chant; but nobody opened the door or paid any attention to him. He rapped again, chanted again, and resignedly went away. Through the lane, burdened camels came stalking, silent, infinitely dignified, returning from the Desert; and their barefooted masters stole along as silently beside them. Beyond the courtyards, an Arab café could be seen, and there, at tables before it in the street, the patrons sat in their ivory-coloured robes, as they had been sitting through all the late afternoon, almost motionless and saying nothing.

Somewhere, in what dim interior, and why, Allah alone knew, a tom-tom beat and beat; and there sounded the far penetrating tinny cry of the African oboe. In the oasis this throbbing and wailing went on eternally, and, like the ticking of an old clock in a farmhouse, could be heard whenever one listened for it. Now, in the hush of evening-fall, it became insistent with a wild and animal melancholy, as if some beast lay up in his lair, whining in time to his thumping heart-beats and brooding upon love and war. There was no other sound upon the air: figures in white and in rainbow robes moved noiselessly up and down a street that ran obliquely upon Ogle's left, as he looked down from the parapet; but there was no laughter, no shouting of children's voices at play; not even the barking of an Algerian dog.

The twilight was deep blue upon the town, but keyhole-shaped windows shone in gold, and golden rhomboids fell upon the street from the lighted open doorways. A portly, white-robed man, pausing beside a door, was blue upon one side and became luminous gold upon the other; figures dappled with gold and blue seemed to swim in the air of that quiet street like gold and blue draperies adrift in azure tinted water. And along another street, meeting this one at a sharp angle and displayed to view from Ogle's parapet, there were rows of houses, each with a little painted balcony above the open door; and in all the lamp-lit doorways, or upon the steps just beyond, painted girls in brilliant scarlet and green and orange and lavender and silver were sitting in the golden lights; for this was the street of the Ouled Nails and these were the dancing girls. Native soldiers passed solemnly; and now and then one of the girls would catch at the burnous of a man from the Desert as he strolled near her, and hold him until he snatched his robe sharply from her detaining hand.

The blue twilight darkened quickly; dusk became night, and the lighted windows of a tower at a little distance were like the keyholes of a giant's house all on fire within. Still the tom-tom throbbed, the oboe wailed, and the iridescent Ouleds sat in their golden doorways—and then, not far from him, Ogle heard again the little voiceless "*Ah!*" of pleasure that he had heard upon the gallery of the tower. For some time he had been conscious of a figure near him, looking down from the parapet; but he did not recognize it for Olivia's until she sighed. This sigh, like that from the tower, was one of pleasure; yet at the sound a curious sympathy he had sometimes felt for her, in spite of her antagonism and his own resentment, became almost vividly emotional within him. He had long since understood that she had been ill-tempered because she suffered; and his guess was that her suffering, in cause, had kinship with his own. Both of them were victims of their own blind gods, he thought; and her sigh seemed to him a little like the call of a sister in the same affliction. He went to her, and spoke her name.

She turned, recognizing him without surprise—
her voice and manner had both become much gentler
since she had so abruptly quitted him in Algiers.
"Mr. Ogle? I supposed you were here."

"You did? Why?"

"I met that French boy, young Momoro—isn't
that his name?—in a corridor of the hotel an hour or
so ago. I supposed his mother must be with him,
and so probably you'd be here too."

"But why should you——"

She laughed amiably. "Because of the 'Duumvir'
—when you danced with me, because you were looking for her. Never mind! I'd admired your taste,
and I'm glad you have it, because now it gives me
another chance to apologize to you. Compared to
me, you've been a Bayard! You see I knew all along,
underneath, that I was misbehaving; and lately, even
when I've wanted to stop it, I haven't been able to
entirely. I went on acting like a surly idiot for
a while when I was really all right inside, and just
out of habit I'm still peckish with my mother and
father sometimes, though I curse myself for it. But
I don't think I'd *ever* be that way with you again.
You've been on my mind, Mr. Ogle. I made a vow
about you."

"I hope you'll tell me."

"That was what I vowed," she said cheerfully. "I vowed to tell you. Could you stand my telling you quite a little?"

In the darkness her voice was warm and kind; and the desolate young man felt the need of kindness just then. He was grateful. "I can stand almost anything, I find," he said. "Especially, I think I could bear a little friendliness."

"You poor thing!" Olivia exclaimed. "I'm afraid the wonderful French lady may have been perplexing lately, perhaps even as perplexing as she seems to an American girl. I'm sure I'd *never* learn to know what a woman who looks like that was going to do next! But I want to talk, not about her, but about myself, Mr. Ogle, and a little about you. My vow was that if we ever did meet again, I'd tell you the *real* reason I couldn't help being insulting to you. The first half of it is simple: I was insulting to everybody, I was in a perpetual temper because I was in a fury with my father. I think I don't need to tell you much about that, because I'm sure you've understood it. You didn't need to be a realistic playwright to understand why a girl of my age on a long voyage is in a state of fury with her father! It always means the father is taking her away from—well, of course from some 'undesirable' person at home and that he believes he can 'cure' her by absence. But just for my pride's sake I do want to explain that I didn't hate my father because he thought he could 'cure' me by the separation. That wasn't at all why I hated him."

"Wasn't it?"

She laughed ruefully. "Don't you know what it is that a woman simply can't stand from *any* man— not even from her father?"

"I've always supposed there were several things of that kind."

"There's one above all," she said, and in the darkness, though he could not see her distinctly enough to be sure, he got the impression that she was blushing. "She can't stand his being *right !*"

"You mean you hated your father because you knew it *would* 'cure' you?"

She laughed again, with a kind of helplessness. "I'm afraid I hated him because it had! Nobody has a right to be right as often as my father is! This is a dreadful confession, Mr. Ogle; but the rest of it isn't quite so humiliating. You understand half the reason I was insulting to you—my disgusting moodiness; but the other half is the reason I made a vow to tell it. You see something—something has had a great effect on me during this African journey. I realized that when we got fairly deep down into the Desert—at Touggourt."

"I think I understand what you mean," he said gravely. "Nobody'd quite understand the effect of Africa who hadn't been here, and I suppose a great many who have been here wouldn't understand. I've just begun to feel the Desert myself—I don't know what change it might make in me; but other parts of Africa have been sufficiently effective."

"It wasn't the Desert that made a change in me, Mr. Ogle," she said. "I realized it at Touggurt and in the Desert; but what *made* the change"—she hesitated, and a ripple of laughter in her voice was a sound not of mirth, but of embarrassment—"well, I think places only help us to realize things in ourselves; they don't make them happen. What made the change in me wasn't a place at all, but a person. It was—it was you!"

"I!" he cried. "I made a——"

"Yes, I think so," she said. "You see I belong to

a very curious sex. We're most curious of all in the way we lump yours together. When one of us hates one of you, she's just as likely to abuse another of you as the one she hates, and it relieves her almost as much as if she'd actually abused that one. I was angry with my father—and the queer truth is, I was angry with the person at home from whom I was separated. You mayn't understand it at all; but along with the rest of what she feels, a girl always is angry with the person from whom she's separated in this particular way—it seems weak of him to allow it. And then, you see, my father showed himself so much the stronger of the two; the contrast wasn't favourable. Well, so there were two men I was furious with—and I took it out on you! I struck at the whole sex through you, and when I had time to think it over I saw I'd had my revenge and began to feel a great deal better and be decent to people again. So you're really my 'cure,' because I really did hit you."

"Did you?"

"Don't you know it yet?" she cried; and although he comprehended what she said as a reproach to his dullness, his conceit and his pride, she seemed friendlier than ever. "Why, of course I did!" she said. "I told you the truth about yourself, the insulting truth.   But the *real* reason I wanted to is that—well, that, after all, you're so nice!"

"What on earth do you mean?"

"Just that.   The insulting truth only covers a little of you.   The insulting truth about me, for instance, is that I've been a self-centred, bad-mannered, evil-tempered, little shrew—but, dear me! that was only a little of me.   So's your literary hauteur, or your New Yorkishness, or whatever it is, only a little of you.   What the rest of you is, I know from the beautiful way you've stood my insults.   I know you're really a very gentle, chivalrous, fine person just deluded into the likeness of a cold-hearted snob. You made me furious because you had that Arab eye: I wanted to shake you and to shout at you, 'Good heavens, you ingrowing blind Mr. Ogle, don't you realize that the rest of us are part of *humanity?*   Do you think you're *not?*   Don't you know that we're all the same *person* really, and that you're only a little of all of it?'   You see it was because I knew you were really so much nicer than you seemed that I was enraged with you.   That's what I vowed to tell you, if I ever met you again, Mr. Ogle, because I owed you a debt of gratitude.   Can you bear my having paid it?"

"I don't know," he said seriously. "Tell me one thing. You said I didn't need to be a 'realistic playwright' in order to understand——"

She interrupted him. "Oh, yes; I saw your play in New York. My father and mother went to it and came home terribly shocked—at least Mother was and Papa pretended to be. I knew they hadn't understood it, so I went to the matinée the next day without telling them. I wasn't much shocked, of course—I saw what you were trying to do——"

"'Trying'?" he said mildly.

"Yes. I thought so."

"Then you didn't like it?"

At this her voice became non-committal, a little evasive. "I shouldn't say just that. What I got from it was the idea that the man who wrote it could do something a lot better, something really important." She hesitated. "I thought he could—maybe."

The hesitant "maybe" was the worst of what she said; and so much needless honesty had an unfortunate effect. One of the most uncompromising of the novelists had written of "The Pastoral Scene" as "perhaps the most important play since the sweeping away of all previous forms of art; perhaps the founda-

tion play of a great new school"; and Ogle, now recalling this passage, failed to see that the enthusiast's
"perhaps" was as cautious as Olivia Tinker's "maybe." But "The Pastoral Scene," besides being a
triumph with the Few, had become instantly an in-
stitution with the Many; a severe weekly periodical
had called it "one of those great popular successes
that affect not only the art of a country, but the life
of a country." It was his first substantial achieve-
ment, and he thought of the play, since it was recent,
as his "magnum opus";—having used that expression to himself without a blush. And here was a
little Midland girl telling him that what she got from
it was an idea that he could do better—maybe!
Suffering from wounded love and from betrayal as he
was, the young playwright found time to add to his
other emotions a sense of outrage, to regret the
sympathetic inclinations that had led him to Olivia's
side, and to withdraw them utterly.

"You're very kind," he said.

An infinitesimal bit of what he felt was expressed to
her in his voice; and she wished to be as kind as she
could. "I haven't ever mentioned to my father or
mother that you wrote it," she said. "You see, I
went to school in New York until only last year, and

besides our going to the theatres some of the girls who'd been abroad in the summer would bring home copies of French plays, and we'd read 'em; but of course my father and mother don't know what's going on, and they'd never understand that the only reason you write that way is because so many other people are doing the same thing too. But you mustn't think I was really critical. I thought it was—well, honestly, I *was* interested in parts of it."

She was indeed too kind, and he told her so.

"Too kind, Mr. Ogle?" she said; and she was troubled, understanding that if she had ever hurt him at all, she had hurt him now, when she honestly meant to be friendly. "I'm afraid you don't say that as if you mean it. I don't know a great deal about plays, of course: I only know——"

"Don't!" he interrupted her. "You're going to say you only know what you like, yourself."

"I was going to say I only know what I feel about them. The only other thing you can know about plays, where they're all pretty well done, is what somebody else feels about them, isn't it?"

For a moment he stared at her through the gloom; then he said icily: "I suppose so."

"Well, what I felt about your play——"

"Never mind," he said. "Let's not talk of that any more. I'm a little curious upon one point. Something I overheard you say on the steamer to your mother gave me the impression that you didn't know I——" He checked himself, and reformed his sentence. "On the 'Duumvir' I think you weren't aware that I am a playwright. Were you?"

"No. I didn't know until yesterday that you were the author of that play."

"Until yesterday? How could you have learned it here, in Biskra?"

She laughed. "That's simple. My father——" She stopped speaking, and leaned forward staring down from the parapet. "Why, how queer! There he is now."

Mrs. Tinker spoke from a little distance behind her. She was approaching over the roof with Mr. and Mrs. Shuler. "Your father, Libby? Where do you see him?"

Olivia answered quickly, "I don't. I was mistaken; it's someone else." She had been looking down into the street of the Ouled Nails, but immediately she pointed in another direction. "Look at that tower, Mamma, with those curious Moorish windows blazing. Isn't it wonderful?"

But Mrs. Tinker leaned over the parapet. "Where did you think you saw your father, Libby?"

"Nowhere. Look at that——"

Mrs. Tinker uttered a sharp exclamation. "It *is* your father!" she said, and pointed downward to the left. "Certainly it's he. Who in the world is that he's got with him?"

Tinker, beautifully unconscious of the splendid view of him afforded by the roof of the hotel, was sauntering through the street of the dancing girls with Mme. Momoro.

XXIII

MR. SHULER immediately cackled with delight in so happy a confirmation of his joke. "Didn't I tell you to keep your eye on him, Mrs. Tinker?"

Mrs. Tinker said nothing. The long building of the hotel was but two stories in height, and the five people now in a row close to the parapet of the roof looked down as from a theatre's darkened balcony commanding a lighted stage. Among the robed Arab supernumeraries moving in many colours upon this stage, the two people in European dress were as conspicuous as any obvious hero and heroine in a play. Mme. Momoro, already dressed for the evening, lacked the Hellenic stillness once imagined of her by a poet;—in ivory satin, with her mantle of Venetian green brocade thrown back from her long and shining figure, and her head bare except for a veil of chiffon transparent enough to show the pale bronze gleamings beneath it, she was a charmingly animated Parisian in Islam.

No woman would have doubted that here was a tall lady who well understood how to be at her best and had decided to be at her best to-night. Almost affectionately arm-in-arm with her companion, she was talking rapidly, talking gayly, too, and smiling as she talked—and her brilliant eyes, continually upon him, emanated a soft radiance plainly far from distasteful to him. Of the affability of his mood there could be no question whatever.

Near the corner of the two streets and only a little way from the intensely observant darkened balcony above, they paused before the last house of the Ouled Nails; she drew her arm from his and stood facing him, still smiling upon him, but speaking in a low voice and apparently with some seriousness. The painted girl, lolling upon the doorstep close by, like a figure dressed in a few yards of rainbow and splashed over with gilt, leaned forward in a glittering movement;—deeply interested, she watched them fixedly, though not with an attention more concentrated than that bestowed upon them from on high.

Mr. Shuler, however, remained humorous; he supposed the encounter of his admired compatriot and the tall lady but a chance one of friendly tourists; and he made no doubt that the lady was some worthy acquaintance of Mrs. Tinker's to whom she had introduced her husband. Tinker had probably just happened upon her in a stroll about the neighbourhood, and they were obviously returning to the hotel, being, in fact, but a few yards distant from a corner of the building now. Therefore, Mr. Shuler, entertaining the ladies, pushed his humour as far as it would go, and had no more thought of preparing a catastrophe than when he was similarly merry, at the Church Bazaar at home, upon the subject of the aged Pastor's gallantries.

He made his cackle breathy, rather than loudly vocal, and again informed the silent Mrs. Tinker that he had warned her to be watchful. "Your husband's certainly proving he's got a good eye this evening!" he continued. "I hate to think what Mrs. Shuler'd say if she caught *me* carrying on with as good a looking woman as that! After dinner I'm going to have a little fun with him about what Charlie Wackstle told me in Naples. I guess you must have been a little off your guard with him on the steamer, Mrs. Tinker; Charlie told me about some fine-looking French lady you had on board that the other gentlemen were all jealous of your husband on account of. Said he never gave a one of 'em the chance to meet her; just shooed 'em away and used to sit all afternoon with her up in a corner of the boat-deck every day. Charlie said he wouldn't even play cards after the first afternoon or two; he was so afraid he'd miss that taity-tait; said it was a perfectly terrible scandal! You wait till I get a chance to twit him about it."

Then, laughing under his breath, he improved this theme; planning an after-dinner discomfiture for Tinker which should be assisted by a pretended severity on the part of Mrs. Tinker; and as he talked jubilantly on, Ogle, standing next to Olivia, was conscious of the increasing rigidity of her attitude. It was his impression that she became frozen with horror and that she was horrified for her father. In spite of his own emotions, which were various and all poignant, Ogle had not failed to notice the hurried anxiety with which she had striven to draw her mother's attention from the street of the dancing girls and to fix it in another direction.

Yet, from the viewpoint of both the girl and her mother, what reason was there for Olivia's anxiety? Ogle understood the marital attitude of the type he thought of as the "Middle Class wife"; but surely even by such a person nothing especially ruinous need be thought of a middle-aged man's walking about the neighbourhood of his own hotel with a lady not intimate with his wife. Of course, after Mr. Shuler's merry revelations, even a wife not decisively "Middle Class" might warrantably become somewhat excitedly inquisitive; but Olivia's manœuvre was before Mr. Shuler spoke. It seemed to be plain, therefore, that although the daughter herself had probably no criticism to make of her father's behaviour, she was alarmed for him because of something familiar to her in her mother's character. Indeed, by the time Mr. Shuler's plans for a pleasant evening were perfected, she seemed to be more than alarmed. Unless Ogle's impression was at fault, her anticipations were preoccupied with an accomplished calamity.

"Look at *that!*" Mr. Shuler exclaimed. "Didn't I tell you?"

But his half-suppressed chuckling was the only sound upon the roof. Leaning nearer to her American friend—and it might be thought almost tenderly—as they stood smilingly face to face, Mme. Momoro did something that upon the instant of her leaning Ogle was sickeningly sure she would do. She gave Tinker a pat or two upon his stalwart right shoulder, and, with the last of these friendly caresses, let her white hand linger pleasantly in its descent of his brown coat sleeve. Then she took his arm cosily again; they plunged into the dark lane beneath the parapet; and the cheerful murmur of their voices rose to that slight but frigid altitude as they went on in the direction of the entrance of the hotel. The Ouled Nail, more interested than ever, half rose to stare after them.

The fatal Shuler's cackle grew louder. "There! What did I tell you, Mrs. Tinker? Didn't I——"

Mrs. Tinker, without a word, turned from the parapet and strode toward the stairway that descended into the hotel.

Shuler called after her: "Now, remember, Mrs. Tinker; we want to make this a good one. Don't say a word to him till after dinner. As soon as we come out to the hotel parlour we'll——"

Ogle heard the whisper, hoarse and fierce, of Mrs. Shuler: "Hush up! Haven't you got *any* sense?"

"Why, what——"

"Hush up!"

Then they disappeared in the darkness.

Olivia had turned to follow her mother; but Ogle detained her. "Just a moment."

"Yes, Mr. Ogle?" she said in a troubled voice. "I mustn't stay long just now, I'm afraid."

"I won't keep you. I asked you how you had learned I was the author of 'The Pastoral Scene.' You said your father——"

"Oh, no," she interrupted. "That didn't have anything to do with my father. By the way——" she paused, and laughed apologetically— "I was going to say something too impulsive, I'm afraid!"

"Please do."

"Well—you mustn't think anything important about Papa's getting his shoulder patted just now. He's really an old dear, you know: he isn't *really* kittenish; he never means anything. I don't think you need fear your fascinating lady will flirt *too* hard with him!"

"If you please," Ogle said;—"she isn't 'my' fascinating lady. I was asking you——"

"Oh, that? A lot of American papers were sent to Papa here, and I happened to notice in one of them that Isabella Clarkson, who'd been playing in Laurence Ogle's 'Pastoral Scene,' was rehearsing for 'Hedda Gabler.' So I knew who you were. I hope it won't make any difference in your play."

"None at all. I suppose she's going to do a special

Ibsen matinée. That's often done by an actress, even when——"

"I'm afraid I'd better run, Mr. Ogle," Olivia broke in nervously. "You'll forgive me; I'm afraid there's something important I ought to be doing."

He followed more slowly as she sped lightly away through the darkness; and then, descending to his room, he found he had added one more to his list of troubles. Isabella Clarkson was the wife of Lehren, the manager of "The Pastoral Scene"; and the playwright wished that her husband held a tighter rein upon her. How could she play well in the evenings after doing special matinées? Besides, she should have been satisfied to be known as the "Anna Struger" of "The Pastoral Scene." If she wanted to do "Hedda Gabler" later, after three or four years, no one could find fault with her for it; but just now adding an Ibsen rôle might diversify interest; and people who saw her as "Hedda" might not care to see her as "Anna." What was the matter with Joe Lehren, that he could never show any firmness or intelligence with Isabella? And, indignantly, as he dressed, Ogle went so far as to picture himself returned to New York and saying to Isabella: "See here! You sit down in that chair and listen to me.

You may be able to do what you like with your husband; but I'm not that sort of man. You're going to do exactly what I——"

But just then an Arab servant brought a note to him.

My dear, I'm going to ask you to forgive me if I let you and Hyacinthe dine alone together this evening. You have seen me at so many meals I must not flatter myself that I am not giving you a little vacation which you may be unkind enough to find a relief! You shall thank me when I see you again, and in the meantime you are a dear boy and I am so fond of you that I send you a pat upon the shoulder. But do miss me a little!

Ogle interrupted his dressing not only to read the note, but also to sit down on the side of his bed and take his head in his hands. Recalling what he had just been saying to Isabella Clarkson, he was able to produce a feeble and nauseated laughter before he rose; then, returning to his mirror to perfect his neckgear, he made with precision the neatest semblance of a black butterfly below the two white triangles of his collar. After that, before going down to join Hyacinthe, he gave a little time to the well-favoured but somewhat stricken-looking portrait within the glass. He sneered at it. "You withdraw your remarks to Miss Clarkson, I gather!" he said aloud; and added, muttering as he turned away: "No wonder you 'try' to write tragedy! Doesn't it rather strike you that you *are* one yourself?"

At their table in the large dining-room he was as silent, for a time, as Hyacinthe, though there were several subjects he wished to discuss with the youth, and he intended to open them before the conclusion of their meal. However, he waited, and in the meantime took note of Miss Olivia Tinker, dining alone just beyond the intervening table of Orthe the Eighteenth and his cheerful princess. The bridal table, though incognito, had been covered with flowers, and from Ogle's view Olivia's pretty head and shoulders, as she sat directly beyond, seemed to be growing out of a small rose garden—not inappropriately. She looked serious; but now that he saw her in the light he perceived that her sullenness was all gone, an improvement almost startlingly becoming to her. Then she turned her head, as if she felt and recognized his gaze, and her seriousness disappeared for an April moment;—she was suddenly all of such charming sunniness, as she smiled and nodded to him, that she even had a lopsided smile from him in return.

He flushed a little with the effort he made to produce even that semblance, and then as she turned away and became grave again, he decided that the time had come to speak to Hyacinthe. The waiters were placing the dessert upon the table.

"Did your mother mention to you where she was dining to-night?"

Hyacinthe's eyebrows and shoulders expressed a tendency to disclaim responsibility. "My mother? I did not see her since we arrive at the hotel. She was very tired, you know. I think perhaps she may have something to eat in her room."

"Do you?"

Hyacinthe looked up, meeting Ogle's eyes mildly, yet with what seemed to be a covert apprehension. "You think she went to some other hotel?"

"I don't know." And as it seemed apparent that if Hyacinthe knew he intended to look upon his knowledge as confidential and not to be imparted, Ogle let it go and tried something else.

"I wonder if you'd mind telling me——"

"Why, no," the youth said. His eyes met Ogle's again mildly, but with a faint surprise. "What is it you like to ask me?"

"Why did that Englishman, Broadfeather, fly off the handle at Bougie? What made him leave there two hours before we did?"

"Why? I thought my mother told you. He drank too much old wine, and it went into his head. We had to stop playing, and I think he must have been ashamed for my mother to see him again."

"What did he say when you stopped playing, Hyacinthe?"

"It was nothing," the boy said; but a faint colour came into his pale cheeks, and his lower lip was thrust forward slightly, producing an expression a little obstinate and a little scornful. "I did suppose my mother told you. He thought himself a great bridge player; and both at Bougie and at Michelet it was he who asked to play with us. At Bougie he had too much Beaune, and he was too confused to understand how he could be outmatched both evenings;—he said I counted wrong. How silly! As if I would do such a thing when there was no need! He is a third-class player; perhaps a fourth-class." Hyacinthe's colour heightened, and he reverted to something he had just said. "When I say I would never do such a thing when I am in a game with a fourth-class player, it isn't the same as to say I would ever do it."

"I understand," Ogle rejoined; and he added, though not with absolute conviction: "Of course not." Then it seemed that he divined something; —the one diversion of Mlle. Daurel and her sister upon the "Duumvir" had been to play cards against Hyacinthe and Mme. Momoro. "Your mother has told me something of your difficulties with Mademoiselle Daurel, Hyacinthe. She was angry with you much as the Englishman was, wasn't she?"

"Much," Hyacinthe said bitterly. "What she lives for, it is bridge and religion—and to make my mother unhappy! Me, I don't care, if that old woman would let my mother alone. My mother must never speak to anybody; she must be ready to run for something every moment like a lady's-maid; she must promise to become a religious. That is a terrible old woman! She makes you presents of a gold cigarette case or a fur coat, and you must give her your life! But never in money two sous! If you had money, you see, she thinks you might escape. What you have in money is the little you win at bridge at fifty centimes the point, and even at that she becomes insane, if you win   Well, what is there to do? She is a poor player, and you can't force her to win just to be obliging; because you can't afford it.

All you can do is to let her become insane and accuse you of everything disgusting! She was horrible in Algiers. I tell you I would refuse to let her adopt me now, even if she wished to! There are some things nobody can bear. I would refuse!"

He spoke with more vehemence than Ogle had heard from him; and there were gloomy lights in his dark and averted eyes as he made this final declaration, which was one his listener found somewhat informing. At least it confirmed the gossip of the *femme de chambre* at Algiers, and it strikingly did not confirm the account Hyacinthe's mother had given him of her quarrel with Mlle. Daurel. Evidently there were reticences really to the credit of both the mother and the son. The two did not plan deliberately together, saying, "Let us agree upon such and such a story"; they had been opportunists, but by no means plotters. Moreover, it was plain that their life at "Colline des Roses" had indeed been one of those purgatories known to the households of opinionated old rich women; that they had endured it in the hope of Hyacinthe's adoption and prospective inheritance; and that there had been a quarrel over the too great talent of this young Mozart of bridge. Something like desperation had been the result, and

Mme. Momoro had shown herself a dramatic artist in the moving presentation of partial truths.

Ogle did not press the boy to say anything more; he was sorry for him, in truth; and as for obtaining further enlightenment he was sufficiently sickened by what he had. It was enough: he could piece out the details from his dramatist's imagination, if he cared to; but he had no wish to engage himself in that occupation at present. Then Hyacinthe added something that startled him. "They are here, you know," the boy said quietly.

"Who are here?"

"Mademoiselle Daurel and Mademoiselle Lucie. They are at another hotel. They guessed that we would come to Biskra. The concierge gave my mother a note from them when we arrive this afternoon before she went to her room. They insist to see her at once."

Ogle stared at him. "Then that's where she's gone to-night."

Hyacinthe gave him a piteous look, wholly genuine. "If she is not in her room, it might be. I am afraid so." He swallowed painfully, and there was no doubt of his despair. "If she promise them for us to go back with them——" He rose abruptly as if he found it impossible to remain longer in a room full of people; then immediately he remembered his manners and sat down again.

"I beg your pardon," he said pathetically, "I did not notice you still have your dessert to eat."

XXIV

AS OGLE sat after dinner, finishing his coffee and beginning a cigar in the public room of the hotel, a long, orientalized apartment with a cosmopolitan population prevalently English, two ladies entered at a door and stood looking about them as if in search of a friend. More accurately, one of them wore the expression of a person looking for a missing friend, though apprehensively; while the other had the air of an aroused feudist trailing an enemy. Her dilated eyes swept fiercely over the room; her lips were bitterly compressed; her colour was that of war. She saw Ogle, who sat in profile to her, unaware of her; and after hurriedly conferring with her daughter, she departed swiftly by way of the door they had just entered.

Olivia came to a vacant chair beside Ogle and occupied it before he knew she was near.

"May I sit here a little while?" she said, and though she looked anxious, she smiled brightly upon him. "I've been instructed to find out something from you so tactfully that you won't think anything's gone wrong; but as you couldn't help knowing it anyhow I'm afraid my diplomacy may be thrown away. I'm going to obey my orders though, and I hope you'll admit afterwards that I've done it with tact."

"What is it I couldn't help knowing? I'm afraid there's not much I know;—I've come to that conclusion lately."

"Dear me!" Olivia laughed and shook her head ruefully. "What a very great deal you've changed! I suppose you think that's a spiteful thing to say, though, don't you?"

"No. From you I take it as the greatest flattery you're capable of. You've made it fairly clear that you'd regard any change whatever in me as an improvement."

"No. I shouldn't," she returned. "I know I've given you a right to think I'm that stupid, Mr. Ogle; but I'm really able to appreciate more things than you have any cause to guess I could. One of them was your smile when I spoke to you at dinner. It was heroic."

"You're a little severe," he said, and again produced the contortion.

But at this she made an outcry of protest. "Don't

try to do it again! It's like Hamlet trying to smile in the scene with his mother. You poor thing, does it upset you as much as that whenever your fascinating lady dines somewhere else?"

"I've told you before that she isn't 'my' fascinating lady."

"Well, she's certainly fascinating," Olivia explained; "and as you're travelling with her——"

He interrupted her. "Do you mind not putting it just that way? I happen to be motoring with her and her son."

Olivia assented cheerfully. "Yes, indeed! I forgot that she's so much older than she looks. You're really not much more than the age of her son, of course, while Madame Momoro is—well, almost a contemporary of my father's, for instance."

He frowned. "I don't know that I'd——"

"Will you make a bet?" she asked gayly. "My end of it is that she's at least five years nearer Papa's age than she is yours." Then without waiting for him to respond she went on: "That makes it all the more conventional for you to be motoring with them, of course. She's really a sort of motherly chaperone for you and her son."

"You're very kind to be so interested," he said

with sharp annoyance; and the gayety went out of her expression at once.

"You owed me that," she said quietly, "and I certainly deserved it. I'm afraid I'll have to admit even more. From the first, I've said hardly a word to you that hasn't been terrifically personal, and I realize my atrociousness thoroughly, Mr. Ogle. It mortifies me all you'd wish, when I'm alone and think it over."

Something in her tone, something genuine, hinting of real emotion, compelled him then; and for a moment they looked at each other frankly and with an odd, grave, friendly curiosity. "I don't wish any such thing," he said. "And as for being mortified about anything concerned with me, I'm not worth anybody's bothering that much."

She may have been tempted to tell him again that he'd changed a great deal; but she restrained herself, and merely nodded, once more smiling.

"I was bothering about myself, not about you; though since you speak of worth, you're worth bothering about any amount more than I am." And as he made a sound of protest, she checked him. "Why, certainly you are! You've done something in the world—your best; and all I've done has been to make myself disagreeable—my worst. We can't argue that! What I really want you to tell me now is the meaning of a word. Our courier is away to-night, or I'd ask him."

"What word?"

"I've heard it before, and I think it's Arabic; I'll show it to you in a moment, in writing—Papa's writing! This is the end of my tactful approach to the subject I'm to question you about. If you think I've led up to it properly, will you tell me where your fascinating friend is dining to-night?"

He was surprised. "I think she's at another hotel with the two old French ladies who were with her on the steamer."

"Do you?" Olivia said; and she seemed skeptical. "Did she tell you so—or did her son?"

"No. I had a note from her saying she wouldn't be joining him and me at table. She didn't say where she was going; but I have good reason to believe that she went to wherever those Frenchwomen are staying. She must have gone there very soon after we saw her come into the hotel with your father, before dinner."

Olivia shook her head. "She and Papa didn't come into the hotel."

"What?"

"No," she said. "My mother hurried down to meet him then; but the concierge said they had only stopped in the doorway a moment and then gone on."

"They did?"

"Madame Momoro left that note for you then. I heard the concierge telling my mother so when I got there."

"He was telling your mother——"

"Yes," Olivia said, and she looked at him gravely. "Mr. Ogle, would you be willing to give me a little help?"

"Of course."

"I thought you would," she said. "I'm afraid you do seem to be mixed up in it a little, besides, through being here with Madame Momoro. You see my mother got a note, too. It was from Papa, and it's really for Papa I'm asking your help."

"You want me to——"

"Wait," she said. "I'd better show you what he wrote to Mamma, if you don't mind, and after you've read it I think you'll agree with me that Papa's going to need help."

She had the note in her hand and gave it to him. He read it.

DEAR HON: I'll be in early but some parties I've got acquainted with in the hotel are waiting for me in quite a hurry and anyhow I don't want to wake you up if you're lying down. They want me to go eat dinner with them at a place where they have this celebrated Arab Koos Koos. So just as soon as this Koos Koos dinner is over I'll be back. You and Baby go right ahead and have your own dinner. Lovingly, Earl.

P. S. We may sit around and talk awhile after the Koos Koos, but anyhow I'll be in early.

When he had read this missive Ogle sat staring at it as he held it in his hand; then he asked her, "Is that the word you meant?"

"Yes. What he calls 'Koos Koos.' What in the world could he have meant?"

Ogle frowned as he explained. "Cous-cous is a dish of chopped meats and rice sprinkled with a kind of powder. I think the powder itself is called cous-cous. The Arabs are said to be fond of it—I loathe it myself." But there he spoke ungratefully, for when Mme. Momoro had taken him to eat cous-cous in Algiers just before their departure, he had praised the dish with honest fervour.

Olivia looked at him anxiously. "You see why his note might make my mother feel rather upset, don't you, Mr. Ogle?"

"I do," he said. "I do, indeed—under the circumstances."

"And since your—since Madame Momoro——"

He looked up at her grimly. "No; I don't think Madame Momoro is dining with her French friends. Not after reading this!"

"But you mustn't——" she began quickly, and stopped as abruptly.

"I mustn't what?"

"You mustn't misunderstand Papa, Mr. Ogle," she said earnestly. "I'm afraid you might. It's easy to see how long it would take a man like you to understand a man like him. I don't know if you *ever* could."

"Perhaps not."

"You see in the first place——" She stopped again; then she said impulsively: "You see you live in New York and that would make it almost impossible for you to understand how really *good* Papa is."

She was right about that, for Ogle's skepticism appeared to be elaborate, although he limited his comment to two words and spoke them quietly. "Is he?"

"Is he?" she cried. "He's more than good, he's innocent! He's childlike! The poor goose tells stories to my mother that an eight-year-old boy would know better than to tell in getting out of mischief he'd been up to. And the mischief Papa gets into is just as childlike. He's worked all his life like a galley-slave, and of *course* he has to be up to a little mischief now and then, just for a rest; but it's the most infantile mischief in the world. He wouldn't know how *not* to be innocent, and he absolutely adores Mamma. And Mamma——" She stopped again, and shook her head ruefully. "Well, Mamma——"

"Yes?"

"Well, Mamma *is* a little strict with him," Olivia admitted. "She didn't know what on earth this 'Koos Koos' meant, of course, in his note; and it's upset her terribly. She's nervous anyhow in this rather wild place, and Le Seyeux warned us not to go about much without him, especially after dark. So she's nervous about Papa's wandering around on that account; but a thing she just couldn't possibly understand would be his going out to dine with another woman, especially a woman she doesn't know, and above all a beautiful exotic person like this one. She couldn't understand that he'd be just flattered and interested by Madame Momoro's seeming a little flirtatious with him——"

"A little?" Ogle interrupted.

"Oh, dear!" Olivia exclaimed; and she uttered a laugh of lamentation. "That patting she gave the poor old goose on the shoulder! And he so blandly *pleased* by it—with Mamma looking straight at him and almost close enough to him to push a chimney over on him!" She laughed brokenly again, put her hand to her head, then let it fall helplessly in her lap, and became serious. "Mr. Ogle, I had the impression you meant to stay in Algiers. Would you mind my asking you if——"

"Ask what you wish to."

"Well, was it your idea—this motor trip you've taken that's brought her here?"

"No; it was hers."

"Then of course it's on Papa's account that she came."

"Yes," he said in a low voice, "I think so."

And upon this she looked at him compassionately. "I'm afraid that must have been a painful conclusion for you to come to."

"Well, a little," he said; and Olivia seemed to appreciate his honesty.

"We do get over these things—in time," she informed him gently. "I'm an example to you, though on the steamer and in Algiers I was a bad one.

However, I don't suppose you care to talk much on the subject, and anyhow we haven't time, if you're going to help me try to be of some use to Papa. Of course Madame Momoro has a special motive. Anyone could see at a glance that she's intelligent, and she wouldn't be absurd enough to think she could supplant my mother. She merely wants to get something out of him, as everybody else does."

"Everybody?"

"You'd think so," Olivia said emphatically, "if you lived with him. At home it's all day long, letters and telephoning; trustees after endowments; charities after him incessantly; old friends coming to him for 'help' and strangers coming to town to get him to go into 'movements' and businesses—it *never* lets up! Heaven knows what it costs him; *he* certainly doesn't! And over here—well, he's been like a sack of sugar spilled in the sun for the bees and ants. Even this Mr. Shuler wants him to put money into a coffee business he owns in Detroit! *Everybody* wants something, and why has this very finished and distinguished-looking Parisian lady followed him to Biskra if she doesn't——"

"Oh, certainly," Ogle interrupted gruffly. "You needn't elaborate it. It's conceded."

He did not look at her as he spoke, but sat staring under darkling brows at the wall before him, and Olivia, naturally resentful of the roughness with which he had spoken, drew herself up stiffly in her chair; then understanding better, she leaned a little toward him, and in a small and gentle voice said: "I'm sorry."

He did not respond to this Christian overture at once; and there was a silence between them.

They were the only occupants of the room now, except for a party of three Russian ladies, who were just rising from their after-dinner coffee and preparing to go forth. From the roadway outside there came the beating and squealing of tom-toms and oboes and a barbaric revelry of yelling: the dancing girls were passing in a torch-lit procession, headed by the negro conjuror, on their way to execute their contortions. Stirred by these sounds, suggestive of erotic and iridescent deviltries, the Russian ladies threw their wraps round them, and, laughing, hurried out, eager to miss nothing. Olivia and the sombre gentleman with her were left alone in the room.

"Yes," he said, when the Russians had closed the door, "I think I'm rather a fit subject for your contemptuous pity. I'm here in the position of a man who's escorted a lady to make an attempt to 'get something' out of your father."

"Poor Mr. Ogle," she said softly. "You do mix yourself a bitter drink to swallow, don't you? You'll have to exonerate me from feeling 'contemptuous pity' though; you know perfectly well it isn't contemptuous. The women in your play were the best things in it, I thought; and that makes me wonder what couldn't she do to Papa, if she can do all this to *you!* I'm afraid you're wasting time feeling sorry for yourself, because there's somebody to feel a great deal sorrier for than for you; and that's Papa. You don't know my mother, Mr. Ogle."

"I seem to be too busy getting to know myself a little!" Then, improving somewhat upon the tragic smile she had asked him to forego, he turned to her with an air as nearly brisk as he could make it. "You thought I could be of use to you. What do you want me to do?"

"You *are* kind," she said; and she nodded as if confirming to herself an impression there had once been some doubt about. Then she looked at him half humorously, half solicitously, and was reluctant.

"I hate to ask you to do it. I'm afraid it would be—well, at the best, embarrassing for you, and at the worst——"

"Don't mind what it might be at the worst. Either at its best or its worst, if you ask me to do it, I'll do it."

"Oh, dear!" she said; and so unexpected was the effect upon her of this impulsive statement of his that a quick high colour rushed in her cheeks;—for a moment her eyes were startled and almost tearful. "Did you really mean that?" She recovered herself, and laughed. "For two such unkind-mannered people, we do seem to be paying each other strange compliments! But I'll take you at your word and ask you to do it."

"What is it?"

Olivia glanced over her shoulder at the closed door of rose-coloured glass behind her, and she shivered. "Mother's waiting for me, and I've got to go and tell her what he meant by 'Koos Koos'; and you told me Madame Momoro was dining with those two old French ladies who were on the boat with her, and that's what I'll tell Mother you said. In the meantime, Papa's likely to walk in before very long with an account of his doings that will merely ruin him. Of course the poor thing hasn't the faintest dream we saw him with Madame Momoro—and that shoulder patting—or that we know they didn't come into the hotel except to leave those two notes. He's got to say that he just walked over to the French ladies' hotel with her and then went on to his 'Koos Koos' party." She choked, laughed, and seemed inclined to sob in the midst of her laughter. "When you think of him—coming back as he will, pleased to death with himself for being a dashing diner-out with a pretty lady and thinking that note of his has made everything all right for him—oh!" she cried, "doesn't it make you *shudder* for him? Do you think you *could* find them?"

"I don't know."

"I do hate to ask you," she said. "It's treating you rather awfully, I'm afraid—under the circumstances—to ask you to go out and break up Madame Momoro's little dinner-party. It might put you in a queer light with her, of course."

"I know. It doesn't matter."

Olivia gave him an appreciative smile for that, and her hand with it, as they both rose. "You'll *never* know how grateful I am! There aren't many hotels here, and I think you'll have to take one of those dragomen at the door. Just tell Papa you've come on an urgent message from me, and get him aside and tell him for heaven's sake not to deny he was walking with her before dinner. And tell him——"

She stopped abruptly. Before her there was a second door of rose-coloured glass, giving admission from the ground-floor corridors; and what checked her instructions was the opening of this door. The person who opened it was Tinker, a little flushed with his consumption of cous-cous, accompanied by Burgundy; in high fettle over his skittish performance, as Olivia had predicted; and also pleased, it might have been guessed, because of some charming things he had been hearing about himself. His comely broad face, pleasantly pink and smiling, brightened even more at the sight of his former table companion of the "Duumvir," and he advanced with a cordial hand extended. "Well, well, *well*, Mr. Ogle!" he exclaimed. "I'm mighty glad to see you again. I just been out to try some o' this celebrated Arab Koos Koos, and I certainly been havin' a grand——"

"Papa!" Olivia cried. "Go away from here. Go quickly!"

"What? What do you want me to go 'way for? What's the——"

Olivia turned quickly to Ogle. "Take him out in the street and tell him. Hurry!"

Ogle took a step to obey her.

But it was too late. The other rose-coloured door had opened and Mrs. Tinker was already in the room. "Earl Tinker!"

"Well, Mamma," he said fondly. "You got my note all right, didn't you, Hon?"

XXV

I DID, indeed," Mrs. Tinker answered dangerously. "Indeed, I did!"

"Well, *that's* all right then," he returned, beaming upon her. "That's fine!"

"Oh, it is?" she said. "Indeed?"

If he had needed warning other than that of her flushed, unsmiling face, it was in her voice; and undoubtedly he realized that all was not well with him domestically. In his hand he held a long cigar, just lighted, which he was about to place between his lips; but his hand wavered upon its way, and, coughing sonorously, he dropped the cigar upon an ash tray. Then, with the ostrich optimism of uneasy men confronted by such warnings, he offered mere loquacity as an alibi for himself and a sedative for her. "Well, I certainly am glad you got my note all right," he said heartily. "You see, I been kind of anxious to try some o' this Koos Koos for quite a while, and I didn't want to miss the opportunity. I didn't want you to worry about me or anything, of course; and I thought I'd like to give this Koos Koos a trial just once—you hear so much about it and all—I thought I'd just find out for once what there was *to* it. John Edwards has been at me all the way down here to get me to try some. 'You needn't eat it,' he says, 'unless you like it; but just give it a *try*,' he says. Well, I'll tell you about it, Mamma. I don't know whether you'd like it or not, because you haven't shown much appetite for these foreign dishes so far and been missin' home cooking so much and all; but the way *I* look at it——"

"I don't believe I care particularly to hear how you look at it, thank you," Mrs. Tinker interrupted. "Are you coming up to our rooms now?"

"Now?" Tinker said inquiringly, and he seemed to think it a debatable question. He still maintained at least outwardly the affable jauntiness with which he had entered the room; and nowhere in his expression or posture was there an admission that he perceived a hint of trouble in the air. "Now? Well, no. No, I believe not for a while, Mamma. I was thinking I'd just sit down here and have a nice smoke with Mr. Ogle. I tell you what *you* do, Honey: suppose you and Libby just slip up to bed, and Mr. Ogle and I'll——"

"No, thank you," she said. "I'll wait for you. Were you expecting to go out again to-night?"

"Me?" He laughed indulgently. "Why, where in the world would I——" Unfortunately, in his fond amusement, he extended his hand as if to pat Mrs. Tinker upon the shoulder.

She drew back, visibly incensed. "Kindly keep your hand to yourself! What makes you so interested in patting people on the shoulder all of a sudden?"

Tinker looked shocked. "Why, dearie!" he said reproachfully. "Why, Hon! Why, what in the world—why, what's disturbed you? You haven't been worried about me, have you, just because some gentlemen invited me to go and eat some of this celebrated Arab——"

Olivia uttered a half-choked outcry. "Papa! You——" But when he turned inquiringly to her, she found herself unable to be more explicit.

Ogle had brought his hat with him when he came into the room; it was upon an ebony tabouret near by, and he took it up. "I think I'll say good-night," he said.

But Tinker caught his arm, genially detaining him.

"Going out for a walk, Mr. Ogle? Well, that's a good idea. I believe I'll just——"

"I believe you'll not," Mrs. Tinker said. "Who were the gentlemen that invited you to dine with them?"

"Why, Honey, I explained all that in my note to you. I told you——"

"I know what you told me," she said. "Were they the same gentlemen that sent you a note when you were up on the roof?"

"Well—practically," he said. "Practically the same."

"And then you went walking with them, didn't you? You took a walk with them through these Arab streets around here, didn't you?"

"Around here?" he repeated, and, still retaining Ogle's arm with a firm right hand, he used his left to pass a handkerchief over his brow. Then he said reflectively: "Around here," and appeared to deliberate geographically. "It would seem so," he answered. "It was in this neighbourhood—practically."

"Who were the gentlemen? What were their names?"

"Names, Honey? Why, you wouldn't know 'em if I told you. There weren't but two of 'em anyhow —besides us."

"'Us'!" Mrs. Tinker cried, and she took a step nearer him. "Us? Who do you mean by 'us'?"

At that he laughed confidently and with the heartiest indulgence for a woman's fretfulness. The unfortunate man had just determined upon a bold and radical course of action. He had been standing near Ogle when Mrs. Tinker entered the room; he had continued to stand near him, and now held him familiarly by the arm. Ogle's hat was present, which appeared to be a strongly corroborative circumstance, and Tinker's own impression was that Ogle had just come in from some outdoor excursion and had stopped casually to talk to Olivia. Moreover, Mrs. Tinker's conception of their former table companion as a harmless, dull young man would now be of service: Ogle had taken no part in the early smoking-room gayeties or subsequent card games upon the "Duumvir" and she had spoken approvingly of him, on that account, to her husband. Tinker felt that he was about to achieve a little triumph.

"Us?" he repeated, continuing his easy laughter, and then, to his daughter's almost hysterical dismay, and to the horror of the owner of the arm he clasped, he explained heartily: "Why, Mr. Ogle and me. That's who I mean by 'us.' It's simple enough, isn't it, Mamma?"

"Indeed it is!" she returned; and she delivered a terrible blow. "Mr. Ogle was walking with you and those other gentlemen 'around here' while he was up on the roof talking to Libby this afternoon, was he?"

It staggered him, and his bright look began to fade pathetically. "Walking with me?" he said. "Walking with me? When do you mean, dearie?"

"I mean when you were walking with those gentlemen who invited you to dinner. Mr. Ogle was with you then, too, wasn't he?"

"Oh, you mean *then?*" Tinker exclaimed, and he brightened again, in his relief. "No, no! He wasn't there *then*. No! What I was talking about was only this Koos Koos affair. No; he didn't go *walking* with us."

"Are you sure? Are you sure it wasn't Mr. Ogle you were walking with?" She stepped closer to him, and her voice, growing louder and sharper, threatened to break. "Wasn't it Mr. Ogle you were sitting with up on the boat-deck all afternoon every day on the steamer? I'm *sure* it must have been Mr. Ogle that patted your shoulder for you on a public corner this afternoon."

He stared at her incredulously. "Patted my shoulder?" he murmured. "On a public corner?" It seemed to daze him that she should have used the word "public," and he repeated it as in deep perplexity. "Public? Did you say a *public* corner, Mamma?" Then, with a visible effort, he became reproachful and spoke with a quiet severity. "I'm afraid you're a little confused. I never said I sat on the boat-deck with Mr. Ogle or anybody else, or that he's been patting my shoulder on a public corner; and I should be pleased to be informed who's been talking such nonsense to you. I only alluded to Mr. Ogle's being at this Koos Koos affair."

"He was?" she cried. "You dare to stand there and tell me he was with you?"

Tinker's grasp of the playwright's arm tightened in one of those appealing signals not uncommon when men, battling with ladies, become desperate. "Why, I'll leave it to him, himself," he said. "*You* tell her, Ogle."

But Ogle was spared this suddenly projected ordeal; Mrs. Tinker uttered a cry of rage, and, relapsing into an easy chair, at once became vehemently hysterical. Olivia darted upon her, scolding her, exhorting her to remember that this public room was no place for emotional explosions, while Tinker stared goggling at the stricken woman, and said over and over, in pained remonstrance: "Now, Mamma! Now, Honey!"

She was stricken, but loudly voluble. "You turn your wicked eyes on *yourself!*" she cried. "Don't you look at me! Don't you *dare* look at me! You *awful* thing, don't you *dare* call me Honey! I'm not! I'm not! I'm *not*——"

She was screaming, and voices were heard outside. Olivia pointed to the door by which her mother had entered the room. "Get her upstairs," she cried to her father. "You can go this way, and probably nobody'll see you. Somebody's coming! Get her out!"

"Let me help," Ogle said, and moved toward Mrs. Tinker.

"Never mind, young man," Tinker returned brusquely. He reached his wife's side in two strides and stooped over her.

She beat him furiously with her open hands. "Don't you *touch* me! You let me alone! Don't you touch me, you terrible, terrible, *terrible*——"

"Open that door!" Tinker said sharply, and, as Olivia rushed to obey, he took his wife up in his arms as if she were of no weight at all, tossed her over his shoulder while she still beat him frantically, and strode out through the open doorway. Ogle, dumbfounded, had a last glimpse of them as they disappeared down an ill-lighted corridor toward a stairway: Mrs. Tinker's head and arms were swinging loosely upon the ruthless back of her husband, somewhat as if she had been a wild animal's skin worn by a savage chieftain. Her hair had come down, and she seemed in a state of collapse.

Olivia closed the door just as the concierge and an Arab dragoman opened the one opposite.

"Is something the matter?" the concierge inquired.

Olivia smiled pleasantly and shook her head. "No. Only some people laughing." And when the two men had withdrawn, she turned wanly to Ogle. "Too bad to let you in for this! But please do remember——" She stopped and half laughed, half sobbed. "Poor Papa! He's *so* outrageous—and so——"

"So what?"

"So *good !*" she said. "That's what I wanted you to remember—in spite of his outrageousness. But he's in for it now just as much as if he wasn't! Poor Mamma! What a terrible family you must think us!"

"I don't," he said honestly. "I'm too terrible myself to be thinking anybody else is."

"No, you're not." For a second she looked him lustrously in the eyes. Then she laughed lamentingly. "I must run after them, and see how many tortoise-shell hairpins I can find on the way."

"Couldn't I——"

"No, no!" She gave him her hand quickly, laughed again; and with an upward glance somehow imparting her meaning that she alluded to Mme. Momoro, "You have your own troubles," she said, and departed hurriedly.

XXVI

LAURENCE OGLE, having lain awake hour after hour that night in Biskra, finally fell asleep only to dream miserably. He was a Greek slave, he dreamed, a Greek from Syracuse, captured in battle by Punic mercenaries and sent down to work in the Desert with other slaves, brown and black and white, all of them sickly and drooping with weakness. The Carthaginians had decided to build a great city in the Sahara; but first the sand must be cleared away from the whole Desert, and that was the task of the slaves. Laurence himself had only a little tin spade and bucket to work with, toys such as children use in play at the seaside beaches in summer; and when he filled the bucket there was no way to empty it except to toss the sand up into the air: then the wind would disperse a little of it; but the rest fell back near him on the ground. Yet the task had to be done before the Master came. Fat black Nubians stood over the toiling slaves, cracking their whips and bellowing: "You git all that sand shovelled away before the Master comes!"

After an eternity of labour, with the awful spaces of waste land as sandy as ever, the Nubians all shouted together in a great voice: "He's coming! He's coming!" And the slaves cast themselves upon the ground, writhing as the silhouette of an advancing caravan appeared upon the horizon.

It came on, swift as light, thunderous with roaring drums and clanging cymbals; it was like a rolling purple cloud shot with scarlet and with flashing brass and silvered steel; the earth shook under the wild hordes of horsemen in flying red cloaks, camel-riders tossing bright-headed spears in the air, and black footmen in jackals' skins, running and leaping. But before them all charged a gigantic white elephant galloping like a horse. Upon his back, instead of a howdah he bore a great green globe, marked properly with the seven seas and the five continents; and upon the globe rode a stalwart, broad-faced man, standing at his ease. He was wrapped in a leopard's skin; but from the head of the leopard long human hair waved on the wind; and the man stood with his right arm extended, bearing a figure upon the palm of his hand, as antique statues sometimes bore a statuette.

But this figure was not a statuette: it was a tall woman, whose ivory-coloured robe was sculptured by the wind like the blown draperies of the Nike of Samothrace; and her immobile face was like white marble under her golden helmet.

Standing upon the hand of the man, who bore her without effort, her imperial gold head was in the pale blue sky and grew ever brighter and more and more dazzling as she was borne nearer. The black Nubians prostrated themselves, crying loudly, "The Master!" and Laurence stood alone in the sand, with his little tin shovel and bucket, directly in the path of the elephant. The broad-faced man upon the globe was laughing cruelly, he saw; but the woman upon his hand was expressionless and imperturbable. Her helmet blazed with a blinding and unbearable brightness, and then, just as the long tusks of the elephant touched the agonized dreamer's breast, that incredibly brilliant head, so high in the air above him, blew up. There was a dazing explosion; the sky filled with brazen arrows; and Ogle moaned in his bed, and rubbed his eyes. He had wakened himself by coughing.

It was one of those dreams that cling and make a day's mood. At breakfast in the sunshine by his window, he found himself drifting back into his nightmare fancies and again condemned to clear all the sand from the Sahara with a child's tin shovel; then, looking out of the window, he saw standing below, across the roadway, the big white camel Tinker had ridden into Biskra on his return from Sidi Okba in the rosy sunset of the day before. The sight of the great beast, placidly waiting for tourists, made Ogle shiver: he saw long and cruel tusks projecting from this innocent camel. For a weight as of horror was upon the young man's soul; and beneath it were layers of emotion, all uncomfortable: resentment, jealousy, the hot sense of being not only used but ill-used; and, hardest to bear, a furious kind of shame brought about by remembering that he had once thought himself a "man of the world"!

At noon he went for a walk eastward toward the Desert, hoping to dispel some portion of these humours in the strong sunshine; but, being alone, he was presently so beset by beggars and the pedlars of daggers that he turned back toward the hotel, more wretched than when he set forth. The Arabs turned back with him, increasing their importunities with every step; and although he gave money to the beggars and bought knives of the pedlars, the beggars whined the louder for more, and the pedlars instantly produced other knives, exactly like those he had bought, and, clamouring passionately, held them almost against his face. He was short with the harpies and pushed them from him, only to have them cunningly press closer against him until the dirt and smell of them were unbearable. He halted and swore vehemently—a performance ideal in its futility, since to the recipients of his curses he was but making sounds that indicated their success. Experienced, and pathetically in need of what he could give them, they knew that they had only to persist; for this man with the angry dark eyes was small and neat, of a kind that would always give more if sufficiently pressed upon and handled. He did give more, after his encouraging profanity; and for a moment he broke away as they paused to squabble over the loot. He walked rapidly, almost running; then they were again hurrying after him, and he recalled with regret that Hyacinthe had forgotten to teach him the Arabic phrases with which the youth had dispersed a similar tormenting group.

Warned by the blatting of an automobile horn behind him, he sought the side of the road; and a superb French closed car rolled by, all fleckless black and crystalline windows, with a European chauffeur and a white-robed Arab servant on the box, and Mlle. Lucie Daurel and Hyacinthe himself in the enclosure. Ogle had only this glimpse of them; but his impression was that Mlle. Lucie's eyes were tearful and that Hyacinthe looked tragically harassed, yet obstinate, as if she were pleading and he refusing. The automobile left the pedestrian obscured in a turmoil of dust, and when he emerged from it his tatterdemalions were upon him again.

They clung to him until he reached the long arcade of the hotel veranda, maddening him, so that he went into the building and into the great *salle à manger* in a dumb fury; and in that same sort of fury ate his lunch, alone. Few people were in the room; the table where Olivia had sat the night before was unoccupied; and neither Mme. Momoro nor her son made an appearance. But just as he had finished his meal and was about to rise, Hyacinthe came in and sat down at the table. He bowed formally in the respectful way he had with Ogle; but he smiled as he bowed, which was unusual; and the cheerfulness of his pale face was noteworthy: never before had Ogle seen him look cheerful.

"I have a message for you from my mother, if you please."

"What is it?"

"She has *déjeuner* in her apartment; but I think she
will be finished by this time.   She told me to find you
and ask if you will be so kind and come to see her
there."

"Now?" Ogle asked, rising.

Hyacinthe jumped up and made his quick bow
again.   "If you will be so kind?"

"I will," the American said grimly, and, without
adding anything to that, he walked away.   He had
begun to breathe rapidly and deeply, his great desire
being for a final interview with Mme. Momoro—as
there were some things he wished to say to her.   He
had been rehearsing them in his mind all morning,
and even when he was cursing the Arabs phrases
were developing in the back of his mind for this last
interview.

He wished her to know definitely his reasons for
closing the episode of their friendship and parting
with her forever.   At the end he would say: "I have
one last means of convincing you that I understand
you, Madame Momoro.   I am sure you are already
aware that Mr. Tinker and his party are going from
here by easy stages to Tunis; I am returning by rail,
myself, to Algiers.   I wish you and your son to take

the automobile we have travelled in and use it as you originally planned, though without my own unnecessary society. You will be able to see your friend and continue your campaign at every stage—unless his wife prevents. You need give yourself no uneasiness whatever in accepting this slight continuation of hospitality: the expense of the automobile and chauffeur has already been provided for, through to Tunis." So bitter he had become, he found himself not only capable of saying such things, but trembling with impatience to say them; for, as he left the dining-room, he was in truth trembling.

To go to the stairway he had to pass through a corridor where there stood a counter covered with postcards, photographs, trinkets, and Arab knives, souvenirs for which the concierge acted as salesman. Leaning upon the counter, and engaged in conversation with this personage, Tinker was pointing out some civic deficiencies of Biskra.

Whatever the place may have lacked, he himself proved to eye and nose that it possessed a barber. Within twenty feet of him anyone would have known that if here was a man in bad odour with his family, he had sought to alter that condition by the most direct and immediate means possible, so powerful was what the barber had mingled with his new-cut hair. He was shaved intensively, pomaded, brushed, massaged, powdered, and almost holy-stoned. Never had such sleekness appeared upon every inch of him; and if at the same time there was something subdued about him, something a little baffled and spiritually sat upon, some hint of the fugitive temporarily at large, he was still able to offer municipal advice from heaven's most favoured spot, the one cherished and perfect city at the heart of the world.

"What you need here is a good, live, snappy Board o' Health," he was saying to the concierge. "You take all these smells, for instance—why, over at that town where I was yesterday there wasn't anything *but* smell, practically! In Algiers I ran across a smell I thought had anything *I* ever smelled stung to death, poisoned, coiled up in a knot and laid away to rest. Why, if a smell like that broke out in *my* town, we'd build a gas-works over it and sell it by the cubic foot to the War Department. But I see now I was just fresh from God's Country when I was in Algiers. I didn't really know what could be done in the line of smells and rags and sores on people. This Siddy Whatcha-call-it place could give the Arab quarter in Algiers cards and spades and just sit back and laugh!

Why, in my town you can sit down anywhere in the city and eat ice-cream right off the street pavement with a silver teaspoon! In my town you could offer an Irish setter a life job with a fee of five thousand dollars for every smell he could find within a radius of twenty miles from the heart of the city and he'd die in the Poor House not worth a nickel! In my town——"

Here, seeing Ogle approach, he stopped short, and his expression became solemn; he left the concierge and went to meet the young man. "I certainly had a wonderful busy night of it!" he said. "You happened to see Babe anywhere this morning?"

"No, I haven't."

Tinker rubbed his scented and glistening head. "I just wondered if she'd *said* anything to you, maybe. She certainly hasn't to me. Maybe she thinks her mother's sayin' enough, and I guess she *is*. Murder!" He moaned slightly and turned to rejoin the concierge; then an after-thought stopped him. "Listen," he said. "What's an impresario?"

Ogle looked at him strangely; but replied without giving any other evidence that the question inspired a train of thought. "A manager of an opera company, or of concerts, or a musical conductor. Why?"

"Nothin'. It's just one of those words a person keeps hearin' all his life and never *does* know what it means, unless he asks somebody. I heard a little about one last night, and I thought I'd ask; that's all."

"Last night?" Ogle said; and there was a gleam in his eye. "You mean after I saw you?"

"After *that?*" Tinker groaned. "My soul, no! My folks weren't talkin' to me all night about impresarios!" He took the young man by the coat lapel. "Listen! I got to go back up to our rooms in a minute;—I been out of 'em longer now than there's any safety in. I got an idea I may be leavin' here for some other place in about an hour; I haven't been told yet, and I know better'n to ask for any *say* in the matter—under the circumstances. Murder, no! But if I'm still here by evening, for heaven's sake send up and see if I'm alive, and if I am, say you got to see me on business, or to go to a fire, or *anything*. And listen! Did you see that petrified man up in the museum at Algiers that they boiled in tar or something? What did they do that to him for?"

"He was a Christian martyr, I believe."

"Is that all?" Tinker said. "Golly! I thought maybe he went out and ate some o' this Arab Koos

Koos with a woman his wife didn't know, or something serious like that. Anyhow, *he* got off *easy*—comparatively!"

Again he would have turned away; but he was arrested by the pallid appearance of his young acquaintance. "What's the matter with you?" he asked. "*You* haven't got anybody to boil you in tar if you break away and eat dinner out, one night in your life, have you? You look like a man that's goin' to be sick."

Ogle shook his head. "The change of climate, perhaps," he said; and he moved to the stairway.

Tinker was solicitous. "Listen! Don't go and get sick 'way off here away from home and everybody like this. You let me know if you feel anything comin' on, young man, and I'll look after you."

His hearty voice showed a friendly concern, and his solicitude was evidently genuine; but Ogle returned only an indistinct "Thank you," and went on up the stairs. A moment later, when he opened the door of Mme. Momoro's salon, upon her bidding, he was even paler than he had been.

XXVII

SHE stood near a window, where she had been watching the fantastic life of the roadway below; and neither Diana of Poitiers nor Mlle. de L'Enclos, nearest and most famous rivals of Aurélie Momoro, could have looked more imposingly and mysteriously beautiful in a brown travelling suit made by a modern tailor. Travelling bags, packed and locked, were upon a table, and the two fur coats she had with her during the excursion by motor hung over the backs of two chairs.

She gave Ogle a smile somewhat inscrutable, though there seemed to be a wistfulness about it. "Come to the window for a moment," she said. "A long caravan is just passing; shaggy old camels and worn-out donkeys and lean goats and dogs—Nomads coming in from far down in the Desert. You must see them."

"No, I thank you," he said, and, after looking at him quickly, she turned from the window to face him; but she no longer smiled.

She waved a hand already gloved toward the travelling bags and fur coats. "I am leaving you, my friend, you see."

"Are you? Do you think your other friend will be able to get away?"

She looked at him again, longer this time. "Let us sit down, if you please," she said; and they sat, facing each other. "What 'other friend' do you speak of?"

At that the pale young man laughed harshly. "How absurd! I met him downstairs not five minutes ago and he told me he might be leaving this afternoon—'in about an hour,' he said. He was waiting to be told. Haven't you sent him word of his good fortune yet?"

"What good fortune?" she asked, and she frowned. "Upon my word, I understand you no more than if you were speaking in Magyar, a language I haven't acquired. What do you mean to be saying to me? Who is it you saw downstairs?"

"Merely the man you came all this distance to meet."

At that, the faintest pinkness in the world overspread her composed features. "Why do you say such things? You are angry, my dear."

"Please don't call me that!"

"Very well," she said, with a little agitation. "It hurts me that you are angry with me. You have meant to be kind to me; I have wished to be kind to you. But, no! At the last moment you are in a fury. Yes: anyone could see it; you are white with fury. Do you know how pale you are? Why should you be in a rage with me?"

"I don't know that I'm in a rage with you," he answered heavily. "It seems to me that my rage is with myself."

She shook her head. "I think not. Women have those rages with themselves sometimes, I think it is true; but men possess a great talent for pardoning themselves everything. What you wish to say, I think, is that you complain of me and that you hate me. What for? What have I done to you?"

"You ask that?" he said with bitterest meaning.

"Why should I not ask it? Ah, I know well enough what you wish to say, Mr. Ogle; but because you feel that a gentleman wouldn't say it, you will not put it into spoken words from your mouth." She had begun to show greater agitation; her long hands clasped themselves tightly together in her lap, and her voice became louder. "What is the difference between saying it and thinking it? Are you a better gentleman if you have such things in your heart to charge me with, but do not speak them?"

"I charge you with nothing."

"No, not with your spoken words," she said. "But to me, isn't it the same? Wait! Don't speak! I will say them for you. You are telling me in your heart that I have accepted everything and given nothing, that you have done all for me and I nothing for you. Well, I tell you that is not true. You even think that I have borne nothing from you; and I tell you that is another thing that is not true."

"What have you 'borne' from me?"

"You ask me that!" she exclaimed, thus turning his own reproach upon him; and she sprang to her feet, looking so tall, as she stood before him, that her head seemed almost as high above him as had the golden head in his uncomfortable dream. "What haven't I!" she cried. "What haven't I borne!" And she began to walk up and down the room with her hands pressed against her temples. "What haven't I!"

Nothing could have surprised him more completely; he had not come to be put upon the defensive; but already he found himself inexplicably in that unfortunate posture. "Didn't you just tell me I had been kind to you?"

"I said you had meant to be. There is a difference. You were kind in your own intention, and I would have liked to part with you letting you think that your intention made a real kindness. But you wouldn't have it like that; you are come to me hatefully, full of accusations in your mind, and so I am willing to tell you that some kindnesses can be torture."

"My kindness to you, I suppose you mean?"

"A thousand times I mean it!"

He had risen, too, and stood beside his chair, looking at her as she paced swiftly up and down the room. "I suppose you'll tell me why."

"Indeed I will." She came and faced him. "From the moment we began to go up into the mountains of Kabyle you assumed the attitude of an unwilling person who has been tricked into doing what he doesn't wish to do. Day after day you have kept that attitude. You would sit saying nothing at all, and always with that peevishness upon your face. Ah, yes, it was! Peevishness! And I was your guest; but you made me earn my way! I must entertain you; I must be always charming! I must get that peevishness out of your face! Do you know how a woman feels when she must sit all day beside a peevish man, trying and trying and trying to make a pleasanter expression show itself upon his face? No, of course not; no man can know such things! But I tell you when we have arrived here in Biskra I was exhausted with the struggle. Not with the days of driving—that could have been a delight—but with the effort to earn my way as your guest by making you cheerful. One more day of that, and I would be ready to cut my throat! I had enough of it, my friend, before we began this journey: I had enough of it in the house of Mademoiselle Daurel, and it is what I would give my life to escape from. And what right had you to be peevish with me?"

"See here," he began huskily. "I asked nothing of you——"

"Ah! Didn't you?" She interrupted him with a sharp and bitter outcry. "All you asked was a complete supervision of my affairs, and on what ground?"

"What?" he said; for she confused him.

"You were jealous of me, just as that old woman was jealous. Do you deny it?"

"I do, emphatically. When was I——"

"What?" she cried. "Even that absurd old Englishman with his little round wife at his elbow every second; you couldn't endure that I should spend a moment with them. At Bougie and when we left there you were unbearable. You think I presume too much in calling it jealousy; but that is what you showed me. I should know jealousy when I see it, by this time."

"Yes," he said. "I should think so, Madame Momoro."

She took his full meaning, and her colour still deepened. "You are kinder than ever, since you imply that I've seen it so often. Well, if I have, it is somesing I comprehend very well, and I will tell you that nothing is commoner than jealousy without love. You have felt it for me, and I think you feel it now; but you were never in love with me, my friend."

"How do you know?"

"Because that is another thing I have unfortunately seen often enough to comprehend a little. You had jealousy, but no more. You had——"

"Let me tell you what I had," he interrupted roughly. "I had jealousy, yes; but it was not of you."

"No?" She laughed aloud. "It wasn't? You were not in love with me; but wasn't I to pay you for this journey by never thinking of anybody but you? You were to have all of me that is worth anything; you were to have all of my thoughts. If I thought of anything else you were enraged. You don't call that jealousy?"

"Not of *you*, I said."

"Then of what?"

"It was of——" His voice began to tremble; he bit his lip, and sank down in his chair, with his elbows on his knees and his head in his hands. "It was of my ideal of you!" he groaned.

She was far from being mollified by this definition;—on the contrary, she spoke with repressed but sharpened hostility. "Of your 'ideal' of me? Will you condescend to explain yourself?"

"I thought—I thought you were above every human sordidness," he said miserably. "I thought you were—I thought you were the highest and brightest—well, if I must talk like a schoolboy to make it clear, I thought you were the most goddess-like creature I'd ever seen. But what I found——"

"Pooh!" she said, startling him with abrupt laughter. "You know nothing of yourself and nothing of what you thought; but I am a woman of some experience and I can tell you what you thought and what your 'ideal' of me is worth. Your 'ideal' was a woman who appreciated Mr. Laurence Ogle. What you thought was that such a 'goddess-like' creature could never prefer a man like Mr. Tinker to a man like Mr. Laurence Ogle! In that is all your trouble, all your peevishness and all your disappointed emotion now, my friend, all of it!"

"What?" He looked up, staring at her. "You tell me——"

"I tell you the truth. It is time! Don't you think so?"

He rose again. "Yes," he said slowly, "I suppose it must be a luxury, now that you feel you've no more use for me."

At that she drew a deep breath, and her eyes concentrated upon him dangerously. "I must ask you to explain yourself again."

"I'm only making it clear that I understand the situation."

"What 'situation'?"

"You came here to find him, and now that you have found him indeed, you can dispense with me;

I was only a convenience by the way. He's preparing to leave and you're preparing to leave."

"You think," she inquired, "we are preparing to leave together—Mr. Tinker and I?"

"I don't know. Possibly not. But wherever he goes, I think——"

"You think he'll find me in Tunis, perhaps, at the end of his automobile journey?"

"I should think it very probable, Madame Momoro."

"And if he did, that is your affair?"

"Not at all!"

To his astonishment tears appeared in her eyes; but they were tears of anger. "You see you have the power to incense me," she said. "I must use a harsh word: it is your stupidity that does it—that unbelievable stupidity women ought to expect from jealous men, but never do, because it *is* unbelievable. You say it is not your affair what I do, and at the same time you make it your affair by accusing me. You are not in love with me; you say all that angers you is my destruction of your 'ideal' of me, and you stand here looking at me like Death, furious with me because you comprehend no more what is in your own heart than you do what is in mine."

"What is that?"

"What is in mine, at least, is my own affair," she said. "What is in yours—well, I must use another harsh expression: it is nothing in the world but a vanity that has been damaged."

"Because you prefer——"

"Yes," she said bravely. "Because you see that anybody would prefer him to you."

But at that, Ogle broke into helpless and painful laughter. "You call me stupid, and you think I'm all injured egoism—I see you really do think it— and I don't know why I still care to try to make you understand what I feel. You think I'm piqued merely because you've made me a convenience and because you preferred to ask him to help you out with your plan for Hyacinthe instead of asking me. By the way, why didn't you? I'd have given it to you."

"You'd have given me what?"

"What you needed to set Hyacinthe up in that impresario's office. Why didn't you ask me?"

"*Ask* you for money?" she said, and her stare at him was as blank as the tone in which she made that inquiry. "Why didn't I?"

"Yes. Why didn't you? I'd have given it to you."

For a moment she was silent; then she said: "You think—you think I have asked Mr. Tinker to give me the money for Hyacinthe?"

"I don't know about your asking. I think you may have mentioned the need for it."

"As I did to you," she said quietly. "But I did not dream of such a thing from you—nor did you."

"But from him——"

"You think he has given it to me?"

"Either that, or he will," Ogle answered. "Yes, I think it extremely probable. I think that's why you're following him."

"Following!" she echoed; and she looked down on him from her fine height. "You use such words, Mr. Ogle!"

"I'm using only what words seem true to me," he said unhappily. "I've been trying to make you understand that a man can suffer more from a damaged ideal than from a damaged vanity."

"How has your 'ideal' of me been so damaged?"

"How? Why, upon my soul!" he cried. "To have thought of you as I did think of you, and then to see that you had just one sordid idea in the world! To see——"

But she interrupted him fiercely. "Sordid? Is it

sordid to wish to escape from hell? Is it sordid for a mother to do anything—anything in the world—to try to get her child out of that same hell? Is it sordid——"

"You admit it then."

"I admit what?"

"That you have followed this man, this gross——"

"Who is that?" she asked coldly. "Who is 'gross'?" Then she sat down, folding her arms and looking at him from beneath half-lowered eyelids. "You needn't say any more, my friend. You make what you feel about him perfectly clear."

"'What I feel about him'!" Laurence echoed in sharpest scorn. "What do you feel about him, yourself? What does anybody feel about him? You know what he is as well as I do."

"What is that?"

"A great barbarian."

"Yes," she said quietly. "That is what I thought of him when I first saw him on the steamer. I saw him in that light—a great barbarian, precisely. I saw him in the most amusing contrast to you and your two little friends."

"What?"

"Wait!" she said, speaking louder, and she opened

her eyes widely, looking at him steadily. "You must listen now. He is a great barbarian, not caring a sou what anybody in the world says of him, not thinking about himself at all. He is a great barbarian with great power. Power? That is money, my friend, and nothing else. Money has always been power; and people who don't know that, understand neither power nor money. He is as careless of his power as he is of everything else. Do you remember how he won that money on the ship and threw it away, and how he bought all the fruit in the boats at Gibraltar, and tossed it to those poor people in the steerage? And in Algiers, you don't know how many people talked of what he had given; and here in the Desert he has been raining money like some great careless thunder-cloud charged with silver and gold and pouring them down. Wherever he goes the people are on their knees to him, and there is a rain of money. He——"

But Ogle could endure no more. "Yes, they are on their knees to him indeed—for money!"

She sprang to her feet. "You see nothing!" she cried. "They respect him! They look up to him!"

"Yes—for his money! As you do!"

She leaned down, so that her face was near his,

and she answered him fiercely. "As I do? You say that bitterly, because your vanity is in ruins, not because you had any right to make some silly 'ideal' of me. You say that of him so bitterly because you began by thinking him a nothing, and ever since then you have seen yourself growing smaller and smaller while he grew larger and larger until now you know he is a colossus. You accuse me of following what any woman would be proud to follow and what no woman could make follow *her!* You say we respect him and get on our knees to him for his money. What have *you* to offer? Anything? As an American you are absurd. Don't you know what we really think of you? What *else* have you to offer us that we can go down on our knees before? What do we respect *any* of you for except for your money?"

She overwhelmed the wretched young man who had so strangely misunderstood her until now; she daunted and dismayed him. He stepped back from her, staring incredulously. "What?" he gasped. "You *say* it! You say——"

"Yes!" she cried. "Once! I say it once, but not again." She followed him as he stepped backward from her. "I want you to go now; the porters will be here for my luggage, and you will be in the way. If you think of me after this, regretting the expense of our excursion together, please remember I have done my best. In return, I have given you at least part of an education."

He came back a step toward her. "And I'd like *you* to remember——"

"No! No!" she cried. "Not another word! The last is said." And as he persisted, trying to speak, she took him by the shoulders, pushing him toward the door. "No! No! No! The last is said, I tell you! If you don't go——" She began to laugh loudly, and, as she opened the door and pushed him into the corridor, "You dear little fool!" she cried. "If you don't go, I'll tell you how old I am!"

Then the door closed sharply upon her continuing laughter.

XXVIII

ALL that day there were no tourists for the great white camel to carry, nor any for the two tall brown camels, also of superior breed, his companions in waiting. The white camel was not actually white, the colour of his fine long hair being old ivory deepening to creamed coffee; but he was famed as "the white camel" and so called by the Arabs and by the travellers who came to this oasis. Moreover, the white camel was distinguished among his kind not only for his colour, but for his voice. The voice of any camel has a wide range in pessimistic eloquence; beyond question a camel has a vocabulary and can say many things, all of them discontented. Without flattery it can be said that this master of patience is at the same time the world's supreme artist in the expression of discontent—a seeming paradox hinting that at least the one virtue is not its own reward—and discontent is always inharmonious. No one has ever thought the camel's utterance musical; in it there is too much that is prehistoric, and, in spite of his long association with man, too much that is uncultivated. It was an oriental ear, accustomed to the painful speech of camels, that rejoiced in a perfect contrast when the voice of the turtle was heard in the land.

Compared to the voice of the white camel the voices of other camels were the voices of doves; and it is difficult to resist the impression that he recognized his own talent and frankly wished for the applause of the many. Throughout all this bright February afternoon the dissonances of his querulous oratory caused acute anguish to a person whose suffering was already sharp enough without any assistance from camels. Laurence Ogle's open windows in the second story of the hotel were directly opposite the white camel's station across the road, and not sixty feet away, whereas the white camel was easily audible at six hundred. The afflicted gentleman lay upon his bed fevered and prostrated by an outrageous headache that had come upon him almost without warning during those last brief moments of tragi-comedy at Mme. Momoro's door. Stumbling away after his expulsion, he realized that his own head, not her golden one, was the scene of an explosion; and thus he had gone woefully down the corridor to his own room; and there he fell at once upon his hed.

His windows, long doors of glass, were open, and for a little time he preferred them to be so; then, as his head grew worse, the ejaculations of the white camel became blows of pain. He would have risen to close the windows and shut out a little of the sound; but the mere thought of lifting that stricken head of his was unendurable; he could only lie upon his back and do his wincing by clenching his hot hands. Even the light buzz of the tiny flies in the screenless room brought added pain; and when he half opened his dreary eyes he could see them, dozens of hateful little egoistic specks of life, irregularly circling about his chandelier. The chandelier was of brass, somewhat dulled, and he wished that it might have been of any other metal, except pale gold.

Twice during that purgatorial afternoon there were great commotions outside. The first was the result of inspirations derived from the white camel by two passing donkeys and an Arab dog. The two donkeys brayed, beginning their uproarious protests with the suddenness of unpremeditated murder; the two brown camels added their raw voices to that of the white one; and the dog barked with a falsetto passion of shrillness in regular half-second intervals until even the ears and temper of some stoic Arab were impaired; the dog completed his staccato with a shriek that became faint in distance abruptly achieved. This was only a casual disturbance among the lower orders, however; but the second one, not long after the first, had a basis of human intent and calculation. Automobile engines racked the air before the principal doors of the hotel, just below Ogle's room; there was a thumping as of trunks upon the roof of a closed car; porters were noisy in argument; there were many outcries of Arabs and French together, and a tom-tom approached hurriedly, growing louder, accompanied by a stentorian negro voice incessantly bellowing "*Hi! Hi! Hi!*" There was then the sudden yelling of a crowd, as upon the consummation of some expected great appearance, and then the tinkling of many thrown coins and a wild laughter that astonished the agonized listener above. Were Arabs laughing? If they were, it was the first time he had heard them.

The automobile horns blatted insistently; the acute Arab yelling became impassioned; more and more coins tinkled. French voices cried, "Merci! Merci,

monsieur!" and "You come soon back, please!"
Then the little horns were heard from a distance;
the tom-tom thumped jubilantly away toward the
Arab quarter, growing fainter;—only the white camel
did anything obnoxious; and the neighbourhood
settled down to phlegmatic eventlessness in the warm
February sunshine.

The sufferer understood that a stirring and unusual
departure had just taken place; it might possibly
have been Orthe the Eighteenth and the Princess;
but the dimensions of the disturbance indicated
something much more important. Ogle became
convinced that Tinker and his family had just set
out upon their journey to Tunis.

After nightfall, when a *valet de chambre* came to
his room, he had the man bring him some tablets of
aspirin, and so presently slept; but when he awoke
in the morning he was still feverish, though of the
pain in his head there remained only a dulled reminiscence. He felt weak, and, having no interest in
anything he might accomplish by rising, remained
in bed. However, he sent to the bank agency for
his letters and at noon they were brought to him
upon a tray of toast and coffee. Only one was of
importance to him, and that was the only one he

opened;—it was from the manager of "The Pastoral Scene."

DEAR MR. OGLE: I suppose by the time you get this if you have been receiving the New York papers you will not be surprised to hear that the bottom fell out of our business pretty disappointingly. None of us here expected anything of the sort from the way it went at the start and it is only another warning that in this business you never can tell. After those big weeks we started with and even doing fine business the worst week in the year when every one of the best attractions fell off worse than we did just before Christmas there wasn't a man in our office wouldn't have bet all he owned that we were set for a full season and probably two. Of course we realized our advance business had not developed the way it ought to but the way the box office showed up every night right along we were absolutely positive the advance would be coming in strong right away.

Well you can't account for it unless it was just that the public satisfied its curiosity and we didn't have enough to hold them after that. There have been 17 openings in the short space of time since our own and they all hurt our business more or less. Some of them are freak shows that arouse more curiosity than ours but everybody is going to them just now to see if they can guess what they mean and others of the new shows are so raw that if we were getting people in on that account these new ones are so much rawer that they're getting them all. Anyhow the whole theatrical situation is bad, except for a very few. Both of Geo. Ebert's productions are already in the storehouse and most of these 17 new ones will be there soon as well as some of the old standbys.

I hope you will not think our hard luck is due to any lack of effort on my part. I had faith in your play and I still think that if the theatre would have shown a more liberal policy about the guarantee we might have pulled it out. But we had to do over 10,000 to stay as I am in no position to stand any more drain on my resources and I am out a pretty heavy loss on the venture. When the theatre wouldn't abate a cent on the guarantee they made me give them there was nothing else to do but let the company have their notices. Of course it is no use trying to do anything on the road.

As we are closing next Saturday night and it looks like a business of only about 3,300 this week unless the Sat. business pulls it up a little your royalties of course will be pretty small. This is a personal disappointment to me, as I had hoped and fully expected to be sending you big checks to spend over there but as a matter of fact I will probably have to borrow about $4,000 myself to clean up. If anything goes through to pull us a little way up out of this deep hole I will let you know but present prospects would not warrant any great confidence in it.

I will send you a complete statement in a few days but as you would probably like to know how we stand I will give you a rough idea. I advanced you $1,000 on acct. future royalties the Sat. before you sailed as you will recall everything being squared between us to that date. This left you owing me the $1,000 advanced which we both fully expected would be practically covered by the next week's royalties, but that was the week we had the drop. I figure that the total royalties due you by Sat. night next when we close will amt. to about $750 to $800 which will leave you owing me between $200 and $250 or somewhere around there. Anyhow you will receive the complete box office statement very soon after this and you can remit me the exact amt. at your convenience.

I am sorry I haven't better news, but we are all pretty down in the mouth about this and the only thing we can say is that it is just the luck of the theatrical business and nobody's fault. I would add that I have not lost faith in yourself and any time in the future if I am in a position to produce a new play and you have a script to submit I will be glad to give it my best consideration. With all good wishes I remain

Yours faithfully,
Jos. Lehren.

Ogle relapsed upon his pillow. "That's the answer!" he murmured. "I've written for the Few, after all!" And the sound of his whispered laughter might have driven a nervous listener from the room.

He had counted upon a noble brood of chickens because the first had been hatched so prettily; but, after the first, no more at all were hatched; and his mistake was serious. He had assumed with unquestioning confidence that Lehren would be sending him weekly drafts from New York—large, comfortable sums such as those few first generous weeks had produced; he had felt no doubt in the world that he would receive them regularly for a length of time so pleasantly indefinite that it had appeared to his sanguine youthfulness as virtually permanent. At least it had appeared permanent enough for him to indulge himself with one of the more expensive cabins on an expensive steamer and to embark upon an elaborate voyage with his supplies actually in hand limited to a small letter of credit—a provision just amply sufficient until his drafts should begin to arrive from Lehren. But now, until he could write another play and get it "on," or do other kinds of writing there would be nothing. Moreover, he had paid M. Cayzac for the automobile and the chauffeur's expenses through to Tunis in advance; the hospitality he had extended to a luxurious lady and her son had been far from niggardly; and upon his letter of credit there now remained at his disposal the sum of sixty-seven dollars.

Out of this and some French money in his pocketbook he must settle his account at the hotel, which doubtless would include that of Mme. Momoro and her son, since they had been his guests in this inclusive manner throughout the excursion. Then he must get to a seaport, either Algiers or Tunis, and thence to Marseilles or Naples by sea, and still have enough money left to pay his passage back to New York. This was his immediate problem and the answer appeared to be of an overwhelming simplicity;—it could not be done.

What employment, he wondered, could be found among the Saharan oases by an American playwright who knew but the one trade and had failed at that?

How long did it take to become sophisticated as a
camel driver? Could he write realism for the Ouled
girls to play, since they were indeed realists too,
though their ambition was frankly for the Many?
And then, remembering his first talk with the poet
and the painter in the smoking-room of the "Duumvir," when they had all three posed for the statu-
esque French lady and for one another, airing themselves and their nonsense about Art, the prostrate
Laurence groaned in sickened revulsion. It was
that ancient bit of naïveté, "For the Few," that
brought this sound of nausea from him; and again
his whispered laughter competed with the buzzing of
the tiny Biskra flies about his chandelier. For, in
his misery, he had at last asked himself a sardonic
and distinctly clarifying question: What "Few" had
he written for? Who actually were those Few? In
the name of heaven, what did he care for *Macklyn!*

A few minutes later he laughed once more the same
self-cauterizing and voiceless laugh, for he recalled
his grandiloquent bitterness of yesterday when he
had told the faithless lady that he would have given
her the money to establish Hyacinthe as an impresario, if she had asked him for it. He had been
gloomily pleased with himself at the moment, as he

realized now; he had thought to show her something of the scorn of an Armand hurling gold upon the crushed lady of the camellias, though with the background difference that there was no golden shower and that she wasn't crushed. Nevertheless, he had felt the pleasure of making a large gesture; but suppose she had taken him up. Suppose she had said: "All right, I'll ask for it now!"

It was when he thought of this possibility and of his sixty-seven dollars that he laughed, and this laughter, more uncomfortable than weeping, was continued as he faced other folly of his. He had always thought a carefulness with money, or much consideration of money, the outstanding symbol of vulgarity, a viewpoint now appearing to him as a little "extreme." More than this, he perceived that it was a viewpoint not happily compatible with an attitude of exclusiveness;—people who are happy-go-lucky with money should be also hail-fellow-well-met with other people. Happy-go-lucky may need a loan.

As it happened, he had been so self-sufficient that the only soul in the world from whom he could hope to borrow without shame or the risk of unbearable rebuff was Albert Jones; and he had no knowledge of this old friend's address; nor could he think of any means to obtain it;—Albert had been living in Paris most of the time since they graduated together, and his recent club affiliations in New York were those of a guest, not a member. Old proverbs, older than that most ancient of Ages, the Victorian, though it cherished them, echoed chasteningly in the mind of this modernist; and the one that most afflicted him concerned the Devil. He paraphrased it: "When the Devil was rich, the Devil a devil would be; when the Devil was bankrupt, the Devil a saint was he." For Laurence Ogle, possessed of a proud devil all his life until now, perceived that having become bankrupt in Africa, he was in a condition of humility. He had been too exclusive; he had indeed looked with the Arabs' eyes upon his fellow-beings. Unquestionably it was a mistake.

He had to take account of his assets, a matter of the utmost simplicity yet involving some degree of desperation. He had the sixty-seven relics upon his letter of credit; a thin watch of white gold, some bits of gold and platinum necessary to his dress; he had his clothes and black leather bag and steamer trunk; and he had the few hundred-franc notes in his pocket-book. These, with a desk, some chairs, a four-post bed, and a case of books, in storage in New York, made the complete list of his present possessions in the material world. Then, bethinking him, he remembered that there remained to him his chartered right in M. Cayzac's automobile. It was at his disposal, engaged to carry him to Batna and Timgad, to Constantine and Bône, all on the way to Tunis, where it would finally deposit him; and this was already paid for.

Then to Tunis he would go. He did not seek further into his motive for this decision: it was enough to say to himself that the automobile would save his railroad fare; and yet a curious little guiltiness, like the faint sly sting of some slightly poisonous insect, penetrated his consciousness as he set himself upon this course. He did not look himself over to find the small wound; he preferred to ignore it. He was doing the only sensible thing—he was sure of that—and toward the close of the afternoon he felt able to dress, and went downstairs to ask questions of the concierge.

"It is too late for you to start to-day," the man told him. "Besides, your chauffeur tells me you are here until to-morrow by M. Cayzac's arrangement for Etienne's own expenses. It is Etienne who is your chauffeur; yes, he tells me he is. So to-morrow morning you leave here nicely after breakfast; you lunch at El Kantara, a fine place; and long before dark you are in Batna, or, if you prefer, at Timgad, which is close by there. The next evening you are at Constantine, the next at Bône; then you must make another long day's drive and you will be at Tunis. Everywhere excellent roads, and it is all perfectly simple."

"Yes," Ogle said thoughtfully. "It seems so." With a hand still feeble and a little tremulous, he passed a kerchief over his forehead. "By the way, I was ill yesterday and last evening. I suppose my friends got off all right?"

"The lady and young gentleman who arrive with you? Madame Momoro? Oh, yes; I have purchased their tickets for them myself; they have first-class to Tunis. It was on the bill."

Ogle stared at him blankly and swallowed dry air. "You mean on—on my bill?"

"No, no!" The concierge laughed indulgently. "On their own bill that the young gentleman paid. They went to the train at two o'clock in the afternoon yesterday."

"I see," Ogle said. He paused; then asked: "And

my other—ah—my other friends? They were leaving too, I think."

"Which was those?"

"Mr. Tinker and——"

The face of the concierge brightened to excess and he laughed. "Aha! Mr. Tinker!" he cried. "Mr. Tinker is a friend of yours, yes? Hah! Mr. Tinker and his family and the courier and the two chauffeurs and two cars, yes, they have left for Tunis at three o'clock yesterday. They go the same way you do; you will be only two days behind them. You will see Mr. Tinker in Tunis then? But it is likely you are going there for that reason, of course. You must please give my respects to him, if you will do that, and from the proprietors also; they would wish to send their regards. You will certainly see Mr. Tinker in Tunis, you think so?"

"I don't know," Ogle said. "If I do, I'll give him your message. I may run across him there, or I may not; I can't tell."

But as he turned away to go back to his room, he felt that faint and poisonous sly sting again. This time he resented it. "I'd never do such a thing in the world!" he said, with feeble indignation, to the staircase.

XXIX

THE long, long gray road that led toward the high plateau of the Atlas wound itself up interminably upon a smooth-running spindle beneath the automobile; and the pale, dark-eyed young man seen through the windows, elegant in dress and opulent evidently, since a fine landaulet was needed for his comfort in travelling, engaged himself in winding up, as well as he could, some long threads of his own. But he lacked the precision of the mechanism beneath him; his threads got into snarls, tangling themselves more and more inextricably until he gave up the task, and, sighing, permitted his mind to become flaccid. Upon this, one of those snarled threads promptly and neatly wound itself up without any effort on his part at all. That is to say, he was freely presented with the answer to a question that had been harrying both his curiosity and what was left of his vanity.

As he came out of the pleasant hostelry in the rock gorge at El Kantara after lunch, the sunshine, pouring down an orange light between the tumbled walls of the gorge, struck silver stars and black glitterings from a French automobile approaching at moderate speed over the road Ogle had travelled, the road from Biskra. Behind the wheel sat a French chauffeur and beside him an Arab servant in white; the American identified this luxurious equipage at once, and, when it stopped at the garden gateway of the inn, he was not surprised to see the sisters Daurel assisted to descend. But the appearance of the elder sister did surprise him;—she had become decrepit. The chauffeur upon one side and the Arab servant upon the other were needed to help her out of the car and get her to the doorway of the inn, while Mlle. Lucie hovered anxiously behind, a crystal vial in her hand. The group, which somehow had the effect of a solemn, small cortège, all in black except for the white turban and burnous of the servant, passed close to Laurence, as he paused in the garden; and the face of Mlle. Daurel, like the last scene in a tragedy, held him motionless. Frostbitten and the colour of chalk this face had been whenever he had seen it, but indomitable, the face of an arrogant woman sure of imposing her will. Now it was that of one defeated and physically shattered by defeat, the face of a woman no longer just elderly, but old and more than old; Mlle. Daurel had suddenly become ancient.

She had lost something vital, something upon which she had depended for existence; and she knew she had lost it, and lost it forever. The smitten face of crumbling white chalk was like a strong illuminant to the melancholy observer in the inn garden, it clarified so much for him. He perceived that at least something of what Aurélie Momoro had told him was true and that it had indeed been this old woman's very life to have her tyrannical way with the object of her benevolences. But most brilliantly clear was the answer to his question. Everybody wanted to "get something" out of Tinker; Mme. Momoro had won her passionate struggle to be free of her tyrant; so the answer was yes. She had already "got something."

The lonely young man in the garden of the inn watched the solemn group until it disappeared within the open doorway; then he nodded slowly, as in some affirmation to himself, and went out to M. Cay-zac's car where it stood waiting for him upon the long road to the north. A few moments later he was again swiftly on his way and preoccupied with a new question in place of the one that had been answered.

Mme. Momoro had already "got something"—something substantial enough to establish Hyacinthe in Paris—and she had shown a superb confidence in her future, certainly, when she broke Mlle. Daurel like that. Would she be awaiting her great barbarian in Tunis to "get something" more? If she did thus await him, the great barbarian might have some questions of his own to answer and "*Delenda est Carthago*" gain a new appropriateness.

In the meantime, Laurence Ogle knew that for some inconceivable reason there was in all the world one breath of human kindness for himself. Far ahead of him upon this long gray road, a friendly young spirit took thought of him, and he guessed, humbly enough, that Olivia understood more than she said and was a little sorry for him. Just as he left Biskra the concierge had handed him a postcard from Batna.

You're coming this way aren't you? I think you'd like stopping overnight at Timgad, which you *mustn't* miss, *really*. Won't you be at Tunis before we leave there for Italy? If you won't, please don't forget how much good you did me! I wish I might do some to you in return, but probably you——

Here the writing had deliberately run off the card, the small space for the communication of messages

being filled; though the initials "O. T.", almost microscopic, were visible in a corner. He had not thrown
the card away; he took it from his coat pocket several
times that day and glanced over it with a thoughtful
melancholy, but amiably.

In the Desert borderland of bleak hills Etienne had
difficulties with the brakes; there were several long
halts by the wayside while he worked; and the landaulet rolled into the bare little town of Batna in a
disheartening lemon-coloured early twilight. Against
the cold wind of the plateau the barefooted Arabs
wore the hoods of their thick brown burnouses pulled
up over their heads; and the veiled women hurrying
by upon the side pavements inspired the traveller to
breathe none of the romance so stimulating to him
when he had seen them on that first happy day of
his landing upon the magic continent. He observed
that most of these wind-blown ladies, although oriental as far down as the ankles, which were encircled
with brass rings, wore French slippers with the high
heels scuffed down upon one side; and the anomaly
so displeased him that he shivered. However, it
was easy enough to shiver even within his enclosure,
the chill of the plateau wind was so keen; but when
the car stopped before the door of the hotel, he told

Etienne to drive on to the inn at Timgad. Darkness had fallen before they reached it; and that night he saw nothing of the city the Romans had built, and Olivia Tinker, some eighteen centuries later, recommended to his attention.

Outside there was a wind-swept starlight; but he kept under shelter, and, as he dined, regaled himself a little with the singular appearance of the other guests of the inn. There were only two, a man of sixty and a girl in her twenties dining together at a small table and talking eagerly in a language so beset with outlandish consonants that Ogle could by no manner of means identify it or guess the nationality of the speakers—nor was he assisted by their peculiarities of dress, which to his eyes seemed extreme. The man had a large head, with thick white hair and a lined, round face, sunburned but rosy, not tanned; his intelligent small hazel eyes, in constant quick motion behind silver spectacles, were shrewd and kindly; unquestionably this was an occidental head. But upon it there was a tall red fez with a long black tassel; and underneath a jacket of Scotch rough tweed this fanciful old person wore a tunic of green silk embroidered with small red flowers. As a final eccentricity, his trousers of brown corduroy were tucked into high light boots of Morocco red leather; and the girl with him had as lively a taste for opera bouffe, the playwright thought. She was small and dark, with short curly black hair; and she wore a long black velvet coat, an embroidered white blouse, black velvet knickerbockers, dark blue silk stockings, and silver-buckled patent-leather slippers with curved high heels. Nevertheless, Ogle admitted that she was highly ornamental.

As he ate his dinner, he was aware that her elderly companion showed a recurrent interest in him: the restless eyes behind the silver spectacles were frequently upon him; and once the girl turned frankly to look at him, as if under the impulse of her friend's mention of him. They rose from their table while Ogle was still seated at his own, and to his surprise they stopped beside him on their way out of the room.

The man bowed genially. "You are an American, I think, sir," he said, and so far as his pronunciation went he might well have been an American himself. "I like to speak to Americans when I have the chance. I once lived several years in the States, most of the time in Rock Island." Then he added, as Laurence had risen, "Please don't let us keep you standing."

Misfortune and suffering are indeed the principal

education of man; and in Africa Laurence Ogle had acquired, at least temporarily and it might even be permanently, a little education. A few months earlier he would not have encouraged the friendly advances of this bizarre person; he would have said with a coldness covering a slight indignation, "Ah— I have never been in Rock Island," without adding anything except frigidity to the statement. Now he offered his hand. "I'm glad to meet someone who is almost a compatriot. I imagine you don't find Timgad very like Rock Island, though."

"There are some resemblances," the other said, smiling as if upon some hidden thought;—"resemblances not so subtle as they might appear. You haven't seen the ruins yet?"

"No. I got in after dark."

"They are all about us, out there in a thin and very chilly starlight. My pupil and I are just going to take a ghostly walk among them; but I should advise you to wait for the morning sunshine. Permit me." Here he bowed and offered Ogle a card upon which was engraved "E. D. G. N. Medjila, D. Arche. Inst. Coll. Bass'a." Ogle mentioned his own name, and the donor of the formidable card continued: "You see I am Doctor Medjila, an arch-

æologist; we are here for several weeks every year
to study Timgad. Excuse me, I should like you to
meet my pupil." The girl nodded composedly; Ogle
bowed and murmured; and Dr. E. D. G. N. Medjila
seemed to feel no need of any further definition of
his pupil. "We are keeping you from finishing your
salad," he said. "We must wish you good-night,
but we are sure to meet among the ruins to-morrow;
we are always there. You will not find here all that
you will at Pompeii, but Timgad is still Roman,
and is enough." With that, and an affable "*Au
plaisir*," he and his ornamental pupil departed for
their ghostly walk; while the young American, tired
by the long drive, and still shivery in the unheated
inn, took his advice and waited for the sunshine.

When it arrived and he set forth, he comprehended
breathlessly and at once what the archæologist had
meant by saying that Timgad was enough; and as
he walked the straight, stone-paved streets of the
ruined town in the brilliancy of the morning, he
understood, too, that Timgad was "still Roman."
He had stepped out of the Mohammedan Orient into
a city of the imperial Cæsars; and for all his depression and anxiety, he found some excitement in taking
so vast a step. During an hour's wandering he saw

not a soul; the dead town of stone remnants, foundation walls, and broken columns lay upon the barren slopes in the ancient silence it had kept through the centuries, and Ogle was pleased to have it apparently all to himself.

Prowling at hazard, he found the theatre, explored it thoughtfully, then climbed to the top of it and sat looking down upon the stone stage. Had a nervous playwright ever watched a "first-night" from this same seat, he wondered. How stately the Roman audience must have looked, he thought, and how astonished they would have been if they could have known that a being like himself would ever sit there, a man from a country built mainly of flimsy wood and stucco. What would be left of an American city after fire, capture, sacking, earthquakes, sand storms, and centuries of Arab lootings. Of an American city, he asked sourly, would even its Yawp be left for a comic opera archæologist to decipher?

Then, as he thought of this singular person, wondering why it happened that one encountered so many strange people in Africa, the man himself and his pretty pupil came from behind a wall and appeared upon the ruined stage below. Dr. E. D. G.

N. Medjila bore less than ever the appearance of having been at one time a resident of Rock Island, Illinois: he had added a brown burnous to his costume of the evening before, and his pupil a small black felt hat to hers, so that even more pointedly they suggested, especially in that place, a moment of theatrical fantasia.

They saw Ogle upon his high seat, waved to him cordially; then climbed up and sat beside him.

"You were thinking of what comedies and tragedies have been played down there," Dr. Medjila said, wiping his large and rosy forehead, and breathing with some heaviness after the ascent. "If you know what dramas the Romans played, you agree with me that most of them were for the idiot mind. But we are strange people, we moderns. We see a little carving on an old wall and we say, 'What ignorant fellow did that?' Then somebody tells us it was done two thousand years ago, and we begin to shout, 'What magnificent art!' The travellers who come here shout as loudly over the bad things as over the good things."

"I suppose we do," Ogle said. "I was thinking of all this Roman solidity, though, and wondering what would be left of an American city after ages of such misfortune. I wondered if you could find even what we call its 'Yawp'? The 'Yawp'——"

"I know very well," Dr. Medjila interrupted, and he laughed. "It is the brag. You think perhaps the Romans didn't have it? Heavens! What braggarts! You find the imperial Roman Yawp in thousands of inscriptions everywhere—everywhere! America has so much that is the same as these dead people: the great Yawp, the love of health, the love of plumbing, the love of power, of wealth, and, above all, the worship of bigness—that old, old passion for giantism. What is strange, you find at the same time a great deal of common sense. In all the different times I have been here I have seen just one tourist who understood Timgad instantly, and that was because he was really a Roman himself. He was here only the other day."

"An Italian?" Ogle asked.

"No, no! One of your own people, of course. You have been to the Forum and the Arch of Triumph this morning?"

"Yes; before I came here."

"Then you can understand," Dr. Medjila said, and he chuckled. "This fellow, he had a guide;

but it was he who told the guide everything. 'Never mind!' he would say. 'I know how it is without your telling me.' And it was true. He did!" Dr. Medjila laughed aloud and slapped his knee, he so enjoyed this recollection. "That fellow, he was rich! He said he guessed *he* knew how to lay out and build a town, and the Romans had done it the same way *he* would—only not so good!"

Ogle's instantaneous premonition was well-founded; and in a kind of despair he suffered a renewal of his previous conviction that it was impossible to be upon the same continent with Tinker and long escape him. "I should call *that* something of a Yawp," he said feebly.

"It was," Medjila admitted. "But it was like the Roman Yawp because it bragged of what was true. This fellow, he told us how much finer his own city was than Timgad—or than any other city, ancient or modern. He told us of all that was made there, of the 'public utilities' and of the climate that is owned there. But he had a great appreciation of Timgad too. He would look at the Arch of Triumph over yonder; then he would say, 'Yes, sir; they probably had to pay for that out of a bond issue; but of course they had to *have* it! They couldn't let the boys get back from the war and not give them a good big Soldiers' Monument near the Square!' He called the Forum 'the Square.' 'Yes, sir,' he would say, 'you can see just what it was like. Here is where the farmers hitched their teams on Saturday while they sold their market produce and did their shopping and had a few drinks to keep them company on the drive back home.'"

Ogle uttered a sound of distaste. "It must have been rather grating, Dr. Medjila. For an archæologist to stand in a Forum of the Roman Empire and have to listen to——"

But Medjila again interrupted. "No, no," he chuckled. "It was precisely the truth, if we omit the technicality of the word 'Saturday.' This man was able to reconstruct the Roman city as it really had been; he saw it as something human. An artist comes here and sees it as a picture; Flaubert is called the founder of realism; but he would have seen Timgad as all blood and drama;—this compatriot of yours alone was the realist, and I would give all the little knowledge I have for use in my decipherings to be able to look at such a place for the first time and understand it as he did. How curious it is! See what the Arab did to this city and this country: it was splendid land about here once. He burned, he massacred, he enslaved, he carried away whatever he could use, as he did everywhere. In the great bazaar of Tunis you will see how he brought marble columns from Carthage and painted them like barbers' poles. But, worst of all, he deforested. Then when hundreds of years had gone by, some soldiers and some gentlemen of my profession came and dug here and uncovered what was left. And at last the new Roman comes in an automobile and is the first person to walk in and think correctly of those poor dead people who were here so long ago and to see that they were human beings like himself. Of course that is because they *were* like himself, the same kind of people."

"Are you sure?" Ogle asked skeptically. "You don't think him a barbarian or, at the best, Carthaginian?"

"No, no! Roman! That feeling about his own city, it is nothing but Roman. The Carthaginian had something of it, but not the pride or the passion. You will find it in the old Florentine, but nowhere at its height except in the Augustan Roman and in such men as this one who was here. We are too likely to think that Rome was all Virgil and Horace

and Pliny and Cicero.   It is only the memory of dead
things that is kept by literature and by art; the
things themselves, when they are alive, are made to
live by such men as those who built Timgad and this
other one who understood it because he deals in living
realities himself.   He is a Roman, and an important
one."

"Is he?" Ogle asked curiously.   "Important?"

Medjila nodded gravely.   "It happened I knew a
little about him.   When I lived in Rock Island I
heard of some undertakings of his that were spoken
of in the papers sometimes.   He reorganized a street-
railway and then a number of factories that made
paper.   The other day before he went away I told
him I remembered, and he was as pleased as a child.
I told him, too, that he was a Roman; but he didn't
know what to make of that."

"I suppose not," Ogle said; then he looked at his
watch, and rose.   "I am afraid I must be off.   I
have to be in Constantine before evening."

Medjila got up also, and shook his burnous loose
from a cranny between two stones where it had
caught.   "We'll walk back to the inn with you if
we may," he said, and he nodded to his silent pupil,
who jumped up like a well-trained child and accom-

panied them in that same manner, looking amiable and saying nothing. "Yes, that compatriot of yours is a great Roman," he insisted when they had reached the ancient street below. "What is more, the world treats him as one. How the Greeks and Orientals laughed behind their hands at 'Roman civilization' and at 'Roman art' and at 'Roman manners'! But laughing behind your hand is bad manners; and the poor Greeks had to see most of their own art carried off to Rome. When a great Roman travelled he was received as this man is received. Everybody hoped for something," Medjila chuckled. "When this new Roman goes over to Europe from Tunis, he will be presented to royalties and dictators and who not, if he wishes. There will be hopes of his making investments, benevolences, largesses. Even I——" He broke off, chuckled again; then added: "But I think you know him, Mr. Ogle."

"I suppose so," the young man assented gloomily. "I do, if you mean Tinker."

"I thought so. Do you know how long he will stay in Tunis?"

"No."

"If he is to be there for some little time," Doctor Medjila said reflectively, "I would shorten our stay

here a day or two because I must go to Tunis anyhow, on my way across to Girgenti where there is
some new digging just now. I would like to have
another talk with him. At a first meeting one doesn't
like to broach such matters; but I thought possibly I could interest him in a little expedition I have
in mind to some buried temples in the south—not at
all expensive. Well, we shall see." He sighed.
"It is an old dream of mine."

"What made you think I knew him?" Ogle asked.

"That?" Medjila's twinkling quick eyes became
mirthful; he shook his head, laughed gayly, and spoke
in his outlandish language to the pupil. She replied,
laughed too, and glanced brightly at Ogle. "I will
tell you, sir," the archæologist said, after this cheerful
interlude. "It is amusing. We were walking back
to the inn just as we are now—Mr. Tinker and his
daughter and the courier and my pupil and I. Mrs.
Tinker didn't go into the ruins; she was waiting in
one of the automobiles yonder by the Museum, and
I think she must have been impatient to go on with
their journey. People who wait a long time become
fretful; that is natural. Mr. Tinker and my pupil
were walking a little way in advance of us, and unfortunately she speaks neither English nor any of

the Romance languages; but Mr. Tinker kept talking to her in English just the same, laughing and
pointing out houses among the ruins and telling her
what fine young men lived in each one, asking her
if such-and-such a one wouldn't be coming to call on
her that evening. He was teasing her, and she understood that, although she didn't know a word he was
saying. Well, she has a strong sense of the absurd-
ities, so she must begin laughing too; and just as we
came to the gateway of the Museum she laughed so
heartily that she gave him a little slap upon the
shoulder. Mrs. Tinker jumped out of her automobile like a young girl, and I think she must be very
severe with her husband sometimes. She made him
get in at once, and they drove away so quickly that
they forgot their daughter, though the second automobile was still waiting, filled with their luggage;
and the courier waited too. You see the young lady
had something she wished to say to me. She said
it before they came back for her, so this was how I
knew you were acquainted with Mr. Tinker."

"What was it she said?"

"She was very pleased with my telling him he was
a Roman and why I thought so, and she wished to
ask a favour of me. She said that possibly a young

man not very tall and—well, that is to say, she described you, and she mentioned your name. She said that possibly you might come to Timgad within a few days, and, if you did, she asked me to be sure to talk to you and tell you what I had said about her father's being a Roman.''

"That was all?" They had come to a halt before the inn where Etienne and the automobile stood waiting, ready to take the road.

"That was all," Dr. Medjila informed him. "She was very serious. In fact," he added, and his rosy face became rosier with mirth, "they were all three serious—oh, very serious!—after her father and mother came back for her. So I have told my pupil she must never slap another American gentleman's shoulder again under any circumstances whatever!"

XXX

THEN as the landaulet began to move away, the departing traveller, speaking his farewell from the window, looked forth upon two faces suffused with a jocose enjoyment so cordial that his own ready colour heightened embarrassingly. Dr. E. D. G. N. Medjila called godspeeds in four languages, and his pupil, with laughter brilliant in her eyes, shouted something all consonants, which made them both the merrier. The automobile began to gather speed; but the two odd, friendly figures remained where they were, calling after it and waving their hands. They were still there and still waving, dwindled by the distance, but strongly coloured against the gray ruins behind them, when the young man in the car looked back for the last time and waved once more in return before the curving road carried him from their sight.

"Incredible people!" he said; but withdrew the adjective since nothing was incredible upon this continent. Strangely, he liked them; unaccountably, he felt a little actual affection for them and knew he should often wonder about them and never forget them, although he had but this glimpse of them and was never to see them again. They were two merry yet wistful queer figures such as Wonderland Alice, wandering in Africa, might have encountered, he thought; and Miss Olivia Tinker was almost as odd as they were to have wished him to hear from Medjila that her father was really a Roman!

That idea belonged indeed to an archæologist who had no place except in a book of airiest whimsy; but as Laurence thought again he was not so sure; for he remembered how he had seen from the minaret in Biskra the return of the caravan from Sidi Okba in the Desert. He remembered how the figure of Tinker in his scarlet robe, riding in barbaric pomp upon the great white camel at the head of the caravan, had at first seemed ridiculous; but as he came nearer with his wild escort in tumult about him and princely rulers upon his right and left, and himself careless of both tumult and princes, there had appeared to be something formidable—something of the great Carthaginian—about such a man. But Medjila would not have him Carthaginian: he had insisted upon "Roman," and "Roman" meant gigantic.

Then suddenly the young man in the landaulet winced;—he made in his throat one of those sounds of protest that dentists sometimes hear from their patients. For Mme. Momoro's final sharpness again operated upon an exposed nerve of his. Was it true? Had he seen that barbarian of hers grow larger and larger until he became Medjila's "Roman," while he himself grew smaller and smaller until he became only a little petty-souled bankrupt—a bankrupt in vanity as in everything else? Could it possibly be true that Tinker was large, was formidable, was gigantic, was indeed the new Roman?

His thought of the man became concentrated. He thought of that outbreak of semi-riotous, middle-aged men on the "Duumvir" with Tinker as their ringleader; he thought of "Honey, how's Baby?" and of "Mariar," and of the poker table in the smoking-room and the sly cunning that had won all the chips; he thought of the infantile helplessness that sought to appease a wife's anger with barber's unguents and with deceptions and evasions a child might have employed; he thought of the man's surreptitious and barbaric gallantries—but at least they had not been rebuffed! And he thought, too, of the weakling husband meekly submitting to be bundled into an automobile and indignantly hurried away because a frolicsome girl had slapped his shoulder. Was this inept creature, this childishly loose, childishly tricky creature, this over-lavish, careless, bragging, noisy, money-getting and money-worshipping creature a "new Roman?"

Laurence drew a deep breath, his shoulders relaxed, and he leaned back against the cushions more comfortably: he saw Tinker in little again. Then, after a time, his frown returned and his shoulders renewed their tensity; for he thought of Mme. Momoro in Tunis, already in possession of "something" and in all probability waiting in the hope of "something more." Even poor E. D. G. N. Medjila hoped to "get something"—and why was he himself on the road to Tunis? He could have arranged with Cayzac by wire for Etienne to drive him back to Algiers without additional cost: the distance was actually shorter. Wasn't he on the road to Tunis because his affairs were desperate and because there he hoped to find the only man he knew whose heart was careless enough of money and big enough with humanity to rescue him without mortifying him? For, in spite of his denial on the stairway in Biskra, Laurence knew all the time that he, too, expected to "get something" out of Tinker. Was it then from a small man, a money worshipper, that he sought a rescue?

Olivia wished him to think of her father as the "new Roman"; she was pleased with that and wanted him to hear it. One thing was clear: she had adored her father even when she hated him; she had always adored him, and now she wanted this critic of him to admire him. Medjila's talk was really a message from her, and, seeing it in that light, Laurence was touched; there was something both whimsical and fond in what she had done. The fondness was for her father—and perhaps there was a little for the critic too; though he was well enough cured of fatuousness not to be sure. It wasn't fatuous, however, to be sure that she cared a little about what he thought, and since she wished him to think of her father as the "new Roman"—— But here Laurence again remembered "Mariar." He would have done anything within his power that Olivia wished him to do; but when he decided to be obedient and to think of the man who had sung "Mariar" as a Roman, he found he couldn't.

He couldn't make up his mind about Tinker at all: Tinker was entirely too much for him.

Tinker was too much for many others, and if Ogle had known it, he had good company in thus being overwhelmed. For years, excellent people in their mutual native land had found Tinker too much for them; so had people not so excellent; and in Africa some of both kinds of people were in a like condition. Among the excellent ones was the courier, Jean Edouard Le Seyeux, who easily recognized his present undertaking as the most remarkable of his career, and one moment held the opinion that his employer was mentally defective and the next that he was a great man. Sometimes he suspected him of humour.

But a part of the time Le Seyeux was merely stupefied by his strange experience, and his thoughts became too confused for him to give them definition even to himself. Coincidentally, such a time was upon him that afternoon. While the disturbed young American on the road to Constantine found Tinker too much for him, Le Seyeux, at the tomb of St. Augustine upon a Mediterranean hillside, found Tinker too much for anybody. This was a hillside up over the town of Bône, and several hundred kilometers beyond the stretch of road coursed by the other person just now most poignantly of Le Seyeux's mind in respect to Tinker. Olivia and her mother, who was tearful (not because of St. Augustine), sat waiting in an automobile before the church at the top of the hill, while the two men descended to the stone-covered grave of the great Bishop.

"Who'd you say he was?" Tinker asked, for the third time.

"It is Saint Augustine."

"What'd he do, John?"

"He was the great ecclesiastical authority of the Fourth Century. He was Bishop. He was the great religious power of his time."

"Preacher, I expect," Tinker said thoughtfully. "What denomination was he?"

Le Seyeux's eyes showed a little wildness; but he answered simply, "He was of the Church."

"Which one?" Then, seeing that the courier seemed to have a difficulty in comprehending him, his employer kindly explained the question. "You know in our country, John, we got Methodists and Presbyterians and Unitarians and Episcopalians and Catholics and Christian Scientists and Baptists and Quakers and Seventh-Day Adventists, and Camp-bellites and Dunkards and Shakers and Lutherans and I don't know what all, just the way you got all these Mohammedans and Catholics and probably a good many others over here. Well, you say this man here—— Wha'd you say his name was?"

"Saint Augustine."

"'Saint,'" Tinker repeated reflectively. "Catholic, I expect. He isn't in the Bible, is he?"

"Bible? No! Fourth Century! He was Bishop. He wrote the great 'Confess˙ons.' He has establish' the doctrine of original sin. He has establish' that if a child is not baptize' it is to go to hell."

"Oh, *that's* it, is it?" Tinker appeared to be greatly enlightened. "*I* see. Well, sir, that's just like my own father. *He* was an old-time Presbyterian."

"No, no! Saint Augustine is not Presbyterian. He is *old* Christian—of the *old* Church. He——"

"Never mind," Tinker said. "I meant my father was a Presbyterian, not this old fellow here; but it looks like they believed a good deal the same way." He looked reflectively at the round stone platform, nicked the end of a cigar with a small gold instrument upon his thin watch chain, shook his head, and remarked pleasantly, "Out o' date."

"Sir? Saint Augustine is buried fifteen hundred years ago."

"That's what I meant," Tinker said. "Plum out o' date. I mean the whole business."

"Sir?"

"It's like this," Tinker explained as he lighted his cigar: "What was the name of that other old fellow we saw his tomb over at the mud town that had the big smells?"

"Sidi Okba, the great Mohammedan conqueror."

"Yes. You said he'd been moulderin' there thirteen hundred years, and this one you say fifteen hundred. That old Sidi Okba was a Mohammedan and wanted to kill everybody didn't think the way he did, and here's *this* old fellow wanted to send everybody to hell didn't think the way *he* did. Listen, John. It's all out o' date."

"Sir?"

"Listen," Tinker said indulgently. "What's it all about? I mean everything—all these mountains and the ocean and the Desert, and all these Arabs and French people, and us? I'm talkin' about the whole possetucky—the whole blame kit-an'-boodle —everything and everybody. What's the big idea? What's the object? Well, one man's guess is as good as the next man's. This old fellow didn't know any more about it than that other one did down there in the mud town with the smell and the sore-eyed children.   Fact is, *both* of 'em guessed wrong.''

"Sir?"

"Listen," Tinker said; and he became profoundly serious.   "There's only just about one single thing been really cleared *up* in a religious line, you might say, in all the time these two old fellows been lyin' in this soil, and what is it?   Listen, John—it's simply this: the human race has got to make progress. Well, you might ask: 'What for?   Where's it got to progress *to?*   It don't seem much use to be *goin'* unless you're goin' some*where*, so where *are* you goin'?'' Well, that's a sensible question, and both these old dead fellows would probably 'a' given you the same answer.   'Goin' to try to keep out o' hell and get to heaven,' they'd 'a' said.   So listen—that's out o' date.   The only hell we worry about nowadays is slippin' back in our progress; we got to show a bigger and better business this year than we did last year."

"Sir?"

"It's like this, John," Tinker said benevolently. "The Almighty doesn't care a nickel about anything except our *makin'* that progress.   He'll wipe us out in a minute if we don't make it.   He'll wipe us out and go on about His business and never give us another thought, because what *He's* looking for is a good live crowd that's got the brains and the push and the go-get-it to keep goin' *ahead*. That's every last thing He cares about! Look how He's wiped 'em out, one race after the other, the way we've seen since we left Algiers! The kind He patronizes are the boys that got the plans all ready for a bigger and better city the morning after the earthquake, the kind that *like* an earthquake because it gives 'em the opportunity they been waitin' for! The *other* kind, He just passes an eraser over 'em; and we've seen where some awful work's been done with that eraser in Africa. Well, to-day *we're* here and we've got our chance; and the one single and only thing in the universe that's *plain*, John Edwards, it's this." Here he became solemnly emphatic, and put his heavy hand upon the courier's shoulder. "The somewhere we're goin' to, and *got* to go to if we don't want to get wiped out, it's somewhere everlastingly and eternally *ahead!* It's like to-morrow; when we get there we *aren't* there; we got to keep goin', and we got to everlastingly and eternally *keep* goin'—and goin' *fast!* If we don't, the Almighty hasn't got a bit o' use for us; He turns us right into dust and scattered old bones, and nothin's left of our whole country and our finest cities except some street paving and a few cellars with weeds in 'em. You get me, John?"

The courier wiped his brow. "Yes, sir. I think the ladies may think we keep them waiting too long."

"I expect so." But Tinker looked at the odd round platform and still lingered. "I suppose he lived in this town here."

"Yes, sir. Bône. It is ancient Hippo."

"Shouldn't think anybody'd want to have his city called either one o' *those* names. Looks like he was a good citizen, though, and thought a lot of the place —wantin' to be buried here and all. Yes, sir; any man's city can get along without *him;* but no man can get along without his *city!*" Thoughtfully, he began to walk away, ascending the upper slope of the hill, the courier beside him. "Did that old fellow ever do anything besides what you told me, John?"

"He wrote some other books. One is called 'The City of God.'"

"Is that *so!*" Tinker was strongly and favourably impressed. He paused and looked down at the roofs and gardens of Bône between the hill and sea. "Is that *so?* He did?" For a moment it was evident that he discovered some point of high congeniality between himself and the great Bishop: he glanced back at the tomb approvingly, then down at the town again. "Called it 'The City of God,' did he? Well, sir, if he thought so much o' *that* little place, it's a pity he couldn't 'a' lived to——" But a second thought dimmed his brightened interest, and he walked on almost gloomily. "Book about spiritual matters, I expect," he said.

"Yes, sir. Saint Augustine lived in Fifth Century also; he wrote this book in thirteen years from four hunder' thirteen Anno Domini to four hunder' twenty-six. In the year four hunder' thirty the city of Hippo was besiege' by——"

"Never mind, John," Tinker interrupted soothingly. "You can tell us about it in the car. What time you think you're goin' to get us into Tunis to-morrow?"

"If we start very early in the morning we arrive by five o'clock."

"All right," Tinker said, and he glanced upward apprehensively.

Mrs. Tinker was leaning out of the window of the automobile, sternly watching his slow approach; her tears were vanished, and she had now gone into the second of the two moods that had been hers, to the exclusion of all others, during the entire journey from

Biskra. Having wept, she was now become grim, and her eye upon her husband was that of a school-teacher upon the worst boy in the class.

Tinker found it unbearable;—he set a powerful grip upon the arm of Le Seyeux. "Listen, John," he said. "You say Tunis is a place where you can buy anything. Well, it *better* be! What I want you to do when we get to the hotel, I want you to get there in the other car before *we* do, and when we come in the first thing I want you to do is to have everything ready and get the ladies up to their rooms the very minute they step into the lobby. I don't know, but I've got kind of an idea there might be a reason it'd be just as well if they didn't poke around any just at first, but went right upstairs and took a nap or something. You understand?"

"Yes, sir; but there is no reason to be uneasy: Tunis is entirely safe for ladies, especially in the French quarter. There would be no danger of any——"

"I certainly *hope* there isn't, myself!" Tinker said fervently; but he seemed dubious about it, and he halted at a little distance from the automobile, keeping the courier with him. "You do as I say. You get them right up to their rooms; that's the main thing I want you to have on your mind. And as soon as you get it done you go out and get me a couple o' those big Arab jewellers you been talkin' about. You tell 'em I want to see 'em at the hotel and tell 'em to bring the best they got right with 'em. You understand me, John?"

Le Seyeux comprehended with the greatest pleasure. His eyes brightened; he smiled and nodded eagerly. "Without fail! In half an hour after we arrive I will bring them to see you. They will show you some of the most splendid——"

Mrs. Tinker's voice, shrill and strained, interrupted them. She leaned farther out of the window and fumbled with the handle of the door as if to open it and descend. "What are you talking about *now?*" she called fiercely. "Earl! Do you hear me? What do you have to have all these mysterious conferences about? Will you kindly inform me?"

"Mother!" Olivia said imploringly. "*Please* remember——"

"Be quiet, Libby; let me alone!" Mrs. Tinker became impassioned, and she renewed her inquiries to her husband as he drew nearer. "What do you have to talk to the courier so much in secret about? What are all these mysterious——"

"Now, Mamma," he said plaintively. "Now, Honey——"

"Are you going to answer me? Who do you expect to have pat your shoulder in the *next* town? What are you——"

"Now, Hon——"

"Stop calling me that! What was all that secret planning you were doing just then?"

Tinker tried to look dignified and reproachful, partially succeeding. "We were talking about this Bishop," he said. "It was the tomb of this old Bishop we went down there to look at. He was a Bishop."

"Bishop!" The word infuriated her. "Do you have to *whisper* because you're talking about a Bishop?"

"Well——" Tinker said gently, and then, casting about for some means to set himself in the right and Mrs. Tinker in the wrong, he had an inspiration that was a misfortune. "Well—he's *dead*, isn't he?"

Mrs. Tinker leaped straightway into her other mood. She wept aloud and was with difficulty restrained by Olivia from continuing to weep in that manner through the more populous modern streets upon the site of Augustine's ancient see of Hippo.

XXXI

TOM–TOMS were throbbing in Tar-Barca and five hundred unsmiling Arabs chattered in the open market square of caked dry mud among the trees. Hung from the dusty lower branches, shoulders of mutton, hunks of goat meat, and carcasses of kids were for sale, and there were great bloody quarters of camel, with hide, hair, and hoof unremoved; other meats also were shown, not easily identified and better for the mystery of their origin. Merchants sat cross-legged with small masses of dates upon the ground before them and dust from the road close by blowing over man and merchandise; other merchants offered to sell so much as a whole goat, lean but still alive, or even a live donkey, not well but admirable, if only for his resignation. Still others sold rusty tin cans, empty bottles, bits of brass and iron, old skins and strips of worn cloth; though there were many at the market who neither bought nor sold; and these, being idle, were the greatest talkers of all the concourse. It was they who made the most to-do over the passage through the crowd of the long automobile from Bône at noon.

In the strong sunshine where there were no trees a brown man in a tunic of rags and a headdress of tatters sat with his bare legs and feet projecting into the crowded road, so that often people and careful donkeys stepped over them; for he was too profoundly engaged to think of withdrawing obstructions from the highway. He was staring straight up into the intolerable face of the African sun, his never-winking and tearless eyes, not blind, bearing the unbearable; and at intervals of thirty seconds—intervals so unvarying that they might have been regulated by a clock—he spread wide his arms, then brought them together, clapped his hands, and uttered in a high-pitched monotone an urgent petition to Allah. For more than an hour he had been doing this, never swerving his direct stare from the supreme blaze of the disk itself, and without anyone's paying the slightest attention to him except to step over his legs. Nothing distracted his hypnotized gaze until the arrival of the automobile from Bône on its way to Tunis.

The chattering crowd covered the road; they made way for the insistent machine slowly and with hard looks for the occupants; while the chauffeur, who was in a hurry, unremittingly urged them with his blatting brass horn. They had no respect for the horn; it annoyed them; and as the automobile drove slowly through the thickest of the press they moved from its path with a more and more hostile deliberation. Finally a sullen group stepped aside with such grudging reluctance that not until too late to avoid a contact did the chauffeur see the legs of the sungazer, who had been concealed from him by the long burnouses of this obstinate group. One of the front tires touched a thin brown shank in the white dust; the monotonous invocation to Allah changed abruptly to a squeal that became a shriek, and the startled devotee rolled over, writhing;—he had suffered no injury whatever.

But the Arabs instantly mobbed the automobile. They leaped upon it, screeching; they covered it hungrily; the windows filled with demon masks contorted to every expression of ferocity, and the two ladies within felt themselves enveloped in sudden nightmare. Meanwhile, the unfortunate chauffeur outside seemed in a fair way to be torn to pieces, pieces all of them minute. Shouting fiercely, himself, he had thrust his right hand into a breast pocket;

but twenty impassioned brown fingers on his arm made him unable to withdraw it. Then a door of the closed interior was thrown open with a violence damaging to the indignant Arabs upon the running-board, and a big, red-faced, bare-headed man leaped out of the car and roared.

His roar was in a tongue unknown to the persons addressed; and, in fact, the words employed were unimpressive, being merely "Get out o' here!" But the Arabs were not aware of anything lacking in his eloquence. Never had they heard such a voice, neither one so masterful nor one so thunderous as they heard in this single great bellow. What was more, upon the very instant of its utterance the big red-faced man put his hand in his pocket, then swept that hand in a semi-circle above his head, and the air filled with glittering riches; silver coins began to shower down like Allah's sweetest rain. The Arabs recognized a stupendous personage.

When he roared they leaped from the car; they scrambled from it; they fell from it. When he rained wealth their garments fluttered as they scrambled; and instantly there was a clear space about the machine with room for it to go forward on its way. The big man jumped upon the running-board, and put his hand in his pocket again: he shouted with laughter, and again there was a shining rain from heaven. Groans of thanksgiving were heard from the scramblers, and the sound might almost have been interpreted as a cheer for the personage; but even as he laughed and sought in other pockets, a clutching gloved hand, slender but imperious, drew him— jerked him, indeed—ingloriously from sight, except as he might still be seen in abrupt subjugation through the glass of the window. His laughter went from him, and his expression relapsed to a plaintive patience, for he in turn was mastered.

The automobile passed on and gratefully left the grateful market behind it. Olivia, still trembling and pallid herself, spoke severely to her mother, intending the severity as a restorative. "Mother, stop that sobbing and jerking! You've already got yourself to the verge of a nervous breakdown without indulging in hysterics because a few poor Arabs get a little excited for half-a-minute. We weren't in the slightest danger."

"We—we weren't?" Mrs. Tinker sobbed. "Then what—what did you scream for?"

"I was startled. But right away I realized Papa would know what to do—and he certainly did!"

Mrs. Tinker continued to weep; but her sobbing subsided, not impeding her utterance. "Yes, he knew what to do. He always does, aud it's always the same thing. The only thing on earth he knows how to do is to hand out money!"

"But it wasn't the money that stopped them;—he just threw them the money *besides*. It was that tremendous yell when he told them to get out. I never heard anything like it. They knew they *had* to, of course. Heavens! I think it would have stopped a war.'

"He thinks he can do anything with just making a noise," Mrs. Tinker said; and then to save her consistency she added: "And handing out money! That's his one remedy for everything in the world— throwing people money!"

"Listen!" Tinker said; and he spoke with the feeble irascibility of a badgered man who feels that the badgering is rightful and warranted. "It works, doesn't it? All I got to say, it works. It did, didn't it?"

"Let me tell *you*," the unhappy lady returned fiercely, "there are *some* times when it won't! There are a *few* things you've done that all the money in the *world* wouldn't——"

"Now, Mamma!   Now, Hon——"

"Stop it!" she cried.   "Don't you *dare* call me that!"

Olivia moaned.   "Oh, dear!   Can't you *ever* quiet down, Mother?   How many more days of this have we——"

Her mother paid no attention to the remonstrance; she began to talk wildly.   "I expect he'd have been *glad* if I'd been murdered!   All those screeching faces and horrible glaring eyes—they *wanted* to murder me! You think you know that man, Olivia; but you don't. If I'd been put out of the way so that he could be a fine rich widower with French adventuresses flattering him and patting his shoulder and getting him to sneak out to meals with them and——"

"Listen!" Tinker said.   "There wasn't any more chance of those people murdering you than there would be of a chicken's murdering an elephant. They just got excited for a minute, and if John Edwards had been with us even that wouldn't 'a' happened."

"Why *wasn't* he with us, then?   You're very sweet to call your wife an elephant!   What did you let him start so long ahead of us for?"

"Because you weren't ready at the time we planned

to get off this morning. I wanted him to be in Tunis ahead of us so's to see there's no mistake about our having the rooms engaged for us You'll be tired when you get there, and I want him to have everything fixed for you so't you can lie right down and take a nap soon as you get there."

"So thoughtful!" she said with sarcasm. "Send the courier ahead the one time when we need him to protect us, and leave us alone among these wild——"

"Wild?" Tinker interrupted, and he laughed ruefully. "Mamma, if they were just one millionth as wild as *you* been lately——"

Olivia foresaw how unfortunate the effect of this sally was to be, and impulsively she clapped her hand over her father's mouth. She was too late: Mrs. Tinker again was seized with a loud and convulsive sobbing.

"Oh, lawsy! Oh, my landy me!" Tinker groaned. "And we're goin' to be late gettin' into Tunis besides! We're certainly in for one *day* of it!"

They were indeed; and poor Mrs. Tinker's condition remained emotional throughout the long afternoon of swift travel through a strange landscape. They passed among hills of golden brown sand, and toward sunset came into a vast and curiously tawny country, once congenial to lions later bewildered in the shouting oval amphitheatres of Carthage and of Rome. Beyond this, in the twilight, lay a wide gray plain with mountain profiles like gigantic haphazard cuttings of blue cardboard set along the horizon;—night fell before the travellers were across these levels. Then presently the wide road began to jolt them incessantly; the surface was rough from the traffic it had borne, and they knew they were near a populous city.

When at last they came into it they seemed within a city shaped out of the stuff that Eastern dreams are made of; coloured even in the night with pigments brushed up from the melting of Scheherazade's jewels and dwelt in by hordes of actors dressed for the wildest of pantomime extravanganzas. Orange-lighted low doorways showed green-faced people in striped gowns, sitting cross-legged upon the floor, stiff as idols; within dark doorways turbaned gnomes were silhouetted crouching over sparks like the sparks in the hearts of rubies; sudden Arabian Night vistas opened and closed, showing arched tunnels rosily lighted and fantastic crowds tossing silently, fiery with colour;—then the car would glide through a street all dark, where pale domes rose vaguely in the starlight, and great palm fronds drooped along white walls; while from hidden gardens hautboys sang their ancient themes of cats in rapture, cats in despair, cats in love.

. . . Le Seyeux waited anxiously at the entrance to the large hotel in the French quarter; and he understood, even better than his employer did, why it was advisable for Mrs. Tinker to ascend immediately to the apartment ready for her. She was more than willing; and as she passed through the entrance hallway to the elevator, with the courier talking eagerly beside her, fatigue and Le Seyeux together happily prevented her from being as observant as she might have been. Her daughter, too, was tired, and failed to see what the courier had seen and what Tinker now saw with undeniable yet conflicting emotions. He entered the hotel a few steps behind the others, which was fortunate, since otherwise Mrs. Tinker might have noticed the slight change in his expression as he happened to glance toward a wide open doorway upon his left. This doorway gave to view one end of a large public room where tea tables were set about a broad central

space of polished floor used for dancing. The dancers and the tea-drinkers had all departed except one;
for the dinner-hour now approached, and even the
one person who lingered had long since done with
tea. In fact, after lingering to supplement the more
innocuous beverage with a tiny glass of white cordial,
she was in the act of drawing on a doffed glove as
she frowningly preparing to depart. She was a tall
lady in cloth of gold and brown velvet of Venice,
and of an aspect so superb that she might have been
thought Olympian rather than Parisian.

As the newly arrived travellers passed through the
hallway she turned toward the open double doors;
then, when they had gone by, she slowly drew off
the glove she had partially replaced upon her right
hand, and leaned back again in her comfortable chair.

Mrs. Tinker waited at the elevator for her husband
to enter it before her. "What's the matter?" she
said querulously. "What are you hanging back
for? Never mind! Get in! Get in before I do;
certainly!" And after he had meekly complied and
the elevator was in motion, "What are you so red in
the face for?" she inquired tartly. "What are
you——"

"I'm not," he said in a dogged voice. "I wasn't 'hanging back.' I only wanted to see if those porters——"

"Never mind! I don't want to hear——"

"Oh, dear!" Olivia moaned. "Mother!"

"Nice day," Le Seyeux ventured cheerfully. "Fine ride. This our floor here. Lovely suite for you, sir. Big rooms. Fireplaces. Splendid beds. Everything good."

The apartment was as excellent as he promised; and Tinker was pleased to find a desk in the room set apart for himself. He congratulated the courier warmly upon the selection of these pleasant quarters; then surreptitiously shook his head at him as a sign to be gone upon his secret errand;—Le Seyeux gave him a look of complete reassurance on that point, and departed. A few minutes later Tinker went cautiously to the desk and sat down in a chair before it.

Mrs. Tinker called instantly from the bed where she reposed in the adjoining chamber. "What are you doing *now?* What do you have to be moving around so much in there for? Why can't you lie down like a Christian and let people get a little rest? Are you fixing to go out somewhere by yourself?

Because if you *are*——" The bed rustled as with a movement of preparation.

"My goodness! I'm just *sitting* here, Mamma! I don't want to lie down. I'm not doing any harm just *sitting* here, am I? Wouldn't you like to have your door closed, Hon?"

"I would not!" she replied with a decisiveness beyond argument.

He sat motionless, doing nothing whatever for several minutes; and the silence was as soothing as he hoped it would be. Presently her breathing became audible—though this was something she never believed of herself—and with slow carefulness he took from an inner pocket of his coat a small, black-bound pad of bank cheques. He cautiously removed one, slid the book back into his pocket, and, bending over the desk, wrote briefly. After that, discovering a single envelope in a pigeon-hole before him, he enclosed the written slip within it, and rose to his feet.

Across the room from him was a door opening upon a corridor. Tinker looked at it fixedly; then, moving with an elaborate delicacy, he made his way craftily over the floor in that direction.

. . . The tall lady sitting alone in the tea-room

faced the doorway as he walked briskly in. A perceptible glow of additional colour came upon her cheeks,
and, not speaking, she extended the hand she had un-
gloved for him.

Tinker shook it heartily. "You're lookin' fine!"
he said. "Fine! How's your family?"

"Hyacinthe? He is happy," she answered. "As
I am. Will you sit here with me?"

"About a minute," he said, glancing over his
shoulder at the vacant doorway;—then, as he sat,
he spoke hurriedly, but genially, "Listen! You
want to get me scalped first and boiled in oil afterwards?"

"No."

"Well, I already *have* been scalped," he informed
her. "All I'm lookin' out for now, I don't want to
get boiled in oil! I told you——"

She stopped him gently. "My friend, you are
angry with me because you think I have stayed in
Tunis to see you. You mustn't be afraid: I shall not
compromise you. I know the customs and ideas of
American ladies perfectly: it is amusing, but of
course could be very painful. I am not stopping at
this hotel on that account, because I was sure you
would come here. I shall protect you, but——

Will you let me confess I did so very, very much wish to see you once more?"

She smiled a little sadly, and then leaning toward him, "Forgive me for wishing it," she said, and lightly patted the heavy shoulder nearer her.

At that, Tinker again looked hastily toward the doorway; but it remained vacant, and he was reassured. "Listen," he said confidentially, "I got something I want to——"

"Wait," she interrupted. "I have somesing I have so wanted to say. In Biskra you wouldn't give me time to say it. You don't understand the gratitude of a woman who is taken out of purgatory, and how much she might wish to do for the man who did such a thing for her. You don't know—perhaps you wouldn't care to know—how much she might like such a man and how difficult it would be for her to think she must say good-bye to him for a last time." She had looked at him steadily as she spoke; but suddenly her fine-lashed eyelids fluttered; she looked away from him, and bit her lower lip. "You——" She could not continue immediately.

"Listen!" he said hurriedly. "My family's takin' a nap, I *think;* but I don't *know.* I got to——"

"Please—it's only a moment," she said; and recovered her composure at once. "I ask you to let me hope to see you in Paris when you come there."

"Sure! Sure!" he returned cordially. "I can find you in the telephone book. But right *now* I——"

"Yes," she said. "The apartment Hyacinthe and I will take, by that time it will be upon the list. But I would write to you——"

"Write?" he interrupted, staring at her incredulously. "Listen——"

"No, no, no! I won't," she said. "I won't write to you. I see you don't wish it. And you are disturbed now; you are nervous. But to-morrow——"

Tinker leaned a little toward her and spoke earnestly. "Look here: I've thought it over, and I realized you only told me what you needed to get that boy o' yours started in the show business, or whatever it is, and that's all I—all I lent you. What I didn't think of at the time, I just lent you the round sum, and you told me how close those old ladies you lived with were when it came down to cash. What I got to thinkin': why, you might not have enough to *go* on for the next few months unless you broke into the round sum you have to use for this show business. For all I know, you mightn't even have enough to pay your fare up from here to Paris, outside o' that, so I—well, this'll fix it up." He pressed the envelope he had brought with him into her hand. "Here! This'll make everything all right. You can get it cashed at the branch bank right here in Tunis to-morrow morning."

She looked down at the envelope in her hand and shook her head slowly. "I can't take it. It is dear of you to offer it. Of course if there were any way I could——" She paused and looked at him inquiringly.

"Why, sure," he said. "That boy of yours'll pay it all off after he gets goin'. You put that in your bag. Do as I tell you!"

But she still shook her head. "No, I can't——"

"Listen!" he said. "My family isn't any too sound a sleeper, and I got to get back upstairs or I'm liable to be in the creek where the cows can't wade it. John Edwards told me there's a steamer from here to Marseilles to-morrow."

She looked at him gravely. "You wish me to take it?"

"Murder, yes!" he said; and they both rose.

"You wish——" she began tremulously, and faltered.

"Look here!" he said. "Give me that!" He took from her the envelope she held loosely in her long fingers, and from the table a little bag of meshed gold and platinum that lay beside her glove. "Here!" He opened the bag, put the envelope within it and snapped the clasp shut. Then he thrust the glove and the bag both into her hands. "There!" he said, beaming upon her. "You take that, and get your young son down to the ticket-office as quick as you can to-morrow morning. And then, for heaven's sake, get out o' here!"

This enthusiasm startled her; and again her remarkable eyelashes fluttered. "You want me not to see you again—at all—until you come to Paris?"

"Well, I should say I did!" he said. "I don't want to be walked on with spiked shoes all the rest o' my life just because it happens you're the finest lookin' woman in the world! That's the trouble: if you were a little homelier, I guess I could make out to see more of you; but the way it *is*—why, you're about eight-hundred per cent. too good-lookin', Mrs. Mummero!" And with that, beaming upon her more cordially than ever, he lifted his large right hand and brought it down with a hearty and sounding slap upon her lovely velvet back, squarely between the shoulders. "You know it!" he said.

She stared at him wide-eyed, amazed. For an instant a line appeared upon her forehead;—it faded and she seemed to be lost in an inward wondering. Then, slowly, she began to smile, and her gaze became one of the truest utter admiration and fondness. "I think I adore you," she said. "I shall be at sea to-morrow, as you command me." And without any farewell whatever, she turned and swept from him with her splendid gliding swiftness;—she walked straight out of the room and out of the hotel.

Alone in the big room, Tinker waited for one minute by his watch, which he took from his pocket to observe; then, with a debonair easiness of manner, he strolled back into the entrance hallway. Mrs. Tinker was just stepping out of the elevator.

Her expression was both grim and anxious; but it became merely indignant as she caught sight of her husband. She came toward him, hurried, nervous, and threatening, walking as rapidly as she could on her high heels and in her tight skirt. "That was a nice trick!" she said. "Slip out the minute I was beginning to get just a little bit of rest after nearly having my back broken in two on that horrible road we took because you didn't know any better than send Le Seyeux ahead where he couldn't be any use to us. Where've you been?"

"Now, look here, Honey!" Tinker remonstrated. "Can't a man even go get his hair cut without your——"

"You haven't had your hair cut."

"Well, I didn't say I *had*. Can't you give me time enough to tell you I'm lookin' for the barber-shop?"

"You don't need to find it. If you want a barber, you can tell them to send one up to your room."

"Now, Mamma——"

"You get in that elevator," Mrs. Tinker said dangerously.

The bright-eyed Arab boy in charge of the elevator giggled pleasantly; and Tinker, though becoming desperate under so much discipline, felt it might be best to comply with his wife's desire.

"Well——" he said resignedly; but at that moment, glancing round, he began to hope. The relief to which he trusted was in sight. Le Seyeux, radiant with pleasure, had just made his appearance, coming in from the street, and with him were three men of solemn presence, followed by three Arab servants in

cleanest white. Two of the three solemn men were
graybeards; one of these two wore silken robes
striped like a barber's pole; and the other, whose
majestic white beard hung to his waist, was in black
and saffron, gloriously embroidered in orange, green,
and gold. The third of the jewel merchants was
a warped and wrinkled yellow person in an English
frock coat, pale lilac trousers, an embroidered velvet waistcoat and a fez. The three paused aloof
while Le Seyeux came forward.

Tinker became urgent in his plea to his wife.
"Listen! I'll be upstairs in half an hour. I can't
go now."

"Why can't you?"

"Well——" He glanced toward the three merchants. "I got business with those gentlemen."

"Business!" Mrs. Tinker said angrily. "What's
it about? A Fancy Dress Party?"

"Honest, I have, Honey," he insisted; and he was
cunning enough to add mysteriously: "You might be
sorry some day! I mean you might be sorry if you
kept me from a conference with those gentlemen.
Mightn't she, John?"

"I think it would be certain," Le Seyeux said, with
laughter intentionally sly. "I am sure if you talk

to them everybody is going to be very happy—oh, very happy, Madame Tinker!"

Mrs. Tinker looked undecided; and perhaps she caught some inkling of what was in the wind. In spite of herself her voice became more moderate, even almost friendly. "Well, you see that he gets upstairs in time enough to dress," she said. "I'll trust him to *you*, Mr. Le Seyeux."

She was borne aloft alone; and Tinker, with a great sigh of relief, turned to the waiting magicians who were to assist in the dispersal of his troubles. It may have been true, as his wife said, that he had but the one remedy for everything; but, on the other hand, as he himself said, it usually "worked."

XXXII

WITH the one diamond point of the first evening star set in a watery green twilight sky behind her, the steamer stood out to sea from the Tunisian shore and pushed her bow toward the bright west. She bore northward too, for she followed the old sea path of the Carthaginian fleets when they sailed for the Golden Shell or to meet the Roman galleys in the great water fighting of the Punic Wars; for this is an old, old harried roadstead, and, embedded in the sea floor, there are statues of gods, encrusted with shells; there are ancient shields and javelin heads and broken swords and dented golden helmets. There was a golden helmet upon the steamer, too, this evening;—at least, that was the interpretation offered by a young Italian returning home after a winter in the Tunisian oases. He pointed out this helmet to the friend who was his travelling companion.

"That beautiful, very long, but very graceful woman standing alone there and looking back at the shore," he said, speaking in French. "She has been inspired to leave her hat in her cabin and step out on deck for a farewell to Africa; and we should be grateful to the inspiration. You don't see how perfectly her head with that smooth hair is a golden helmet? Never in my life have I seen a woman who stood so well poised; and under that crest of old pale gold she is—ah, I have discovered it! She is Diana helmeted! I have these extraordinary thoughts of people, and you never appreciate them. Don't you see she is Diana?"

But his companion was a Scandinavian of the abysmal school, and he shook his head. "I know Diana with a bow and quiver, but not with a helmet. The lady there is just a woman. Probably her husband is an officer on duty in Africa or an adviser of the Bey of Tunis and she is wondering what sort of girl he has begun to flirt with since seeing her off at the dock."

"No. She is thoughtful, a little impassive; but she is radiant."

"Then she is thinking of the man, not her husband, who will meet her when we disembark."

"Not at all," the Italian insisted. "She is not thinking of any man. She is Diana. This is a tremendous thought I am about to have now, Gustav. Listen attentively. Yonder shines the light on that hill of enchantment, Sidi Bousaid, and, below it, there is Carthage. Diana is passing by Moloch. Moloch's fires are out; the god is in the hideous barren dust over yonder that will hardly support a weed. They ground Moloch up as fine as that. But classic beauty survives the barbarian. Classic beauty survives forever, and here is Diana, beautiful and alive, passing over this old sea into which some of Moloch's dust has been blown. Moloch's dust was blown here, and so were some of the bacteria breathed out by Saint Louis dying of the plague close by the ruins of Moloch. Eternal Diana is now being wafted over both the bigot hero saint and the monster. How do you like that for a thought, my friend?"

"Very little. Nothing survives forever except motion; and the most intelligent people are in doubt about even that. European classicism is now as dead stuff as Chinese classicism, and only a few dried-up old men worry about it. There isn't any Diana. Whatever isn't in motion is dead."

The Italian laughed. "Africa hasn't brightened your outlook. As for me, it is a great experience to sail in the same boat with a woman like that one yonder. She isn't in motion, yet she seems more alive than all other people. How still she is! No. She has moved, though only at the lips. She has begun to smile as she looks at the shore. Now tell me the truth, Gustav. Look at that happy, triumphant lady, that gold-helmeted Diana smiling, and dare to tell me the universe is not all bright and glorious!"

"No," said the steadfast Scandinavian. "Everything is dark. It would need more than a tall Parisian lady smiling her good-bye to the coast of Africa to make me believe in a meaning to the universe or in the existence of happiness."

Here the gloomy young gentleman was in a striking coincidental conjunction with a second gloomy young gentleman just then a few leagues inland from the deep blue Carthaginian coast line. What is more, a view of the farewell smile of that same tall lady would have lightened the melancholy of this second dour traveller even less than it lightened that of the first, who was actually looking at her. For, as Aurélie Momoro stood on the high deck, a statue vaguely gilded in the afterglow, Laurence Ogle's landaulet bumped him over the bad roads of the outskirts of Tunis.

She passed down the coast and was borne evenly out to sea, still standing where she was and still smiling as she swept on westward. He, with his anxious face to the Orient, drove miserably into Tunis, carrying his entire fortune, now equal to twenty-eight American dollars, in his pocket.

Of this, he must give Etienne a *pourboire*, well understood, amounting to not less than twenty dollars; which would leave nothing inspirational for a courageous confrontation of the staff of a fashionable hotel. And the nearer the landaulet drew him to the absolutely necessary interview with Tinker the more was his soul filled with a grovelling anguish.

Etienne stopped the car at a street corner, descended, and opened the door.

"Hôtel, Monsieur?"

"Uh—" Ogle coughed, swallowed, coughed again, and said: "Vous savez—vous savez est-ce-que M. Le Seyeux, le courier de M. Tangkaire, a dit à vous à quel hôtel M. Cayzac avait engagé des appartements pour M. Tangkaire?"

"Oui, oui, Monsieur. Je sais bien que——"

"Allons là!" Ogle said desperately. "Allons donc là, Etienne!"

Then, as Etienne returned to his seat and they moved forward again, the imagination of the flushed passenger became active. If his calculations were correct he was only twenty-four hours behind the man he sought; but Mrs. Tinker might not have liked Tunis. Her husband was now in a state of cringing subjugation to that nervous and irritated lady, and she might have insisted upon continuing their journey—with what destination it was useless to guess. For Ogle had no means to follow any farther; and if they had departed he would be left pleasantly installed in what must undoubtedly prove to be the most expensive and cold-hearted hotel in the city. He wondered if the American consul in Tunis ever made personal visits to the jail on behalf of unfortunate compatriots.

But his arrival reassured him immediately upon the one point: Tinker had not left Tunis. Before the great doorway of the hotel, Le Seyeux was making a passionate oration to a magnificent group of men who stood in stately patience to hear him. They were dressed in silken robes, striped like sticks of peppermint candy; in robes striped in green and lemon and lilac and purple; in robes of white cloth and tunics of embroidered saffron; their finger nails were stained with henna and their feet thrust loosely into embroidered slippers; their turbans, nodding together, were like a bed of immense flowers. With them there were two or three dapper men in European clothes and fezzes, and two or three others, hawk-nosed and olive-skinned, in enormous green trousers and embroidered short green jackets—immaculate, scented men whose eyelids were blackened with kohl.

They wished Tinker to buy sapphires and diamonds and emeralds and rubies and ivory and fine rugs and embroideries and brocades and carved amber and carved jade and carved crystal and old silver inlaid with gold, and old copper inlaid with silver, and glass and perfumes and curious bird-cages and ostrich feathers and curved daggers and tasselled spears and round steel shields and cigarette-holders, a foot long, and burnouses and beaten brass and ebony stools inlaid with mother-of-pearl. He had already bought some quantity of all of these things during the day; but the merchants had called, hoping that he would buy more, and the courier was trying to make them understand that at the moment he couldn't, as he was now in the bath; and that after he came out of it he would go to his dinner. He couldn't buy anything while bathing or eating; and in fact he wouldn't do any more buying until early to-morrow morning.

The relief Ogle felt when he saw Le Seyeux was so great that he missed a perception he should have had. In his writing he was fashionably fond of the ironical, and surely he should have seen a fine sample of irony in that very relief of his. All the way from the Sahara to this corner on the Mediterranean he had been pursuing the man from whom he had so often complained in his soul that it was impossible to escape; and now that he had found him he was confident of salvation. Mentally he was not himself, or he must have set his teeth on edge with this engaging paradox. Physically, however, he was himself enough to be quick at blushing, and, as he made his way through the courier's gorgeous audience, the colour of his cheeks was almost that of a red burnous against which he brushed in his passage. Not only merchants waited there, in high hopes of Tinker: mendicants hovered upon the fringes and it was with them he felt that he should have taken his own place.

Probably few sensitive people have shrivelled within themselves more wretchedly than this prospective supplicant did when he thought of the interview before him. He knew that he ought to get it over quickly; but when he considered the direct course of sending a note to Tinker's apartment asking him for a few minutes as soon as possible, his gorge rose and he knew that he couldn't force himself to write such a note. Since he couldn't, he fell back upon opportunism and gave himself a respite until the morrow; —groaning aloud, he postponed the interview until then.

An hour later, as he sat at a small table against the wall in the hotel dining-room, he postponed it permanently. With no other help visible in heaven or earth, he definitely abandoned that appeal to Tinker which was the purpose of his journey, and abandoned himself with it. Common sense was all against such an abandonment; nevertheless, his reasons were creditable.

The many tables in the room were chattered over by embellished cosmopolites piquant in variety;— every racial shade of swarthiness, of ruddiness, of pallor seemed to be displayed as if in some decorous competition for a prize. Richly dressed and handsome golden-skinned ladies dined with covertly wild-eyed sleek brown gentlemen; flamboyant ladies, enamelled dead white and wearing tall ivory combs in polished jet-black hair, dined with sallow little dandies who were smoothed with brilliantine and touched with scent; there were flaxen Danish families, pink frosted English families, dark Latin families, olive and ivory Jewish families, pallid American families, restless with curiosity; and there were two tables of flawless Japanese gentlemen on a mission. Just outside the open glass doors, in the dance-room beyond, an excellent orchestra discoursed the customary subjects from Carmen, La Bohême, Tosca, and Pagliacci; but suddenly, in the midst of "Mi Chiamano Mimi," there was a disconcerting breakdown of that touching melody: strings, brasses, woods, and piano performed gymnastics upon the astonished air for some seconds, then gloriously united themselves again into a vehement jubilation. "Yes, We Have No Bananas" had reached Tunisia at last and was there conceived to be the preferred national anthem of the land from which it sprang. This orchestra played it with supreme dash, yet grandly; everybody looked round; and the *maître d'hôtel* raced to the wide doorway; but his two chief assistants were already there, bowing ceremoniously. Then the Tinker family came in and were escorted to a table covered with flowers, where all the waiters in that part of the room instantly gathered.

Ogle had expected a plaintive and anxious Tinker, a querulous and injured Mrs. Tinker. On the contrary, the expression of the big, broad-faced man was placidly dominant, the expression of a man who knows himself to be not only the master of many fates, but the head of his own family. As for Mrs. Tinker, she was radiant—and in more ways than one; for her throat, her bosom, and her wrists shot white and coloured fires with every movement she made.

No doubt she wore too many jewels for the occasion; but, as they were all new, it may have been impossible for her to choose between them. When she came thus brilliantly into the spacious room, smiling upon her consort as she walked beside him, the diners stared at her, dazzled;—she was startling even to a banker from the Argentine, who half rose from his chair for a better view of her. But when she had been seated at her table, she was visibly a true and devoted wife; anyone could see that it was her husband's admiration she wanted first of all. She moved her sparkling wrist gracefully under his eyes, pretending to pass things to him; she coquetted tenderly with him, beamed upon him, teased him sweetly. Upon his part, he received her attentions benignly, like a big kind old dog pleased with a kitten's gayeties, yet withal a little absent-minded.

But it was at Olivia that the lonely young man across the room looked most fixedly. She blushed as she came in with her father and mother, seeming to be a little troubled by the attention drawn to their entrance—perhaps dismayed, too, by the tribute of the orchestra; and she kept her eyes downcast, holding them so after she had taken her place at the table. She sat in profile to Laurence; but he could see that she was preoccupied, and when she did look up, he had a disturbing impression that he comprehended a thought of hers. Perhaps it was at first more a disconsolate bit of hope than an impression; but what brought it to him was the manner in which she glanced rather quickly over the room as if she hoped, a little breathlessly, to see someone she knew. The glance did not reach him quite, and she looked down again at her plate;—there seemed to be disappointment, a little sadness, in her preoccupation then.

She had never before looked so charming. Moreover, Laurence had never before thought of her as charming, precisely, though he had thought of her as many things both disagreeable and agreeable; and of late he realized that he had the habit of thinking of her more and more. In the inevitable rebound of his emotions she had begun to have a great effect upon him, and he knew it;—she had been a thorn-bush from which an elusive perfume hinted spring, and of late wistful little petals had blown to him. To-night it was as if the bush were all in bloom—and then drooped because he was not near. For suddenly Laurence knew positively, without knowing how he knew it, that it was indeed himself whom she had hoped to see; that it was for him this deep, eager, gentle glance had gone quickly over the room; and he knew it was because she thought he had not come that she was sorrowful. Then, when he knew this, he knew that he could never ask her father to lend him any money.

He had finished his dinner; but for a time he sat staring at the depths of his despair, which appeared to be in the finger-bowl on the table before him. He made no decision; he had no control in the matter, which had thus been decided for him; and he understood that being unable to ask Olivia's father for money did not enable a stranded bankrupt to ask for Olivia: he had now no chance for either. He was in some measure an artist, at times almost supernaturally shrewd, but not usually practical, and, in this stress, wholly lacking the resourcefulness of an ordinary man of affairs. With their situations exchanged, Tinker would have felt no distress whatever;— he would have been admirably sanguine of securing both the girl and the money; and indeed he would have had both; but Tinker's imagination was that of the builder of roads and mover of mountains.

The imagination of the playwright, finer and in its delicacy infinitely feebler, presented him with nothing whatever except a tragic view of his own helplessness; and he found nothing to do except, in his shame, to keep out of Olivia's way. If she looked for him again she might turn her head far enough in his direction to see him; and as soon as he thought of this possibility he got up and went out of the room. He was near the doorway and no one noticed him.

The triumphal struttings of the Toreador, flung out with gusto by the orchestra, accompanied him as he crossed the vacant dancing-floor of the room beyond; and he thought that he would ever afterward hate that song—if indeed there were any "afterward" for him. He could see none;—what vision of his future he had was limited to a vague, soul-shrivelling picture of himself being manhandled by hotel porters hustling him to the street; and in this passage across the shining floor on his way to the entrance hall, where he meant to take the elevator and go to his own room, he touched the bottom of his misery.

But, having touched bottom, there was only one direction in which he could move; and as the ancient salvation of souls at the bottom is the fact that motion is the one perpetual necessity of all things, then upward he must go, willy-nilly. In that happy direction, therefore, he was going, though he had no hope or thought of it when he walked out into the hallway with the Toreador prancing so hatefully behind him.

In truth, the gods of comedy who had ridden the storm out of the too frolicsome northeastern seas and had espied him, happy, self-content, and newly prosperous, on that noble ship, the "Duumvir", took now a surfeit of him. They had pursued him furiously, allowing him only such moments of peaceful fatuousness between their harryings as should make his anguishes the more pungent and their mirth the keener; but, having had their fill of him at last, when even they could drive his spirit no lower than its lowest, they gave him over to mercy and departed from him for this while with the same abruptness of their pounce upon him out of the heart of the north-easter. The malicious beating of their pinions should have been heard down the coast of Barbary and the long reaches of the Mediterranean, that night, as they rode the darkness back to the Herculean Pillars and onward to their home eyrie over the top of the winds. For from there, assured of their gratification, they would watch the vessels puffing merrily out of New York Harbour and select new comedians to writhe and grimace for their antic humour.

The young man in despair at the bottom was saved by an agency he despised, one that within the space of a youth's life bears greater weight in the world than is borne by stupendous philosophies developed through the centuries: this mighty force, at least touching the affairs of almost all men in one way or another, became now the complete salvation of Laurence Ogle. Lehren had been shrewd enough to guess something of the effect the "The Pastoral Scene's" withdrawal might have upon its author, for the manager had a long and sometimes severe experience of people who buoyantly conceived as perpetual the temporary theatrical incomes passed to them through his office. Therefore, while he feared that the disappointing career of "The Pastoral

Scene" might bring about an extreme embarrassment upon foreign shores, he had written of the matter with great caution. Even though Lehren had a hope of reimbursing himself for his own loss and of extricating the playwright from what might be a predicament, he did not think it wise to extend this hope to Laurence. Because of his severe experience he feared that the playwright might cable him requesting an advance in cash to be repaid out of the hope; and the negotiations with the moving-picture corporation had not yet reached a conclusion.

A few days after his cautious letter, however, the matter was set down and made fast upon legal paper; money was passed, and half of it, except for a slight deduction, belonged by contract to the author of the play. Lehren's second letter had been forwarded by rail from Biskra, and one of the concierge's assistants in the hotel at Tunis handed it to a tragic-looking, dark and smallish, but handsome young gentleman with "burning eyes" indeed, as he was just stepping into the elevator.

Laurence looked at it broodingly, and, when he reached his room he tossed the missive upon his dressing-table, accompanying this action with a slight hissing noise from his lips. Then he sat down in a chair, took his head in his hands and rubbed his hair into a tumult of disorder, renewing this desperate massage at intervals during the next half hour. Finally, with the thought in his mind that the last accounting for "The Pastoral Scene" could not possibly make him more unhappy than he was—since nothing could—he opened the envelope. It contained the promised account, a letter from Lehren and a blue slip of paper—a draft readily negotiable at the office of M. Cayzac's agency in Tunis.

Laurence did not read the letter or examine the account;—he stared and stared at the draft, reading it over and over with slowly dispersing incredulity: it was for four thousand, eight hundred and twelve dollars and seventy-one cents. Then, after a tremulous glance at the letter, he understood what had happened. He had always thought and spoken with detestation of moving pictures and of their effect upon the populace and upon "art" and "literature"; they were indeed and repulsively for "the many," and his conviction of their vulgarity was a profound one.

Now he sat trembling, looking at Lehren's draft; and his eyes grew bright and watery. "Thank God for the movies!" he whispered brokenly.

A few moments later he jumped up and looked at

the happy and distracted person in the mirror over his dressing-table. "You better brush your hair, you little fool!" he said, omitting the "dear" Mme. Momoro had used when she called him that.

When he came downstairs presently, a new man, the tables about the central dancing space in the large room beyond the hallway were filled with diners sipping coffee and cordials while the orchestra thrillingly crooned an Argentine tango. From the doorway he saw where Olivia sat with her dominant big father and glittering mother to watch the intermittently gliding and pausing couples; and in the daughter's look there was a pathetic blankness;—it was the look of a girl hurt by some cruel omission.

When he came near her and she saw him, there was a change in her at first pathetically eloquent, then altogether lovely; one that showed how dangerous it is for a girl to be too personal (even abusively) in her contact with a young man easily mistaken by other girls for a Spanish poet. She sank a little into her chair; she seemed stricken and about to weep; then instantly she straightened;—she was all of a rosy and glowing gayety.

"Well, I should *say* so!" she answered, when he asked her if she would dance with him.

XXXIII

UPON the southern side of the hotel, at the height of the second story, a broad veranda ran the length of the building and overlooked the street. Under a green-and-white striped awning, great urns, green plants, painted iron chairs, and a balustrade suggested the pleasant leisures of a garden terrace; and here, in the filtered warm light beneath the awning, a critical conversation between two American travellers took place on the first afternoon in March, This interview, though not so appalling to the younger of the two as that other he had undergone only in his imagination, was nevertheless an uncomfortable one; and although both parties to it had for some days realized that it was inevitable, neither of them would have submitted to its embarrassments except as a necessity.

Ogle was pale, but Tinker the more obviously showed the nervousness he felt; and the strain upon him may have been heightened by his ceremonial costume, which included a silk hat, a tailed black coat and an annoying collar. His big comely face was flushed; he frowned, wiped his brow as he talked; and his general air was one of complaint. He made it clear that he acted under pressure. "I can't take much time to this," he said, looking at his watch as the two seated themselves near the railing. "I got an appointment pretty soon, and I don't know as there's rightly long enough to talk the proposition over with you the way it ought to be. I promised this gentleman—I don't know his name; but one these Turkish Jew jewellery men introduced me to him and he's been to call on me a couple o' times—well, anyhow, he said he wanted to come and get me and introduce me to some Lord High Muck-a-Muck Grand Panjandrum they got here, I don't know who; but he's some kind of Persian king or other—I couldn't make out what. Anyway, I put on these clothes, and they're too warm for the weather." He glanced down with distaste upon his excellent attire, and ineffectively fanned himself with the silk hat. "Mrs. Tinker made me wear 'em," he explained discontentedly. "She don't know any more what it's all about than I do; but she was bound I had to." He lighted a cigar slowly, taking all the time he could; then he said: "Well, John Edwards tells me he's got everything fixed up for us to clear out o' here day after to-morrow. I suppose that's agreeable to you, too?"

Laurence understood that Tinker was putting off their inevitable topic as long as possible; but now as an actual supplicant the young man had more courage than he had shown as a prospective one. "It will be agreeable to me if what I have to say is agreeable to you, Mr. Tinker."

Tinker sighed heavily and audibly;—it was a groan. "Oh, murder!" he said. "I suppose we might as well get down to it. Of course Babe's told me what you want to talk to me about. Well, sir, it isn't so awful agreeable; no, sir, it's not. When you come right down to it, it's not so agreeable."

The applicant bit his lip. "I don't know that I——"

"Listen!" Tinker said; and he leaned forward earnestly toward the young man. "Look here! I haven't got a word to say against your character or your family. Babe's told me everything about that and how your father was a college professor and all; and I'll admit right now, when we started on this trip I had a kind of hope that something like this might happen. Not that *I* wanted such a thing, you get me; but I mean on *her* account. She thought she liked a young fellow at home—a right bright sort of no-account young nothin' he is, at that—but I knew what he was and she didn't. He's kind of a bad egg, and I had to tell her so. Well, she knew I was tellin' her the truth, and she knew I knew what I was talkin' about; but, my *soul!* how it did upset her with me! Well, so my wife thought o' this trip—he kept hangin' around tryin' to see her—and I made Babe come. Of course she was in pretty low spirits, and I admit I thought it might be kind of a good thing if she'd maybe take a fancy to some first-rate young fellow, if we happened to run into anybody like that. So I don't say what's happened may not be all right. But there's several things——" He paused, frowned more deeply, shook his head, and leaned back discontentedly in his chair.

"I understand from her that you have some objection to my profession," Ogle said.

Tinker's deep frown continued in position upon his large forehead. "I don't exactly object to it, you might say, and Babe's pretty near talked my head off about that show o' yours I saw in New York. She says you insisted on my knowin' you wrote it, and I consider that honourable and above-board with me, Mr. Ogle. Well, she's made me understand you didn't write it the way everybody seemed to be takin' it—and the way I'll have to admit I took it myself. She's told me the whole story of it a dozen times, I expect, tryin' to prove how you *had* to make those actors and actresses say what they did and behave the way they did; and I guess she's pretty well proved her case to me. Anyway, I believe you meant it the way she says you did. But see here——" He leaned forward again and set his large hand upon Laurence's knee. "Listen! You don't have to put on any *more* shows like that, do you?"

Ogle ruefully shook his head. "No. Not like that!"

Tinker seemed to be somewhat relieved. He tilted back in his iron chair, put his feet upon the railing, and contemplated his cigar. "I'm glad to hear it. I can take a night off myself and see a show like that; but I wouldn't exactly care to have anybody in my own family—especially my own daughter's——" He waved his hand, as Ogle tried to interrupt "Wait a minute! I understand you didn't mean it that way; but there's too many people *take* it that way for anybody to want it in his own family. And another thing: Babe says the show's off now and won't ever be heard of again, so we agreed it'll be just as well if

Mrs. Tinker never hears that you had anything to do with it. *She* never *would* understand! So that's all there is to say about *that*. Let's get on to something else."

"Very well," Ogle said in a low voice. The colour had returned to his face during this disposal of "The Pastoral Scene";—in truth, he was now as warmly flushed as Tinker, and a frown as deep as the latter's had appeared upon his forehead. "What else, if you please?"

"I understand from Babe," Tinker said, "you're going to do other kinds of writing as a regular business and try plays on the side, as it were, because you don't consider theatre work reliable enough in the way of income. She says you already have done this other work and got yourself enough established in it so't you can count on it. Well, that's all right, and I don't want you to think I haven't got any respect for literature, because I have. I don't know all this and that about it the way my wife and Babe do—I been too busy—but still I think it has its own place. I'll say this to you, Mr. Ogle: while it might 'a' seemed more satisfactory to me if you'd been in something regular and substantial, something kind of more like *men's* business, as you might put it, still,

I'm not goin' to stand out against my daughter's happiness just because you didn't happen to be built to shine in that way."

Laurence Ogle drew a quick breath and looked briefly at the man beside him; but Tinker's troubled eyes were averted. Then the two sat in silence for some moments, preoccupied.

What preoccupied Ogle was a problem he foresaw in the long future. He was himself again;—at least, with a renewed purse, he was almost himself again; though he had suffered some enlightenments and improved his knowledge of himself. Nevertheless, in the last few minutes he had returned to his old opinion that Tinker was irrecoverably a great barbarian and the problem foreseen for the future concerned the barbarian's happiness as well as his own. Tinker often came to New York and would come oftener when his daughter lived there: Laurence trembled within when he thought of what the people he knew would think of his father-in-law, and of what they would think of himself for having such a father-in-law. They would never be able to understand that although Tinker was a barbarian, he was a great one; and the difficulty would be to conceal him from them during his visits—and also to conceal them from Tinker.

Tinker made it plain what his own preoccupation concerned. Suddenly he slapped his knee. "Well, sir," he said, "the first time I saw you if anybody'd 'a' told me you'd ever be my son-in-law I'd 'a' killed him!"

Thus the two preoccupations had not been so dissimilar in fundamentals as might have been supposed. But when the older man, having thus released his profoundest feeling, turned his head and saw the sensitive face of the younger again grow pallid under this shock, a more genial sentiment began to prevail with both of them. Tinker stretched forth his arm and set his hand upon Laurence's shoulder.

"Now, don't you take that to heart," he said. "My daughter's just the world and all to me, next to her mother, of course; and I expect I'd 'a' been just as grudging whoever it was I had to give her up to. I oughtn't to of said what I just did, even if it *is* the God's own truth. Anyhow, I didn't feel that way long. When you came to sit at our table I didn't think you *knew* much, it's true; but I see Babe's right about that's only being the Eastern way you were brought up—timid and afraid you might do something wrong, or get mixed up with strangers and all. Well, in a way I began to kind of take a sort of fancy to you, because you were so quiet and modest. I tell you, modesty's something you don't see in so many young men nowadays, and yours is the main and principal thing I like about you. Yes, sir; it's what makes me think we can manage to get along with you in the family about as well as if it'd been somebody different, Mr. Ogle. Yes, sir; I'll say *this* much for you, myself: you're quiet and you got nice manners, and you're perfectly honourable and you 'tend to your own business, and, what's best of all, you're modest. Well, those things make up for a good deal; indeed they do. And since I got to give my daughter up, I'm glad it's to a man that's got *those* qualities *anyhow!*"

With that, his troubled face relaxed; he sent forth thick wreathings of blue smoke, and, sighing loudly, seemed almost content. Behind him, in the open French window that gave admission to this high veranda, there appeared a witness to his increased geniality: a little, ancient, hawk-nosed English lady in black taffeta and an Indian shawl. She looked thoughtfully at the figure of Tinker and at his

gleaming large shoes upon the railing of the balustrade before him. "Ha!" she said to herself, but
audibly. "The magnificent Goth again!" And
she went away.

This was a new definition for Ogle, who already
had several; but Tinker did not hear her. "Well,
sir," he said, "I expect we better call it a day. You
and I can get along all right because I've seen how
you feel about my little girl, and I know how she feels
about you. I'm glad you want to get right back to
work; and we'll see you off on your steamer from
Naples next week. We aren't goin' to be very long
behind you gettin' back home. All I'm goin' to do is
just give the family a little motor trip around Italy—
Rome and Florence and Venice maybe—then we're
goin' to come straight back to Naples and sail from
there ourselves."

Laurence was pleasantly surprised. "I understood you were going to continue northward and sail
from a French port. I thought the ladies had Paris
in mind as——"

"No, sir!" Tinker's tilted chair and his feet came
down simultaneously with a bang. "We're not goin'
anywhere *near* Paris," he said. "If Babe and Hon
want to go to Paris, they can come over some other

time—with you, maybe—and see all they want of it; but if I got anything to say about *this* expedition— and I think I have—we're goin' to sail from *Naples !*"

Both men stood up then, relieved of their heavy duty, but still a little embarrassed with each other, and Le Seyeux came from the doorway. Behind him, in the dusk of the interior, a charming head appeared;—it was Olivia's, prettily anxious.

Tinker called to her, "Come out here!"

She came, and her mother with her.

"See that?" he said. And he took Laurence's hand and gave it a hearty shake. "Satisfy you?" he said

But unexpectedly his lips began to tremble; he swallowed painfully, and, to conceal the big tears that rose in his eyes, he turned his head away. Then he turned again to his daughter, kissed her hurriedly, and strode into the hotel without another word.

"Don't go," Mrs. Tinker called after him tremulously, "Earl, don't go."

"He must go now," Le Seyeux explained. "The gentleman has come for him down there."

"Down where?"

"You will see," the courier said; and he pointed to the street below them, where now was heard a great trampling and clanging of iron-shod hooves. "Look! You are going to see him."

They leaned upon the railing and looked down upon a many-coloured jostle of turbans, bare heads, tasselled fezzes, pith helmets, and the ragged head swathings of mendicants. These were all busily clustering about a semicircular cleared space where stood an open red touring car almost intolerable to the eye in its splendour of mirroring brass; and drawn up, facing this equipage, were a troop of cavalrymen in violent uniforms, brown men with flamboyant mustachios and long curved sabres as amazing. Their harness clanked and jangled with the nodding of the restless Arabian chargers; the fantastic crowd pressed about them, murmuring; child beggars squealed and wept;— then, at a signal invisible to the observers on the veranda, one of the troopers blew a trumpet, and a little dark old gentleman, dapper in European dress, but with a fez upon his head, came out from the hotel. And with him came the resplendent Tinker, overshadowing everything with his broad shoulders and tall hat.

He passed through a group of reverent and gorgeous merchants, the sellers of jewels, of perfumes, of amber, of ivory, of silks, of velvet brocades, of embroideries, of wrought metals, of glass, of ostrich feathers, of inlaid ebony and sandal-wood, of carved jade, and of domed bird-cages. He acknowledged their salutations heartily as he stepped into the car; the dapper Eastern gentleman got in beside him; the trumpet sounded again, and the pageant began to move.

Half of the cavalry troop galloped forward, clearing the street; the other half split into two sections, one on each side of the automobile, and thus with a glorious clattering and a noble pomposity of colour, the astounding procession came beneath the eyes of the watchers upon the veranda.

But there was something that astonished Laurence Ogle more than the procession did; and that was the humourless calm of Mrs. Tinker, though Olivia laughed delightedly. "Gracious!" the daughter said, "it's almost like the day he had to escort those French marshals and admirals and people up Jefferson Avenue to the stand in the Court House Yard."

"Who's that with him?" Mrs. Tinker inquired of the courier, and a slight frown appeared upon her forehead. "I mean the funny little man he's got in the car with him."

"I think it is a Pasha, who lives here," Le Seyeux

answered. "I don't know certainly. I think he wish to take Mr. Tinker to meet the Bey of Tunis."

"Who's he?"

"The Bey? Well, he is suppose' to be the ruler of this country," the courier explained. "That is to say, he governs it excellently under the advice of the French. But he has his own army, you see, and most of it is taking care of Mr. Tinker to-day, I think. Look! He sees us!"

The cavalcade had passed down the length of the veranda; but Tinker, conscious of the eyes upon him from on high, looked back over his shoulder and communicated with the friendly watchers by means of a wink easily visible at the distance. Not feeling this to be sufficient, however, he stood up, removed his hat and waved it sweepingly. Then, with the strange security against being understood that foreign soil affords so many of his compatriots, in the use of their native tongue, he employed a bit of street currency from home to express his evidently jocular sentiments. "Good-bye, folks!" he bellowed at the top of his big voice. "I don't know where I'm goin', but I'm on my way!"

"I do wonder," Mrs. Tinker said fretfully, "what that Bey, or whoever he is, wants of him."

But the courier protested. "No, no! He will want nothing. It will be that he has heard of Mr. Tinker since he has come here, and he feels he would like to speak with him and maybe especially"— Le Seyeux paused, coughed explosively, then completed his thought—"and maybe especially he wish to look at him!"

Mrs. Tinker shook her head. "No; I know he wants something. They always do."

With Olivia's light and gentle hand upon his arm, her betrothed leaned forward to watch the glittering car and its gorgeous outriders as they passed on down the street in a thin cloud of dust of their own creation. Tinker's whole course across Barbary had been like this, a jocose kind of pageantry, Laurence thought. And, in the end, what *was* the man? "Barbarian," "Carthaginian," "Goth," he had been called; but with qualifications: a barbarian, but a great one; a Carthaginian, but a great one;—a Goth, the little old English lady had just said; but she called him a magnificent one.

"Wave to him, Mother!" Olivia cried. "Look at him! He's still showing off for us—to make us laugh. Wave to him, Mother!"

As she said, Tinker was still standing up in the car,

and gloriously waving his shining hat. The sun was behind him, outlining him in dusty fire; and his figure, now at a distance, seemed to rise above the tossing heads of the chargers about him and beyond him like that of some mockingly triumphant charioteer riding home to glory in the arena of the Circus Maximus. After all, it was Medjila who had been right, Laurence thought;—here was neither Carthaginian nor barbaric Goth, or if he was, he was above all other things, the New Roman. Then, all at once, that problem for the future appeared less difficult, and the young man felt it might not be so important, after all, to conceal Tinker from the Macklyns and Albert Joneses.

For, in the cloud of dust against the sun, the powerful and humorous figure, still standing and waving as it rode on toward long-conquered Carthage, seemed to have become gigantic.

THE END

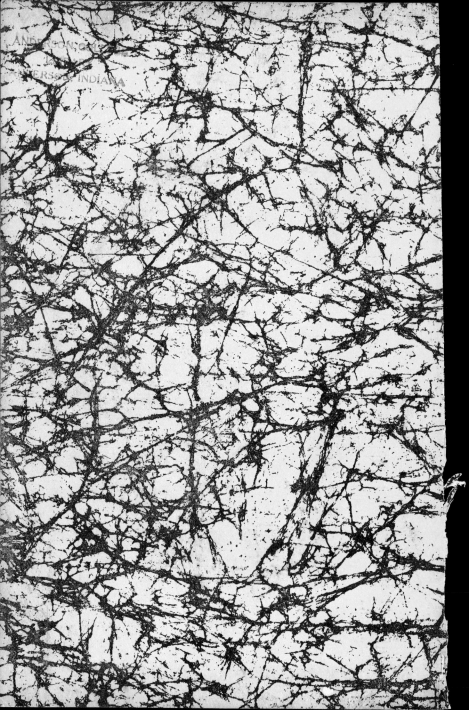